WILL CARVER
DEAD SET

arrow books

Published by Arrow Books 2013

2 4 6 8 10 9 7 5 3

Copyright © Will Carver

Will Carver has asserted his right under the Copyright, Designs
and Patents Act 1988 to be identified as the author of this work

First published in Great Britain in 2013 by
Arrow Books
Random House, 20 Vauxhall Bridge Road,
London SW1V 2SA

www.randomhouse.co.uk

Addresses for companies within The Random House Group Limited can be
found at: www.randomhouse.co.uk/offices.htm

The Random House Group Limited Reg. No. 954009

A CIP catalogue record for this book
is available from the British Library

ISBN 9780099551058

The Random House Group Limited supports the Forest Stewardship
Council® (FSC®), the leading international forest-certification organisation.
Our books carrying the FSC label are printed on FSC®-certified paper.
FSC is the only forest-certification scheme supported by the leading
environmental organisations, including Greenpeace. Our paper procurement
policy can be found at www.randomhouse.co.uk/environment

Typeset in Palatino by Palimpsest Book Production Limited
Falkirk, Stirlingshire
Printed and bound by CPI Group (UK) Ltd, Croydon, CR0 4YY

Mum, this one's for you.

'The easiest way to attract a crowd is to let it be known that at a given time and a given place someone is going to attempt something that in the event of failure will mean sudden death.'

Erik Weisz, also known as Harry Houdini

The Truth

---

*I*n November 2006, Dorothy Penn consented to have sex *with the man who would take her life. She was discovered standing naked, tied to her bed, which had been flipped upright, and shot through the mouth at close range.*

She was the first.

She was Girl 1.

Over the next two years, this man continued to kill. Each victim chosen for their name, each from a different London borough, each killed with increasing theatricality, taking inspiration from the world's greatest magic tricks, mutating them into scenes of morbidity. The press called him 'The Zone Two Killer'.

His real name is Eames.

The night before Dorothy Penn died, Detective Inspector January David saw something. In his sleep. A dream, a vision, an intuition of a giant, dark figure occupying an empty black space in his mind, feeding him clues about the woman who would die within the next twenty-four hours.

This apparition would visit him the day before each victim would be taken, delivering his message through a perpetual grin, giving the detective enough time to stop the murder. January David called him 'The Smiling Man'. He disappeared the night that Eames was captured.

Five innocents died at the hand of Eames. One survived.

Girl 4.

Audrey David.

The detective's wife.

This was not through luck or a mistake; she planned it this way. She planned everything. Manipulating the mind of a serial killer to do her sinister bidding in a warped attempt to be noticed by her husband, to be loved. Loved more than the sister who has been missing from his life for over twenty years.

She failed.

And now she is gone. Left without a word. January David does not know of his wife's involvement, he knows not where she is, only that she is not alone. The baby will be eighteen months old by now. Her baby. Eames' baby. She naively believes that this is all behind her. That January David no longer cares.

She wants him to care.

But The Smiling Man has returned; another girl will die in the next twenty-four hours.

For now, Eames remains incarcerated in a high-security psychiatric hospital.

With four more tricks on his list.

4

Prologue

When a perfectly coiffed reporter perches himself inside a cell and throws a question across a flimsy wooden table, believing he already knows the entertainment value of the answer, that's not me he's trying to bait. If it were, his adrenalin would lose its battle with fear.

When this journalist's adversary claims not to remember murdering anybody, when they eventually cave, stating that *killing is like a drug*, that *we all go a little mad sometimes*, that occasionally *I feel like a vampire*, that is not reality. That is not something I would say.

I am not a sound bite.

I don't want notoriety.

Just leave me to do my job.

I'd rather disappear.

In the beginning, when I gave myself up, when Detective Inspector January David took the glory of capturing me, when he thought it was the end, everyone wanted an interview: they needed the exclusive conversation; they had an idea for a true-crime story or a novel; they were making a documentary.

Think how lucky the filthy reporter will feel that I didn't jump across the table and strangle him, the relief he'll experience as the door is locked behind his back on exit; when he gets to go home and tell his wife that she is safe, I am still locked away.

Think how protected this hack convinces himself he is with the camera pointed directly at my face, and how naive he truly is to believe that I care.

I've been in this place for nearly two years now. You can't call it an asylum. We are no longer known as lunatics. Political correctness. Or the rather weaker reason that there has been an evolution in the attitude towards mental health. It is a hospital. You must refer to it as a hospital.

For the criminally insane.

You have to whisper the last part. Or say it in your head.

But there is no space in my mind for anything other than Audrey. The last time I saw her she was barely conscious. Folded in half, waiting for her unappreciative husband to arrive and not save her again. Not be there in her time of need.

When the saw dropped.

That was January David.

Detective Inspector January David.

That is not who I am.

When the columnist asks about your childhood, whether it was normal, whether it was loving, his knees bounce nervously under the table I could easily tip over. His hands tap silently against his thighs beneath the thin wooden top I could force down on his neck as he lies on the floor, his windpipe crushed and clamped together before the man with the camera feels the impetus to react. He wants me to say that my father hit me. That he left. That I suffered some kind of abuse, which manifests itself as violence and hatred towards women. But that is not me either. I'm nothing like all the others.

I am Eames.

They know of five people that I killed. What they should want to know is why I let Girl 4 live. They should want a reason for Girl 7 to still be breathing. But they speak only of my mother's death and the families of my victims. Because that is good television or magazine copy. Maybe they can rile me. But they do not ask why Girl 4 and Girl 7 are the same person. Why they are both Audrey David. The detective's unfaithful wife; the woman I love. Why is she still alive? How can I love this woman?

I have not finished with her.

She was not supposed to die then.

That is the simplest of answers.

But her time has come.

When January David uses the term 'career case', that's me he is proud of. It is I who define him. When this same detective believes enough time has passed to place part of history in a locked compartment of his brain, just as the faces of the five victims he failed to protect start to blur in his mind, as the scent of his wife finally fades from the material of their formerly shared home, that will be the optimal moment for a demon to return to his life and reopen those wounds, unlocking that compartment.

That monster is me.

Imagine his confusion when he finds Girl 8.

CE23.

Think how terrified he will be that I could walk straight out the front door.

Detective Inspector January David, when will you realise that Audrey was not the final trick? That this is far from being over? That things have changed. Altered. Metamorphosed. That there are four more.

Your wife was not the reveal.
She was merely misdirection.
It was never the plan to stop at Girl 7.
That's not me.
I can't stop.

Part One

Pledge

Girl 8

———✦———

Wednesday
CHELSEA, 22:53

I'm meeting Eames at the theatre.
   This afternoon I laid the foundations of my imaginary illness to my colleagues and my boss. My head hurts. It might be a migraine. I feel sick. My neck is stiff. Is it hot in here?

I'll call them in the morning and fake a sore throat. Maybe I'll cough for good measure.

I've been vomiting all night.

My gut keeps cramping.

I'm sweating but I feel cold.

The framed poster on my living-room wall says *Amen Avenue*. Written and directed by Kerry Ross. That play was over two years ago, when Eames was still killing people and we were reading the newspaper articles thinking it could never happen to us. That was before I'd forgotten his name.

The experimental theatre company I once belonged to is no longer inflicting its horror on small, discerning crowds in Chelsea since our performance space closed two Novembers ago. The Old Sanford Meisner Theater would only seat seventy-three people at capacity and is, at best, off-off the theatre district. *Amen Avenue* was the first and last play I wrote that was performed.

Until now.

My old theatre company website is still active and has the contact details of each member listed. Nobody has taken the site down because it is a record of the things we achieved as a group. We're all still proud of it even if we aren't in touch as often any more. That is how Eames found me. I don't even use that email address any more, I just kept it in the vain hope that I may need it again some day, when I can leave my fledgling PR career and move back to the theatre. I don't hate my job; it's great. It's just not where I want to be in five years. Or ten. Or the rest of my life. So feigning sickness is hardly a crime.

My nose just started bleeding.

My skin won't stop itching.

I think I need to take the morning off.

Every couple of weeks I go into the email account to keep it activated. As usual, everything is junk. Job offers, pills to enhance my apparently dreary sex life, discounts and free shipping applied. And what seems like a philanthropic gesture to fund a play. Somebody contacting playwrights and directors in the area with the hope of resurrecting the Sanford Meisner Theater as a performance space for lower budget exploratory ventures.

This is the ticket.

A once-in-a-lifetime opportunity.

I am being presented with my dream in order to take away my life.

Too wired to sleep, I flip open my laptop and email the former members of our troupe, hoping they, like me, retained their accounts and empty them weekly of trash.

Desperately, excitedly hoping that they, like me, still allow themselves to dream.

Tomorrow, I will call in sick. Women's problems. Ear infection. I'm having trouble sleeping. I will be picturing the next production. Getting the gang back together. Filling those seventy-three seats. I won't be worrying about e-shots and website banners. I won't be distracted by a distant memory of the name Eames.

Tomorrow I will know what a mistake I have made as I lash out, kicking my legs hard against the floor for leverage, waving my arms about hoping to hit something, fighting for breath. I will remember Eames.

Tomorrow, when they find my body, when they see that I have been made to look exactly like one of his previous victims, that I have been chosen as the understudy to Audrey David, everyone will be reminded.

And they will recognise me as a fool.

The Foot

———✦———

Wednesday
CAMDEN, 23:57

Alan Barber is not important to Aria Sky's life story, at least not as a person, a personality; it is only his actions that carry significance. And he only knew her in death.

He has a list of sins throughout his life, he has even added some this evening, but he is incapable of murder. The first time he noticed the young girl it was late and he was pissing all over her.

It begins in Camden.

And ends in Regent's Park.

The Taittinger gathers dust on the top shelf. Below that, the Disaronno is crying out for some wannabe trendy sophisticate to order it with orange and ice while winking at a female stranger across the room. The Macallan whisky doesn't look like it has been opened on the shelf beneath, but just under that is the place Alan Barber calls home. Somewhere between the Gordon's, Plymouth and Tanqueray.

'I can't get fat on gin and tonic,' he tells the other two men at the bar. They are a decade or two older than he

14

is and are sticking to ales and bitters. 'Clear spirits are the key to staying slim while having fun.' He doesn't tell them the effect that the tonic water has on him. That he spends half the next day on the toilet losing liquid and calories.

Recumbent bulimia.

Dysentery of excess.

Two hours pass and Alan Barber alternates between the three available gins on offer so nobody can tell he has had an entire litre to himself: each bottle has only gone down by one third; it's barely noticeable.

Then his friend finally arrives.

His name is irrelevant; in fact, his actions are negligible. The one thing he does is keep Alan Barber drinking into the late hours, testing his constitution, forcing him outside with that woman then walking him through the park late at night and waiting while Alan Barber relieves himself through a fence which has a four-year-old girl on the other side.

'What can I get you, (Insignificant Friend)? The usual?' Alan asks.

His friend nods and sits down.

Alan Barber orders a Disaronno with orange and ice for his friend and a Plymouth and tonic for himself. He lays a ten-pound note on the bar and excuses himself to go to the lavatory while the barmaid completes the order.

At the furthest urinal, facing the corner at an angle, an older, more portly gentleman leans with his left hand against the tiled wall, his right hand by his zip, whistling. Alan Barber never sees his face.

This is unfortunate because, unlike Alan, *he* is important.

He is significant.

He is capable of murder.

Alan Barber is so drunk that later, when the police question him, he will not be able to recall this seemingly arbitrary encounter. At first.

Though he does not need to clear his throat, Alan coughs as he approaches the urinal furthest to the right, thus alerting the other patron to his existence.

'When you get to my age, you have to whistle sometimes just to get things moving,' the faceless killer jokes, masking himself from view, fixing his eyes on his flaccid, unused dick.

Alan Barber grunts an acknowledgement towards his left then stares down into the bowl, looking at the yellow cakes, which smell of bleach, piss and lemon. He does not avert his eyes even when the notable character to his left finishes, walks behind him, washes his hands and leaves.

When he returns to the bar, his friend is sitting with a girl. He has bought her a drink with the ten-pound note that Alan trustingly left, and there is now nothing in the way of change.

'Hey, Alan' – his friend stands up from his stool – 'this is (a female name Alan Barber instantly forgets).' He does remember that they went into the cold, empty beer garden after closing time and that she sat on the bench, unzipped his jeans and performed an impressive oral dance on him, complete with humming interludes. He omits this portion of the night from his original testimony, too. He doesn't mention that he walked away, unable to ejaculate.

Leaving the Edinboro Castle pub, Alan Barber and his friend, who has been waiting patiently at the end of Delancey Street, stumble around the perimeter of Regent's

Park until they spot a young girl walking on her own and, in their inebriated state, think it will be hilarious to follow her for a while.

Stop.

It's not her.

She's not the one who dies.

Part of the way into the park, Alan Barber decides to stop pursuing the woman. He needs to empty the gin from his bladder. He knows there is a toilet nearby on one side of the small coffee shop, which is closed.

This is the point where his life gained some meaning. Some clarity.

He jogs on from his friend, turns right at the bush, which was suggested as an adequate urinal, then turns left up the path to the brick building partially covered by the undergrowth.

The lights are on but it is locked. Alan Barber pushes and pulls at the door in frustration before being overtaken by a state of urgency. He pulls at his trousers violently before poking his penis between two of the iron bars of the fence, which runs around the ground to the right of the building.

Dropping his head backwards, he looks up at the sky and naturally arches his back enough to change the trajectory of his open-air urination. It hits a muddy slope and begins to splash against something flat. He looks to see what it is.

Toes.

Pale, white, tiny, delicate toes.

Instead of pulling back or stopping or jumping over the fence, he continues to empty his bladder, circling around the exposed digits, revealing the outer arch, part of the ankle.

He screams the name of his friend.

Still, he doesn't move. He doesn't react. Adrenalin does not force him to vault the fence and take a closer look or dig through the mud with his hands. He becomes a grotesque statue of an inconsequential, drunken life. His hands drop to his side, his flaccid penis drips between his legs, his eyes fixate on the excavated-by-gin-sodden-kidney-waste foot.

He can see it is a foot.

A child's foot.

And he assumes that she is already dead.

At no point does it occur to him that this was recent and that he could still help in some way, that the last time he evacuated his bladder he stood next to the man that buried this body.

He is the one to call the police and he waits behind the fence gazing at the dead, porcelain foot until they arrive.

So forget about Alan Barber. He is not a suspect. He has a witness to corroborate his actions. You can forget about him too; he's an idiot. There is CCTV footage of Alan at the pub he admitted to drinking at with his friends. It is time-stamped to confirm his story. He is just a man who was on his way home and found a girl who was never expected to be found.

This is what Paulson and Murphy have been missing.

What they have been waiting for.

This is the front line.

January

——✦——

Wednesday
HAMPSTEAD, 23:59

I saw my sister.
    I saw Cathy.

She was standing in the corner of my living room, her head bobbing slightly as she faced the wall; it looked like she was counting. I knew it was her. Her hair was the same. Her manner the same. She was wearing the same polka-dot dress she had on the day she went missing.

That spring in '85.

When everything withered.

And then she just disappeared.

It has been just over six weeks since I saw her. Since I have slept well enough to dream. Since I was last at work. My democratically enforced sabbatical has afforded me the opportunity to arrange the journals my mother left to me after her death, and gain insight into the intuition we seem to have shared. I drink less. The dark shadows under my eyes are ever-present, whether I am rested or not. I've had time to reflect. And I'm ready to go back. Return to my job.

To lie.

I will admit to my superiors that my drinking had escalated on the last case, the hunt for Celeste Varrick, and I won't use the excuse that both of my parents had died and my wife had left me after sleeping with a fucking serial killer. I'll explain that I was exhausted when returning home the night I solved that mystery, that everything had conspired too abruptly, that I must have been hallucinating or projecting as a result of the alcohol level in my body and the emotional fatigue.

That it was a shadow or a trick of light. A wind-blown curtain.

That, whatever it is that I think I saw, it could not have been my sister.

I will lie.

Because everyone but me thinks my sister is dead.

And these are the things they want to hear.

I know what I saw. I know Cathy. And it is time that I return to lead my team. Chief Inspector Markam needs to bring me back in. Not because a man named Alan Barber has numbed himself with gin and will foolishly trail an innocent girl through Camden in the early hours, unaware of his impending discovery. That is not my case. Not yet.

I just need to work. That is who I am. It is all I am now. My parents are gone. I accept that the unresolved issues with my father will remain unresolved; I can bear the slow erosion of unanswerable questions. I have locked Eames in a box in my mind; Audrey's compartment has been placed in the opposite corner of my memory.

A point of equilibrium has been reached. The sabbatical I never wanted to take has worked in the way that nobody truly expected it to. I'm ready. Ready for work, for the next case. Ready to dream.

But, if that is so, I must also prepare myself to experience nightmare. And nightmares have the power to unlock the chambers of grief and torment and misery and murder that a person like me hides in the recesses of his mind.

They can bring back the very incidents you have been trying to forget.

I have been ignoring Eames. I've overlooked Audrey. And said goodbye to their infidelity.

It will soon be tomorrow.

And The Smiling Man wants me to remember.

The Front Line

Thursday
REGENT'S PARK, 05:23

Murphy considers himself to be the inspector in January's absence.

Paulson would never refer to him in that manner.

As *Acting Detective Inspector*, Murphy revels in echoing the message he had received only moments before from his unknown supporter to Paulson, the man he now regards as a subordinate.

'We've got one. And it's going to be huge.'

'What are you talking about, Murph?' Paulson, his mobile pressed to his ever-decreasing cheek, pants heavily as he continues to march on his new routine, thumping along the London pavements in his early-morning, pre-work power-walk. Nobody is out at this time. Nobody can see an overweight man trying to sweat out the excess kilos.

'A case. We've got a case. A young girl has been found.'

'Oh fuck.' Paulson hates those words. Why a *young girl*? Why does it have to be another young, innocent girl?

'We don't know how long she has been dead for. Discovered by a couple of drunks. A shallow grave.'

Paulson remains silent, put off by Murphy's verve.

'Meet me at Regent's Park. The corner of Broadwalk nearest to Park Square Gardens. We'll go in together.'

Detective Sergeant Paulson ceases his exercise and rests against the concrete wall surrounding the stone front garden of one of the houses on his street, his lower back pushing against the bricks to support his weight. And he despairs. The moment he heard it was a young girl, and that there is no evidence yet to suggest how long she has been buried, he thought about January David and, more specifically, his missing sister Cathy.

With his real inspector on indeterminate leave, DS Paulson feels burdened. Murphy may have the title but Paulson is taking on the anguish. Fearing he will be the one forced to inform his friend that his missing sister has finally been found after all these years.

That she is dead.

And her bones are still small.

And the lack of sensitivity that Murphy displays only adds to the frustration.

This is the kind of thing January David has to contend with each day.

Paulson knows that they have to deal with the violent cases, the extreme cases, and that a certain level of desensitisation occurs in everyone after prolonged exposure to the scenes they encounter, but Murphy seems excited. This is what he has been waiting for. The opportunity to tackle a high-profile case without January David's input.

All that Paulson can muster in response is, 'OK.'

And he ends the call.

Before he realises that there is nobody at the other end of the line, Murphy punctuates his call by repeating, 'This is going to be huge.' He knows he should not be smiling as he says this but it doesn't stop him. He has become someone even he no longer recognises.

And it's too late to turn back.

The severity of the situation only turns to reality at the crime scene. Alan Barber, the man who unearthed the child with his gin-soaked urine, still sobs into his own lap, a friend uncomfortably laying a hand on his shoulder, nervous though he has done nothing wrong.

Two police colleagues, assigned to a missing person's query nearly two days ago, wait in front of the tape which separates the path to the public toilets and the patch of dirt where a four-year-old porcelain doll lies at rest.

It is the girl they were assigned to locate.

Aria Sky.

The gentle child.

Paulson spots the body through the gap between his failed colleagues' shoulders. She is wearing a muddied, white, child-size boiler suit. Her hair is straight and scraggly and blonde. Her feet are small and clean and pale. But at least she has skin and muscle and eyes and hair. This is recent.

It cannot be the body of Cathy David.

Detective Paulson breathes a sigh of relief.

And this time he feels like the monster.

January

---✦---

B lindfolded and tied to a chair.
    That's how it always starts with him.

He pulls the scarf away from my eyes, his giant frame looming behind me, no shadow, no sound of breath, just the empty expanse of black before me stretching into for ever.

I don't need to turn around to know that it is him.

Again.

The Smiling Man.

The apparition that leads me to Eames.

I want to wake up. I don't want him back because it reopens the wounds I felt were healing since he disappeared from my intuitions. Mother's journals state that she was able to pull herself out, get back to consciousness. To reality. I want this now. But he starts to shift behind me, his left foot then his right, bobbing from side to side in this dust-covered purgatory he calls home.

And I realise I am stuck.

I can't get out before he delivers his message.

Not this time.

When the image of my missing sister appeared to me

25

following the last case, my pain was emotional. She looked the same as she did all those years ago, a ten-year-old girl in a polka-dot dress innocently playing hide-and-seek. Her presence wrenched at my heart but I was never in danger.

The Two who guided me on the last case were threatening. The apparition of that young boy and girl working in perfect syzygy, always edging closer to me, increasing their menace with each vision, but they just wanted to communicate, to convey the information that would help me capture Celeste Varrick.

The Smiling Man is different. He tied me up, hit me, placed bullets between my teeth, stuffed my mouth to its maximum point of elasticity with hundreds of cigarettes. He abuses me physically. He gets off on torturing me.

I'm anxious.

Still, I have not turned around but I know it is him.

The lack of air is the same.

His presence incites a horror within me akin to no other emotion I have ever felt. Though he exists as merely dust and figment, our connection surpasses reality.

I don't question his motives for returning to my mind. I don't think about Eames yet, or Audrey, or the five people killed the last time this sinister giant occupied a space in my subconscious. I just want to know what he is going to do to me this time. I'm thinking about myself.

One of his large, dark hands grazes my right shoulder as he floats into view and ignites the sound of an out-of-key piano being played badly.

It has begun.

I inwardly judder at the first note but the startle does not manifest itself into movement; I'm frozen rigid.

He controls me.

The long leather raincoat he once wore, which made him look like a nightclub bouncer, has been replaced by a blue velvet suit, which makes him look like a pimp. His legs are thin but his back, which is turned to me still, is a broad, stalwart triangle.

Then he starts. His trick, his charade, his torment. And cold runs through me. My organs goose-pimple.

His strong arms stretch out to form a crucifixion much like he did in my vision of his levitation, but his hands are delicate. Womanly, even. With a gliding fluidity his wrists circle around and eventually stop to reveal his forefinger and thumb touching at the tip to form two rings of dark flesh and bone.

And he starts to turn around.

Somehow I feel more paralysed; I can move my body less than not-at-all. His feet have ceased their usual shuffle and are clamped together at the ankles. It seems as though the floor moves to rotate this giant figure ahead of me like a sinister music-box ballerina.

From the side I can see how his jaundiced eyes protrude from his skull; I know every bloodshot vein. He turns further and my gaze is drawn in to his yellow gravestone teeth. He is smiling. Of course he is smiling. Still, the piano plays its series of flats and sharps.

He stops and fixes his unblinking stare on to mine, scorching my retina with his disquieting beaming expression. I can't look away. I don't dare. With a subtle flick of his wrists towards the gloaming above, I feel my body jolt into a standing position. He is controlling me. Like a puppet my limbs dangle floppily as though being held up on display by two rods underneath my armpits.

As he brings his hands closer together, his arms still outstretched at chest-height, my elbows begin to lift so that the backs of my hands are now resting against my stomach. The nearer his looped fingers get to each other, the nearer my elbows are to one another.

Eventually both shoulders pop from their sockets in order for the elbows to connect. I grimace and shout but the only sound in this place is a B-flat, which should have been played as an A. He smiles at my agony.

He smiles at everything.

He lifts the two circles of fingers, which are now touching, up to his face and peers through them like joke glasses. He lowers them, then lifts them.

Lowers them.

Lifts them.

Then links the circles.

My right arm appears to push straight through my left as though one is a hologram but I feel the bone pass through bone, the muscle entwine with muscle, before my broken-doll knot of an exterior mimics his intricate hand gestures.

Before I have a moment to convey my pain he is flinging his arms towards the non-existent ceiling and my flimsy legs are taken from beneath me to hoist me into the dust-drenched air.

The Smiling Man steps closer to me, resuming his original dance, bobbing from left foot to right, left foot to right. I sense what I think is his glee but it is not his emotion to have: this belongs to the person he represents. The killer I must apprehend.

The giant stands below where I float so I know I am at least seven feet up. We make eye contact again. This time he tilts his head to the left for a moment as if apologising for what will come next.

He gently places his linked fingers below my Adam's

apple. His remaining fingers touch lightly at the sides of my neck. I note a tendon tense in his own neck to bring his head back to mirror mine. He is giving me all the clues I need.

Then he squeezes. Bracing my oesophagus.

And I wake up.

In bed. The bed I once shared with my wife, Audrey. The wife whose scent once lingered in this room, a ghostly reminder of our failed relationship. But she is not the person I think of; I have learned to deal with this loss.

I picture Eames, sitting in the hallway of his house two years ago, awaiting my arrival, seemingly happy to be caught. Glad to be rid of his secrets.

All rationality leaves me when The Smiling Man is involved in my thoughts. He is my link to Eames. He represents Eames' actions. Someone, undoubtedly a girl, a woman, will be killed in the next twenty-four hours.

Fuck.

How did he get out?

How can I get back in?

The Call

—✦—

It has been six weeks since the last case ended, since Detective Inspector January David took the bullet for the conduct of that final operation. Where he had apprehended the perpetrator of those ritualistic murders only to allow his guard to drop for a moment, resulting in a struggle and the eventual death of the suspect. Detective Sergeant Paulson has been losing weight from that day.

The day January David was praised for apprehending the perpetrator, only to be rewarded with an indefinite sabbatical. Reprimanded for the death of Sam Abbadon, though there was nothing he could have done to prevent it.

At least he wasn't fired.

Thank God Paulson is still around to keep an eye on Murphy.

That fucking snake.

'Jan won't recognise you if he ever comes back,' Murphy spouts towards Paulson, who is pouring a coffee on the other side of the office.

'When. *When* he comes back, Murph.'

Murphy rolls his eyes as if he knows something

30

Paulson does not. They have fallen effortlessly back into their archetypal roles of principled policeman and corrupt cop. Aria Sky's body was only discovered a little over two hours ago.

'And when he comes back,' Paulson adds, 'he's gonna be pissed off to find you sitting at his desk.'

Murphy has taken a more active role in leading the team from the moment of January's departure. He spread his files over his inspector's desk but his gumption fell short of emptying the drawer that January reserves for his missing sister's case file. He's stupid but he's not an idiot. Chief Inspector Markam had offered the temporary upgrade in status to the thinning detective Paulson, but he expressed a preference to be on the front line.

There had been no front line. At least there hadn't been for a couple of months. There was no sociopath looking to outsmart Detective Sergeant Paulson. No mass-murderer trying to one-up Detective Sergeant Murphy. Nobody knows who they are. They are support. Lackeys, at best.

Only the scalp of January David will do.

And Eames feels this is his property.

Paulson's phone rings. Not the one on his desk or the mobile phone he has for work. The other one. The one only a few people know about. People he likes. People who owe him favours. People who owe him money. People with information.

Murphy does not have this number.

He looks at the screen and sees January's name flash in bright blue letters. 'I'm going to take this into the hall.'

'You can talk freely in here.' Murphy doesn't even look up from the desk as he speaks.

'I'd rather go outside, all the same.'

'Checking up on me, is he?' Murphy grins knowingly and flicks through a handful of papers he's not even reading.

Paulson, though slimmer than usual, still possesses an intimidating frame. He turns to the desk, steaming coffee in his left hand, and faces his irritating colleague. Staring through him apathetically, he lifts the phone to his cheek, flips it open to answer the call and simply says 'Go!' to the person at the other end.

Murphy peers on, dumbfounded.

Paulson walks out casually without saying a word.

And he won't be back for the rest of the morning.

He is being asked to drive out of London and head west on the M4 motorway. Phone confirmation won't do. It isn't good enough to hear from a nurse. It won't work to believe a voice on the end of a line. Paulson must travel in person. Sign in at the front desk. Be escorted down the corridor. Wait in a guarded room.

See him with his own two eyes.

January trusts Paulson. That's why he called him. He will rely only on Paulson's verification that Eames is still there, locked away in his cage. He needs to know for certain that nobody is going to die. That The Smiling Man is not real this time. An aftershock, at best. Residual memory.

'Jan. This is ludicrous. He's there. We'd know by now if he'd escaped.'

'Will you just do it for me, please? It's important.'

Paulson agrees to the trip. Says he'll call back once he has seen Eames. But he worries: his friend should be feeling better; he should have recovered. In the car, he turns the ignition and rests his head back.

The time away from the station and the pressure of cases is supposed to clear his inspector's mind, give him a chance to regroup, face some lingering demons.

What if Murphy is right?

Maybe January David is never coming back.

Eames

—◆—

They test the alarm every Monday morning at 10 a.m. Two minutes of an air-raid siren followed by another two minutes of a single tone to signify the all-clear. For the first year, I thought this would be the best time to escape.

It's not.

Imagine how futile it will be to sound the alarm thirty minutes after I walk out unnoticed. Think how stupid you will all feel for, once again, buying in to the misdirection.

I've already taken your card while you focus on shuffling the pack.

A male nurse comes to retrieve me.

You can't call him a guard. This is not a prison. He says I have a visitor.

'There are no visits on a Thursday before two,' I tell him, lying on my bed, hand behind my neck, gazing at the ceiling as though it is the first sky I have ever seen.

He's visibly uncomfortable; he is told that we require a regimented structure to our days, weeks, months. Lives. He is afraid to disrupt.

34

Shh. Don't refer to me as a maniac.

I'm ill. That's all.

'It's a policeman.' He speaks coyly yet succinctly.

I sit bolt upright and the glorified orderly sent to collect me steps back and widens his stance in preparation. I smirk without looking at him. I'm not going to hurt him. I won't attack him. I've just been caught off guard. I wanted to be prepared for this meeting, know everything I would say and how I would act, but now I can't do that.

He is here now.

Detective Inspector January David is here right now.

He's a day earlier than I expected.

Nobody has died yet.

Kerry Ross is yet to call in sick for work today.

I shut my eyes and breathe deeply, perched on the edge of my mattress.

'Ready to go?' my escort questions.

I take three more breaths, stand, nod, then open my eyes.

He moves his well-over-six-feet, looks-like-a-prison-guard body to the outside of the room and I exit. He walks next to me, towering over me, slightly behind. So he can always see my hands.

There is no doubt in my mind that he could stop me with ease if I tried to run or hit him, yet still I sense his fear. That is my gift. Terror keeps you safe. Trust ensnares. There are people here who would fight just to take a chunk out of him; some would not hesitate to bite through his neck, spoon out an eye. That's not me. That's impulsive. It requires no thought, no control.

We plod down the hall to begin with but I find myself

picking up the pace in anticipation of a meeting with my favourite opponent. I want to look into his face and smile. I want him to wonder what it is that I know. I want him to torture himself about it in the same way he will for ever be tormented that I have been inside his wife.

The overgrown carer opens the door to the visiting room. I have never been in here before. Nobody has come to see me. There is nobody. Just letters. Or cards. Or code. But nobody real. Nothing is real.

And my excitement dissipates in an instant.

The room is filled with tables, each surrounded by four orange plastic school chairs. Every chair is empty but one. He stands up when I enter the room. Echoing around the giant space is the sound of the chair legs screeching against the floor as he pushes it backwards.

'You're not him.' I whisper this sentence in the same way I say *lunatic*. In the same manner I utter *asylum*. In the same way I call this place a prison.

He takes four steps towards me.

'You're not him,' I repeat, this time audible to the fat man opposite me.

'No. But you certainly are,' he responds smugly.

Then he walks past me as if it is the end.

'Hey,' I call out to him, as though speaking to a friend. He is no friend. He continues to walk away.

'Hey.' This time louder, my venom aimed at his broad back. Still, he is unperturbed. He has what he came for. A positive identification. I am still locked away.

'Hey!' He turns around this time. My voice warbles slightly and the man who is apparently not a prison guard widens his stance once more, his low centre of gravity planting him firmly into the ground. Unrockable.

The overweight detective turns but does not speak.

'Where is he?'

Nothing.

'Where is Detective Inspector January David?'

He is consistent in his indifference.

'I need you to give him a message.'

He doesn't blink. He doesn't even move. I wait a short time and monitor him, hoping he will give in and ask what the message is, but he shows mettle.

'CE23,' I state confidently.

His eyes squint ever so slightly as he digests the information. The movement is minute, but I notice it. I was looking for it.

We wait again. He thinks this is a stand-off, that he is a match for me, that we are in some kind of cerebral confrontation. But I have already won the battle. I step closer to him and he is predictably unflinching.

'You can leave now.' My smile stretches across my face without showing any teeth.

He turns back and strides to the door. At one point he stutters, stops as if to say something, thinks better of it, and continues.

And then he is gone.

Back in my empty room, my cell, my prison, beneath the uncomfortably thin mattress, bending against the springs, there is a single playing card taken from a split-spades deck. The eight of spades.

It starts now.

Girl 8

—✦—

My boss shows no sympathy for my alleged illness. He wants me to feel guilty for having the day off. He employs the same tone when people are really sick yet still come into the office.

I click through my emails again with the telephone receiver tucked beneath my chin, my voice hoarse, sniffing as I speak. I have sinus pain. Conjunctivitis. There's a lump in my breast.

None of the old theatre troupe have responded to me.

They will, I'm sure.

It's what we always wanted.

I sip at a mug of chai tea while navigating the old theatre company website, smiling at some of the production pictures we plastered over the Internet for people to enjoy, but hardly anybody bothered. My reminiscences fill me with the warmth of creative innocence and naivety yet at the same time I feel a sense of loss at the group's long-defunct camaraderie.

I refresh my emails.

Still no answer.

I'm meeting Eames in less than an hour.

My boss tells me to rest. He says he hopes I'll feel better tomorrow morning. He doesn't know that I won't feel anything, that yesterday was my last full day. I hack into the mouthpiece for good measure and croak, 'Me too.' Then I hit the red button on my mobile phone to cut him off for good.

I have time to quickly read through the various updates of my so-called friends on the several social-networking sites I can't seem to drag myself away from. I want to write something about my meeting today, how my life could be turning around, how I'll be back in the theatre very soon, but I can't: I have to maintain the illusion and instead opt for a lie about how sick I feel today. Someone I went to school with but haven't seen for ten years feels compelled to comment with words of condolence that I read as disingenuous.

I don't shut the computer down, I just log out. I'm sure the authorities will be able to crack my password when I don't return; it's the name of the play I directed followed by the date of opening night. Then they'll be able to go through my files, my pictures, my emails.

And they'll know who killed me.

They'll know Eames is back.

My outfit is somewhere between the smart, city-savvy look I don for work and the casualness I adopt away from the office. I want him to know that I am creative but also commercially astute.

I exit my apartment to the familiar sight of blue

construction boards covered in white stencilled lettering ordering *Post No Bills*. I do not live here for the view. I'm here because it is affordable, there are no tourists and I'm somewhere between the theatre district where I dream of belonging and the Chelsea area I must conquer first.

I cross at the corner where my road intersects a major avenue, keeping parallel with the iron bridge, which now runs trains directly over my head. In the distance I see decrepit office blocks with ageing wooden water towers across the rooftops. Back over my right shoulder are the brighter lights I long to live amid. For now, the graffiti-stained concrete ahead is all I have to look forward to.

I glance at the rubble beneath the railway bridge as I walk and think of every detective show I've ever watched, every film about small-time crooks and organised crime. I wonder whether there are any bodies buried in there; it seems an ideal spot. I don't walk around here at night. In my head I start to create a story of crime and malevolence that ends on the broken stones underneath this bridge. It could be my next play. It doesn't seem right to be smiling as I imagine this storyline but nothing can bring my mood down today; I see beauty in everything.

In thirty-five minutes I will be attacked.

And killed.

And stripped of dignity.

And nobody will know for hours.

January

———❖———

'He's still in there.'

I say nothing but my mind breathes an extended sigh.

'I saw him with my own eyes, Jan,' Paulson continues, hoping to elicit a response. 'He looks the same. Unde—'

I jump in. 'I don't care how he is or seems to be, I just want to know that he is locked away.'

There is silence at both ends of the line while I think of a way to speak about Eames, the man who took away half of my life, without getting agitated and thrusting that disquiet in the direction of my only friend. Paulson could confirm again that Eames is secure. He could moan about something Murphy has done at work. He could tell me not to worry about The Smiling Man. But he doesn't do any of these things.

'When do you think you'll be back?'

'I can't say for sure. I thought things were picking up. I've served out the sabbatical' – my eyes roll at the word, flimsily disguising its true meaning of suspension – 'and Chief Markam says it's up to me now. This false intuition is making me think that I may need more time. I had thought I was ready.'

'But you are . . . coming back, aren't you?' he asks nervously, Murphy's earlier words still invading his thoughts.

I allow myself a moment to smile, exhaling a short puff of laughter.

'What else am I going to do?'

'We've got something. You could come back and run it.'

I'm silent for a second, not sure how to react. I don't know whether his desperation for me to return is for my sanity or his.

'Young girl. Shallow grave. Regent's Park,' he continues, waiting for me to bite.

'Have you spoken to the family yet?'

'Today. With Murph. No need for them to identify the body. We know.'

'How long has she been missing? A day or two? You think it's the family?' I fire the questions out as though he's on the wrong end of an interrogation.

'Yeah. It usually is.' He seems confident in this summation. I think it's laziness. They do need me back.

'Not this time. I don't believe it. The burial seems rushed. And why take the body to the park? Seems risky. If results come back and say she has been there the whole time, then lean towards the relations; but if she was kept alive for even a day, you could be looking at something else entirely.' I can't assume Paulson is still thinking laterally; with nobody there to make him up his game, he could become complacent like Murphy.

I keep him sharp.

He is helping me. I will help him in any way I can.

We talk for a while as friends. Paulson explains a little about his eating and walking and breathing exercises, which seem to be helping him regain some health while dropping the weight he has carried around for as long as I can remember. He says he's still heavily involved in the online poker community and that he has hooked his workstation up to an even bigger flat-screen.

Then he says, 'Gosh, I nearly forgot.'

'What? What is it?'

'He had a message . . . for you.'

'Forget it. He's trying to get inside my head. Keep it to yourself. I don't want to know.' I string the sentences together as though speaking one long word.

'OK. OK. You're probably right. Sounded like gibberish, anyway.'

'Look, Paulson, thanks for driving over there. He's incarcerated. His words have no significance any more. Nothing good can come of entering into this game with him.'

He agrees and I hang up.

Eames

———✦———

J ack of hearts.
   Five of hearts.
Five of diamonds.
Five of diamonds. Each diamond surrounded by a hand-drawn circle in black ink.
Queen of diamonds.

These were the last five cards I received. Each delivered to me in a separate brown envelope with my name written on the front in a silver marker. Someone opens the envelope before I am allowed to see what is inside. They used to take the cards away, afraid I would slit my wrists, until I told them that they may want to take my teeth away, in that case.

The letters could have been delivered to me in any order and it would not make a difference.

I would understand.

I would know that Kerry Ross is dead.

That she is Girl 8.

That everything is still going to plan.

That there are now only three.

44

January

—✦—

I step into the en-suite and splash my face with water
from the cold tap. My reflection is not as old, it's not
as tired. One thing my time away has afforded me is
physical and mental recovery. I'm not under any
pressure. For once, I don't have to think of anyone else
but myself.

The perfume bottle behind the sink is empty. Audrey's
scent has nearly disappeared from this room. I have been
spraying a few squirts each morning as a reminder.

It ran dry three days ago.

Yesterday, the last molecule of my estranged wife
evaporated.

She must have known.

I face the mirror, scrutinising the reflection. Peering
into my own eyes. Water clings to my two-day stubble,
and I see the futility of my actions. I know what is coming.
I note the brow of the man who looks just like me, his
interest piquing. But in every wrinkle and crease, every
darkened patch of skin, we both uncover the ingrained
disappointment. The heavy heart. Back in the bedroom, I
pick up the mobile phone from the bed; the battery is

still warm from conversation. I scroll down to the number only a handful of people know.

'Jan? Everything—'

'Just tell me. Fucking tell me what he said. What is his message?' My voice is identifiable as perpetually-aggravated-by-Eames'-existence.

'CE23,' Paulson exclaims.

'That's it?'

'That's all he said, Jan.'

'And he said two, three? Not twenty-three?' I query.

'Yeah. C. E. Two. Three.'

I don't say goodbye or thank Paulson, I just cut the call, throw the phone on the bed and run down the stairs repeating 'CE23' over and over until I reach the kitchen. Inside one of the silent-closing drawers is a collection of leaflets and menus and coupons and a map of the London Underground system.

I check the grid reference. This is how he would preface his kills before. This is how he taunted us with their location. But the numbers do not fit. It's not the same.

Everything is backwards.

I'm letting him screw with me again.

I throw the map down onto the granite surface and pace around to the journal room where I keep Mother's scribblings and Cathy's file and a desk now and my whisky. I still drink most days, but not as much.

Sitting in my new desk chair I rest my left elbow on the arm and my forehead in my hand while I stare at the floor.

Eames is imprisoned.

He's confined.

Detained.

And he knows exactly where Girl 8 is going to die.

The Skys

—◆—

There are two pictures above the fireplace. To the left, the entire family unit – mother, father, deceased daughter and her older brother – and on the right side an image, too overly posed to look natural, depicts just the siblings together. Both photos were clearly taken in a white-box studio as so often seen advertised by overzealous sales-people in shopping centres.

Paulson stares at the image on the left and feels awful, even guilty. He focuses on the face of Aria Sky and almost doesn't recognise her as the frail, ashen doll unearthed at Regent's Park. There, lying dead in the dirt, no blood coursing through her veins, her right foot spattered with the urine of a local alcoholic, she seemed pure and at peace. In the photo she appears playful and carefree as any young child would be, but she isn't pretty or dainty or cute. Though she has been missing for almost two days, Paulson wonders why he cannot recall anything in the newspapers, why the parents have not been replayed over and over on television pleading to their daughter's abductor. Cynically, perhaps, he tells himself that Aria Sky just didn't have the face.

47

Until she died.

Paulson looks at the mother and sees the woman Aria could have become. Her eyes are tired yet unblinking. She has been awake for over fifty hours. Her eyelids are afraid to close for fear of wasting time that could be spent productively looking for the missing girl. The three frown lines on her forehead indicate to Paulson that she is deliberately forcing her eyes wide open in anticipation of the news she doesn't want to hear but cannot escape.

The father seems removed, almost placing himself a step back from his wife; she is in charge of their investigation. Some might feel suspicious at the scene, sensing fault had been passed in his direction, but Paulson understands that the mother's unsinkable call to action is both maternal instinct and a debilitating sense of self-blame.

They are both young, mid-thirties, and seemingly healthy. Aria's father has a slouch to his shoulder and a concave crater to his chest where his heart used to be. Everything about his posture says he is submissive, not in control.

That he has already given up.

He knew she would never be returning to the Sky household.

'Where are the two detectives who were here before?' another voice asks.

He is sitting on the couch while the rest of them stand. It feels as though a great crowd parts at the centre to reveal his presence, though in actuality there are only five people in the room.

It is Aria's uncle.

He is an obvious relation, bearing a striking resemblance to the cowering father who falls further into shadow as his brother's voice booms through the imaginary horde. He inherited the full head of hair, which shows no sign of receding despite being around five years the elder.

He stands up, seemingly in possession of his brother's backbone as well as his own, and stretches out a welcoming hand to both detectives; Murphy first, then Paulson. He seems less aware than the parents of the news about to be broken. The blur between denial and guilt.

In just over an hour, Detective Sergeant Paulson will be back at the police station, rifling through old files, hoping something will jump out to suggest a link to this case, Detective Constable Higgs will be checking to see whether anything similar has occurred around the country recently, and Murphy will be waiting for his next instruction, someone to tell him he has to wrap this up or pin it on one of the people he is about to upset in the room in which he nervously stands.

The awkward father seems a more likely suspect than the confident uncle or resolute mother – if Murphy were forced to 'make something stick', as will be suggested by his enigmatic sponsor.

'Detective Sergeant Paulson and myself are taking over this case,' Murphy responds, shaking the uncle's hand and signalling with his eyes for him to sit back down.

Paulson thinks of the elder brother and how he will handle, emotionally, the loss of his sister. He has seen how consumed January David is with his own sister's case. Perhaps it is harder because she has never been found, he reflects, dropping his attention away from the Sky family for just a moment.

'So we have to recount the details all over again?' The uncle rolls his eyes in pseudo-frustration.

'We know the details, sir, that's not why we are here.' Murphy displays a degree of authority Paulson has never witnessed before. He is slipping effortlessly into the role vacated by January David and is making all the right noises. 'If you'd like to sit back down. Mr and Mrs Sky,' – he gestures towards them with an open palm – 'you may like to be seated also.' Murphy exudes an authority he has never had the opportunity to display until now. His body language tells the Skys that the other two officers were dealing with a missing person's enquiry. Murphy and Paulson are something different. Something more austere.

Mrs Sky drops down on to the single-seat sofa cushion, and her husband perches on the arm of the seat beside her.

'In the early hours of this morning, a gentleman by the name of Alan Barber . . .' He pauses to see whether there is any reaction to or recognition of this name – there is none. He gives a knowing glance towards Paulson. 'Alan Barber,' he repeats, 'quite through chance, located your daughter Aria.'

This time Paulson surveys the faces, the unattractive faces that genetically hindered a young girl's chance of national media exposure, to gauge their varying responses to Murphy's impending announcement.

On hearing that she has been found, Aria's mother seems lighter. The tension released. Only her eyelids carry weight. The father looks resigned, as though he is the realist of the room; he knows that the next sentence to leave Murphy's lips will confirm the worst. And his brother, Aria's uncle, fleetingly portrays panic or trepidation or disbelief.

Then Murphy informs them all that she is dead.

That he and his partner work in violent crime.

That Aria is gone.

Their daughter and niece has been killed and dumped and buried and pissed on.

Mrs Sky slips from the edge of the sofa cushion, her knees crashing to the floor, and wails, releasing a sorrow she has been fooling herself would never have to be realised. Her husband remains stalwart in his apathy while Aria's uncle looks on in confusion, not knowing whether to comfort his sister-in-law in an all-encompassing embrace or shake his brother violently into feeling something other than nothing.

Aria Sky, the gentle child, has passed, and leaves a family, understandably, in a state of hysteria and grief.

Whether this is true or forced, genuine or contrived, the two detectives who find themselves in the midst of the moment, yet also peripheral figures, must maintain their critical eye. Through the anguish and delirium, they must exert a professional level of comfort and consolation.

But a young girl has died.

She was four years old, five in June.

Paulson and Murphy have little to go on at this point.

Alan Barber found the body. That is all. That was his role. He has an alibi and witnesses to his whereabouts at the time Aria was abducted. He is a stranger. The smallest percentage of kidnappings are committed by someone unknown to the victim.

There appear to be no enemies. There have been no threats, no incidents, no disagreements with neighbours or co-workers or cousins or siblings. Over a quarter of these cases find guilt in an acquaintance.

And half are uncovered to be a family member.

So these three people, each with a profound absence, each with a different way of handling the grief, the suffering, each hiding a truth, are now suspects.

Audrey

—◆—

He has his father's eyes. I hate that about him.
My son is eighteen months old. He is innocent
and curious. His speech consists of mispronounced
nouns. He is the one thing I always wanted in life and,
from the moment of his birth, I have loathed looking at
him.

Because I just see Eames.

And all I wanted was January.

The nanny arrives ten minutes early, just as she does
every morning. I hand over my child and she smiles
as she greets him. She does not see the killer in his eyes.
She cannot peer into the blue and be reminded of the
mistakes I have made. She sees only the purity that I
cannot.

I head straight to my en-suite shower while the fresh-
faced, petite, blonde waif I hired takes my son by the
hand and walks with him to the playroom. I got him out
of bed first thing this morning, gave him milk, changed
him, chose his outfit for the day, toasted some bread for

him while I drank my first mug of coffee in front of the television; I'm not completely devoid of connection. He knows I am his mother.

But I know his father.

That is the reason things are so difficult. I have been forced back into my old routine. Nothing has changed. I have gone back to being *that* Audrey. The businesswoman who heads a company, who handles large recruitment contracts for blue-chip corporations, who longs for stability and balance between her personal and work lives. I am the person who must accomplish everything I set out to achieve; I complete and conquer.

But the joy of success is momentary. Failure is the only thing that persists and holds true meaning.

As the scorching water blasts me in the face, I push my hair back and relive the catastrophe of the plan to make my husband love me more than his undoubtedly dead sister. I miss him every day. I wish my little boy had his eyes. Those brown, tired, sad, longing eyes.

I turn the heat up and allow the water to beat down against my breasts. Each droplet stabs into my flesh and adds a dot of pain to the gathering cluster. This is insignificant penance for my faults. This is part of my new regime.

The glass partition to my right is fully steamed. I hit the button on the wall, which controls the speakers in the ceiling, and turn my back to the punishing shower head, hoping the music will distract me from my thoughts even if only for a short while.

The first chord causes my skin to goose-bump instantly and, instead of averting my attention from January's whereabouts, I wonder how often he thinks of me. I contemplate him in the shower we used to share, the water at a temperature designed for comfort and cleaning: he has nothing to be punished for. I imagine him imagining me, asking himself whether enough time has passed, whether he can forgive me for being with Eames when I should only ever have been with him.

And I'm touching myself with my left hand. The image of January's face, his body, the smell of his hair, his breath: all are so real in my mind. I desire him. The hot water digging into my back reminds me that I should not be feeling pleasure; I don't deserve it. I halt the motion of my fingers and dig my long nails in like brakes.

Then I flick off the water and I am angry.

Why has he not tried to contact me? Does he not want to find me? Has he given up? Is he with someone else? In our house? This is the irrational Audrey. It is nothing new. I have always been this way. This is an everyday occurrence. Part of my procedure.

Next, I am wrapped in a giant towel blow-drying my hair. Soon, I am dressed and made-up and three inches taller in my heels, which alert the beautiful, opposite-of-me nanny and the toddler with intrinsic sociopathy to my presence as I click across the kitchen's marble floor.

'Mum-mum-mum-mum-mum,' he repeats, waddling from the playroom with a teddy in his right hand, the nanny a few steps behind him, smiling as she always does.

'Hang on a second, darling,' I say without looking at him as I reach into the top cupboard for my aluminium coffee cup.

I place the cup on the granite work surface and flick the switch on the coffee machine at the exact point my son reaches me, grabbing my legs from behind, nestling his head against the inside of my right thigh. He says

Mummy as though I am a toy that has been missing for weeks and has mysteriously reappeared. He does this most mornings.

Routine.

Endless, laborious routine.

Carefully, I manage to turn myself around without knocking him over on to the hard surface; it is completely impractical with a small child who is unsteady on his feet, but this is the kitchen I wanted. I curtsey down until my knees rest on the cold floor and I am closer to his level.

'Now, Mummy has to go to work this morning.'

I look directly at him, straight into Eames' eyes as I say this. He stares back, his face more serious, his pale white skin the same as mine, and repeats back the word 'work'.

'That's right.' I smile. And so does the nanny from a distance. Then I pick him up, jut out a hip for him to perch on, and speak to him about the wonderful things he will do today with Phillipa, the ever-optimistic nanny.

The machine beeps twice in the background and fills my cup with a sweet espresso roast coffee. I screw the lid on with my right hand while still holding my son with the other and carry them both to the front door where Phillipa is already waiting.

'OK. Give Mummy a kiss.' He leans his face into mine and I kiss his cheek. I hand him over to the nanny and step outside the door with my coffee.

'It won't be a late one tonight. I'll be home at half-past five,' I inform her. She, of course, smiles back at me with her faultlessly pristine incisors. I reciprocate but my lips do not part.

'Say goodbye to Mummy,' she whispers softly into

Walter's ear. I named him after January's father. I know that he will hate that. I think it may be my way of apologising. Or trying to keep a part of him with me.

'Bye,' he utters, unconcerned, waving me away. He used to scream when I left him.

I ponder Walter's nonchalance in the lift and momentarily push aside the recurring, tormenting thoughts of January with another woman and his apathy towards my whereabouts. I don't drive to work any more; it is easier to travel by foot here, or take a cab if the sky seems grey. As soon as the air hits my face, Jan is back in my mind.

Perhaps he has looked for me.

It's possible he just isn't ready.

Maybe the only way for him to find me is for Eames to find me first.

I exhale heavily and take a sip of the too-hot coffee while walking. Already I am less than enthused about work. My only motivation is to get through the day. To return home safely. To bathe my son and put him to bed. To sit down on the sofa with a large glass of red wine after Phillipa leaves. To bolt the door shut after she has gone. To lock it from the inside.

To be secure.

To not end up like the girl they will find in Chelsea this evening.

The girl who looks just like me.

The way I did two years ago.

When I was Girl 4.

I need you, January.

Find me again.

Girl 8

---❖---

Thursday
CHELSEA, NEW YORK, 15:30 EST
London, 20:30 GMT

A middle-aged man with a hefty moustache perches outside a store listening to his radio. The right side of his face is drooping as if already drunk or mid-stroke. He fishes through a white plastic bag of God knows what and his only companion appears to be the large box of unopened ice-cream sandwiches.

I remember all these details about him. If I noticed on the evening news that he had been killed today, I would recognise him. I'd be able to call the police and inform them of exactly where and when I saw him last.

But he merely glimpses the blur of another young girl of average attractiveness in flat shoes with straight, dark hair and immediately forgets what is not important to him.

The horn of a huge purple truck startles me and takes my focus away from the lopsided man who will never help in the investigation of my death.

I curse out loud.

He remains unaware.

I continue down Eleventh Avenue. There are bags of

58

trash on the street; there are no police patrolling or hanging in packs of six on the corner. This is not a part of the city people come to visit; this is where we live and work.

And die.

Opposite the Terminal Warehouse a UPS driver abandons his truck in the road and walks a trolley full of parcels along the street ahead of me. I smile at the recollection of an old theatre friend who called them 'Ups' rather than separating the letters individually. I check the emails again on my phone to see whether she has responded.

Nothing.

At the next corner I stop to allow the traffic through. A vehicle passes by hauling a trailer with a huge screen on the back of it. The lights flash the words: 'In a Palestinian state: No Jews or gays.' I'm neither of these things but I still wonder who paid a company to drive around town with this message. This stands out; it's very brazen. And I am standing right next to it.

Others must notice it.

Surely they see me too.

The delivery guy turns left with his parcels and I watch him from behind. I don't remember his face, just his lean dark legs striding along the path in those short shorts.

Just before I die, those legs are the last thing I see.

Eames has arrived early and is waiting for me.

I'm almost there.

Nearly dead.

Six heavily overweight black women congregate outside the police human resources building, drinking various sugary sodas. One wags her finger at another and says, 'That don't make it right.'

'Well, I never said it did,' comes the other woman's retort.

Roadworks force me off the sidewalk and I miss the remainder of their debate.

Is it possible that not one of the half-dozen Rubenesque, dark-skinned ladies observed a solitary, skinny white girl in confused attire pass them by on their break, clearly eavesdropping on the journey to her ultimate demise?

How can it be that the one person who can help is currently over seventeen hundred miles from the place where I stand right now?

The legs of the UPS delivery guy are behind me now. As are the six stomachs of those fat ladies and the sagging cheek of the ice-cream-obsessed stroke victim. I leave the image of the girl who did not have the body to wear that opaque purple dress with all the other non-witnesses and I arrive at 164 Eleventh Avenue.

The Sanford Meisner Theater.

I am Girl 4's reflection.

I'm excited and anxious. My hands are clammy as I approach the front. The white lettering that simply states the address rather than the theatre name is still present and untouched but I feel a pang of melancholy at the state of the surroundings.

The silver shutters are down and somebody has sprayed graffiti, which resembles a pink lipstick-drawn LA. You can't write LA here, not in this town. Not on my theatre.

A sign to the right says *Retail Space For Lease* then a phone number and the instruction to ask for Levinson ext. 205. This is not a retail space. This is a creative expanse, an area of dramatic experimentation. Stupidly,

I believe that Eames feels this too and has chosen to save it, preserve it. But this is a one-person, one-act play.

This is opening night.

And final performance.

Next to the door are the frayed and stained-with-age remnants of an old poster. I choose to believe it was from one of our plays. Somebody has taken the time to stick plain white stickers over it and write *Zen Dog* and *DSense* in black marker on these labels.

It's not a sales outlet. It's a place for personal expression.

The nickel-plated speaker to the left of the door has two buzzers. The bottom has *Spencer STAATS* etched into the metal. The top has words carved in too but a white label has been placed over the top. The name simply says *Eames*.

There is no need to press my shaking finger against the buzzer, the door is open. The detectives will not find my fingerprint there. They will know that my killer was waiting for me.

Disguised as a dream, as opportunity.

A picture of a pushbike with basket, resting against a bush, is fixed to the door with tack for a reason I cannot fathom, but once in the open doorway, familiarity returns.

My world turns to black and white.

All I can see are the pale stairs leading upwards to a space and time in my life I had compartmentalised. They appear to narrow at the top, warning me that the thing I desire should remain out of reach, asking me not to venture upwards. Things have changed. This is a different world.

Nobody paid attention to me walking here. Everyone I know believes I am sick. I can't keep anything down.

I'm feverous.

I have a chest infection.

I ascend. The dark walls closing in around me squeeze me higher and higher up the stairwell. I'm aware of the sweat on my palms as the temperature drops. I can taste the dampness. The sound of footsteps around the corner forces me to hesitate; it should be a pause for reflection, recognition, recollection, but I smile in the anticipation of meeting my new sponsor.

Denying that this was ever a bad idea.

Ignoring the signals that point towards danger.

Forgetting the mythology that surrounds the name on the buzzer.

Is that really how quickly it takes to forget?

Panting slightly, I reach the top of the stairs I will never have to walk down and turn left into the derelict seating area with space for seventy-three spectators. The stage is lit in a blue flood and there are four chains dangling from the ceiling in the centre. I move closer to examine the scene; my breathing slows but my heart rate increases.

I'm excited and scared and bewildered and optimistic and wondering where the sound of those footsteps came from. I rest the tips of my fingers on the stage and look up to interlocking links of metal and allow myself a moment of reverie for what the future may hold.

And the person I am here to meet wraps a fifth chain around my exposed neck.

We fall backwards and the chain tightens. Those strong thighs clamp me to the floor and the back wall, washed in blue, begins to fade.

This is not the end for me. There is more in store. I cannot be found like this.

I am the mirror image.

This is art.

Eames wants me to look like her.

To show he is not finished. He is coming.

There is no time to contemplate my own stupidity or the lie I told to co-workers and alleged friends. I don't have the awareness to imagine the dismay and devastation of my proud parents. My play and any new ideas fall out of consciousness. I recall only the final moments walking back up those stairs my feet have not touched for years. I remember those six female police administrators and the hunched-over man with the old radio and plastic bag. And, as the bulbs and glistening, hanging chains dissipate into darkness, I see the legs of the UPS truck driver.

I never looked at his face.

January

———◆———

An hour after somebody discovers another floating corpse, my home phone rings. The hideous antique phone perched under the hallway mirror that I have hated since the day Audrey showed it to me.

The one my father called to tease Audrey.

It isn't Paulson.

'January David?' a voice asks in an American accent. Brooklyn or Boston or Chicago, I get these muddled; it's difficult to differentiate.

'Speaking.' I don't want to give too much away in case it is some kind of sales call or a survey or something equally irritating, preventing my planned evening of red wine and my sister's case file.

'This is Special Agent Marquez. Is this a secure line, sir?'

'Is anything secure?' The ensuing silence makes my British sense of humour somehow seem even more British.

He jumps straight in, telling me that a woman has been found in a theatre. That she was naked, with pure white skin, deep crimson lips and dark straight hair, which hung down to disguise her face, at first.

64

I ask him what this has to do with me.

'She was suspended above the centre of the stage, Detective Inspector David. Four chains held her body in the air around seven feet from the floor. With the lights off you couldn't see the chains but you could make out the shape of her body. It looked like she was—'

'Floating,' I interrupt, completing his sentence. My mind flicks back to Audrey and all the air seems to escape from my lungs.

'Her neck is badly bruised. All evidence points toward a strangling but whoever killed her tampered with her after. She is wearing a necklace that she could not have been wearing when strangled; there are no marks to suggest this. It was put on her when she was dead.'

I wait for him to finish. He waits for me to acknowledge that I am listening.

'A tight, delicate silver choker. Five linked circles at the front.'

The Smiling Man was real.

And his message was true.

But Paulson checked the asylum; there's no way my old adversary can be involved.

'Where, Agent Marquez? Where was she found? Do you know who she is? Are there signs of intercourse?' Eames floods my mind.

He explains about the old Sanford Meisner Theater: a small venue away from the main theatre district, it was used to house an experimental theatre company which disbanded around four years ago.

164, Eleventh Avenue.

Manhattan, New York.

'That's a little out of my jurisdiction, Agent Marquez.'

'I'm just glad you're home so I can cross you off my list of suspects.' For a moment, it's awkward and stilted.

He explains that I will act as his consultant, that I have a certain amount of invaluable experience, that I know this case. His first procedural step was to search for similar cases nearby, then extend the search across the States and finally overseas. He came across the Eames case, the Zone Two Killer, he calls it – and that image of the fourth victim. He feels I can aid with the investigation. But my help will not be official. Nobody wants to bring me in – my reputation for the unconventional appears to have travelled – but he feels it is necessary if he is going to take this killer down. He believes in me. I respect his honesty.

He says, 'Sometimes you have take a risk and make a name for yourself, Detective Inspector David. You have to make things happen.'

He has no choice. His reputation has also been bruised.

I recall the things The Smiling Man did to me last time – stuffing my mouth with cigarettes, forcing a bullet between my teeth – and I remember the agony of my contortion from the last intuition.

When my shoulders cracked.

And my arms passed through one another.

'Wait. One second,' I command, leaving the phone on the table and blasting into the now organised journal room. The old phone is not cordless; it's completely impractical but I keep it because it belongs to Audrey.

I open the second drawer down. The one below Cathy's case. This is where I keep the information and research gathered from the time Audrey was strung up in a similar manner to this girl.

Finding the sheet of paper I was looking for, I speed back to the phone.

'Agent Marquez?'

'Yes?'

'Ross. Her surname is Ross, isn't it?'

'How could you possibly know—'

I interrupt in half-excitement and explain the Richard Ross Linking Rings trick. I tell him with complete certainty that somebody is trying to finish the list. That there is only Paul Daniels, Robert Harbin and Lance Burton left.

I tell myself that there can't be another David Copperfield illusion.

I try to convince myself that Audrey is safe, wherever she is.

With the help of The Smiling Man, I would know a day before anyone which trick the killer was aiming to emulate and distort – as long as I could decipher the vision. This would give us a surname. We could narrow it down quicker than before.

But something poignant is occurring in London: a young girl has been found. This is my town. This is where I belong.

'That's not all you need to know, Detective Inspector David. The buzzer outside, the theatre itself, they are both linked to the same person.'

I pre-empt what he is going to say but I do not trust myself with this knowledge.

'This person is going by the name Eames.'

I fall cold as he finishes his sentence and feel my scalp turn to goose flesh at the mention of that name.

And it is sealed.

I will remain on my forced sabbatical and fly out to aid Marquez, without question. Paulson and Murphy will have to deal with things here in my absence; this is the challenge they require. I cannot ignore The Smiling Man; I will never be able to put Eames firmly into my past.

I choose this case.

Though my life is somehow implicated in both.

Unknowingly, for the first time ever, I am choosing something over my sister.

Just as she wanted years ago, Audrey has become my priority.

I want to see her.

But not like this.

Nobody wants this.

Eames

—✦—

Thursday
BERKSHIRE, 21:30 GMT
New York, 16:30 EST

I am not allowed to mingle with the other patients.
Shh! They think I am a maniac.
They mutter the word *madman*.
They label me *psychotic*.

I'm not like the others. I don't claim to hear voices or speak directly to a deity. I am not in denial about the things that I did, the people I have killed. I am not violent towards the meatheads who claim they are doctors of the criminal mind. Those pop-psychology charlatans. Those head-shrinking snake-oil salesmen masquerading as medical professionals.
I am not the fraud.
Eames is not a fake.
They ask, 'Do you freely admit to killing those women and abducting the investigating officer's wife?'
Yes. And I have killed more.
'Do you feel a sense of remorse for the families who have been left behind as a result of your unlawful actions?

Do you understand that these acts of lust and anger and vengeance are wrong?'

You want me to say that I do not comprehend the emotion of guilt, that this feeling holds equal weight with the non-sense of pleasure I gain from cutting a person's life shorter than they had anticipated. You wish me to adhere to the research you were too lazy to perform. You hope I tessellate effortlessly into the laymen sayings of your sub-doctorate-level textbooks.

You write: *Eames conforms to standard prescribed psychopathy.*

You scribble: *Eames is not in control.*

Imagine how baffled they would be if I imparted my ability to love; if I explained how my body knows when to kill in the same way it tells me when to eat.

I tell them what they need to hear.

When Detective Inspector January David is too weak or misguided or scared or intrigued to visit me himself, I will tell his overweight minion nothing. Not this time. Not what he wants to hear. Not yet.

I lie back on my too-thin mattress in my solitary confinement and remember all the women I have loved, all the mothers, daughters, sisters I have killed. And I look forwards, to the seeds, to the lamp post, to the underpass, to my next victim. Girl 9.

The time is 21:30.

The lights are out.

It is 16:30 there.

So I think of the woman hanging from the ceiling of the Sanford Meisner Theater and how Detective Inspector January David is probably just finding out.

And I imagine Audrey's face as she opens a newspaper or turns on her television.

When she hears the name Kerry Ross.

But only sees herself.

Audrey

—✦—

I leave the office dead on five, as planned.

I notice the smug look on some faces as they congratulate themselves on projecting a positive image by staying at work later than they have to. They smirk at colleagues who leave at the same time as the boss, but these are the people whose names I remember; the ones who have a family, a personal life. The ones who can manage their workload efficiently and factor in their undoubtedly more enjoyable existence outside this building.

I bid farewell to Carey, my new assistant, who has no choice but to remain after my departure. He is my first male assistant yet is perhaps a little more feminine than any of his predecessors.

'Goodnight, Ms David.' He smiles, teeth all sparkling and straight. 'Getting home to see your little man?' He cocks his head to the side and adds, 'He's such a cutie.'

It's a little sickly.

I want to say, 'Cute with the eyes of a killer' but his sentiment is genuine. 'Thanks, Carey. I'm hoping to get back in time for his evening bath.' I force a smile and he mouths *awwww*.

And I look human.

There are people on the street – there are always people on the street around this area – but I feel paranoid today, like everybody is looking at me. I see them read the screen of their phone, perhaps a text or an online article or one of these news apps, then take a glimpse at me. Like they know I am Girl 4 and I'm in for a shock when I return home to my bastard son and his perfect nanny.

The past is not always the thing that lies behind you.

I quicken my pace, keeping my head high and looking only in the direction where I am heading, trying to appear as though I belong in this part of town. Aloofness results in imperceptibility.

It is the new muscular Asian man on the door of my building today; it was the giant Polish guy when I left for work. He slinks out from behind the desk and greets me on the steps, holding the door open for me to enter.

'Good evening, Ms David.'

'Evening.' I throw out a perfunctory nod and smile of acknowledgement. I can't remember his name, though I am sure he told me the last time he worked – he should be wearing his badge. He's short but stocky. He's polite and his moustache is neat. But that's all I know about him. He knows my name and the fact that I have opted for Ms instead of Mrs.

Too many questions.

The lobby is minimal. Off-white walls and pale carpet. There are three canvasses hanging, each one a black silhouette on a brilliant-white background; one looks to be poppies blowing in the breeze, the others depict an array of twigs, which paint a stark scene of what the world would look like after a nuclear holocaust. Only the twigs would remain.

I turn a key in the elevator rather than pressing a button for my floor and it takes me to the top. When I enter, Phillipa is wiping Walter's face to clean away the stray splatters from his fruit-pot dessert. She smiles at me in her unflustered, takes-it-in-her-stride style.

She looks amazing. Like she put my son down for his afternoon nap, jumped into my shower, used my products to exfoliate and soften and condition, then reapplied her make-up to appear glowing and in control. Her cheeks are the faultless shade of rouge I aspire to for a night out, not that I ever really have a night out any more. I'm changed.

'Ah, you made it.' She smiles, displaying those glowing gravestone incisors, and pulls Walter up and out of his highchair so that he can greet me.

I suppose she has reason to doubt my words, to be surprised that I have shown up when I said I would. There have been numerous occasions over the past six months when I have called to apologise that I am running late and have asked her to stay on a little longer. She always obliges with her usual tone of grateful optimism.

'Look who it iii-iis.' She spins my son around to the big reveal of his largely absent mother.

'Mum!' he screams excitedly.

I look into his killer's eyes and my heart melts. I think back to the large corporate contracts I have captured and finalised in the past, all my great achievements in life, but nothing compares to the fact that my son recognises me, and calls to me by the name that only he can use.

He knows me.
Just as Phillipa knows me.
And the muscular Asian man knows me.
The delivery guy knows me.
The cleaner.
January.
And Eames.

I take Walter from her grasp and hold him on my hip.

'Everything OK today, Phillipa?' I ask, kissing Walter's cheek, hoping there has been some mishap. A bumped head. A spilled drink. Anything. But every day seems to be flawless and fun. I dump my bag on the floor with my spare hand and put my coffee container on the kitchen surface, then walk into the lounge.

Phillipa slides her arms into her jacket. Sometimes she sits around and has a tea while we talk. She fills me in on the landmark moments a mother should experience with her first child and I pretend that I am grateful to hear that he is developing and thriving without too much input from me. But this evening she just wants to leave.

Sitting on the sofa, I kick off my shoes while balancing Walter on my knee. He slides himself down and stands on the floor between my feet, resting his back against the cushion, and his arms are draped over my legs in languid comfort. My stunningly beautiful nanny fastens the front of her coat as I switch on the television and change immediately from a cartoon to one of the many news channels.

A male news reporter stands in front of a downtown building with his freshly gelled hair and his anti-glare glasses newly polished. The text at the bottom says *Sanford Meisner Theater, Chelsea.*

The voice in the doorway says something like, 'OK. I should really go now.' I do not respond and instead raise the volume of the report. Walter sways unknowingly and innocent against my knees.

Phillipa becomes more agitated at my distraction.

'I'm off, then.' She glances at the screen then at my expression of dismay.

The news explains the murder of a young girl in an off-off-Broadway theatre that has been left to stagnate for many years. She was in her twenties. They describe her appearance.

They describe me.

Her name is not divulged but I find myself holding my breath, waiting for the next piece of information to drip out through the speakers.

Phillipa senses my distress, my fear, and she softly moves over to sit beside and comfort me. My immediate reaction is to pull my son into my chest to shield and protect him.

'Are you all right?' she asks, genuinely, her eyes full of concern. 'You seem—'

'Oh it's just . . . so . . .' I interrupt then stumble for an excuse. 'It's just so sad.'

'I know. I know.' She rubs the top of my arm tenderly and Walter rests his cheek on my other shoulder.

The man in the glasses explains that she was found hanging above a stage and I flash back to that Perspex coffin below me, blood dripping into it from the cuts on my body and wound on my lip. I recall being in her position, and living.

Some people are better dead.

'Would you like me to stay a while?'

'No. No, Phillipa. It's fine. Honestly. You go. Thank

you for today. I'll be fine. I'm looking forward to giving Walter his bath this evening.'

I stand up with Walter still in my arms. He takes his head away from me and rubs his right eye with the back of a scrunched hand. I escort Phillipa to the front door as I hold tightly on to my son. He waves as she exits and I fasten the chain and two huge bolts on the door: one at the top, the other at the bottom.

I lean my back against the door and Phillipa descends in the lift. The muscular Asian man opens the front door for her and hails her a cab.

This city was supposed to be an escape, a new start.

A place where I had no known history and no husband.

But somebody here knows more than just my name.

January

—✦—

I arrive at Newark Airport.

My ESTA is still valid from the gambling trip Paulson had planned months before but which never came about. I pulled out. No need to fill in new forms to authorise my entry.

The earliest flight I could get myself on to was the 20:20, UK time, the day after Marquez called.

The day after Paulson and Murphy started working the Aria Sky case.

I spent thirty pounds to upgrade to a seat with more legroom. The plane is almost empty; everybody else is more comfortable than I am as they stretch across three or four seats with the armrests folded back.

I can't sleep.

So I drink.

At passport control, a webcam takes a picture of my retina and another contraption flashes an image of the fingerprints on my left hand. I'm asked what I am doing in New York, how long I'll be here. What my occupation is.

78

I breathe a mist of whisky-infused travel-breath towards the border official – his name badge says *Manny* – and tell him I'm here for a week.

To get away for a while.

I'm a police officer.

Agent Marquez did not want to draw any attention to my involvement so I honour that by lying to the first agent I encounter. I haven't met Agent Marquez yet. There's no way I can disguise my arrival in this city; they just swiped my passport. I just have to lie low and help where I can.

Manny smirks in my direction. It is either knowing or patronising. I don't care right now. I'm through. I've arrived.

Nobody is here to meet me. I perform a quick scan of the placards being held up by the crowd waiting for loved ones or business professionals. None of them display the name January David.

This is the furthest I have ever travelled. As a kid, we stayed in the UK. A holiday was a trip to wherever my father was performing. After Cathy was taken, we never went anywhere. We had to wait at home. Always. My first time on a plane was my honeymoon. With Audrey.

I don't really know where I am. And I'm alone.

There was no time to arrange for a transfer so I follow the signs hanging from the ceiling, which point me towards the taxis. En route, a man steps towards me and asks whether I am looking for a taxicab. I say that I am. He tells me his name is Maroum and that I should follow him.

We walk over to a lift, rather than outside where the signs are directing arrivals to the taxi rank. He asks where I am from, I tell him London. Usual taxi-driver pleasantries, but I do begin to wonder where he is taking me.

A deserted car park.

Maroum, if that is in fact his real name, talks continually, explaining that there are renovations or that they are trying to move the parking levels upward, but I'm not really listening, I am looking around to spot anything untoward, scoping for people or vehicles or anything unsavoury as I drag my suitcase behind me. The situation and fresh American air are sobering.

We emerge on the other side; the official yellow taxis are lined up to my left but we head straight into the car park. He opens the boot of an MPV and throws my case into the large open space like a dead body.

And still I get in.

On the road, he spots me turn up my nose at the smell seeping into the car.

'That's Jersey,' he offers.

'Sorry?'

'Jersey. The smell. They dump all the trash here.'

We head towards another toll point before going through a tunnel under the East River. Cars are stopping and handing cash over at various points but he drives straight through an open barrier on the right-hand side. He harps on about the cost every time he goes to and from the airport; he whines about the port authority and their moneymaking. He moans about the road they always catch people speeding on with their cameras. And he asks me what I do in England.

Then it is awkward for a moment when I let him know I am a police detective.

He still bills me ninety dollars.

Inclusive of the twenty-four dollars for tolls.

My phone rings.

Marquez.

It's as if he is watching me; he knows that I have arrived.

'Detective David. You're here in our great city. How was your flight?'

'Fine. Thanks. I haven't checked in to the hotel yet, the cab has just dropped me off.' I wait a moment, expecting him to say *I know*. 'You want to meet tonight?' I pull my phone from my ear to check the time on the screen. It's approaching midnight here. Almost Saturday. Five in the morning for my body.

'No, no, no. You get your rest. We'll meet in the morning. If you look left from the front of your hotel, there's a diner on the corner. I'll see you there around ten. OK?'

'Sure. See you then.'

Bleary-eyed and a hundred bucks down in my first hour of visiting the city, I'm greeted by less-than-average hotel decor and worse-than-that service. A Hungarian giant helps me up in the lift with my bag and informs me of some of the famous people that have allegedly stayed here.

The lift door opens to the sight of a large fire hose hanging from a cracked brick wall; it is as barren as the car park I traipsed through with Maroum but not nearly as luxurious. I tip him two dollars; the in-flight magazine said that was standard.

I don't unpack, hang up my clothes – with the exception of two shirts and a jacket – or get into bed.

I don't want to rest.

I want to walk the streets, feel the city, gain an under-standing of my surroundings and the people who share the paths and crossings with me. I need to get into the mind of this murderer, feel as immersed in the city as I do in London. I have to understand how Eames is doing this from his padded room in Berkshire.

I turn left out of the hotel entrance, heading towards the lights, noting the meeting point for tomorrow morning. Audrey David, the wife I have not seen for over two years, is only twenty-seven blocks behind me. While I sample a lager brewed in Brooklyn, she is tending to her crying child, rocking him, holding him tight, pacing around her apartment which has already had a third bolt fitted to the front door this afternoon.

So that she can feel safe.

Secure.

But she can not be protected from Eames. Not this time.

And she won't keep me away either.

The Gentle Child

—◆—

A ria Sky is four years old.
     If you asked her age, she would tell you, 'Five in June.'

She will never be five.

Currently, she lies on her back, unable to feel the cold of the sterile metal slab beneath her. Just as she could not feel the dirt beside a public toilet, or the man who delicately brushed the earth away from her smooth white skin as though excavating a never-before-seen fossil. Just as she could not be blinded by a temporary light erected in order for the crime-scene photographer to capture accurate images.

She had been buried for only a day.

But missing for two.

And now she is being cut open and prodded and tugged about and swabbed and weighed.

Because it took too long to find her.

Those first forty-eight hours are the most crucial. At this point, the investigating officers would start to fear the worst. The parents and families go on believing; they have hope. Something inside January David is telling him that his sister is long dead, but he locks that emotion away; he holds that rationality in the dark nowhere of his mind.

Aria Sky's parents, her uncles and cousins, will no longer possess this luxury.

Uncertainty will be replaced with loss, grief and the need for vengeance.

There is small consolation in the fact that examinations will indicate that Aria was not interfered with in any way. She does not appear to have been touched or to have suffered any form of sexual abuse. Her face looks the same as it did when she was alive, only paler. She appears restful and cold. She was not hit. There are no cuts.

When the body was eventually moved, the bruising on her back was exposed. The coroner now knows how she was killed. That this man, this strong, overbearing sick fuck, suffocated her. He squeezed the life from her body. Her ribs were cracked, her lungs were compressed and not given the opportunity to inflate. Paulson will feel relieved that she was not raped or forced into performing a lurid act on this unhinged child-snatcher. But his revulsion will take a new shape as the coroner's report will suggest that Aria Sky was *hugged to death*.

This monster. This ageing, mentally unbalanced, repeating infant-predator does not see it that way. Yes, his arms locked around the back of the dainty girl. Yes, he gripped that breakable ribcage with all his adult male strength. Yes, he has bruising on his thighs from her writhing to escape his clutches. Yes, he fought through her kicking until she went limp in his grasp. But he does not blame himself.

He never set out to kill Aria Sky.
He felt that they were together.
Convinced there was some kind of relationship there.
That all he did was love her. To death.

In his deluded, battered-with-loneliness, twisted mind, he truly believes that he has not felt this way about another person for some time. He has not killed for years. A decade, maybe. But this is his cycle, his comfortable routine.

That is why he had to spend one last perfect day with the body.

It is the reason he eventually had to dump it in the park with all the others.

January

—✦—

Saturday
MIDTOWN MANHATTAN, NEW YORK, 12:25 EST
London, 17:25 GMT

T here were five cops on every corner when I arrived. They're here throughout the day. They patrol in the evening and in the late hours of night to early hours of the morning. I heard the police dogs barking in the vans as they stopped to intimidate the inebriated population on the border of Hell's Kitchen.

The city felt safe.

But, of course, it's not. And many of the girls here are still unaware. Too many of them have that it-won't-happen-to-me attitude, that same there-are-eight-million-people-in-this-city outlook that cost four women and one man their lives in London two years ago.

I stayed out late last night, drinking at a bar called Emmett's. The barmaid flirted at me with her eyes and said 'You're welcome' in what could have been interpreted as a sultry manner, but I was too tired to even think about fucking her, too exhausted to feel guilty about Cathy and Audrey.

And this morning, I feel fine. Like I have beaten the

journey and emerged completely accustomed to my new time zone.

I arrived at the Ben Ash Delicatessen on time. Marquez walks in eight minutes late.

He's shorter than I expected. Under six foot, maybe by a couple of inches. But he's smart, as you would anticipate a federal agent to be. His suit is dark and fitted around his slender, athletic frame. His hair is straight and also dark but not as short and tidy as I'd have imagined. It is parted loosely on the left. And his skin is white. With a name like Marquez, I had assumed some Latino lineage, but the link must be distant.

He advances with an expression of austerity and the merest hint of forced geniality. His hand stretches out to greet me and the severity embedded in the lines of his face appears to soften as we introduce ourselves properly.

The waiter approaches and asks whether we would like any drinks. Marquez nods at me to go first.

'Er, I'll take a cup of black coffee and a glass of water too, if that's OK.' The water is to replenish liquid after the whisky and local ale; the coffee is to kick-start the day.

'That's fine, sir.'

'Thanks.'

'You're welcome.'

It's at this point that I realise the waitress was not coming on to me last night; I would thank her and she would follow it every time with a polite *you're welcome*. Waiters here are programmed for good service. They live off their tips. I can't remember what the guide suggested for restaurants. In London I tend to tip at around twelve per cent. If I give twenty here then I hopefully won't cause offence. They won't notice me as irregular. I won't stand out.

Marquez orders a Coke and drinks it through two thin straws when it arrives. We both eat the 'Six Silver Dollar Pancakes' with maple syrup. I place the first bite of my second sugar-drenched pancake in my mouth and Marquez produces a black-and-white still of Kerry Ross's naked body hooked through the flesh of her shoulders and muscles of her calves. They show her attached to chains, which are hanging from the ceiling.

It is not identical to the way that I found Audrey in Putney. Kerry Ross's arms are not perpendicular; they hang down in the same way that her long dark hair does, and blood from her right shoulder makes its way down her tricep in this particular picture. It's not the same but it's similar enough to understand the message.

The theatricality of the Eames murders is present but at a less accomplished level.

It is the off-off-Broadway production.

It is Eames with budget constraints.

Two Jewish guys in their early forties talk in numbers over Marquez's right shoulder. Behind them, another two younger men in hooded tops drink coffee and laugh loudly. I swallow the mouthful of food and my eyes tell me that I see Audrey walk past the window on the far side of the restaurant.

'You OK?' Marquez queries.

I turn to him for a moment to acknowledge everything is fine and, when I look back to the window, she is gone. This case is triggering something I thought I was ready to move on from.

What I saw was guilt.

What I felt was longing.

'Yeah. Sorry. I thought I saw someone I knew.' I shake my head and blink to disperse the cloud of disbelief.

'Small world,' he offers, shovelling in another forkful of breakfast.

I turn over the photos of another floating corpse, so that the images now face the tabletop, and continue with my own plate of food.

'So what do you think?' Marquez asks, swallowing a piece of pancake. 'Same MO as your case? Can't be the same guy, obviously, because he's locked up. Must be a copycat.'

I don't know whether it's too early in our relationship to divulge everything I know. Eames is still involved. It cannot be coincidence that he suddenly appears on the radar at the time of this murder. He had a message for me.

CE23.

I have my own questions. I want to find out whether there is any significance to Eames' words or whether it is merely another one of his games.

'You find anything out of the ordinary?' I ask to warm him up.

'Apart from a naked girl hanging from the ceiling?' He stifles an incredulous laugh.

I look directly at him, dropping all emotion from my expression.

'She's at OCME right now.' He senses my lack of comprehension. 'The Office of Chief Medical Examiner. They'll identify the cause of death and run the autopsy, tox report, examination for sexual assault—'

'She won't have been assaulted,' I proclaim assuredly. 'If there was any sex it would have been consensual. If there wasn't . . . then that would be something out of the ordinary.'

Marquez adds, 'You think he's trying to do that David Copperfield flying trick like before? What came after that?'

'The Pendragons. Metamorphosis.' I'm referring to the classic magic trick where the illusionist Jonathan Pendragon locks his wife, Charlotte, in a chest. He stands on top of that chest, throws a curtain into the air and, in the split second it takes the material to fall, he appears to vanish and metamorphose into the woman he has only just locked in the chest below.

Eames used this to kill Richard Pendragon in London. He cut off his penis, made him up like a woman, stuffed him in a chest to bleed to death, then delivered that chest via courier to his place of work, dumping him at Canary Wharf. It was the one death that didn't quite fit with the others. It is both the least and the most important illusion of them all.

But I'm too busy looking at Girl 4.

'That's the one,' he responds almost excitedly. As though seeing that trick for the first time in his mind.

The way magicians want you to respond to their magic.

The way Eames wants you to marvel at his murders.

Horrified yet somewhat impressed.

It is art. And fakery. And mystery. And illusion.

'You think that'll be next?' he continues. 'We should be looking for a man to die this time? That's what we have so far.'

'It's not a copycat killing, Agent Marquez,' I say with the same authority and certainty I would say it with to Detective Sergeant Murphy, who always falls back on the copycat argument for each case. Marquez screws up his eyes and stops himself short of taking another bite of food.

'For a start, we haven't seen the first three murders. Have you had a body turn up with a bullet through its teeth or an arrow through its thigh or stuffed full of cigarettes and contorted?'

He shakes his head.

'This is not trying to recreate the work that Eames put in two years ago. It is a continuation. Whoever is doing this, whatever sicko looks upon Eames as a role model or hero, they are continuing his work, not duplicating it. They are finishing off the list. I explained this when you first called me back in London.' I'm aware that I'm coming across frosty but there is always a degree of butting heads when two different areas of the police force join ranks. We are still getting the measure of each other.

'I know. Those were your initial thoughts but you've had some time to think since I put you on the spot, Detective David. I'm trying to cover every angle, that's what we do here. We're not Scotland Yard or the NYPD.' He exudes some frostiness of his own, at the same time playing up his position as superior.

I question the need to have me over here. If it is merely to contest his theories, it could have been done over the phone and I could be back in London ensuring Eames remains locked away from civilisation; I could be helping Paulson and Murphy find the man who killed that girl in Regent's Park.

I could be locating my sister.

He tells me that they've used psychics on cases in the past.

'I'm not psychic,' I inform him, with even more conviction than my previous rebuttal of his copycat-killer theory.

'Look. I am not sitting around behind a desk relying on conjecture and theorising over the multitude of possibilities, Detective – I can't afford to. I won't wait for another murder. I want to make things happen. That is why you are here.'

He must think there will be more to follow.

He knows it.

Over his left shoulder I notice a glass cabinet containing a cake stand. There must be fifteen whole cakes in there on display. This place looks like every diner you've ever seen in a movie. On every wall there are black-and-white pictures of the Empire State Building, and James Dean and baseball stars I do not recognise. Marquez turns over another black-and-white image on the table and pulls me back to reality.

He tells me that I should take a look at the theatre where Kerry Ross was found. That I should ingratiate myself within the surrounding area. And I should report back to him. In an equally unsubtle way he suggests that I call him should I have a feeling that something is going to happen.

I metaphorically roll my eyes.

'What is the best way to get to this theatre, Agent Marquez?'

He informs me that it is located over on Eleventh Avenue so I could take the M23 cross-town bus to get to that side of the island. First I should jump on the subway.

'Take the C train or the E train to 23rd Street.'

CE23.

Eames knows.

The Smiling Man is telling me *how*. He is telling me *who*.

Eames, like before, is playing a game, but his amusement notifies me *where*.

My intuition tells me *when*.

Marquez leaves me with the photos and the bill.

And I decide to walk. This city needs to be mine.

Girl 8

—◆—

I'll soon be forgotten.

I may have borne a passing resemblance to Girl 4, but I am not as significant.

I was used to bring in January David. Summoning him into the world of Eames while simultaneously wrenching him out of it. Plunging him into the metaphor, the mythology, and dragging him from what is physical.

He's here now.

Time to get on with more killing.

Agent Marquez is so scared of screwing this up, he has resorted to desperation; he thinks he is being set up to fail. He can't escape the mistake he made on the last case that cost two people their lives. He is out to prove something. He wants a tick in the success column. He needs a huge case and he must be the one to crack it.

Detective Inspector David is here to confront his demons. To lay some ghosts to rest. To end Eames' reign of terror on his professional and private life. He wants

94

to beat him again. January David wants to look into the eyes of his adversary and tell him that he will never be free. That this is the end.

And Audrey David, also known as Girl 7, also known as Girl 4, is only known as Ms David here. She has set up a new perfect life with her perfectly unknown past and her perfectly beautiful and qualified nanny taking care of her child perfectly in that perfectly furnished house. But I have sparked a perfect recollection of her time in the role of floating corpse – in the mind of January David, at least. Audrey does not need another reminder of her failure, though, of how she wants January back but cannot fathom a time when he will ever forgive her transgressions. It's all about them and their ambition and kudos and a perverted little love triangle.

Is no one here for me?

Kerry Ross.

Girl 8.

I was strangled to death for no other reason than my name and my vulnerability in the face of nearly obtaining my dream. I was choked and stripped and hooks were cleaved through my soleus muscles and anterior deltoids in order to hang my naked body above a stage.

Nobody remembers seeing me take the journey from my apartment to the theatre in Chelsea. Was I followed? Was my killer there the entire time? How did they get my name? A fluke Internet search or something else entirely? Why was I chosen? Why now, after all this time?

Who is even asking these questions?

I don't care if Audrey David thinks her son is the spawn of something evil, or if she still cares for the husband she so obligingly betrayed. My mother feels nothing for Agent Marquez; she does not sympathise with his shame. She empathises with the family of those left behind. My father is not concerned about January David and his intuitions or his past sparring with the locked-up criminal Eames. He won't waste his time thinking about how the detective fights the urge to locate his wife every day; that he could forgive her.

We don't give a fuck about any of this.

We want to know why.

We want to know who.

We want justice and punishment.

The evidence is available to those who make the correct queries. But I have a shelf life: three more days in the forefront of the public's mind. My fifteen minutes of fame.

Five minutes per day.

Then it is no longer the case of Kerry Ross. It transforms. It mutates. It re-emerges as the case of Eames once more.

I become the afterthought.

Another piece in the grotesque puzzle.

Support of theory.

Replaced by Girl 9.

That misleading liar.

January

Saturday
MIDTOWN MANHATTAN, NEW YORK, 13:22 EST
London, 18:22 GMT

I turn left, following the path of the woman I thought I saw earlier; the apparition of Audrey. Stalking a trail of vapour with the scent of past deceit, the mist of unanswered questions.

The same guy who accosted me last night on this route, asking me for spare change for the homeless, placing my ten-dollar bill in the slot of the Perspex box behind him, throws out a laughable English accent. He calls me *mate* and *old chum*. He asks for yet more money from me. The guide did not mention this; it wasn't descriptive of the homeless situation here. Do I have to give something every time I pass? What about the four alleged veterans I spot ahead with their cardboard placards?

I smell Audrey's perfume in the air and zone out, walking blankly past the pastiche pronunciation of *me old mucker*, transported to my Hampstead en-suite and a time three years previously. I pass the alleged veterans silently, all the while imagining walking into Times Square with Audrey by my side. I know the emotions I thought I felt for Alison Aeslin, the woman who helped me crack the Varrick case, were fleeting; I was lonely, desperate.

She was there.

Never seeing her again has not been painful; not as painful as I thought.

There's only Audrey. That is how it has always been. And, suddenly, she is everywhere.

I turn right at Madison Square Garden. There's no sporting event on here this week. Maroum, my extortionately priced airport driver, said that I should not miss out on a Knicks game if I haven't seen one. I don't plan on staying for that long. Help Marquez, solve the case, get back to London. That's the plan. My jet-lagged realism.

The buildings grow shorter and the streets less bathed in shadow as I veer away from the more populated areas of interest in the city. The number of police diminishes proportionally. There is only me, and I have no authority on these streets. I'm armed with an idea and a brown envelope of crime-scene photography.

I step out into the road to avoid the workmen digging a hole and spot the postal building I have seen in so many films. This is like London in so many ways; I could almost be stepping out of Leicester Square and into somewhere like Balham. This is where people of New York work; this is where they live.

Where Kerry Ross lived.

Girl 8.

I walk by the blue boarding that surrounds an area of development. To my right is a brown glass building, which somehow looks as though it is simultaneously sloping away from me while also arcing over my head towards the sky. It dizzies me and I support myself against the blue chipboard behind.

And I see her again.

The woman in the black dress with the dark hair and pale skin that I thought I saw through the cafe window.

It looks like Audrey.

It can't be.

My coffee was drugged. I'm hallucinating. Another vision.

I hold back and tail her. I want to be sure. I've chased ghosts before.

I follow her down Eleventh Avenue, past the store where Girl 8 was not seen by the man with the radio. I note the mysterious woman's gait, how her tiny, heeled feet cross over slightly in front of her as though she is walking along a tightrope. The way this forces her buttocks to inch effortlessly from side to side. This is how Audrey walks. I romanticise out of all proportion.

She passes the police admin building where the workers on their cigarette breaks inconveniently failed to recall the image of an eavesdropping Kerry Ross. They are not outside today; they will not notice the woman I am stalking from a distance of one and a half blocks.

Two Hispanic women in dark suits, white shirts and black ties walk towards me looking like a female Blues Brothers tribute group. They are the first people I have properly noticed on the journey. When I regain focus, the woman who looks like Audrey from behind, who dresses as elegantly, who strides so fluidly, has stopped for a moment outside a black-fronted building with shutters. I halt for a second and gaze as she steps close to the glass, raising her hand to her forehead and peering through the glass over the police tape.

Her arm prevents me from seeing her full profile. I

want to see that delicate nose, that smooth chin, those full, bright-red lips. For the first time in years, I want to see my wife.

She turns her head away from the door of the theatre where Girl 8 was hung up to look like Girl 4, to remind me. To trigger that mixed feeling of protectiveness and anxiety. She walks several paces to the corner and makes a left out of my sight.

I look left and right in panic, not knowing which direction the traffic will come from. And I run to catch up with her; I don't want her out of my sight for too long. My pace slows as I reach the theatre and I am walking again by the time I hit the bar under renovation next to it, trying to suppress the sound of my breathing.

When I turn the corner, nobody is there. Just a street lined with apartment buildings and cars, and one of the many art galleries in this neighbourhood on the opposite side of the road.

Audrey is nowhere.

I lose her again.

She is an illusion.

My delusion.

Part of the Eames misdirection.

Audrey

Walter is asleep.

Phillipa did not work today; some bright idea I had about spending time with my son, being able to hold down my career while also being a mother.

Because I think I can do it all.

Have it all.

But it is exhausting.

I took Friday off too, once the news of Kerry Ross's death had been televised, and I've been cooped up here since, ignoring the phone, my emails and the post.

I pull a bottle of Sauvignon Blanc from the wine cooler and pour it ferociously into my oversized glass, just as January would. No need to stand on ceremony, to respect the grape, just pour and drink.

I slump down onto the sofa, languid and bittersweet. The neck of the bottle drips condensation onto my left hand, the liquid from the glass in my right swills inside the giant bowl as I shudder to a stop.

I'm alone. Walter is here in the apartment, peaceful

and rested with the eyes of a psychopath hiding behind those thin closed lids. This is not what I wanted. It is never what I wanted. I can't go on like this. Live like this. Feel like this.

When you think of Audrey David, you think of a victim, a lucky escape. That's not me. I drink down a gulp and think how betrayed January would feel if he knew everything. If he knew who I really was. What I had done.

What I could do.

What I may do in the future.

Would he still be able to forgive me if he knew I had written to Eames since his capture? Could he understand my reasons for calling the man who helped tear us apart? Is there any way he would comprehend that I could not just break it off with him? Would January believe me if I told him that I loved him and that almost everything I do is for him, to get us back together, to keep us together?

Yes, I have been in contact with Eames.

Yes, you could say that I am still, somewhat, under his spell.

But I want to get out.

Only January can save me.

I think about skipping work on Monday. I could stay at home, locked away behind my securely bolted door. I could sit around on my sofa drinking wine like I am now and think of that girl hanging from the roof of the Sanford Meisner Theater. How she looked a little bit like Girl 4. Like me.

But she is not like me.

I'm not even like me any more.

So I decide that I will go to work on Monday morning;

it will look odd if I don't. Like I care too much about this girl. Like I have been profoundly affected by her murder.

No.

I will get into the office first on Monday morning.

Not like Thursday.

I entered the office late. Mid-morning. 11:15.

Thirty-five minutes after I had killed Kerry Ross.

And tonight I shall sleep soundly.

The Cycle

——◆——

ISLINGTON, LONDON, 1952

It didn't start with the skinning of cats or cutting the throat of the family dog or setting fire to a sibling's hamster, as is so often the case, but it began at an early age, nonetheless. His temperament was different from other kids', his illness more subtle. This disgusting malefactor hid his delinquency behind shyness and an inability to integrate.

The sequence he would repeat all his life, that inability to express his emotions and form functional relationships, commenced before his age hit double figures.

He would hurt before he would maim.

He would love before he would kill.

The first girl was called Annie. It was 1952. She was nine. He was eight. And his mother had agreed to take her in after school for an hour on weekdays to help a neighbour who was getting back into work.

'Say hello to Annie,' his mother ordered.

'Hello, Annie,' he sighed, not looking directly at her but soaking up every detail of the girl he hoped would one day befriend him.

Annie was quiet at first but they soon became friends.

That was her mistake.

Initially, Annie said very little. She'd sit on the sofa reading books meant for children several years older than she was. She would rock on her seat slightly, keeping a rhythm with the words she read in her head. The boy would sit on the floor and draw with a crayon or pencil – his back to Annie, leaning over a sheet of paper so that nobody could see his sketches. The mother would make herself a cup of tea in the kitchen, or smoke cigarettes, and leave them alone.

It took three afternoons before she asked him what he was drawing, and another two before he showed interest in one of her books. He was sketching a dragon; she was reading, and not fully understanding, *The Hobbit*.

Time moved on and their relationship progressed. He would show her pictures and she would provide him, always, with a positive critique. Sometimes she would read aloud to him and he challenged himself to remain motionless and concentrate entirely on the words as they escaped her lips. While her eyes flitted over the text, his would gaze intently at her face, which appeared more luminescent with every utterance.

He thought, even at that tender, innocent age, that he was experiencing love, or something more, perhaps.

He remains confused by this emotion still.

He knows not how to be friends.

With one year between them, they rarely saw one another at school. He wanted to find her at break time and lunchtime but never gave in to that temptation. It was too exciting for him to wait until the end of the day; then he didn't have to share her with anyone. She was all his. Even at eight years old he was selfish and unhinged and at sea.

And wanted always to delay his pleasure.

His teachers called him diffident.

Smart and introverted.

They got him so wrong, then forgot he existed.

Sometimes Annie would break away from her friends at the top of his road and catch him up. He would be walking alone. She made him feel special. So, at the half-term break, when he didn't see her for an entire week, he did not see this as the postponement of gratification: it was rejection.

Annie had abandoned him and she knew nothing about her error. There was nothing she could have done. She should have ignored him from the beginning. Why did she need to know about his picture?

After the seven-day break, things regressed. The boy, that troubled, upset, loner, hunched over his pictures again, hiding them, obscuring them from her view. When she asked what he was doing, what was the matter, is everything OK, he said only one word.

Sorry.

Sorry for the way he was feeling. Sorry for the manner of his actions.

Sorry for what he was going to do to her.

The mother, that neglectful, chain-smoking inept matriarch, never took Annie in again after that day; the girl's parents would not allow it.

How could she let something like this happen?

Where had she been?

Why did she not stop it sooner?

The boy never gained pleasure from his actions, for the horrifying things he did to that sweet-natured nine-year-old girl. The twisted reprobate was trying to erase her evil, the thing that had made her stay away from him for so long. That force which would make her forget they were close to one another. It had taken something he perceived to be perfect and made it broken.

His quest to recreate something so unsurpassed continues. He strives for a relationship, a bond as strong as this first experience. Each prospective partner ending in failure, each one making the same mistake as the last. Each being buried like Aria Sky, only deeper.

This search for a friend, a companion who will settle and break this now murderous cycle, perseveres. He has grown older; the girls stay the same age.

He sees them all as Annie.

Part Two

Turn

Girl 9

—◆—

This is all true, in my mind, at least. We all see things differently. And some see nothing at all.

Every bench in the park seems to be dedicated to somebody's memory.

Dave, we will never forget.

To my one and only, love Oscar.

I read these pithy dedications every day that I run through the park, and each time I traipse around the miles of paving, I stumble on a new delight; a heartfelt, three-word poem which somehow manages to convey a longing, a loss, a love and a loyalty within its laconic structure.

Art, until we meet . . .

Too soon. L.

Certain things last.

Central Park is a different place during the day from what it is in the evening. When the sun shines it can seem full and loud; a sudden downpour creates rampaging rivers along the paths leading to Midtown and Fifth Avenue. And the benches remain stalwart, weathering the tide of elemental abuse. The brass plaques repel erosion from the frost and cascading autumnal leaves, keeping alive the memories of those who lament a passed loved one.

Some sit on these benches and talk with a mouth full of bagel or street-vended hot dog. They do not read the sign behind their backs. That is not required for the messages to live on; they are not for everybody's enjoyment. They are curios for all, yet pathos for one.

I jog through Central Park, as I do most days, with my earphones ticking another contemporary pop song into my brain, forcing my legs to keep time with the music. I spot a new inscription, which lingers until I hit the vastness of the reservoir.

I wonder what my bench will say.

Georgina Burton. No more lies.

Killed by magic.

Eaten by birds.

Eames

———◆———

He must still be there. The Big Apple. Not returned.
He knows there will be more.
I will take more.
Girl 9 will die, I have faith.
She will kill again. She's just like me.
She is Eames.
We are all Eames.

I expected Detective Inspector January David to have
contacted me himself, not send his overweight minion. He
must have figured the significance of CE23 by now; it is
the same code I used to bait him with when I killed the
girls in London. He must realise that I am involved, that
I knew where Kerry Ross – the woman he will affectionately
refer to as *Girl 8* – would be killed.

I want the image to trigger an emotion he felt when
he saw his wife on display in the same way at the theatre
in Putney.

I want him to think of Audrey and the son that is
not his.

I want him cursing my name, my existence. I want him to recognise the reason Kerry Ross was chosen and the manner in which she was culled, but know he is still further from solving this case than he ever has been, even if I dangle a carrot of location.

I want him to play my game.

To see me as the set-up, the humorous comment that disguises the sleight of hand. Imagine his surprise when he finds that I am still the flourish, the glide, the Hindu Shuffle. That the things he sees are not the truth; they are not what is real. His waking life is the illusion.

When Houdini asks you to place him in handcuffs, when he tells you to thread his arms through a straightjacket, when he instructs you to ensure the knot is tight on the bag, that the water chamber is to be locked from the outside, it is because he knows he will free himself.

Lower the curtain.

He will emerge unscathed.

This building or prison or asylum or red-brick structure of lunacy or politically correct hospital for the criminally insane is merely a box. You may leave it empty or fill it with liquid or push blades through each surface; this is of no consequence. I am merely waiting for someone to fully close the door.

Throw away the key.

Challenge me.

She sends me the seven of hearts, five of hearts, two of diamonds, five of diamonds with small *m* shapes dotted in the background in black ink to look like birds flying, the seven of hearts, the ace of diamonds and the ace of hearts.

I know Georgina Burton is next.

I know how she will die.
Where she will die.

I am just waiting for the nine of spades to arrive and tell me it is done.

Audrey

——◆——

UPPER EAST SIDE, MANHATTAN, NEW YORK, 09:00 EST
London, 14:00 GMT

It was me.

The news may have quoted another name, a younger woman from Chelsea or the Garment District or wherever, but it is not her that I see. I see the floating corpse. I see the Putney Theatre. I see a past version of myself.

And so will January.

I needed these two days away from the office. To collect my thoughts. To centre myself. To keep the front door bolted from the inside and wait for another story to overtake that of the woman they reveal to be Kerry Ross, a PR worker with a penchant for the dramatic arts.

That woman who was made to look like me but is nothing like me.

I made her that way.

The news footage shows videos of neighbours and co-workers extolling her virtues. Her family weeps at the injustice. They say a bright light has been blown out too early. The TV station continues to run these clichés every hour or so to achieve a sufficient level of sympathy

116

towards the dead girl. Think how relieved they'll feel that I didn't cut her pretty little face.

What would people say if it were me hanging there?

If I didn't get away this time?

Who would speak fondly of my life, my contribution?

My son is my only family, and sentences are a struggle for him; my colleagues are all underlings whom I do not deal with personally, though my assistant does have an understanding of my life away from business. There is only Phillipa. The nanny I employ to take care of Walter knows me better than anyone in this country and, truthfully, she still knows very little. But there is a bond there. There has to be for me to entrust her daily with my child.

Tomorrow, we will fight. We will have our first argument. More accurately, I will shout at her and she'll back down with repeated apology.

I don't think about Phillipa or the girl I left hanging from the ceiling at the theatre; instead I ponder the amount of emails that have piled up since Friday, and how it will take around half the day to sift through them and respond accordingly. I will only see Walter for under fifty minutes tomorrow morning and that is more difficult to take after spending every waking minute together for the forty-eight hours I had us both intentionally detained within the apartment.

It will take more than two bolts, a chain and a peephole to keep Eames away, though.

Having Walter means that Eames is always here with me. A part of him lingers.

He never dies.

*

I call the hospital and inform them that it is Miss Silver, that I need to speak with Eames. They say I can leave a message. I ask them to pass on two words.

It's over.

Then I make another call to London.

'Close it down. Make something stick. He won't be coming back.'

Walter gurgles cutely in his cot and I roll my eyes.

The Sponsor

**PRATT STREET CAR PARK, CAMDEN, LONDON,
14:18 GMT**
New York, 09:18 EST

They're working on a Sunday. A young girl has been killed and buried in the dirt next to a public toilet; they will work every day.

Murphy, as acting inspector, does not have to justify his whereabouts or actions, and Paulson has been tasked with trawling through the archives with Constable Higgs, searching for similar incidents that have occurred in the past.

Detective Sergeant Paulson kills the engine in the police car park and looks at his phone. Murphy has stopped at a location not far from the scene of the crime – an underground public car park on Pratt Street, Camden Town. What Paulson cannot know is the reason Murphy is there and who he is meeting with. A man with no agency, but influence on all. He walks the corridors of power with impunity. He works for money but his leverage comes from knowledge.

*

The usual method for arranging one of these furtive meetings is less than explicit – a cryptic note on the noticeboard, a card in a window, a coded telegram – but Murphy needs to act fast. He requires success before January David returns. A text was sent from a phone that was immediately destroyed. The message gave the location off Pratt Street and came from a number that his phone did not recognise.

There seems to be no stairwell or lift to take Murphy below ground, and there is nobody in the booth at the front to direct him or witness his presence. The slope is steep at first but levels out as it turns right at the corner. He has to duck ungracefully beneath the barrier before beginning his journey downwards.

He is anxious about the ease with which he trusted an anonymous text message, but he has met in many darkened, out-of-the-way locations since his recruitment during the first Eames case. These are the moments when he learns of his own operations: he is instructed; he is advised. This is where he learns that he must hide or interfere with evidence. He must subvert January David's efforts. He must report back on the capabilities of his inspector and whether he is acting professionally and conventionally rather than with superstition and esoteric fantasy.

This is not, nor has it ever been, an operation to further Detective Sergeant Murphy's career. That is merely a by-product. It is about January David.

That is all it has ever been about.

Murphy waits, leaning against the pillar behind parking space 48, as instructed. His body shakes but he cannot pinpoint whether that is due to the cold or his own apprehensiveness.

He waits.

His mind begins to wander but he stops himself just in time from whistling to test the acoustics of the subterranean cavernous expanse. He lacks the focus of January David. He is nowhere near his equal.

He waits.

Growing intolerant of the unpunctuality of the man he expects to meet, he looks around, gazing at the slope he descended almost twenty minutes ago. He ducks his head to see further up the ramp, the ceiling of this level obstructing his view somewhat. He turns back and is shocked to see a figure leaning against the pillar diagonally left of where he has been waiting.

'How long have you been there?' he asks, puffing out his cheeks and placing his right hand against his chest to demonstrate his shock.

'Thank you for coming at such short notice, Sergeant Murphy.' He ignores Murphy's question. He does not answer queries. He reduces Murphy to his real, not acting, rank as a punishment for not adhering to those rules.

'That's fine.' Murphy adjusts his jacket and straightens his back in an attempt to appear professional or attentive or in control. 'I figured it had to be urgent.'

The man he is meeting is impeccably presented. His suit is pressed with the accuracy of a costumier, his hair parted to the side and gelled into place – it is dark but greying sporadically. His face is clean-shaven and chiselled. Though he is not as young as Murphy, indeed twenty years his senior, he displays the healthy glow of affluence.

Chief Inspector Markam has met this man on several occasions.

January David has noticed him twice before.

It doesn't matter.

He is a ghost.

'You've met the girl's family.'

'DS Paulson and myself have only recently informed them. I sent him back to the station archives. I can't remember a case like thi—'

'You need to find something and make it stick,' he interrupts. He was not asking a question. 'And fast.'

He explains that January David is in New York, that he is being monitored, that they picked up on the use of his passport.

'It seems he is consulting on a case. Off the books. Pro bono,' he continues.

'And?'

'And it shows that he is ready to come back. There's nothing we can do. We had the power to enforce his time off, but cracking that last case, even in the manner he chose, meant we couldn't possibly get a suspension.'

Murphy reads volumes into a look that nebulose figure directs his way: that it is his own fault they could not oust January David on the last case or the case before that. He wants to say that it is not his fault, that he did everything they asked of him. But he knows better than to get on the wrong side of this particular well-presented silhouette.

A moment of silence ensues and teeters on the edge of awkwardness while Murphy thinks of a more tactful way to ask, 'What do you want from me this time?' The sound of a car door closing shatters the atmosphere. A slim, blonde woman locks the door of her silver Audi A3 over in space 71. Murphy did not hear her drive in. Has she been sitting there the entire time? He obscures himself behind the pillar and watches as her legs disappear up the slope towards the light outside. She never turns back.

'We want a quick resolution on this one. Make something stick.'

He said *we*.

'We've only recently identified her.' Murphy tries to hide his protestation behind a veil of serious concern.

'Do your job, Detective Murphy. Just have a contingency. Look at the family. The father. Hell, even the mother. An uncle is great if you think it'll work.' His voice croaks with an intimidating quiet.

Murphy doesn't know what to say. Tampering slightly with evidence to delay an outcome is one thing, but pinning something like this on an innocent seems underhand, even to him. He begins to wonder what he has got himself involved in. His ambition only stretches so far. Surely this much effort isn't being expended because the force are embarrassed by January's belief in the fantastical, by the fact that he has visions or intuitions? They can't believe in Murphy this much.

Unprompted, Murphy finds himself suddenly thinking like a detective, unconsciously demonstrating the reason he was originally chosen for January's violent crime team. 'I'm on it!' he asserts.

'Get it done, Detective Murphy. He could return at any moment. Get it done and he won't be coming back.'

And the immaculate man backs away into the darkness and exits through a doorway Murphy had not realised was there.

In order to avoid further descent to a moral depth from which he may not be able to return, Murphy is being forced to do what January David always wanted of him: be a detective; put together a list of suspects; uncover pertinent information; identify a pattern, a logic, a profile of the killer, and then weave this information together into irrefutable argument.

He does not want to have to 'make something stick' if it is untrue, just to spite his estranged inspector.

But he has more time than he knows.

January David has three more bodies to find.

Eames is delaying his greatest reveal.

And Audrey David is no longer safe.

In the greyness of a car park corridor, a call is made.

'It is done,' he croaks.

And he breaks another phone in half.

January

——∗——

I wake to the sound of my alarm.
   I have to change my hotel suite.
'Good morning, sir. How may I help?' The man on reception sounds at once obliging and disinterested.
'There's a mouse in my room.'
'I'm sorry, sir?'
'There's a mouse . . . in my room.' I hope the pause gives him time to register my words and drop his apathy.
'And you are in room . . .'
'1520.'
'The fifteenth floor? I'll send someone up right away.'
I hang up without responding to his question. I don't know how the rodent made his way up here; I just know that I won't sleep if I know it's still in here. The time difference between New York and London hasn't had a huge effect on me but I still need to rest a little.
The Smiling Man is coming.
Another girl will be dead in the next twenty-four hours.

*

Most of my clothing is still inside the small suitcase I travelled with. I hung up a jacket and a couple of shirts when I arrived and I now throw them on top of the already folded trousers. I tip my toiletries into a plastic bag, stuff it into one of the zipped compartments and shut the case. Then I wait.

There is a knock. A nervous knock.

I jump off the bed and head towards the door, expecting an eager porter to be waiting for me with a new key card and an outstretched hand prepared to pull my case to an upgraded room.

I unhook the chain and pull the door inwards to be greeted by a short Mexican man with a stereotypical moustache, holding a rolled-up towel in his left hand and a spray-can of disinfectant in the other. He doesn't say a word. He just stares at me with a trepidatious smile. Still, I invite him in and point towards the area I last saw the mouse scuttle.

The receptionist seems shocked when I call back to inform him that there is a confused, mute employee casting a shadow in my doorway.

'Oh, you'd like to switch rooms?' he asks, idiotically thinking that beating the mouse and bleaching the carpet afterwards constitutes customer satisfaction. *You're welcome.*

Eventually, another helper arrives, this time a tall Eastern European man, and escorts me to my new room. I leave behind the tableau of the Mexican handyman on his hands and knees trying to fit a triangular sticky cardboard trap under the bed, unflatteringly doubling up his duties as the new head of pest control.

My new room is identical in standard, despite having a completely separate sleeping area. I don't have the energy to rehang my clothes so I kick the case underneath my new bed. The pillows and quilt are cold from the air conditioning, and I flop my weight forwards, hitting the bed with a comfortable bounce.

The noise from the streets outside, the perpetual life of this great city still humming along at whatever time you choose to peer out the window, all fades into a steady thrum which seems to rock me to sleep.

Into darkness.

Into silence.

The Smiling Man waits in the dust.

But I do not smell grass.

Or feel moisture to know that the next murder will be outside.

He does not have me blindfolded and bound and standing with my hands fastened behind my back; I can't feel the cold corrugated metal of the pole behind me.

I avoid his teasing and torture this time, the sound of those shuffling feet, that noise which usually instils anxiety.

Left foot to right foot.

Left.

To right.

He wants to whip away my blindfold and propel me into a world of blindingly bright white light that stretches as far as the usual gloaming I am accustomed to finding. The sound of a flock of birds suddenly taking flight does not vibrate in my ear, and I see nothing.

Nothing.

The faint, grey, arched lines in the distance go

unnoticed. I am not extrapolating the clues to help save Girl 9.

He wants to stand in front of me, so close that my face is only at the height of his muscular chest, and I have to crane my neck upwards to view his face: his dark brown skin somehow luminous against the unconventional white background, the yellow teeth in his mouth and jaundiced, protruding eyes unblinkingly gazing down at me. He hopes I feel small and insignificant in his presence, the customary sense of unease creeping its way back to me.

But it does not.

If I could see his head tilt upwards as though looking to a God, I could immediately start to run through ideas of what this could mean. Could it be related to the height of the buildings in this town? Perhaps the financial district. Is he trying to tell me where the next murder will occur?

But I do not see anything.

He looks back down at me. Always with that grin of overtly fake affability.

I do not see the black top hat ten feet in the air, hooked on to a lamp post. Or the high-quality black suit or the white shirt or the cravat. I have no opportunity to ask myself whether this denotes affluence – is he pointing me to the Upper East Side? The Upper West?

The Smiling Man does not reach into his breast pocket and produce a perfectly white handkerchief, sending a memory into a backflip across my synapses, telling me unequivocally that the next victim will have the surname Burton.

He performs none of this.

Not to me.

I am not there.
Something has changed.
Something has turned.

I should be seeing all of this. The Smiling Man is here to help me.
But I don't. I don't see anything.
He is gone. I'm on my own.
All I can do is sleep.

Eames

——✦——

The guard stares at me from the other side of the secure, heavy door as I slap the nine of spades against it repeatedly, shouting about Audrey. I'm calling her a bitch. A fucking ungrateful bitch. A whore. A cunt.

I never call her Audrey.

I never say it is her.

This is supposed to be the woman that I love.

A female doctor joins the tall man in the corridor and monitors my outburst through the safety of the tiny rectangular, inch-thick window. I'm not supposed to call them guards or wardens or whatever. It has to be another mixture of words that includes *health* and *professional* and *practitioner* and *medical*.

They conclude I may need sedating, that I am showing signs of frustration. But nobody wants to come into this room because, beyond the political correctness, they know I just want to kill.

She sent me the card, the nine of spades, with a cross drawn through it in a black marker. She's trying to tell me that she wants out. That she no longer wishes to play this game. She cannot kill again.

I think about that and stop.

I go quiet.

I rest my hands above the sorry excuse for a window to the outside world and I close my eyes for a moment. And breathe. Beyond the glass, they hold their breath. Waiting. Waiting to see how my agitation has evolved, developed.

With my eyes still shut and my heart rate descending, I picture Audrey, on her back, her ankles resting against my shoulders as I peer down at her pale skin. Does she think she is the only woman to ever have looked up at me in that way? The only whore to have had my hands around her neck as I choke out an orgasm? The only cunt I have tasted? The only dog I've spat on? Imagine how naive you have to be to believe you are the only one. That you are different. That you are loved.

My eyelids lift with my head and I smile involuntarily. The two idiots outside my door want to avert their gaze but morbid curiosity can often overpower humanity.

She can't stop.

She can't stop because I can't stop.

I almost laugh.

Girl 9 will die tomorrow, I'm confident of that. She will be found in Central Park, whatever Audrey fucking David believes, whatever she thinks she knows. Girl 9 will die. They will all still die. And, now, as I screw the nine from the split-spades deck into a ball, I know I can't let Girl 4 escape again.

A part of Eames just died.

Girl 9

———✦———

**CENTRAL PARK, MANHATTAN, NEW YORK,
08:01 EST**
London, 13:01 GMT

The rain can clear the whole of Central Park on heavy days.

It doesn't stop me, though.

I can tie my hair back, enter at any point, and get lost in the maze of pathways. Jogging, sometimes I avoid the puddles; sometimes it's impossible. My view is only obstructed by the droplets that gather on my eyelashes. There is hardly anybody around.

But there only needs to be one other person for me to die. To not exit at the other side in my drenched shorts, to the amusement of those who huddle beneath the Upper East Side scaffolding. It only requires Eames to be waiting beneath one of the twenty archways for me to cease being Georgina Burton the person and transform into Girl 9, the trick. The myth. The unfortunate liar. The three-word dedication etched into brass and pasted to a wooden bench for none to see.

I enter the park near Strawberry Fields from West 72nd. Taxis splash their way down Central Park West behind me. Tourists stand unknowingly with their hands held aloft, hoping to grab a lift back down Eighth Avenue into Midtown after their visit to the American Museum of Natural History; they don't realise that they won't get a cab in this weather.

The only people offering a service are the ebullient rickshaw drivers who persist with drumming up business longer than the street vendors who sit drearily underneath their umbrellas, the raindrops bouncing off their faded yellow awnings, vapour dispersing into the air as steam from their hot-dog warmers.

I jog straight through the black-and-white circle of the 'Imagine' mosaic, which commemorates John Lennon and is usually being photographed by somebody at any given time.

I smile at one of the rickshaw cyclists, who cheekily offers me a ride. I blush slightly at his playfulness and continue on my journey to death.

Running to end my life.

At a sign for the East Green I am splashed by a car while waiting on the sidewalk for the lights to change in my favour. I jump to the left, hoping to avoid being saturated, and my left foot sinks into a muddy puddle up to my ankle.

And I think things can't get worse.

I head south-west towards the sound of a carousel. There are people there. It must be safe. Dry. Undercover. I pass a white carriage which has attached itself to a glorious horse that has been stuck with giant red feathers. It seems so cruel and degrading for the animal. It stands there looking majestic and camp; there is no sign of the owner or driver. No sign of a possible witness.

An Indian man makes balloon animals outside the

public toilet and I see three girls on a bench drinking soda and laughing at him. Parents are wary of him so do not clock another jogger in the park.

I continue on to Driprock Arch. It is somehow red brick and gothic at the same time. Beneath it, a man stays dry playing the saxophone. Two of the few people left in the park now that the rain has become even more ferocious and tropical are filming him with a video camera. Neither of them places any money in his case. Someone else takes photographs.

Perhaps I can be seen in the background of the film. Maybe it is time-stamped to allow Detective David and Agent Marquez an idea of the last time I was seen alive.

Another group of people waits at the other end, shrouded in the shadow cast by the overhanging brick-work; they fidget uncomfortably in their wet clothes near a lamp post.

I power past the musician and amateur cameraman wishing I had a buck or two I could throw into his pot for encouragement. I pace on towards the group at the far side, loitering by the post that informs visitors of the structure's name.

But this is not the arch I am attacked in.

That is not the lamp I am dumped under.

You will not find me here.

This is nothing.

The Conversation

Monday
VIOLENT CRIME OFFICE, LONDON, 13:35 GMT
New York, 08:35 EST

It has been four days since the body of Aria Sky was found in Regent's Park. Detective Sergeant Murphy is being leaned on and is, therefore, leaning towards the girl's uncle.

'Something doesn't sit right,' he says, squinting his eyes in faux supposition.

Paulson thinks that Murphy is fulfilling the usual predictable role he does when January David is there: offering the simplest, often most sensational theory. Paulson wants to dig deeper. To be certain. He thinks that pinning this heinous crime on the uncle is too easy.

Sometimes it is that easy.

Sometimes it is the uncle.

Paulson's phone rings. He is standing with a towel around his waist in the changing room at the station. He has just showered after taking a run during his lunch break. His weight has dropped enough through his lengthy power walks that he is starting to feel comfortable enough to jog. Or, at least, plod. For now.

'This is Paulson.'

There is a delay then a voice. 'It's me.'

'Jan?'

'Hey. How's things your end . . . with the case?'

January David is partially interested in the progress, slightly intrigued by Murphy's assimilation into the role of lead investigator, but mostly this is the foreplay before he asks his friend to go above and beyond the call of duty once again.

'This is a tough one, Jan. You know . . .'

January says nothing.

'. . . it's a little girl, for fuck's sake. I mean, you can kind of understand when two men fight over a woman and things turn dark or some lady catches her husband sleeping around and takes a high-heel to his temple, but this . . . I can't get my head around it.' He sounds exasperated yet lethargic.

'The things we've seen over the years, Paulson, nothing shocks me now. That's violent crime. It's what we signed up for.'

'I know. I know.'

'You want to tell me about it? Might do some good to get an outside perspective on things.'

For a moment, a short moment, January David slips back into sleuth mode; he wants to solve a problem, crack a case, give a family the closure he is yet to obtain. Help his only friend. He has not seen The Smiling Man. He doesn't know what has happened. He thinks he still has time. His mind moves away from Audrey and Eames to the little girl found in London.

January doesn't realise that this is where he should be: with Paulson, leading Murphy, running his team. If he were here, where he belongs, not chasing another ghost, he would be the closest he has ever been to finding his sister, Cathy.

He could finally rest.

And maybe the dreams would stop for good.

But January David is not in New York because The Smiling Man alludes to that location, or because Agent Marquez has called on his expertise, or because Audrey David has willed it to happen through dedicated prayer. He is there because Eames does not want him in London. Not yet.

'We've spoken with the family once, back tomorrow for further interviews to corroborate. The mother is distraught and blames herself; she was in the house when it happened. The dad is like a zombie. Says he was at work that day but we found out he wasn't.'

'Suspect?' January interrupts.

'We have footage of him at the bookmaker's at the time it all occurred, and betting slips from the same time.'

'So he wasn't lying to you so much as his wife.' He expels a puff of air in amazement. It is too common for this kind of thing to happen while investigating a case. 'These idiots don't realise that they are obstructing justice. I mean, you are trying to find the person who killed his little girl and he's worried about an argument with his fucking wife . . .'

During the tirade, Paulson switches his phone into his left hand and grips it between his cheek and shoulder. He dries his groin with a towel that he then drops to the floor and stands on to dry his feet. 'Then there's the uncle who was asleep. No one to corroborate but he does work nights as a cab driver so it would stand to reason.' He waits for input but his mentor is silently filing all these details into the correct folders in his brain, compartmentalising the information away from his current consulting position in New York and far away from the locked door marked 'Cathy'.

Paulson adds, 'Murphy thinks it's the uncle.'

'Hah! Well, he would.' They share a silent moment of understanding. Thousands of miles from each other but still on the same team, in the same room.

Paulson feels a certain reluctance to discuss this case with January David. He has searched the archives and found many unsolved cases, several including the abduction of children – boys and girls. Aria Sky was taken from near her house in broad daylight; there are cases that go back over forty years, which include Cathy David in the spring of 1985.

The type of crime, the locality, the manner in which it was performed, the way some victims were found . . . it suggests that each case is different, that the victims knew their attackers. Could it be possible that some had the same murderer? Could he have evaded the authorities for this long? Is the Aria Sky case somehow related to January David's sister's case? The file that has been lying in his top drawer along with a bottle of Scotch since the day he had enough kudos within the force to obtain a copy?

Paulson dare not mention this link though he knows January would certainly have contemplated it; he is always ahead of everyone.

'I don't think it's the family. It's obviously not the dad. I'm guessing the press are trying their best to cast doubt on the mother or the uncle.'

Paulson grunts an affirmation.

'How long was she buried? One day? Or the two that she was missing?'

'Coroner says she was there less than twenty-four hours.'

'There's an element of ritual to it; it's personal. I can't see that the family would take her for a day and keep her. If it was an accident and they are trying to cover it up, they would have done it immediately, and much closer to home.' January thinks aloud and all Paulson can do is agree.

'I know these types of cases are committed by someone who is known to the victim ninety per cent of the time, Paulson. But ten per cent of the time, they are not. Let Murphy waste his time with the uncle.'

'Makes sense,' Paulson responds, wearily, not knowing whether this comes from the January David who likes to turn to more illusory probabilities or the January David who possesses a more than accurate hunch based on experience and keen deduction skills.

'Keep digging, Paulson,' January affirms.

'I will.' He pulls his trousers up and sits on the bench to put his socks back on.

'No. Keep digging the site at which you found this girl. Just because she was found in a shallow grave does not mean there are not more underneath.'

Paulson doesn't know what to say; the thought never crossed his mind.

'I assume someone is watching the area twenty-four-seven. I wouldn't be surprised if your man returns to the site. It may be that this is his first – and I hope it's his last – but, if it is not, there may be more. He may have killed before when he had the time or the energy to dig a proper hole.'

'Fuck, Jan. I kind of hope you're wrong about this.' Paulson feels himself start to sweat.

'I do too. But you need to do this. You should have done this already. I would have made you do this.'

Now Paulson will have to convince Murphy that this is what needs to be done without revealing the source of the idea. He decides he'll take it higher. To Chief Inspector Markam.

'Can you hold on a sec?' Paulson puts his phone on the bench and pulls his shirt out of the locker. He takes a moment to reflect on the notion that he may be excavating more children if his boss's hunch is correct – and his hunches usually are. With each button he feels his large stomach tense. He tastes acidity in the back of his throat as though he has recently vomited. He wants to cheat and eat something unhealthy, erasing all his hard work accomplished through diet and exercise.

Meanwhile, January moves over to his hotel window and stares down at bustling yellow taxis and power suits stalking the sidewalks, newspapers under their arms and coffee spilling out the tiny holes in their take-away cup lids as they pace with purpose.

'Sorry about that, I was getting my shirt on.'

January is too jarred to comment.

'Thanks for the talk, Jan, but I assume you weren't only calling for an update at this end. What do you need from me?' Paulson smiles knowingly as he says this, then forces himself out of the emotion he feels is unsuitable for the situation.

A young girl is dead.

There may be more.

So many more.

'I haven't had an intuition since I arrived in this city. Hell, I slept right through the night last night. That should be telling me that I still have time to work this out but something is niggling at me to say that I probably have less . . .'

'And?' Paulson prompts.

January takes a deep breath as though he is about to swim a length of the pool underwater.

'I need you to go back and see him.'

'Him . . .' Paulson knows who he means. It seems cruel to January that his friend makes him say it.

'Eames. You have to go and see Eames. He has information, I'm sure of it.' He shuts his eyes and scratches at his forehead like he wants to bore through his skull and dislodge the idea from his mind.

'I need him.'

This is the admission he hoped never to make again. It means Eames has already won.

Girl 9

—✦—

I was born in the Roosevelt Hospital, which is arguably Midtown Manhattan, but I am an Upper West Side girl, it's all I've ever known. My father's family have been here for generations. The *real* New York, he calls it. He's still around, still attends the same synagogue on West 86th, still has time for me. Mother has lived in the family home since the divorce. She hasn't left in nearly four years. She reverted to her maiden name of Burton almost immediately and, because I was still young at the time, changed mine too.

Unknowingly signing off my death this evening.

What's in a name?

I don't expect sympathy because I come from a broken marriage, but I don't expect less compassion because my background is more privileged than any of the other girls' on Eames' list.

My parents never fought over me; I just went straight to my mother, no questions asked. When visiting my father he would never attempt to one-up his ex-wife, he

142

would not insult her around me or fish for information; it was what it was. Mother was the same, for the most part. They were kind, generous and fair of heart.

And I lied to them constantly.

That's how it started, how I got this reputation.

I don't know why I did it; I was young. A kid. If I thought it might upset my father to hear that mother was doing well, seemingly better without him, I would lie. I would make up a story to suggest that she was still having difficulty coming to terms with separation, that there was a concern for her health. She looked pale. Tired.

I placated and pacified her in the same way.

He's eating healthily, of course.

I think he started jogging again.

He's definitely lost weight.

The fabrications eventually overlapped and transmuted until I found it impossible to extricate fiction from fact. Perhaps this accounts for my success as a magazine agony aunt. I can say with full confidence to my readers that *I have been there* or *this is very common* or *studies have shown* without actually having been anywhere or seen any studies because it may be true, it may be false. I may not even be an agony aunt.

Is anybody really who they say they are?

Is Eames really Eames?

So, while I recount my demise, I try to remain truthful, but if there are any embellishments, I can't help it. I'm sick. I don't know where the lying ends and I begin.

And I'm sorry about that.

But there is always some truth.

I leave the saxophonist behind me, playing something smooth and jazzy to an unappreciative audience of youngsters too ill-educated to give him a shot; they congregate under the arch merely to keep out of the rain I find so refreshing.

I bounce lightly down one of the paths designated as a 'literary walk'. One bench declares 'In Loving Memory of Papa' and I feel uninspired by the words, although strangely intrigued by the anonymity of them. I bound on towards Dipway Arch, each stride bringing me closer to death, closer to Eames, closer to becoming Girl 9.

A forgotten number.

Mother may have to leave the house to identify my body.

She'll know I lied about father shaving his beard last week.

An average-looking couple pose at the opening to the archway; nothing appears sinister as yet. He holds her from behind, trusting a passing stranger with their camera. As I near, they become more creative, artistic, even. Both of them leaning either side of the entrance, ignoring the scent of car fumes and urine, pretending they are taking a shot for the cover of *Italian Vogue*. She reminds me of a marginally overweight Linda Blair.

Another musician arrives, this time with a French horn. He stops and lays down a newspaper on the ground and places a red bag on top. I stop opposite him and press my hands against the brick, pushing my right leg back to isometrically stretch my calf muscle.

He blows out something in a minor key, inadvertently composing the score to the rest of my short life. The plus-size models retrieve their digital camera from the passerby and flick through the images, giggling and muttering in a European language.

The bricks stretch over me in a perfect parabola; on

the opposite side there are cut-outs, indentations of smaller arches within the wall. Someone has left an empty shoebox inside one of the shapes and a crumpled Footlocker bag in the other. They may have been here for days. What else could be stored in these apertures? Knives. Bottles. Large bags of birdseed. UPS parcels. Heavy blocks of wood used to smash over the back of someone's head to knock them unconscious. Loose bricks. Money. Keys.

The French-horn player makes a note that is so bum he can't even pass it off as jazz, and I jolt back upright, jogging on the spot, kicking my heels up to my buttocks, and give the busker a look that says, 'Keep it up.'

A man in a long black coat appears at the exit of the tunnel and kicks his shoes against the brickwork before leaning back, breathless. I make my way towards him. The horn player is in a musical trance and the young posers have since continued out into the drenched park.

He, the attractive man in the coat, smiles at me. A tender, disarming smile that implies safe passage beyond, that suggests I have nothing to fear from this man, this attractive, mysterious man.

I have no recollection of Eames' identity from the news. It was years ago. Another world. That is how he wants it to be. That is his plan. That has always been the plan.

I bounce back a similar expression in his direction.

And I forget that it is still raining.

You will not find me here, January David.

This is not where I die.

This is where I pretended to be alive.

The Request

———✦———

Detective Sergeant Paulson's collar is too big. It seems the first place he is losing weight is his chin.

Or his neck.

That large hump of fat which connects his chest to his chin and disguises his neck, ensuring he has no flattering angle whatsoever, that's where the weight is falling away.

And his back.

He never realised the amount he was carrying on his back; he looks so front-heavy, his gut overhanging any belt buckle, keeping his trousers high at the front and sagging in the rear. He needs new clothes. He should look fitter. He should appear as healthy as he feels. But oversized garments on a fat man can look worse than clothing that hugs an immense figure.

He seems withdrawn. Grey, even, his skin no longer shot with blood as capillaries fight their way to the surface of his skin to reveal how lacking in nutrition his diet truly is. He is healthier but portrays a greater indisposition, as though he has been forged from dreary, overcast sky hanging depressingly over the public toilets in Regent's Park where Aria was found. Like he washed out his colour in the shower.

After speaking with January, he heads straight to Chief Inspector Markam's office.

'Come in,' the voice booms from behind a door engraved with its owner's name, the level of reverberation directly proportional to the presence of the figure perched behind the desk. Paulson has already cleared this meeting with Markam's secretary.

'Christ, Paulson. You look like shit.'

'I feel fine, sir.'

'I'm sure you do. But you *look* like shit. Are you sleeping?'

'Does anyone in this place sleep?'

'Quite. What have you got for me? Urgent, I hear. Have you spoken to January recently?' He fires out a barrage of questions as though somebody is in the room watching him and assessing his conduct.

Paulson doesn't know how to answer that last question. He could say that he has spoken to January, but not recently. It might seem that the idea to dig beneath Aria Sky's burial spot was his idea, and he doesn't want to claim the credit. Not falsely. Not again. He is still dealing with the praise for the last major case that should only truly be directed towards January David.

But that was the only way they could play it.

That slight shift of responsibility is the reason January David avoided suspension.

The lie saved them both.

He could explain to Markam that he has been in constant correspondence with his inspector, that he is still at his bidding despite the sabbatical that has been imposed upon him. That he has visited Eames, the culprit of the Zone Two Killings, and that he plans to skip out and revisit for further information on a clandestine case being worked on by his erstwhile inspector.

He chooses to sidestep the inquiry and focus on his own case.

'We need to dig below the spot where the girl was found?' He is cautious not to start the sentence with 'I think'.

'What? Disturb the scene? We're still getting samples from the soil, man.'

'There may be more bodies . . .' – there is a long enough silence to add weight to Paulson's final word – '. . . underneath.'

'Why do you think that?'

Paulson relays January's rationale behind this statement, all the time treading carefully around the ownership of such a notion, trudging past any culpability.

'Why is Murphy not bringing this to me?' Chief Inspector Markam is a fair man, a just man. He is in the force for all the right reasons and the position of power he has deservedly attained ensures that those under his command both fear and respect him. He works by the book, insomuch as he understands his station and rank in the overall hierarchy; he will not piss off his superiors. But he will not accept dubiously motivated decisions from 'on high' without a fight, either. As such, he shows himself to be reigning in someone like January David while also giving him the slack and grace to pursue avenues that others would not encourage. Because January gets the results.

Markam is an ally. A strong confederate.

January David does not necessarily realise this yet.

But he will.

'I take it he has no idea you are here,' Markam

continues, holding back a smile, respecting Paulson's gumption. Markam understands the dynamic within the violent crime team. After all, he was the person Murphy imprudently came to with the suggestion that January David was the Zone Two Killer. Markam knew it was absurd but had to act according to protocol. This decision meant another innocent girl died. It was Murphy's insecurity and ambition that created the situation, but Markam still blames himself for how it ended. Perhaps he did not get things turned around quickly enough. The killing of Stacey Blaine – the girl found levitating in a garage with a pole pushed through her stomach – may have been the murder that finally exonerated January David of blame, but it changed Chief Markam.

He won't let that happen again.

And he is watching Murphy.

'I'm not sure where he is, sir. I just don't want to waste time if there are any more bodies. It's more evidence, more clues.'

'Say no more.'

'Thank you, sir.' Paulson exhales a breath that feels like his first since entering the room.

There is a moment of inaction as both men consider their next move. Is that the end of the conversation? Will Markam arrange the excavation? Will he force Murphy to do it? Should Paulson leave? It will take another day to arrange, fill out the paperwork, obtain necessary authorisation.

'Might be best to say that I called you in to talk about this, eh? Keep things harmonious in the office,' Markam says at last, his seriousness masking the complicity of his suggestion.

'Of course. I'm glad you brought it to our attention, sir,'

Paulson replies, playing along with the tacit agreement, aiming for subtlety but missing only an exaggerated comedy wink.

Paulson turns and heads for the door, sensing that this is the opportune moment for departure. Markam will handle the details. He can manage Murphy's predictable response. The chief inspector drops his imposing frame back into the chair behind his desk and picks up the phone receiver.

As Paulson steps out through the half-open door, Markam, already dialling a number, speaks under his breath yet at a volume he knows can be heard. 'Let's hope January is right about this one.'

Paulson turns back to Chief Markam, his face at first betraying shock and then a smile he has no control over.

'Next time you speak to David, tell him to get back here soon, eh? And take the rest of the day off, will you? You look like shit.' These are his final toneless words before he gives the person at the other end of the line his name and rank while shooing Paulson out with a strong single flick of the wrist.

Murphy will feel disgruntled when he receives the information; he'll know this came from Paulson, even if Markam does stick with his line.

Paulson takes the day off as directed.

He gets into his car but will not drive home to rest as instructed.

Eames is still to be paid a visit.

And it has to be today.

Soon, there will be more bodies.

Many more bodies.

Eames

⸻✦⸻

I haven't killed a person for a long time.

I've wanted to.

I want to.

It is something I know I excel at; I'm better at it than anyone else – I make an art of destruction. When I take a life, I give meaning where once there was none. Through death my victims reach a poignancy they would never have been able to attain without my help, without me.

Girl 1 would still be working inside a bank, collecting her Swedish modular furniture, narrowly avoiding the lechery of her boss, serial-dating every loser on even the most niche of match-making websites.

Girl 5 would still have his dick attached but he would remain invisible and unable. He would die anyway at his own hand, giving his life and death an equal amount of insignificance, an identical lack of substance. He should be pleased I de-sexed him. He should be kneeling before me in the blood that gushes from where his manhood once dripped and thank me for making him a somebody.

Girl 4 would still be with her husband, perhaps her child would be his child. She would seem happy, content, fulfilled.

She would be none of these things.

She does not yet know but she can never feel any of these emotions.

She can never be that person.

When they find Georgina Burton dead in the park, everything about it will scream my name. The memory of those first victims will jump to the forefront of people's minds.

Imagine how stupid they will feel to have believed they could forget.

Think of their confusion as they fear the presence of a man they know is locked away. They'll question their judgement, their rationality.

Everybody will recall something different.

A face stuffed with cigarettes.

Shattered teeth embedded into a throat.

A beaten wife strung up and left bleeding to death.

She keeps me alive.

As memory.

As incubus.

Detective Sergeant Paulson is on his way here now, doubtlessly practising his opening line in the rear-view mirror, hoping to deliver it with convincing authority. It's different when you are in a room with the killer. If he'd waited another day, there would be more than one.

Our last meeting was off-timetable. There are set visiting hours and he cornered me in the vastness of an empty room; the element of surprise was his only ally on that occasion. He probably believes he will have that advantage again today when he questions me about the second murder; he's been sent to tease information from me about this killing that I would willingly provide if only the correct questions were asked.

Idiot. He is always here at my behest. I need to see how it will look. I'm running through logistics. Calculating the probabilities. I imagine his face as I slit his throat the next time he visits, his eyes asking me *Why?* Wondering how I came about a weapon. The last thing he'll see is my smile.

I'm sawing a cartoon doorway into the floorboards.

My usual guard's face appears in the small window of my door, the one through which I am endlessly ogled by middle-aged white men who call themselves doctors or psychiatrists.

Shhh! You can't call them wardens.

No, of course they are not abusive, your honour.

This is a medical facility.

He unlocks the door but I do not move from my bed. His expression as he enters is one of relief that there has been no confrontation. I have never been combative here, even towards those on a power trip. I see through their eyes and into their thoughts. This place can turn a regular person into something they are not.

Evil breeds evil.

Over time there is only a small difference between the incarcerated and those who watch over the damned. There is a minuscule contrast between the faux guards, the fake doctors, the fraud psychologists and myself. We all know what we are or have become as a result of our surroundings.

I just don't care.

I'm indifferent.

Not the same as the others.

'Looks like you have another visitor,' he says, one hand still on the door – he is neither locking himself in with me or allowing me passage to exit. 'Very popular all of a sudden.' And he smiles the smile of a nervous person who's trying to appear at ease. We have a rapport of sorts. He seems to pull the short straw every time, and is lumbered with me. He's perfectly affable, likeable even. He doesn't appear to have been corrupted like so many others who work in this madhouse.

It's a *medical facility.*

We're just a little sick.

Come down with a case of the want-to-kill-people.

The guard nods his head backwards, subtly summoning me to stand. When I don't respond immediately he looks at his watch. This is good for me to know; I can break his concentration. There is another doctor here who reacts in the same way yet does not wear a watch. His rudeness aggravates me, but this guard is not doing it out of spite or to demonstrate his freedom versus my isolation.

I stand and saunter towards the door where he remains tall and strong and somehow kind. I look at him for a brief moment and sense no malice. I don't know that he has a doting wife, two daughters and a son. I have no idea of the financial strains he faces or how his working hours will eventually take their toll on his relationships with all the members of the family he is just trying to support.

Even if I did know this, it would not change the fact that he is most likely to be the next person I murder. That I can wait for that one opportunity where his mind wanders or attentiveness wavers, and his life insurance can take care of his family.

I am incapable of guilt. I realise that much.

I feel for him the way I do about any of my other victims, or the guards who deliver surreptitious punches to the ribs, or this bed-frame, or paint on the walls. He is something to someone but nothing to me. Only one person makes me feel.

Audrey.

The one I did not kill. Twice.

Everything is for her.

And now, for our reunion.

I am led down the long corridor once more to the blue doors at the other end; this time I am cuffed. Beyond that there is the sterile wasteland the fat detective summoned me to on the last occasion.

Inside the room I see where the men we are not allowed to refer to as prisoners or psychopaths will sit tomorrow in front of broken families and appeal lawyers. Each of them at a different table, conversing amiably with family members, apparent friends, mistresses and colleagues. Alone, to the rear right side corner, a hefty individual pushes himself to his feet, scraping the legs of his chair against the floor noisily like a petulant schoolchild.

He wants more.

Detective Sergeant Paulson, you believe yourself to be the conduit, the man walking the line between myself and my adversary. You feel superior. Smarter. Protected.

That is not who you are.

You are the butt of my joke.

Nothing but a stooge.

The Revisit

—✦—

Monday
BERKSHIRE, 15:00 GMT
New York, 10:00 EST

The overweight but thinning detective hopes his friend is wrong about the bodies, that they are not about to unearth more pain. It is all he can manage to consider in the monotony of motorway traffic.

Now he has a job to do.

He parks outside the asylum, checking himself in the rear-view mirror before slipping out of the car, putting on a mask of no fear.

Eames is different this time. Even from across the room, Paulson notices a swagger that was not present at their last impromptu meeting.

He knows why I am here, he thinks to himself, dropping back into his seat.

How can he know?

'Detective,' Eames greets, holding out his cuffed hands, his left one a little further forward than his right, as though offering a handshake. He smirks, knowing that Paulson would never accept such a gesture. He sits opposite the detective, whose back faces the wall behind, and rests his forearms flat along the desk that separates them.

'I could get out of these, you know,' he boasts.

'Why bother with them, then?' Paulson responds apathetically to what he presumes is bravado aimed at knocking him off balance.

'I wear them for you.' Any semblance of joviality evaporates with this sentence. He delivers it in pointed monotone that suggests he could have added, 'For your safety'.

So that you think you have the power.

Because I do exactly what I want.

I invent the rules of the game.

Paulson knows how to interrogate. He is trained. He understands that he is to enter into the conversation with an open mind, searching for the truth rather than appointing blame. But Eames is different. He will attest to the murder or at least his knowledge that it has occurred, that he knew when, where, to whom, and how it took place.

Paulson is not prepared for this. He has driven straight here after leapfrogging his acting inspector and requesting the excavation of what he will soon learn to be six children's skeletal remains. And preparation is key in this situation.

He has the lower hand.

He does not see the metaphorical string connected to both wrists and feet that walked him from his car and through the door like a plump marionette.

'Another girl is dead.' Paulson throws any legalities aside and opts for outright confrontation. Then he monitors verbal and non-verbal cues to decipher whether or not he is being toyed with, whether Eames actually has any part in this killing series. Was this the plan from the outset or is this a new group of murders?

'Cutting to the chase. I like your style. It's very January David of you.'

Paulson tries desperately to remain stalwart and convicted.

'I don't need to give you the run-around, Detective. You don't want to hear tube-map coordinates or bus routes, you just want to know her name and where she will be found. You don't know she is dead yet but she is. You'll have to try a little harder than that.' Eames turns his head to one side as if bored already and brings his hands close to his cheek, scratching at the two-day stubble with his left hand while glancing over his shoulder at the solitary guard manning the only exit.

The detective is forced to act quickly, ignoring the now moot steps of investigative interviewing. No time for theme development. No need to overcome denials or defeat objections. Paulson is beyond offering Eames possible motives; he cannot preserve a sympathetic facade. So he reaches across the desk, faster than you would expect for a man of his size, and grips the bar between the handcuffs, pulling his suspect's arms back down to the table and his gaze back in the direction of the man now speaking and taking control.

'Do not look away from me when I am talking to you.' He speaks through clenched teeth, his mouth genial in shape to fool any onlookers. 'I am not here to play your game. Your battle is not with me.'

He has surely gained the attention of the serial murderer who sits three feet from him, their foreheads almost touching, but he is working on the fly, improvising. He thought he was here to glean information on the second victim, but it appears he is too late. He is here to stop the third being killed.

Eames stares for a while, disguising lividness and pushing it deep within.

'The next time you touch me will be the last time you feel anything.' This message is delivered as caustically as his line about being cuffed for Paulson's sake.

And he isn't lying.

The only person Eames is capable of lying to is himself.

'Where is the next murder due to take place?' Paulson pushes aside a threat he considers idle in the current circumstances.

'Do you mean the one happening . . .' Eames pretends to look at a watch on his wrist '. . . right now, or the one after that?' He smirks.

'Where is the next murder due to take place?' Paulson repeats.

'Is that your question? You don't want to know who it will be or when it will be? You want to know where? So you can sit there staking it out, drinking coffee and eating junk.' The last sentence is not a question and is not delivered as such.

Paulson changes tack. 'Who is doing this?'

'Well, I am, of course. I picked them out myself.' He lowers his brow as though stating the obvious.

'Who is killing these girls?' Paulson repeats.

'Eames.'

'You are in here.'

'Did Manson have to plunge the knife in himself?'

The detective's entire body seems to sigh and resign itself and he moves back to his original line of questioning, hoping to avoid his suspect's apparent disillusionment. 'What is the location of your next victim?' He accentuates the word *your* to play on the deluded ego.

'Oh. All over. Anywhere. Everywhere. A little bit here. A little bit there,' he taunts.

Paulson merely stares across at him, unmoved.

'You need to be looking more closely at the police in that city.'

'What?'

'That is what I am telling you. It's what I am telling Detective Inspector January David. You need to be looking more closely at the police in that city.' Eames repeats the sentence, this time with a slight pause between words as though talking to a deaf person who has only recently grasped the art of lip-reading.

'I thought we had stopped playing games.'

'Do you believe everything I say?'

'You want a deal, is that it? You tell us where the next victim is supposed to be killed and you get something in return, am I right?' Paulson is panicking now. He can't handle the rhetoric and his mind keeps ticking back to Aria Sky and the possibility of others.

'No, Detective, use your sense,' he responds calmly, the playfulness dropping from his face once more. 'You insult my sensibility; I just want to help.'

Paulson knows that is all he will get from the maniac opposite him. It is a game to Eames. It always is. And he is demonstrating how comfortable he is in the asylum, that there is no desire to leave. He stands to signify the end of the conversation and Eames responds by sitting further back into his seat – somehow more relaxed than he was in the moment he entered.

'We're done here.'

'Thanks for visiting, Detective. Must dash. Would you come again?' He does not speak smugly, merely with a quiet assuredness that they will go through this at least once more.

Before stepping out from behind the table, Paulson has the presence of mind to ask one more question. He falls back on what he knows, that he should have the suspect relay pertinent details of the offence in order to determine false testimony, to gauge deception. 'What is her name?' he asks sternly, towering over the enigmatic Eames, his frame casting shadow on the suspect's face.

'I'm sorry?'

'The girl who is apparently being murdered by you right now. What – is – her – name?' Paulson repeats the treatment he was recently subjected to and elongates his question with deliberate breaks between words.

Eames pauses for longer than he would want, his eyes distracted momentarily and drifting upwards to the left.

'This is information that Detective Inspector David is probably more than aware of. Please just pass on the message and forget about the doves. You're too late.'

There is a wisp of the incredible about this conclusion and it gives Paulson the greatest insight yet into what January David is up against. Is Eames really involved? Is he falsely claiming these girls to put himself back on the map? Or has he himself become the distraction?

Audrey

—✦—

Monday
**UPPER EAST SIDE, MANHATTAN, NEW YORK,
22:30 EST**
London, 03:30 GMT

'Good ee-van-ing, Ms David,' the Polish giant drools, splitting the last word into three shorter words. 'Everybody working late, I see.' And he smiles.

'Sorry?'

'Everybody working late, I see,' he repeats more slowly, as though I have not understood his sentiment through the accent.

And he smiles again, this time nodding a glance towards the lift and rolling his eyes back to me knowingly.

My own expression must be easier for him to read and he chooses to elaborate.

'Ms Phillipa . . . she has only recently returned too.'

'What?'

His smile drops, pulling his eyebrows down with it into a shape of concern and terror. I pace towards the lift and press the button with repeated aggression.

'She left him alone . . .'

'Oh, no no no no no, Ms David.' He steps back out from behind his booth and for the first time I notice that

162

he is wearing his name badge. It displays the word 'Marek' in black lettering on a shiny gold background. 'The baby was with Ms Phillipa. He was in his pushchair.'

This does not calm me down.

'Awake when they left, asleep when they returned.' He pulls out the dullard smile he gave on my arrival but it does not soothe or cut through the tension.

The lift doors open and I step inside, wishing Marek a good night and thanking him for the information. The next person he sees will be Phillipa as she leaves, crying behind her hand.

'Where have you been?' My voice is raised, my eyes are widened. I jump immediately on to the offensive as I enter the apartment.

Phillipa walks swiftly to greet me, her finger pressed against her lips, almost ordering me to quieten down – in my own home.

'I've only just managed to get Walter to sleep.'

'You took him outside!'

Phillipa looks back over her shoulder tentatively, hoping I haven't woken my son, seemingly unfazed at my knowledge of her whereabouts this evening.

'You took him outside,' I repeat, this time at a lower volume but the pseudo-whisper merely adds more venom. 'On to the streets of Manhattan. At night.'

She looks directly at me, her cheeks seeming to sink back into her skull in shame while her eyes appear to grow larger and darker as her own upset swells inside.

Then she attempts to justify her actions, stating that she did not go far, that she thought the air might do him good after being inside for two days. She notices my body stiffen at this comment as though I find it a personal attack on my skills as a mother, and decides to backtrack.

'This was not like looking after him during the day as I usually do. He was crying then hyperactive then vacant. I took his temperature but there was nothing out of the ordinary. He seemed more restless than I have seen him; I tried everything to get him to go down and stay asleep. The walk was really a last resort. I know how it soothes him when we go out to the park in the stroller . . . during the day,' she adds, trying to pacify me.

As she continues with her vindicating diatribe, I zone out, already forgiving her. Walter is safe; she is a great nanny. She should never have taken him out, that much is true, but it fills me with a warmth to know that she is not perfect, that it doesn't all go swimmingly for her every day, that she is not without fault. This is the happiest and least distracted I have felt since the police discovered Kerry Ross hanging from a theatre ceiling, performing a cut-price version of the Girl 4 tableau.

I act out a weak chastising dressed up as a limp warning and explain to Phillipa that I will see her in the morning, that 'We learn from our mistakes'.

Of course, I do not learn.

Tomorrow morning, while taking a trip through Central Park, a group of schoolchildren will discover Girl 9.

He's getting closer.

He's here.

He's me.

January

⸻✦⸻

Paulson thinks Eames is bluffing. That he has nothing to do with these murders. He just wants us to think that he is running things. I've tried getting through to Marquez but to no avail. Where is he?

Eames, in his cryptic, game-playing way, is telling us the girl's name.

There is nothing on the news, though. And, according to Eames, she died over twelve hours ago. We should know by now. Somebody would have heard. Someone would have noticed.

I drift off, my face down in the pillow, still; my right hand is on the phone in my pocket, its battery slowly dying though the charger lies on the bedside table within reach. I expect The Smiling Man to revisit, prepared to inflict his torment on me.

But he is nowhere.

Or I cannot see him.

The blackness of the dust-covered room he inhabits is replaced by a dark emptiness, which poses no threat.

This should tell me something.

Maniswomanismaniswomanismaniswomanisman.

My hand vibrates and I unfold myself into a sitting position, unaware how long I have been in deep slumber.

'Agent Marquez?' I sound out groggily, coughing afterwards to clear my throat.

'Detective Inspector David. I'm sorry I was unable to get back to you, it has been a very busy night. I'd appreciate it if we could meet.'

'Of course, I have some things I need to discuss.' I find I have to pause and manually encourage my brain to recall what those things are.

'We have plenty to talk about, Detective David.'

'Shall we meet at the same deli? I can come right away.' My phone beeps twice into my ear.

'No, no. I'm uptown right now. Meet me at 202 West 74th. We can talk there. Let's say tomorrow morning at 10:15.'

My phone vibrates in my hand again. I turn the screen towards me and it fades to black.

'Hello? Hellooooo. Agent Marquez, can you hear me?' For some reason I shake the phone violently, as though that will make it work. 'Fucking peace of sh—' I curse, standing up and cutting myself off as I head for the wire dangling limply over the bedside table. It takes the handset a minute or two to boot back up and another minute to realise I am still in New York before I receive any signal.

I call Marquez.

His phone rings continuously. I want to pace while I wait but I can't unplug the phone from the wall so I tap my right heel impatiently.

Where is he? I only just spoke to him. What is he playing at?

I know that the next person on Eames' list has the surname Burton. I know that it will more than likely be a female. I can't say exactly how Eames has planned for her to meet her demise or indeed how he is doing this, but it does revolve around Lance Burton's Doves trick if he is following his previous MO, which he undoubtedly seems to be, judging from the state in which Kerry Ross was discovered.

I know that Marquez must have the resources within the FBI to pull up a list of every Burton on the Island of Manhattan in seconds. But we need the search narrowed and with only one murder so far, which seems to be a cut-rate copycat, it's difficult to calculate an accurate profile let alone decrypt a pattern I am not yet seeing.

The idea of a copycat killer makes me think of Murphy. It's his go-to solution for every case but is rarely the answer. Besides, I know that Eames is involved: he provided information he couldn't possibly know unless he orchestrated the murder of Kerry Ross, Girl 8.

This is the thing that jars, that irks. I could help Agent Marquez hone in on an area as small as one block. We could wait there, stake it out, knowing that we have a twenty-four-hour timeframe to catch this killer – although I have already wasted four of those waiting for my federal colleague to return a call. We could know who and where and at what time. We wouldn't even need to understand the killer's motives – we would be a step ahead. We'd know what he was doing before he even did it.

But I no longer have The Smiling Man.

And I would need Eames.

I would have to ask for help from the man who fucked my wife and twice left her for dead.

The man who ensured I have nothing left but this crusade to find my sister.

What choice do I have?

I'm half a step back.

Girl 9

The lamp post above me is no longer illuminated, but it was when I first got here. A green sign is fastened to the centre of the pole and reads *Balto* at the top in white letters. I don't know what that means. Below that are the words *Dial and Discover* and then a number – *646-862 0997.* Press +03# on your Central Park audio guide.

'Behind you'll find a bronze statue of a sled dog named Balto who, in 1925, transported a serum across Alaska to tackle an outbreak of diphtheria,' it pronounces.

This should be the updated version: 'To your left is Willowdell Arch where Georgina Burton was caught in the shadows, strangled until the white-hot bulb of the lamp post scorched its image into her retina and all she saw was a great white light. Then the darkest of darknesses that signifies demise. Her body was then dumped at the spot just ahead of where your feet are now, the long grass disguising her until up close. Birds peck at the seeds covering her body, revealing the holes where her eyes used to be.'

That last part is a lie, one of my embellishments. Eames did not take my eyes, though the birds are pecking at me.

Sixteen schoolchildren stand at the bronze statue of a dog, most of them attentive with their pencil or pen, poised to take notes of whatever the guide or teacher is trying to fill their brains with. As if any of this is important. If I'd known about the dog, would I not have been killed? Idiots.

They innocently pet the hard surface of the dog statue; some have a photo snapped by a mobile-phone camera. Though the topic is not particularly interesting, both students and educator believe the excursion to be better, more enjoyable, less laborious, than a classroom lecture.

That will change.

They haven't spotted me yet.

In the background is the sound of three young men, all sporting an afro, playing their guitars on top of the rocks in the distance. It isn't raining today, did I mention that? They strum chords and tap the wooden bodies of their instruments percussively. One of the children, those innocent kids, has predictably lost interest in the story of a brave hound battling adverse weather conditions back in a time when not even his grandparents were born. He peers back over his shoulder and rocks his torso in time with the live music.

He peers over my corpse, which is lightly camouflaged by the long grass, probably to negate the necessity for huge bags of birdseed to cover my body. Pigeons tap their beaks against my thighs, on the bone of my ankle; they shit on my chest before flying off to gloat about their feast, their free meal.

The schoolboy doesn't realise how long he has been

listening to the band on the rocks instead of his teacher until she snaps him back into reality, saying, 'OK, students. Now, if you'd like to turn around and walk down the path we'll see what other treasures await us.'

She is talking about Olmstead & Vaux Way, the next stop on their tour.

But a girl screams.

Then three more join her.

The teacher pushes her way through the small congregation of kids to understand what has provoked such a reaction. When she does, her own response is far more stilted and contained – a sharp intake of breath and a hand covering her mouth.

With maternal instinct, she stretches her arms out, attempting to usher the children away from my pecked-at carcass. My neck is bruised and twisted unnaturally, my eyes pointing towards the grey sky, more brightness penetrating my pupils. I feel nothing. I know nothing.

I am nothing.

The three black kids up the hill, sitting on their cold grey boulders, grab their instruments tightly by the necks and pace swiftly yet cautiously down to the growing audience beneath, the occasional vibration of the strings as they run creating a fitting sombre, incidental accompaniment. Most of the schoolchildren look away, too distraught at the sight of my pock-marked, bleeding white skin. One boy takes a picture on his phone and uploads the image to the Internet.

Everybody is too pre-occupied by my presence to notice the top hat and scarf hanging from the sign on the post. My killer has been careful not to leave anything incriminating within the fibres.

They are an accent.

His signature.

A clear message meant for January David.

This is how I got my own plaque on a bench in Central Park. I want everything I have said to be true, to have actually occurred in the way I have relayed the details. Mark it down as evidence. Everything is a clue, whether true or not.

Could this have been avoided had I not gone out for that run in the rain? Had I not gone into that tunnel? Had I remembered Eames at all?

Heck, no. Hardly any of that happened.

When I arrived in the park, I was already dead.

January

✦

**CENTRAL PARK, MANHATTAN, NEW YORK,
09:58 EST**
London, 14:58 GMT

I try to call Marquez again after another night of uninterrupted sleep.

I hose myself down in the shower, leaving the mobile phone to charge, thinking that I have time: The Smiling Man should have delivered his message to me yesterday.

I'm already too late.

As I pull back the yellow-with-age-and-neglect shower curtain, the water hailing down against my stomach and a draught squeezing around the mottled window that peers over Seventh Avenue, I bend my knees slightly to fit under the low showerhead and tilt my face to the spray, letting it beat away my tiredness.

I don't know that time is up.

Girl 9 is dead a few blocks from where I stand now, in this chipped bath, the water running down on to the tiled floor where I forgot to tuck the curtain inside the tub. I cleanse myself while children scream and birds feed and guitars stop playing.

Georgina Burton has been killed, the details not yet

known to the authorities, and the next victim has already been chosen.

My phone is one hundred per cent charged.

The lift doors open to a tall, attractive couple, mid-conversation.

'*Nein. Nein. An der kreuzung*,' she says to him, shaking her head dismissively; I only understand that she said *no* at one point.

I step inside and they say *good morning*, somehow knowing that I am English even though I haven't said anything. I begin to wonder how much I stick out here. How easy it is to spot me as a non-native, an alien. And I think of the killer. The Eames substitute. To walk these streets and go unnoticed, they must be from this town, or American at least. I look suspicious. Even with my head bowed I'm conspicuous on these streets, in these buildings, strolling through these parks and sitting on these benches. In London I can disappear. I can blend and fall out of focus. The city and I know one another.

We hit the bottom floor and my German fellow travellers stand back politely, silently ushering me first out the door with their kind manners. I want to say *goodbye* in their language but the words escape me for a moment. I nod in courteous acknowledgement instead.

The lobby is rammed with people picking up leaflets, throwing cases on to trolleys, collecting room keys and talking with bellhops, all of them unaware at this stage that there are mice in this building with the ability to climb up fifteen stories. That they are being hemmed in by a trail of murder which threatens to blight their cultural or shopping excursion. Luckily, the killer seems to be local and is, so far, only killing locals.

I turn right and on to Seventh Avenue, remembering the words *auf Wiedersehen* the moment my left foot hits the sidewalk. It's too late.

I'm too late.

The hotel on the opposite side of the road looks much better quality than the one I am staying in. I may move there if I am here much longer. I know they even have free Internet over there because I can pick it up from my bedroom if I sit by the window. The action of even contemplating this, of making myself more comfortable, is my subconscious informing me that there will be more deaths. That I won't be able to save Georgina Burton.

Then I see the commotion ahead.

The crowds.

The police.

The line of tape.

I itch impatiently at the next crossing, squinting my eyes and dodging the heads of pedestrians intersecting my path as a green light signals time to walk.

Central Park South is half a block from here now. I pick up the pace. Perhaps Agent Marquez is caught in the throng; that is why he did not return my last call. I manage to force my way to the front through a mixture of confidence and apathy towards others. The cop is acting as a human shield, his arms spread widely or a hand held rigidly to warn people to stay back from the police cordon. *Don't come any closer.*

He sees me out of the corner of his eye. I spot the moment my appearance registers with him.

'Excuse me,' I aim my words directly at his dominating figure, trying to lock myself in a stare with him. 'Excuse me,' I repeat, 'what happened here?'

'I'm sorry, sir. Like I said before, this is a police—'

'I am the police,' I interrupt, hoping to throw him off script and enter into more civilised dialogue.

He sidesteps down the line of the morbidly fascinated horde. 'Look, pal, this is serious here, OK? Maybe you should just—'

I jump in again before he has the chance to dismiss me. 'I'm a British detective over here consulting on a case.' His ears prick up. 'I'm working with Agent Marquez.'

'The Feds? They're not here, sir. What's your name?'

'David. Detective Inspector January David. I flew here from London.' I'm trying to give him as much information as possible because I have no identification on me to verify my position, my job title. It's locked in the safe of my hotel room for now. My presence is unofficial. I have no authority on this island.

He calls over his shoulder to a colleague, 'Hey, Joe.' His accent suddenly sounds stronger, more New York than when he spoke to me. 'Is there an Agent Marquez here, at the scene?'

'Feds?' Joe bleats back.

The muscular mountain keeping me back shrugs his shoulders.

'No. Not here,' confirms Joe. 'Not yet,' he speculates.

'We don't know no Marquez, Mr . . .' He pauses as though trying to remember my name. He hasn't forgotten.

'David. Detective Inspector January David,' I remind him, placing greater emphasis on the rank of my position.

'Mr David, there is no Marquez and there's nothing I can do to help. You'll have to find out via the news channels like everybody else.'

And he turns himself away from me as though that is the end of it. He doesn't want to speak to me or see me again; he just wants to do his job.

My face gets lost in a sea of expressions hoping to catch a glimpse of a dead body. They don't yet know what one looks like and how it stays with you. They think it may be interesting, a good story to tell when they go home, but the lucidity with which you recall your first corpse is terrifying. The only thing more horrifying is the ease with which you can then forget the ones you see from that point onwards. You can reduce them to a number.

Girl 1.

Girl 2.

Girl 3.

I back out of the sea of *Schadenfreude*, that early-morning mere of voyeuristic sadism, and head to the location Marquez gave over the phone.

The cop who dismissed me still acts like a human barrier and has already pushed me to the back of his mind, but soon he'll want to talk.

He'll have to ask me for my help.

Just as I have had to do with Eames.

Girl 9

—◆—

The truth is, it doesn't matter what happened. My final journey towards emptiness is only worthwhile if a clue can be extrapolated from the information given, whether there were any witnesses present. I could have been jogging through the park in the rain; it could have been simply overcast or sun-drenched. I may have marvelled at the occasional busker or gushed over kind words on a bench commemoration.

None of these things could be true.

Or all of them could be.

Perhaps I could have been traipsing up Fifth Avenue with hands being cut into by the weight of the shopping bags from Saks. It may have been a simple mugging or a hit-and-run down a quiet side street.

Is a backstory so vital? My mother and father were divorced; I formed a habit of fabricating events to make them sound more interesting, to ensure nobody's feelings were hurt in the day-to-day process of living my life. Am I to be sympathised with as a consequence of my mother's agoraphobia? Am I more likeable if I mention that I cared for her, that sometimes my lies made me her enabler? But at least she was content.

In truth, none of this matters.

A blow-by-blow account of my final struggle with life, how blood filled the back of my throat, how I was dragged under the archway, how my killer debated taking my eyes then reassessed the situation, holds no gravity.

My journey is unmomentous.

My history irrelevant.

All that matters is now.

January David should be fighting harder to get to me, to see me up close and visualise the inspiration. It is my body lying on the grass, dotted with birdseed, a top hat and scarf draped on the lamp post that is key, not my failure as a daughter. Not my stuttering career. I can't lie now.

It was Eames who killed me, Detective Inspector David. Whether it was the man himself or not, it was Eames. You know this. So you must know that it is only how I ended that is real. That only the spectacle is true. That if I had kept the name Georgina Radner, my father's family name, I would still be alive, and even then, everything you think you know about me would be worthless.

Don't you see, Detective David?

Everything is illusion.

This is all one trick.

And you are looking the wrong way.

Use him like he uses you.

Stop looking for Eames. You know where he is.

January

───◆───

**UPPER WEST SIDE, MANHATTAN, NEW YORK,
10:28 EST**
London, 15:28 GMT

Marquez has directed me to a baseball centre.
I'm late as a result of the Central Park diversion.

I open the door cautiously, confused as to the location. There are caps on the wall and life-size cardboard cut-outs of players I have no knowledge of. An attractive young black girl sits behind a giant glass display case full of gloves and bats and cards of yet more players I've never heard of, more superstars I do not know.

'Good morning, sir, how may I help you today?' She smiles a bright white, straight-toothed smile and blinks her eyes.

'Er, is this 202 West 74th Street?' I edge closer to her, trying to take in my surroundings. One player seems to be everywhere, Derek Jeter. I know nothing about the sport but I have heard his name and I know what the New York Yankees logo looks like.

'It certainly is.' She seems flirtatious. 'Do you have a reservation?'

'I'm supposed to be meeting somebody here, I think.'

'Ah, yes. You are . . .' She fingers down a sporadically highlighted timesheet. 'Mistaaaaaaa,' she sounds out, holding the word until she locates the current time-slot, 'David. Mr David. Your friend has already arrived, he's down there waiting for you. Have you been here before? Do you know where you're going?'

'Um, no. Never been before.' I notice that I suddenly sound even more English in the solitude of this room and against the strength of her borough accent – I'm unsure which. Could be Queens or Brooklyn. It could be anywhere.

I'm a stranger here.

She explains the directions, that I am in the blue area and I can pick up bats, a hat and gloves while I'm down there; I have to wear a helmet in the nets.

'There's restrooms and a soda machine too,' she punctuates. Then she sets the impeccable customer service to one side. 'I love the way you talk. You're English, right?' She nods almost undetectably as she asks, knowing the answer.

'Yes. Yes. I'm from London.' I don't want to be impolite because she has been nothing but courteous to me, but I have just been rejected from a crime scene where I may be one of a handful of people to add real insight into the inquiry and my American liaison has asked to meet me in the most unusual of places. My body starts to excuse itself closer to the door, which leads downstairs.

She eventually trails off her flirtations and her *dreams of seeing Europe one day*.

'Well, enjoy yourself down there, Mr David. You have eighteen minutes left on the clock.' And she lets her grin linger long enough to suggest that she is not merely extending the company's well wishes. My lack of sexual encounters since Audrey left means that, while walking down the stairs, I imagine the petite black girl bouncing up and down on my lap the way that my wife used to, arching her back and touching herself as she breathes heavily into climax. This simple flirtation manages to spark sexual thought.

The sound of machinery is followed by a thwack of wood against rubber and then a guttural curse of self-deprecation, which leads me to Marquez.

The long red pathway which runs down the centre of the room bisects four separate fenced-off areas. The walls are covered in protective blue cushioning and the roof is corrugated to give the sense of I don't know what.

Through the green fence wire to my right I can pick out the figure of Marquez, standing in his standard dark fitted suit and white shirt, his tie tucked between the two middle buttons to prevent flapping when he swings the bat. There are fifty to sixty bright yellow balls peppering the fake grass ahead of him. He stands in a wide stance, swinging erratically, forgoing any form or technique, hoping to connect sweetly with the oversized fake base-ball which is about to be flung at him at around forty miles per hour by a robotic arm.

He misses.

'Fucking hell, Marquez,' he shouts, tapping his bat against his helmet in frustration and setting up for the next ball.

I keep walking until I am level with him. He doesn't acknowledge I'm there.

He swings.

And misses.

'You piece of . . .' he mutters under his breath, waggling the bat from the wrists as if emptying out thoughts of malice from a salt shaker.

I flip the switch sitting just above head-height on the pillar outside the entrance to his cage, which is draped from the roof in a heavy black net.

'Detective David, you're late. Hit the switch, I can talk while I bat.' He doesn't even look at me while saying this.

'Why are we here, Agent Marquez?'

He misses another ball.

'There's been another murder.' Still, he looks ahead at the whirring machine thirty feet in front of him.

'I know. In Central Park.' I pause for a moment. 'But why are we *here*?'

He takes a step to his left and finally turns towards me, looking ridiculous in smart attire and plastic baseball helmet, yet somehow retaining an urban ruggedness. A yellow ball whizzes past him just below his chest.

'You know?' He stealthily ignores my second query batting back his own.

'I just walked past it all. It's pandemonium. I take it you've already been there, seen the body?' I ask this to test him. The police at the scene suggested that there was no Agent Marquez, or at least they hadn't seen one, met one.

'I was there to view the body, work out whether it's our guy.' He turns back to his mechanical nemesis. 'She was lying in the grass under a lamp post with birds pecking holes across her skin. But I guess you probably already knew that too, eh?'

'I have no idea what the victim looks like or how she died, but that description makes sense.' The sound of the ball hitting his bat and flying straight up into the netting above forces a gap in my sentence. 'I spoke to some of the guys down there and they hadn't seen any federal agents all morning.' I let it linger and try to gauge his response. What reason would he have to lie? He, like any agent or detective, is trying to carve a career out for himself.

'I'm not sure what you're trying to get at but I've been there most of the morning, which is why I'm trying to swing out some of the fuckin' stress and frustration that this guy is beatin' us still. So, a couple of cops didn't see me. You've got the New York Police Department and the City Parks Enforcement Control stepping on each other's toes for the first two fuckin' hours, these pigeons are just mutilating the body while they piss up against a wall to see who's in charge of things. I'm in fuckin' charge. They can worry about wrapping some tape around a tree or two and keeping some Chinese kid with a video camera away from the scene; I'll get the pictures taken, the forensics in and the body removed for identification and autopsy.' He steps into the swing this time, launching his body forward and twisting his hips; he connects with the ball and sends it flying back from where it came, hitting a target almost in the centre on the back wall.

I consider myself a decent judge of character. I know that Murphy is a snake and that Paulson is the only person I can trust. I know that this is a game for Eames and that, despite her infidelity, Audrey probably misses me in the same way I have started to long for her. And I can sense that Marquez is on the level. He's screwed up somewhere along the line and he's willing to do whatever it takes to put things right. He sees this case as his opportunity for atonement.

'So,' he continues, 'how about you flip that switch, grab your stuff, get in here and tell me what it is that *you* know?'

I turn the machine off and everything goes quiet. Marquez walks towards me, sweat dripping from the underside of the helmet's peak. He bends down to the floor and lifts the net up for me to duck under. I do so. When I turn back, he is outside with his hand held to the switch.

'Get into position,' he orders. His eyes nod towards the spot where I should be standing. 'Step up to the plate.'

He flicks the switch and the noise of cogs and electricity once again perfuse the room to mask anything we may discuss. 'So, what do you know?' he quips just as a ball hurtles towards me faster than I expected. I don't even have time to swing the bat.

I tell him briefly about The Smiling Man. I explain that I saw nothing this time. No visit. No dream. No intuition. Nothing. I don't tell him that I find this somehow liberating. That I can work on instincts again. I'm not held back by my misunderstanding of subconscious intimations. I notice him baulk slightly when I say that I am in contact with Eames. I explain that he didn't give us a clue as to where it would be on this occasion – we were too late.

'The latest girl was called Burton and her demise was based around Lance Burton's famous Doves illusion. Before that, Kerry Ross was suspended from the ceiling in a sick take on Richard Ross's Rings trick.' I catch the ball early this time, sending it into the left side wall. It hits a logo for The Cubs – the letter C in red with a small blue bear. Three of the fingers on my left hand vibrate against the handle of the bat and my right shoulder starts to burn, but I begin to understand Marquez's need to pummel a shot to the back of the room.

'Look, I know it sounds stupid or made up or weird or whatever, but once I see him and I uncover the message he is trying to convey, I know that I have a twenty-four-hour timeframe to discover the victim and save them.' He knows this, or some sensational version of this, otherwise he would never have called me.

'Fuck me, David.' He laughs at the unbelievability of what I told him and again at himself for believing it. 'I'm surprised you haven't been locked away in a dark basement office of your precinct.'

'They're trying, let me tell you.'

I run through some of the other victims from this case but I leave out Audrey; we don't need to discuss my wife. I hold back some information. I do not inform him that I am still in contact with Eames through Paulson – he need not know that detail – but I run through his profile and suggest that whoever is finishing things off stateside is really a pale version of the criminal mastermind I feel I know so well. Marquez seems visibly put out by this comment. Like this case, his case, is not as important, not as real, as mine was several years ago when I first discovered Dorothy Penn shot through the mouth in East London.

'The thing is, I didn't see The Smiling Man before this murder, before this Burton girl was killed.'

His phone rings and he walks off for privacy, heading towards the solitude of the blue area beyond the cages. The machine continues to spit balls at me for a few minutes while I wait. Eventually, the impish receptionist emerges in my periphery and stops the machine.

'Time's up.' She grins, leaning too close, too sexily, against the stone pillar.

'Really? Where's Mar—'

'Oh, your friend apologised. Said he had to leave suddenly. A work thing.'

I roll my eyes incredulously.

'He paid up for the session at the start,' she says, as though that is what I am irked about. 'There's only you and me left in the whole place until the next group comes in twenty-five minutes.'

I'm not sure whether she is joking around with me or if this is indeed how they do things in this part of the world. Her body language suggests that she is at ease with the words she speaks so matter-of-factly, but I don't have time to play baseball or have a federal agent walk out on a conversation or fuck a complete stranger up against a pillar in the basement of a sports centre.

I need to be immersed in the darkness of the case.

I want to get inside the head and heart of this abhorrent murderer, to locate and swim around in the grime of the New York underworld rather than thump through the brightly lit streets, not scratching the surface of what is reality.

At this moment, I have to be with the body. With Georgina Burton. With Girl 9.

Why won't Marquez take me with him?

What does he have to hide?

I exit the building, pushing out of the glass door into the Manhattan air. I take a laboured breath as though my lungs are more efficient in the city smog. My phone vibrates inside my pocket; a text has been delivered now that I'm in an area with a signal. Marquez pardons himself saying he was called back to the scene. I look to my right, in the direction of the park.

Then left.

In the direction of my wife.

Audrey

---·⊹·---

I watch the report on the television and I cry.
  I feel guilt.

I can sense him with me, in me.

Eames is getting closer.

They can link me to this murder.

It was near enough when that girl was killed and made to look like me downtown in Chelsea, an area of Manhattan I don't know that well, but to infiltrate my immediate surroundings seems too provocative. This is my bubble. I walk past that entrance to the park most days.

The world has become darker overnight.

I can feel it again.

Walter is still asleep after a later night than usual. I wipe beneath my eyes with my middle finger, brushing away tear residue, pressing against the increasingly dark half-moons until my vision is as blurred as my mind. Why have I brought a child into this world? This immoral planet. This appalling existence where countries fight for money or power or religion, where an individual can arbitrarily choke the life from another being simply through boredom or peer pressure or a psychological dysfunction. Where the act of taking someone's life is without remorse. And regret is replaced with thrill.

Imagine his answer in fifteen years when they ask what he remembers most about his mother.

I stare at my son through the open gap by his bedroom door and I wonder what the future holds for him. Have we gone too far? Is it too late for change? Have we passed the mark from which return is impossible?

A knock at the door startles me and instinct tells me to close Walter's door, to keep him locked away from the misery that permeates every city.

It is Phillipa.

I was worried that our minor altercation yesterday evening would for ever alter our relationship, perhaps ending it. But she is here and I respect her greatly for coming back. I am content to forget. I can't hold it against her; she is, somehow, my closest friend in this city.

'Good morning.' I throw on a smile to signify an insouciance for the past. 'The coffee machine is spluttering. Can I interest you?'

'Thanks. That would be great. Didn't have the best night's sleep.' She takes her jacket off and hangs it with her bag in the storage cupboard next to the door.

It's unclear whether she is prodding an acknowledgement of our discussion – I was trying to move past it – or whether she is merely trying to illustrate how much she cares, that she was awake with worry at how her actions had affected me and our relationship.

'Have you seen the news this morning?' I ask, pouring us each a coffee with my back turned towards her. She leans casually against the polished worktop on the other side of the kitchen area.

'No. Not yet. I didn't have time this morning.'

This seems odd to me. She claims that she hardly slept a wink last night. And I've allowed her to start later this morning as I have a meeting on the other side of town so won't be going into the office until after that – it didn't seem worth the trip to traipse in only to leave once my computer has finished booting up.

'I saw a commotion outside the park entrance on sixty-sixth. Something to do with that?' she asks, I presume, naively.

I turn and pass her a white coffee in a tall, white, angular mug of minimalist design. Mine is in a stainless-steel Thermos, replicating the one I left in Hampstead with January; a reminder that I am still here and I won't just go away. I won't just disappear for ever.

My vacuum flask of hope.

'Another girl has been killed.'

Phillipa doesn't drop her drink but her grip on the handle weakens slightly at the news and she spills some of the mug's contents on to my pristine floor tiles.

'Oh, God. They know already? I mean . . .' She gets flustered, snatching at some kitchen roll to clear up her mess. 'I mean, they know it's the same culprit as the one who hung up that girl in the theatre?' She bends down and wipes the floor then the bottom of her cup.

'Looks that way.'

'That only seems like yesterday. Another victim already?' She is still for a moment. A statue of the Madonna with a flat white. Still resplendent in beauty in her time of heartfelt anguish.

'It was only a few days ago.' Her reaction is forcing

me to toughen my own. I fall effortlessly into the businesswoman guise, hardened and stoic.

'I'm sorry, Audrey. I swear I won't take Walter out like that again.' Her eyes glaze and her body seems to shorten so that she can look up at me, pointing her perfectly formed chin upwards and elongating that smooth silken neck. She appears before me as a waif, a suicidal doe transfixed by the headlights that will release her from a personal hell. It would be the ideal moment to break down the walls of our employer–employee relationship, to just be a friend and hug her. Tell her it's all right.

Everything will be OK.

But I am incapable of crossing the boundary that separates my two lives.

I inject my gaze into hers, not intimidatingly or harshly or, conversely, forgivingly, and say, 'I know you won't.'

Seven minutes later I am walking north and then crossing the park on the 85th Street Transverse. There's no way I'll get through further south; you can hear the racket from Madison Avenue. I didn't want to take a cab.

I check my watch while finishing the dregs of my home-brewed Colombian coffee and pick up the pace for my meeting. Then my mobile phone rings and I am informed that it will be delayed by twenty minutes.

My pace automatically slows in response to this message and I find myself taking in the mix of architecture, trying to equate it to a London borough, somewhere like Notting Hill, perhaps, certainly the West End, though the shops look distinctly East End to me.

I order another coffee at a chain cafe along West 75th Street and take a seat. Everyone around me is either tapping at their BlackBerry or scrolling around on a laptop. I tilt my watch face towards me.

Still early.

Two tall, well-spoken Englishmen enter. It's lovely to hear that accent, that simple reminder of home. They marvel at one of the display cases holding packs to make iced beverages in your own kitchen.

'You can't get these in England. We should grab some,' the one with the darker hair enthuses.

'Wait. Wait. Let me take a picture first,' his counterpart chips in excitedly.

A middle-aged woman to my right stops reading for a moment to tut out her distaste for their juvenility. A young studious girl walks in. She is wearing thick-rimmed glasses and her hair is tied up scraggily on top of her head. She holds a yellow clip-folder in her left hand and points up at the board to indicate her chosen drink, a caramel latte.

'Half and half,' she adds as the barista scribbles letters on a paper cup.

Next to walk in is a cop. He's not in uniform but I can tell. He's shorter than I'd expect a policeman to be – below six feet – but well presented in a dark, fitted suit. He may be undercover or simply of high rank, but I know a detective when I see one. I'm still, technically, married to one. And if he taught me anything it's that I am attracted to men of the law and I can sift them out from a crowd.

He orders a tea. Camomile. Though he doesn't pronounce it *mile*, but *meal*.

'Is this seat taken?' he asks, already pulling a chair back from the table for two I solely occupy and where I've been people-watching.

I look at my watch quickly. 'Yes. That's fine. I'm leaving now anyway. Running late,' I lie, feeling somewhat flustered at the thought of entering into conversation with the man my estranged husband knows simply as Marquez.

I'm so close.

I head east down a house-lined street. Each dwelling has stairs leading up to a large front door. Some have multiple apartments, others are huge homes. It reminds me of certain parts of the Village only slightly more grandiose, less bohemian.

I turn my wrist over. No need to pick up the pace.

I swig at my coffee. It's sweeter than the one I made myself earlier this morning. Looking to my right I can see that the building goes down a level so that the kitchen is in the basement and a bearded man plays his piano at a window facing a concrete wall. I have to step out of the way of a woman with fake breasts walking seven dogs at once. I don't know what breed they are. I've never been fond of animals, not even at a young age.

I stroll through another crossing and, after a few metres, check my watch one more time. As I am about to pass a building, a door opens and a man steps out into my path, startling me.

I lift my head up and raise a hand to my chest to signify my fright.

It's him.

He's here.

At this time of the day, in this location, in this city, he stands there, with an attractive shadow and glow from sweating. I stand before him, frozen, open-mouthed and at his mercy.

It's Jan.

It worked.

He came.

There is no need for me to know the hour, the minute, the second.

I'm right on time.

January

**UPPER WEST SIDE, MANHATTAN, NEW YORK,
11:05 EST**
London, 16:05 GMT

Audrey excuses herself as though she has accidentally
walked into a stranger.

My mouth hangs open on the first syllable of her name
with no sound emerging, the utter shock acting as a
barrier to my voice and my thoughts.

She continues to walk east, her pace quickening slightly
but not enough to suggest she is trying to get away.

It was her. I know it was her. Her pale British skin
acting as the smooth foundation for that ludicrously sexy
red lipstick, that dark hair framing her face, presenting
her as artistic sculpture, and that smell, the scent that
has all but disintegrated in the home we once shared.
For a moment, the car fumes were sweet and crisp and
floral and mine.

'Audrey,' I manage to bleat in a vocal that isn't my
own, swallowing between syllables.

She continues on her way.

'Audrey David,' I exclaim, my tone denoting the lack
of inquiry. *I know who you are.*

She glances over her shoulder, maintaining her pace, looking, at first, as though I am inconveniencing her in some way. Her brow is furrowed into a tight frown that insists I leave her alone but softens into eyes betraying longing and sorrow. Then her gaze snaps to the front as she heads closer and closer to Columbus Avenue.

'Audrey, wait,' I call out to her, but she doesn't wait. I step out of the doorway of the batting cages centre. 'We need to talk.' Her pace quickens. She dare not look back now; her focus is fixed on the main road ahead. Where there are people. Where there is life. Hubbub. Traffic.

I want to catch up with her, to grab her roughly by the arm and turn her around so that her gaze can meet my own. But I can't run after her. I don't want to appear threatening.

I want to ask her why she did it: why did she sleep with Eames, where has she been all this time? Why has she not tried to contact me? Why are we still married? I want to shout at her and call her a whore. I want to tell her that I hate her and how she has made my life change so dramatically. I want to shake her. Scare her. I want to scream in her face that she left me with absolutely nothing. Nobody.

But I don't sprint after Audrey as she power-walks to the corner of West 75th.

Because I wouldn't be able to say all of these things.

Because I want to grip her by the shoulders and turn her perfectly smooth face to my weathered, tired eyes. And I want to stay there in silence, drinking her in, inebriating myself in the memory of the way things once were. Because I want to pull her body into mine and kiss her roughly. I want to slap her. And forgive her. And tell her none of this matters.

That I don't need to talk to her.

I just need her.

Watching the way her hips move and her legs cross over slightly at the front as she treads along the pavement, my mind jumps back to the woman I tailed downtown towards the site of the Girl 8 murder. Then it flicks to the image of Audrey suspended from the ceiling of a theatre with high-gauge fishing wire cutting through her skin and I halt, closing my eyes for a moment to black out the past.

Snapping back into the situation, I see a yellow taxi pull up at the corner and watch as Audrey reaches for the door handle.

'Audrey, stop.'

For a second she is lost in ambivalence. I clock her pause and reconsider. I think she is going to stay, turn around. That somehow this thing will work itself out. But my optimism is fleeting. She pulls at the handle calmly and coolly lowers herself on to the back seat, never turning around.

Now I run.

She's not that far away from me. I'm close enough to see her mouth an address to the cab driver. I could get to the door in time. I could pull on the handle. But as I near, she finally turns her head in my direction. It is sad and sorry and it cries without a grimace. And her right hand reaches up to the window so that four fingertips delicately press against the glass as though she has secretly been longing for a moment like this.

I stop short because it feels somehow invasive to progress.

It's not right.

We were not supposed to meet like this.

She heads south towards Midtown. I pull the mobile phone from my pocket and redial the last number. Marquez should be at the crime scene, but he's not. He's three streets back drinking camomile tea at the table my wife just left.

He tells me that he is heading downtown. I should meet him in thirty minutes. He tells me to come to Chelsea Pier.

CE23.

The Perfect Day

—◆—

REGENT'S PARK, LONDON, 11:32 GMT
New York, 06:32 EST

The tiles are green and cold and they slope upward towards the light of day. It's easy for an old man to walk or push a child in their pram. But there are still steps at the end of the slope. The tube is too risky, anyway.

Other families walk in the direction of the zoo. Excited children pace ahead of overweight mothers smoking cigarettes as though ill-health is acceptable; they shave hairstyles on to these children that are too old for them. The sign on the corner says *Marylebone Road. NW1. City of Westminster*.

The number 453 bus exhales dirt as it passes pedestrians. These people breathe in the smog and pollution of the city that will turn their nasal mucus black within a day.

But not Aria.

She is not breathing.

Like Girl 9, she is already dead when she arrives at the park.

*

To the old man, her killer, that sick fuck, the air smells like fresh leaves and damp rubbish.

He counts down the pillared houses across the street.

23 . . . 22 . . . 21 . . .

'That's the Prince's Trust at number eighteen,' he says out loud to the dead girl in the pram. He leans forward slightly over the handles because he wants to make sure that she can hear him. He wants to share with her. He wants to show her that he is not stupid.

St Andrew's gate is open and leads to Avenue Gardens where he hopes they can spend a moment of peace together. As he enters, an elderly Spanish couple run their fingers over the map of the park. The demented murderer does not recognise their language; to him they are merely foreign. And that is enough in his tiny mind.

Next to the sign stating *Welcome to Regent's Park* is a poster that says *RAPE*. Beside the large, red capital letters is the picture of a black male. He is twenty years old. He is five feet seven inches tall. The overweight child predator tuts and turns his nose up at the statement of events. He rolls his eyes at the colour of the man's skin and he mouths the words *sick bastard*.

He thinks he is different from the rapist because he never fucked Aria Sky.

Four years old.

Five in June.

If you know anything or saw anything suspicious, you are to contact the Police Sapphire Team. Aria's killer reads this and smirks. He tells himself he doesn't know why. He looks down at the pale face of the deceased infant, wrapped in a blanket below him, and grips the handles tightly. Nothing will spoil their day together.

A male jogger approaches and smiles at Aria then her killer as he rounds the corner. The pervert mouths a faked *Shhh!* to the runner as though he doesn't want his dead victim to be disturbed. Then he thinks about this interaction, how he can be remembered from it, that there is now a witness to his whereabouts. He starts to feel nervous but this anxiety soon turns into anger, at himself, at the jogger, at how this is ruining their perfect day together.

A squirrel leaps on to a tree trunk and the overweight weirdo jumps in fright. A red leaf drops from above as he continues walking, pushing the pram, and he is startled. Moving closer to the fountain, he praises the relaxing sound of the running water to Aria but the shadow of a pigeon still scares him.

On a patch of grass to the left, this degenerate spots three magpies. He points the pram towards the birds and stops. Moving around to the front he whispers to himself, 'One for sorrow. Two for joy.' He crouches down to his victim, whose cold, pale, limp hand is exposed to an unexpected chill, and says, 'Three for a girl, eh?'

Then he smiles.

And kisses her lifeless hand.

And he wraps it in the blanket as though he is her protector.

The first gate to the play area has been cordoned off with red tape and an orange cone. Moving on to the next gate he thinks about taking Aria to the central pavilion, but he can see the children playing on the roundabout and climbing frames. He doesn't want to take any of them. Not today. The parents are looking vigilant, at any rate.

There are no kids on the swings. The sicko is saddened.

'I used to love the swings when I was your age,' he mutters to the delicate corpse, reminiscing over times spent with his first love. 'So did your aunt Annie,' he adds.

A chalkboard says 'Farm-Made Devon Ice-Cream'.

The crackpot rubs his hand against Aria's stomach lovingly and answers a question that was never asked. 'Oh, of course you can have an ice cream. We'll get one after lunch.' He smiles, and the parents in the park do not notice the wacko passing by.

He thinks of Annie all the time but he never allows himself to wonder. He can't imagine her at a university or married or with children or living up north as he had heard. To him, she is a child. She is nine. And she reads while he draws. And they talk. And they are friends. And his world is perfect. And he has not attacked her yet. He has not hit her face over and over. That feeling of perfection, of safety and belonging, is exactly what he is trying to reproduce today with Aria.

Maybe if he'd been spurned by Annie at a later age, he wouldn't go around killing kids. Perhaps it would be teenagers or young adults. Like the woman throwing a tennis ball on the field for her dog to chase.

The fat fucking freak stares through the woman and into the distance. Things are suddenly peaceful, the wind only touching the top few branches of the trees.

And then he hits Broadwalk Gate.

This is where Aria will be buried with the others.

*

The building in front of the public toilets, hiding them from view, looks like an old, tiny church. The sign says 'Cow and Coffee Bean'. It sells ice cream and hot drinks. And the air is now filled with the word *toilet* as parents check with their children to avoid an accident. The kids are taken even if they say no.

Two mothers try to make their offspring walk while holding hands, but the kids don't want to. This human cancer tells himself that they are cruel; at least Aria wants to be here with him.

He buys a drink and sits down. The scent of coffee and public toilet and baby shit squashed into a nappy cover the aroma of the death-on-wheels.

A family with two-point-four children passes. An eccentric dog-walker holding six separate leads flounces by. An elderly interracial couple sits opposite, the man staring at the tanned legs of a young girl hauling a suitcase through the park. The coffee-drinking killer takes note of two kids turning their heads towards him; he could easily abduct them. A German family stops in front of him and checks their map. Hundreds of witnesses. None seeing anything out of the ordinary.

The child-slayer glares at the ground where the other victims have been buried, and he lays a hand on Aria as though he is sorry. She is wearing her white overalls, just as the others were. Not that many, he thinks. He's kept it under control. The clothes they died in are hanging untouched in a small wardrobe in his bedroom. Each outfit retaining its owner's scent. Their memory.

His memory of them.

*

He eats at The Honest Sausage, ordering himself the seasonal sausage roll. 'And she'll have the apple juice.' He smiles at the discontented student on the counter who doesn't care enough to look down at the bloodless remains of Aria Sky, her overalls hidden by the blanket that swaddles her. There are dogs everywhere. They bark when he is too close.

Afterwards, they take a stroll along a route that neither have been down before. This is a special moment for this murderer; this path is just for Aria. He likes to do this with all the children. All his victims.

It means nothing to Aria. She is dead. Still dead. Always dead. She is waste.

This destroyer of life would like to take Aria down by the boats. She'd like that, he thinks, as though he knows her. It is where his mother took him. Where he remembers being happy and loved. But he is too old to make the trip.

He kisses Aria's cheek and thanks her to mark the occasion but is unsettled by the cry of a man calling his dogs. 'Pedro. Georgia. Come on!' He was becoming too comfortable. Two gardeners are now looking at him suspiciously. He is paranoid. He needs to be. Nothing can be perfect.

No one can be Annie.

The zoo is too expensive so he takes her to a cut-out in the trees. A small semi-circle of gravel next to the path overlooked by a tall iron, pointed fence. Beyond the spikes there is screaming and laughter and the sight of water and people in waterproof clothing and penguins.

This is where he makes his mistake.

The ageing child-abductor presses his thumbs against the belt to unfasten the decaying body of the dead infant he has been pushing around all day. He places his right arm behind her back, his left hand behind her neck, and he lifts her from her seat; the blanket hides her hair. He picks her up so that she is pressed against his chest and he aims her dead eyes towards the waddling birds.

And he laughs and jokes and kisses and tells stories.

Then he places her back into the pram, readying her for that final walk back to the public toilets where she will be buried.

Aria Sky sits in the pushchair, peaceful and seemingly sleeping.

But she isn't sleeping. She isn't resting.

She is at rest.

She is dead. Gone.

The entire day that the unhinged, overweight, aged, lonely Neanderthal strolled around the bisecting paths of Regent's Park, the whole time he was sitting at lunch or pausing for breath on a bench while those passing by cooed at Aria's apparent fatigue, assuming he was her doting grandfather, she was not breathing. His mistaken love had squeezed out the four-year-old girl's essence.

To him, everything was finally perfect again.

For now.

Tomorrow he will drink in a local bar and piss next to Alan Barber before the girl, Aria Sky, the gentle child, is uncovered.

Then his plan is to carry on as normal. Alone. Lonely. Longing. A cupboard full of dead children's clothes to smell and stroke and admire. And remember.

He has no plans to do this again.

All that is left is to be caught and punished.

Or to die without penalty.

Part Three

Misdirection

Girl 10

---◆---

I still have a couple of days before I take Eames into double figures.

Before I become Girl 10.

Leaving Eames with one final trick.

Detective Inspector January David is more compelled by his personal quest than his professional one at this moment. He stalks his estranged wife in the same way my killer has stalked me. He watches her from afar, scrutinising her moves, debating the optimal moment to insert himself back into her life.

What about my life, Detective David?

What about Eleanor Harbin?

What about Zig-Zag Girl?

My roommate decided it was time her boyfriend moved in. He asked her to live with him and she got over-excited at the prospect of this commitment. He doesn't have his own place so he's coming here. We've lived together for two years now but I only have two weeks to get out.

I'm going to see a studio flat over on West 50th Street, between Tenth and Eleventh Avenues. It's a little out of the way but the pictures suggest that there is ample space to fit a sofa, a bed and a dining table – which I do not own. The separate kitchen is tiny but the realtor used the term *cute* to bait me. I suppose it is kind of cute.

Essentially, they are looking for immediate occupancy and it's two thousand dollars per month, which I can afford on my new salary. I don't even need to see it to know that I'll take it for twelve months; I just want to get out of this apartment for a while. They're like a brand-new couple all of a sudden and, even though we are all friends, things are not as comfortable as they were even a week ago.

I need to get out.

It's clear they want me out.

I leave without saying goodbye and head across town. To the one spot in Manhattan that seems to be furthest away from any part of my body the authorities will find.

I have enough to deal with right now: starting a new job, finding a new place to live, moving all my stuff out and transporting it however many blocks away by myself. So fuck them in their content little bubble of adoration, waiting for me to pick up groceries so they can screw on the sofa.

Fuck them with all their relationship troubles they used to dump on me before they decided that more time together would somehow magically save them.

And fuck them in three days when they expect me to be taking all my belongings down the stairs into the van, when the brown boxes are stacked up high near the door and they have to squeeze themselves into the kitchen. When they wonder where I am and why it is taking so long because they want to walk around the kitchen naked, feeding one other a conveyor-belt of phallic and suggestive foods.

Fuck them.

And fuck their guilt when I don't come home to collect my bed linen or hair straighteners or summer wardrobe because I have become the latest addition to the Eames mythology. Because I've been killed and didn't even get laid beforehand like the first seven victims. Because Eames plans to use my body, parts of my body, to taunt the authorities. To goad them into action and panic. To demonstrate his superiority.

So fuck you, too, January David, with your preoccupation with off-the-record consultancy.

And you, Marquez, whoever you think you are, trying to *make things happen*, make a name for yourself again. Just do your job.

I return home after viewing the studio across town to hear my roommate faking yet another orgasm. And I can't wait to get out of here.

Audrey

Tuesday
**UPPER EAST SIDE, MANHATTAN, NEW YORK,
11:17 EST**
London, 16:17 GMT

He found me.
Jan found me.

That's what he thinks. As long as it is true to him . . .

In his mind he would rather it had happened in better, more controlled circumstances. But the important thing is that he is here. And he knows that I am here, also. It was perfect. Wherever we could have met would have been ideal.

I am a silent statue for the entire journey around the park and back home; my fingertips do not leave the windowpane until the car comes to a complete stop. I can't possibly go in to work today; this is momentous. This is what I want.

What we both have wanted for some time.

I am his priority.

I turn the key and catch the end of Phillipa's startled spin around to the door as I enter. She has a teaspoon in

212

her left hand that has been stirring her coffee on the counter, and a mobile phone in her right.

'Look. I'll have to call you back.' She speaks sharply to the person at the other end of the line and hits the button to hang up. Her eyes are screwed up in concern and her mouth pushed to one side in a quizzically cartoon manner.

'I'm back early.'

'Early? It's not even halfway through the day yet. Is everything all right?' She drops the shocked act and we fall into our usual rhythm.

'Yes. Yes.' I pause for a moment, thinking of something I can add.

'That was just my brother on the phone,' she chimes in, guiltily. 'He's very protective over me and he heard about the second murder.'

'Mm-hmm,' I respond, as though I don't really need to know this information.

I'm not as interested in her as she is in me.

'Walter is napping so I was making a coffee.'

She could have stopped talking. It wasn't an issue for me that she was on her mobile phone or that she took some time for herself. It occurs to me that she probably still feels regret over the incident yesterday evening. It doesn't even cross my mind that her call was anything underhand, that the person on the other end of the line was anyone other than her brother, that she may be hiding something from me.

'I'll have one if it's just brewed,' I request innocently as I kick off my heels at the entrance.

Phillipa turns back to the counter, places her phone back inside her trouser pocket and reaches into the cupboard for a mug. She pours my usual from the machine.

'Thanks, Phillipa. You can take the rest of the day off, if you like. It'll probably do me some good to spend some time alone with Walter anyway.'

'Are you sure? I'm more than happy to help if you need the rest or even to take some time to be alone with yourself . . .' She allows her suggestions to trail off naturally.

'It's fine. Take it. I'll pay you for the whole day.'

'I wasn't trying to—'

'Just take it,' I interrupt. 'Get away from the mayhem up this end of town. Get your hair done. Go out. Do whatever it is you young people do.' I smile through my jealousy.

'Well, my friend Eleanor is looking for a new place to live. I might be able to catch up with her today. Are you sure?' Her body language tells me that she wants to collect her bag and go.

'Go now. In case I change my mind.' And I smile to set her at ease, all the while the image of January occupying my thoughts. He looked tired. Defeated.

Has he given up on Cathy?

Had he given up on me?

I wanted to turn back on the street. I wanted to wait for him, sort this out. Move forward. But I need him to crave me, desire me. January has to be clear in his mind. It will not end how I hope and plan it will if I had given in to the temptation of contact on that east-side path.

I know January.

He will find me.

He'll come.

Everything is going as I planned.

Phillipa takes a swift gulp of her coffee while slipping one of her slim arms into a jacket. She relays the current status of Walter's day without really looking at me, gazing up at the ceiling as though trying to remember.

'. . . so he'll probably need food when he wakes up, which should be about another twenty or thirty minutes.'

With her coat now fastened and her information delivered, she asks one more time whether it really is OK for her to be leaving.

I say nothing but widen my eyes in fake sternness.

And she walks past, giving my left hand a soft grip to thank me. It could come off as patronising but I know her. It isn't. She is almost a friend. I debated talking to her about January, relieving some of my burden.

Letting her in.

But she probably already knows about him. About me. We were news once.

I'm not her friend.

And neither is Eleanor, really. But Phillipa is taking this day off to visit her. And in less than two days, her not-real friend will be dead.

I'm sorry, Phillipa.

I'll explain it all soon.

It is not Eames that made me kill.

It is January.

The Dig

⸻✦⸻

Don't dare say that the system failed him.

That they had him; they knew his mental state from an early age.

And they let him go.

Do not blame anyone but the old, fat piece of shit that squeezed Aria Sky until her breath could not be found through inhalation or exhalation. Do not dignify him an open ear to refer to this breathless stasis as a hug, cuddling her to death. Loving the life out of her. Clamping her innocence under the pretence of befriending her.

He was frustrated. And he killed her.

She was four years old.

Five in June.

Paulson stands with an out-of-sorts Murphy in front of the coffee shack in front of the toilet building where Aria Sky was found. He thinks of Eames and his mind games, how he can still be a step ahead of everyone from inside his cage. He pictures his friend and boss lost in New York, chasing down his own past, and hopes

216

that January is wrong about finding more bodies in the earth below the spot where Alan Barber uncovered Aria Sky's foot.

'I know you went over my head on this one, Paulson.' Murphy speaks calmly from the side of his mouth, his eyes never flinching from the scene of the excavation ahead. It is unlike him to be so calm, so calculated. His affronted brow seems to cast a shadow of uncertainty down the length of his body. His normal petty, whining tone has been replaced by something more perfidious.

Paulson says nothing. He doesn't care for Murphy's personal ambition or the path he chooses to arrive at a destination he unrightfully believes he is the natural successor to. He cares about the case. About the girl.

'I told you that you'd have to pick a side and it's clear to me that you have,' Murphy continues, baiting Paulson.

'Markam called the dig, Murph. I'm sure you'd have come around to the same notion in the end,' he bats back, unflustered. 'Where were you this morning anyway?'

'Whether it was Markam or you or January David from afar' – he ignores the question – 'I'm in a no-lose situation. If there's nothing there, one of you has to bite the bullet for wrecking the crime scene, for wasting time, not to mention the bad PR with the kid's family . . .'

'Aria, Murph. The kid was a girl. Her name is Aria.'

Murphy continues to talk as though Paulson is not even there, as though he has rehearsed this speech.

'. . . and if there happens to be another body, which I highly doubt, I'm still the fucking lead on this case.' He finally turns his gaze to Paulson. 'So you will fall in line.'

Paulson is unnerved by Murphy's blatant duplicity. He looks like a man under pressure. He has always thought that Murphy wanted Jan out, but never has he been this explicit. And never has he shown any disdain towards Paulson.

Murphy turns back to the growing hole next to the public restroom and squeezes a tablet of gum into his mouth. 'Let's see which way I get to win,' he utters smugly and quietly, but not quite under his breath. He trusts his sponsor too easily. He has no concept of his own expendability.

The number of spectators is growing. The line of police tape is far enough from the scene to disguise the possibility of a discovery but the two warring detectives are visible to all, and more interesting to some.

Murphy's last comment fuels Paulson's rage, testing the usual straight temperament that he has developed on the poker tables. He grabs Murphy's tie and pulls it down sharply, tightening the knot, bringing their faces closer together.

'Get your fucking hand off me.' Murphy raises his voice and attempts to bat Paulson's mitt away, but to no avail. More members of the crowd divert their eyes to the rumble.

'Listen to me.' Paulson talks softly now, echoing Murphy's earlier Machiavellian diatribe. 'I don't give a fuck about who you think you are or where you think you should be. I don't care how you feel about me or Jan or Markam. But you will respect the girl. You will think of her family appropriately until evidence suggests they do not deserve your condolences.'

Murphy says nothing.

Paulson releases his grip, allowing his acting inspector to straighten himself out. 'We don't have to get along, Murph. We don't even have to like each other. But we do have to care about what we are doing. We have to have some regard for the victims and the people they leave behind. That . . . that is what makes January better than all of us.'

Neither of them talk from this point.

Murphy faces the front and chews his sugar-free gum.

Paulson does likewise, sparking a cigarette.

And the disgusting dolt of a man that killed Aria Sky returns his stare to the digging, along with the rest of the crowd.

January David was right. The killer would return to the scene of the crime. Paulson had forgotten about this aspect of the conversation. He was preoccupied with the dig results.

Of course, January David was right about that too. The mood around the site turns from dreaded anticipation to sickening realisation as Murphy and Paulson are summoned closer to confirm the uncovering of another small victim.

The hum of the audience descends into a cold hush as each spectator expels a breath of air which hangs over the park like a mist of disbelief, killing the sound of everything it touches.

And the old man forces his way through the back of the crowd.

He can't look.

He doesn't have to.

He knows they will find four more.

January

Tuesday
CHELSEA PIERS, MANHATTAN, NEW YORK, 11:48 EST
London, 16:48 GMT

I pass the Sanford Meisner Theater, the place Girl 8 was found, on my way to meet Marquez. The police tape has been taken down but the picture of the bicycle in the window has been replaced with a police notice asking for witnesses to step up.

But all I can think about is Audrey.

I should tell Paulson that I've found her, but he's busy excavating skeletons of lost children.

A red X has been graffitied on the door of the theatre as a warning or a distasteful joke.

It seems so long ago that Kerry Ross was strangled and transformed into another floating corpse.

Eames is locked away. He seems to be involved, he has too much knowledge for someone who is not, but he cannot be committing the physical act of murder.

This is no longer a case of catching Eames the person, the animal, but of thwarting Eames the movement, the belief. The myth.

The lie.

*

I can see the piers complex on the opposite side of the road; the colourfully numbered sections look nothing more than loading bays for goods deliveries, but the innocuous exterior hides a state-of-the-art sporting facility beneath.

I walk underneath the red tunnel, which feels as though I am dangerously entering the exit to a car park. A lorry beeps as it reverses inside and I look over my shoulder to check the distance to the outside should I need to make a run for it.

The buildings inside look as false as any building in this country. There is a restaurant, a shop, a post office; it's like an unreal but functioning village. Directly ahead of me is the golf club entrance. That is where Marquez is waiting. Tucked away. Keeping me a secret.

Off the radar.

Where Audrey has been living for the last year or so, invisibly getting on with her life.

An overweight, friendly Hispanic lady – five feet three inches tall, shoulder-length dark, straight hair, smooth dark skin – greets me with a smile. She asks whether she can help me today and then marvels at my accent in much the same way that the batting-cages woman did.

'Oh, you're meeting someone?' she jokes flirtatiously, throwing a grin to her colleague who is standing by the glass door wrestling with a bag of wayward golfing irons.

'Yes. I imagine he's already inside,' I suggest, trying to move the conversation on.

'Well, there's a private party on the top level and a group coming in on three real soon, but you can take a look down here or on level one. That's just through this door' – she points to her right – 'and left up the stairwell to get to the other levels.'

'Thank you. You've been a big help.' I accentuate my Britishness a little more to leave her with something to coo about.

'You're welcome,' she responds, on automatic pilot, but she means it.

I check the lower level first. An elderly gentleman adorned with a lemon sleeveless jumper and pale blue cap is having a lesson at the far end. In the centre, a slither of a young man dispenses with every club in his bag with the exception of the driver. He grunts with each swing, trading technique for power every time. Perhaps this is his therapy.

There is no sign of Marquez; he's starting to frustrate me.

I find him on the next floor, delicately chipping a pile of balls as close to the first green as he can. There are two more flags further out. It says something about his character that he chooses the option that requires the most control.

'Is this some kind of sports tour, because we do have golf in England.'

Marquez finishes his swing, waits to see where his ball will land then turns slowly towards me as though nothing important is happening today.

'Detective David.' He steps towards me with a half smile.

'What the fuck are we doing here, Marquez?' I drop his title as a sign of our partnership but also as a mark of disrespect. 'Why aren't you at Central Park? Why are *we* not examining the scene? Where are the—'

'Whoa. Whoa.' He raises his palms as though attempting to calm a spooked horse. 'Everything is under control there, we'll have photos soon and toxicology tomorrow morning. She was found hours ago. I was under the impression we weren't here about the case, that it was something more personal, Detective David.' There is a knowing look in his eyes. As though he believes he can read me.

He can't.

But he has also seen my wife today.

'It is about the case. I have a lead,' I lie. 'Can you pull up an address if I give you a name?'

'Just a name? That might pull up quite a few addresses. Do you have anything more to go on?'

I had thought that telling him I had a lead in the case would incite some optimism. I wasn't expecting to hit a roadblock.

'A list of addresses will be fine.' I reserve my cool. I'll know which one to choose.

We are linked.

My thoughts drift off momentarily to the last time Audrey and I made love but these reminiscences are always spliced with that image of Eames, sitting in his hallway, waiting for me to arrest him. Giving himself up. He must have known that it wasn't the end. I think about The Smiling Man. Why has he forsaken me?

'What's the name?' he asks, pulling his mobile phone from a trouser pocket.

'Are we going in to your office?' I test him, knowing he is trying to keep me marginalised, either to protect his reputation by not being seen to collaborate with me or to enhance it by having me solve this and then claiming the credit, thereby reinstating his success within the bureau.

'My office is in Maryland.'

I pursue despite his avoidance tactics. 'Of course, I assumed there would be a local office in New York . . .'

'There's no need. Give me the name, I'll call it in now, get the list sent straight to my phone and we're off.'

I don't like the way he has included himself in this part of the investigation. My investigation, but I need to know where she is. 'Audrey David.' I speak quietly, watching his eyes widen. 'You may want to check her maiden name too, which is Silver.'

He taps the screen of his smartphone and holds it to his ear before repeating her name back to me.

'Yes. She's my wife.' The final word hangs in the air as he waits to be connected. 'She was Girl 4.'

I'm worried about her safety.

I won't fail her again.

Eames

———✦———

I knew she could do it.
She's a killer now.
When you accidentally run into your wife on the street after a two-year relationship hiatus, when you're covered in sweat and she looks like she just stepped out of your idealistic recollection of her image, when she walks away from you instead of confronting the situation, when she leaves you stranded in a foreign land with more than just her memory to cling to, I did that.

I made that happen.
Are you listening, Detective Inspector January David?
I make things happen.

When you go to Agent Marquez for help, I make that happen.

When you find your wife and she invites you into her home, I make that happen.

When you fuck her and wake up the next morning

thinking everything is back on track and are introduced to her son, my son, I make that happen.

And I smile as I do it.

You are not making any decisions. I am your guide.

When you see Audrey's nanny in all her long-haired, perfect-skinned, toned-bodied beauty, when she reminds you of everything Audrey is not, I am your lust. I am the tightening of your underwear. I am your impure thought.

Do not try to tell yourself that you have found her when you must know that I am giving her back to you. It plagues you that I gave myself up in that hallway. I did not fight you. I did not resist. I was mocking you. I still am.

I am Eames. And I pull your strings. I am allowing you this shot at happiness, at forgiveness, at the closure you will surely never find with your sister. I give you consolation. You should be thanking me, Detective Inspector January David.

Thank me.

Look me in the eye and thank me.

Then I can take her from you again.

I open the brown envelope, written on in silver pen, and I pull out the seven cards that tell me who will die next. Two of the cards are the same. The five of hearts. One has been marked with what looks like a bolt of lightning.

The ten of spades will arrive tomorrow.

And I will know that she has killed again.

I told her to cut this girl up.

*

226

She will kill.
Eames will kill.
I live through her.
But soon, she will also have to die.

January

---◆---

I know he could get me the exact address, I know enough about her. He's playing a game. Not letting me get too close.

He needs the control.

Just like Audrey.

He doesn't realise that by only giving a small amount of information, I am the one in control.

Marquez chips more balls at the flag that pokes up from an artificial green sixty yards to the left while we wait for his phone to vibrate. He offers me the club but I decline, choosing instead to look out over the vast expanse of the Hudson River. At the end of the driving range, a boat is docked with a helicopter strapped snugly to its roof. I hear the grunt of the inept golfer on the level below as he tries to hit the protective netting separating us from the water.

My mind drifts off, imagining what my wife is doing at this moment. Does she think of me? Does she empathise with the hurt I feel?

Then I wonder what Cathy would think.

I am here, in New York, trying to catch a man who gave himself up to me two years ago. I am pining over the woman who fucked him and left me alone. I should be in London. I should be leading my team, pushing Murphy out, finding the truth behind the Aria Sky murder so that I may inch closer to the truth about my sister.

Cathy, give me a sign.

The phone buzzes against the wood of the dividing fence that Marquez has rested it upon. I step forward in anticipation but Marquez does not display the same level of urgency and finishes his swing. He seems more compelled to move in my direction when I pick up his phone and start pressing buttons.

He snatches the phone with a nervous smile and starts to scroll through the document.

'A lot of Davids and Silvers in this city, as you'd expect . . .' He trails off as though I should know what that means. 'Here, take a look. See if anything jumps out at you.'

He hands me the smartphone and I swipe my finger against the screen.

'It's very small. Can you forward the document on to me?' I'm trying to sever the tie with him on this. If he needs help with the Eames investigation, that is fine, I'm here. But I can't have him tagging along with me while I search for Audrey. It is personal.

For once I am choosing life over work.

Marquez marches downstairs to the front desk, flashes his badge briefly, which is the first time I have seen it, and gets them to print off the document from his phone.

He peers over my shoulder as I circle random addresses on the sheet with my biro.

'You think she's in the Village?' Marquez inquires, counting the blue ink circles as they mount up on the printout.

'We always talked about living there one day.' I remain focused on the list of addresses.

Audrey and I had spoken about it a few times in the same way we debated living in Paris. It was a romantic notion that I never took seriously. It was a dream. It was nothing real. I do not think that she would move to the Village. I have already seen three addresses on the Upper East Side that I know would fit her lifestyle, but I am trying to steer Marquez away from there. If I can keep him with me in the Village, following dead-ends, there will come a point where he has to leave, where he is called back to the case or he simply realises this is a needle in a haystack, a wild goose chase. I can then pursue my own path.

Marquez adds the list of houses and apartments I have highlighted and smiles to himself. For someone who appears controlled and precise and somewhat desperate to prove his worth, he does come across as laid-back, light-hearted and, occasionally, lazy about proceedings.

'There's twelve or fifteen address on this list already, David,' he exclaims, clearly thinking our relationship has hit a level of mutual friendliness.

'It's our best lead, Agent Marquez,' I respond, letting him know that this a professional affinity. 'I'll sit outside each building until I'm sure I have found her and it's the right time to approach,' I lie, hoping to put him off.

He explains that he needs to check in with the coroner today and push through the results of the tox screen. He suggests that we touch base later to correlate our findings.

'That's probably best. More efficient,' I placate, subtly.

'You want me to drop you at the first place on the list?'

'No, no. You go. I can get there. I need to be on the ground anyway, get to know this fine city of yours.'

I smile falsely.

Marquez leaves me with the printout. I walk back out through the same tunnel I entered and wait at the lights to cross the road. I decide to head to the Village, despite knowing that Audrey will not be there, as I'm paranoid that Marquez will follow me to ensure I am doing as I have stated. Trust is not a part of our ever-evolving relationship.

But Marquez is not following me.

He is heading straight uptown.

To the one address he recognised on the list.

A building east of Central Park.

He's getting to Audrey first.

Girl 10

---❖---

I feel grateful to Phillipa.
   She put herself on the line for me and asked her boss to fix me up with an opportunity for a new job. So that I could afford to get out on my own.
   She couldn't have known that I was being recruited.
   That I was being added to Eames' list.
   The apartment across town is fine. Plenty of space for just me. The realtor tried to palm off the old-fashionedness as *character features*. I pretended to buy her bullshit. I just want out of my place. Well, not *my* place. I suppose it was never my place. I was merely filling a void. Passing the time until Mr Not-So-Perfect decided to fill his mind with romance, my room with exercise equipment and my roommate with his semen.
   As I emerge from the subway, my phone vibrates and makes a tinkling noise inside my purse. It's a text from Phillipa who works uptown as a nanny for some rich, workaholic mother.
   Day off. Cocktails. Village. You and me.

She doesn't even phrase it as a question. It's just what I need. Time to unwind and a reason to stay away from the den of nymphomania.

The phone vibrates again in my hand as another message comes through.

How was the apartment?

Phillipa is the only one, apart from my mother, who has asked about that.

And I've only known her a few months.

We met through the New York Secret Cinema. It's simple – add yourself to their mailing list via various social-networking sites and receive an email detailing a clandestine location in the city where a private screening of a movie will take place. Sometimes there is a large crowd, other times just a handful of people.

I don't see her often because she works strange hours and seems to always be on duty in one capacity or another but we have stayed in touch. I know she loves her job and that kid she looks after – sometimes I think she's even into the woman she works for; she idolises her – but I can't remember the last time she had a full day off. She must need this as much as I do.

So I call her to meet me in an hour.

I walk in to the sight of the only people who really care about me moving and, for once, they're not scratching at one another's backs in coital ardour. Both are perched on the edge of the sofa as though waiting to hear news of the magnificent dwelling I have located.

Their voices fill the room with congratulatory platitudes aimed at making themselves feel less guilty.

'Anyway, I'm heading out for a few drinks,' I say in

monotone as though it's nothing special. I don't want to talk about it.

'Maybe we could all go. Make it a celebration about your new place.' My former roommate over-eggs her eagerness, her long dark lashes batting at me as though I give a shit about what treasure lies between those thighs.

'Actually, I'm meeting someone.'

'Oh, well, say no more. If you don't want us there cramping your style with some guy . . .' the new roommate-with-benefits pitches in, and they laugh with each other.

'No.' I speak straight-faced. 'No. That's not why I don't want you there.'

And I leave the air in an uncomfortable state.

Then an awkward moment longer to push home my point and erase any ambiguity.

'I'll be home late,' I state, breaking the silence. 'So, I guess I'll hear you later.'

I turn and smile to myself, knowing they'll have to double-take before realising what I mean. A small victory.

I eventually settle on an outfit and take a shower to freshen up before meeting Phillipa. I'm hoping for a night of freedom, fun and cocktails. Where I can bitch about the couple who used to be my friends but are now kicking me to the kerb. Phillipa can dote over the boy she takes care of and the mother she so admires.

Maybe we'll even get laid.

God knows *I* need it.

Because I'll be dead in less than two days and an Eames killing no longer comes with a free farewell fuck.

January

✦

Tuesday
UPPER EAST SIDE, MANHATTAN, NEW YORK, 13:27 EST
London, 18:27 GMT

'Paulson?' I question, making sure it is definitely my loyal friend's ear I am speaking into.

'Jan.' He uses my name to respond so I know that Murphy is not close by.

'I've found her.'

He takes a moment to digest my fragmented exclamation, distracted by what he himself has found.

'Cathy?'

This time, I find myself momentarily distracted from the conversation with thoughts of my missing sister. It remains stilted until I plunge back to the present time.

'No. Not Cathy. I'm still in New York. Audrey. I've found Audrey.' I find my excitement quashed slightly by heartache.

'What?'

'I know. It seems unlikely, but she is here. I'm outside her apartment right now.'

*

I went to the East Village, to the first address I had circled on Marquez's sheet of Audrey Davids/Silvers. I even waited outside for a while, knowing that the inhabitant of the red-brick townhouse was not going to be the Audrey I was looking for. I was wasting time. Testing Marquez.

After thirty minutes, I was satisfied that I hadn't been followed and dived into a cab that took me up Park Avenue, stopping at 80th Street and walking the rest of the way.

I think I have time to do this because The Smiling Man is nowhere.

'You're what? Outside her apartment?' His disbelief rings clear. 'Wh— wha— what are you going to do?' he stutters.

'Nothing. Yet. I need to make sure this is the right place before I go knocking.'

'She doesn't know you're there? What, are you hiding in the bushes? Jan, this doesn't sound right.' His protective nature kicks in as it usually does.

'Calm down. She knows I'm in New York, we bumped into each other today on the street. But she doesn't know I'm down here, of course.' I try to speak as though our meeting was casual and everyday but I'm not fooling him.

'Get out of there, Jan. Think this through. You either need to knock on the door or leave it alone. Don't stalk her.'

'I'm not fucking stalking her. She's my wife. I just need to make sure . . .'

I trail off, squinting my eyes in an attempt to focus through the glass doors of the foyer. The tall doorman is facing away from me, talking to someone standing by the lift. Their identity is obscured by a pillar.

Paulson asks me about the case, trying to get me back on point. It is still the middle of the day here but it's late in London and they are still finding skeletons in the ground. He relays what Eames told him on his last visit. That her name would be Burton but he didn't give her first name.

He doesn't need to.

That's not important.

'He said the next victim will be *here, there and everywhere* in the city,' Paulson explains.

'Well, that's pretty vague. It doesn't sound much like he is calling the shots, does it?'

'He seems pretty confident, Jan. He had a message for you.'

'Another one? Great.' My sarcasm disguises my anxious want.

'You need to be looking . . .'

'One second, Paulson,' I interrupt. The doorman is talking to someone else.

I wait but nobody emerges from the building. The gangly concierge moves his lips seriously.

'Sorry. Go on.'

'You need to be looking more closely at the police in that city.'

'Is that it? That's all he said?'

'Yep. That's it,' Paulson confirms, forgetting the rest of the conversation, thinking it was bluster. 'Do you know what he means?'

'No. Maybe the next victim will be a cop. That'll heighten the exposure, for sure. Could be something else, though. You know Eames.'

Nobody knows Eames.

'I'll need you to fax me the file from the Eames case. Send it to my hotel. I'll pick it up . . . Shit. I've got to go.' I hang up swiftly and back into the doorway of another apartment building behind me. I didn't even have the opportunity to discuss the Aria Sky case. I leave Paulson at the other end of the line speaking at the fuzz of the disconnection, asking, 'Is it Audrey?'

No. She is still inside.

It's Agent Marquez.

I leave.

I'm not ready for this.

The Suspects

———◆———

It used to be that the finger would be pointed at the school caretaker or local ice-cream man when a child went missing. The media, the way information can be transmitted and received so instantaneously, has changed that.

For better or worse.

A plea from a grieving and hopeless family for the safe return of their son or daughter no longer needs to air on the national news to travel across the world in microseconds. Viewers tune in on their computers and phones and forget about the ice-cream man or the fifty-year-old teacher who still lives alone or with their mother. They omit the idea of the alcoholic caretaker as they watch Aria Sky's family appeal to the good nature of a man who kills kids and buries them in the park for a drunken idiot to piss on.

Spectators gawp at the uncle in the background and place him at the head of a paedophile ring. They see the timidity of the father hanging a half step back from the foreground and place guilt in his direction. Even the mother is

239

castigated by onlookers in a one-way conversation that brands her as the murderer without any evidence.

A gut feeling based on the false hyperreality of soap operas.

Narrow-minded sensationalism.

And the Skys will never escape this. Even with alibis and proof and the rightful conviction, they will have to deal with the loss of four-year-old Aria and the stigma that will not dissipate. That somehow they had something to do with her disappearance.

The Sky family perch around the dinner table at the home where the girl was last seen alive. Aria's mother starts to cry, realising that she has taken four placemats from the kitchen drawer and has started to set a place for her dead daughter. Out of habit. Or guilt.

Both men, her husband and brother-in-law, stand up to comfort her, or catch her from falling. Aria's father is the slower of the two, his shoulders forced downwards by the weight of death and loss.

Mrs Sky leaves the room alone and returns shortly to silence and trepidation. She places a serving bowl of mashed potato next to the sausages, the peas and the gravy.

And she says nothing.

There is no muttered grace this evening.

May the Lord make us truly thankful.

They each tuck in to the food, filling their mouths as though the mediocre fare is of a quality not worth interrupting.

They do not discuss that Aria's father initially told the police he was at work at the time his daughter was taken. Her mother has nothing to add to her story or her grief.

She says that Aria is her only alibi and that she is not here to defend her mother. And her uncle is persistent with his version of events that day. Insisting that he was asleep. That he works nights. That he was alone and it's not as though he gives much thought to having a witness with him at all times.

They say nothing because they know words have no power. They asked the British public to look for their daughter. Pleaded with the killer to bring her home. They prayed to a God they once believed in. And it made no difference.

So they sit and they eat and they do not speak. Do not mention anything about Aria or the case. Because their words mean nothing. And everybody lied.

Girl 10

Tuesday
GREENWICH VILLAGE, MANHATTAN,
NEW YORK, 19:40 EST
London, 00:40 GMT

I have under three days until I'm supposed to shift my
belongings across town to my new apartment.

But I'll be dead in two.

It doesn't matter where I live; Eames can always get
to me.

Eames could be sitting right next to me and I wouldn't
even know.

We meet at a music bar called Kenny's Castaways on
Bleecker Street. It's a cool place but not trendy. You can
pick up CDs by local bands at the door above a huge glass
jar full of free condoms. Inside it's full of memorabilia and
signed guitars and has a neon light that says *Through these
portals walk the famous*.

And the prices are beyond reasonable.

'Cheers,' Phillipa says, grinning her perfect white smile
at me, holding aloft a flute of Moët, 'great to see you
again.' Lit from above she looks like a cover girl after a
thorough air-brushing.

'Champagne for my real friends and real pain for my sham friends,' I add, drenching the joviality in my bitterness.

We drink.

'Wow. They really did a number on you, eh? Just thank your lucky stars that you're out of there.'

She takes one of her delicate white hands and grips the neck of the bottle, hoisting it out of the ice bucket and topping us both up. Her glass bubbles over-dramatically and she wraps her lips around the entire rim of the glass to prevent spillage. She somehow manages to make this look elegant. I love the fact that she has no idea just how attractive she is.

I give her a bit of background on my soon-to-be ex-roommate's relationship and the reasons I think they are moving in together and how I fully expect it to fail and how she will come crawling back to me in a few months wanting to talk. And I will tell her to go screw herself.

'I think you've got it right, living alone,' I concede, hoping to lighten the mood.

'It's about all I can handle after a day of work. I need my own space by that time.'

We both gulp at the bubbling golden liquid, and Phillipa pours some more, the condensation from the bottle sliding down her thumb and threatening to drip on to the varnished tabletop.

'At least you love your job and your boss. I've just started that new position and I think it could really work out for me.'

Phillipa tells me that she is pleased to hear this news and she taps her glass against mine. I lose myself in the lagoon of her sincere eyes for a moment.

'I do love my job, of course. Little Walter is such a dream and it's such a treat to see him grow up and know that I may have helped to shape who he becomes, even in a small way.'

She is so genuine and understated, I wonder why I don't see more of her.

'In a huge way,' I counter, wide-eyed. 'You're putting in more time than his mother.'

'She's great. And if it wasn't for her I wouldn't have this job. Don't forget that she helped get your job too.' She puts down her glass after raising it to her mouth for a drink, apparently second-guessing herself.

'God, you really love her.' I feign light-heartedness to hide the truth of my words.

'I mean, she's successful and focused and beautiful. And considering everything she's been through . . . she hasn't mentioned anything to me, but I know. Don't get. me wrong, though. It's like any boss. I respect her but there are days when I look at her and think I could kill her.'

I tell her that perhaps that is too strong a reaction but I understand her sentiment.

We both laugh.

We both drink.

We both need this night.

For very different reasons.

'Maybe my old roommate has it all figured out. We need a man in our lives, in our beds,' I joke, aware that we are already coming to the end of our first bottle. I look around and the place is crawling with NYU students holding green cups that give them a fifty per cent discount in the places that signed up for the Fall Pub Crawl. Some of these guys are going to be wasted before we even get going.

'Well, I already have both of those.' Phillipa blushes at the hint of her own sexual activity.

And she goes on to inform me that it has been several months. That he's different. He works hard. He's kind to her. He's tender and giving and they are in tune in the bedroom. The rose of her cheeks deepens to crimson at the mention of their intimacy.

This mystery man I have heard nothing about apparently works demanding hours too. He's with the police or he's a Fed or he works out of Langley, or something. I don't give Phillipa's merriment the same level of attention as her disillusionment.

All I want now is another drink and a guy to take home and bang. I don't even want it for pleasure or a sense of closeness. I want it because I'm angry and I need a release. He can screw me however he likes, he can put it anywhere he wants, he can finish inside me or on my breasts or my face or my feet. I just don't care.

At this moment, I just want out.

Escape.

Feel free to use me.

I covertly scan Phillipa's toned stomach, ample breasts and lustrous golden locks and know that I can use her to entice the men to our table. Men who will ultimately be disappointed at her lack of availability. Men I can use to evade my sad reality.

The way Phillipa is using me.

The way her secret partner is probably using her.

We're all exploiting one another.

But in two days, Phillipa will still be pleasant and perfect.

Her lover will be headline news.

And I will finally come face to face with Detective Inspector January David.

When he finds my discarded head, wrapped in plastic and thrown down a stairwell.

Audrey

—◆—

Tuesday
UPPER EAST SIDE, MANHATTAN, NEW YORK,
21:25 EST
London, 02:25 GMT

I peer out of my window, shooting my gaze over Central Park.

Below me and out of sight is the statue of Hans Christian Anderson. I can't see it, but I know it is there. I stare at its location through the trees and I think of Eames.

The emperor has no clothes.

Today has been a drain. I've been worrying about Girl 9. Imagining Girl 10 cut into pieces. It's all too much to think about. I could have done with Phillipa's help but I can't have her here. Not today. I don't want it to be her that January sees first. Not Phillipa, with her wispy, shining mane and gravestone teeth. Not Phillipa, with her still-young can-eat-whatever-she-wants flat stomach and rounded breasts.

It needs to be me that he views when he walks through that doorway, with my pale, English skin made whiter by the dark shade of my hair. Me, with my thinning red

247

lips and thankfully lengthy eyelashes. Me, with my naturally waif body shape, never knowing when things will head south.

It has to be me.

And he will come.

He will find me again. He knows my address by now and he won't be able to leave things as they were on the street. It would have been easier for him to let go having not seen me for so long, but January craves closure. It drives him. I can thank his sister for that.

My eyes flit over to the right, glaring through the branches and foliage where the Alice in Wonderland sculpture resides, and I empathise with her. I too have been puzzled by myself. Whether I woke up one morning to become a completely different person. Whether something occurred during the hours of sleep, in the gloaming of the night.

Who was I?

And who am I now?

I am not the person who can solve this riddle; I am too far gone. It is not meant for the man in the cage thousands of miles from this spot. The only person who can unpick the stitching, discover what lies inside and put it back together so it is better than before is waiting in the doorway to the building opposite, wanting desperately to look up at me with weary eyes I can only hope are not too tired to forgive.

And I won't look away.

Because I love him. Simply and chemically.

At this moment, there is nothing more important than him.

Not Eames. Not Walter. Nor those poor dead girls.

The Hospital

He drops the zero from the beginning and replaces it with the country code +44.

Then starts to dial 1344 77 . . .

This takes him through to the hospital reception desk. You can't call it a madhouse.

'Good evening, sorry to call so late.'

The receptionist picks up his accent immediately and corrects him. 'It's gone two in the morning here, sir. How may I help you?'

'Yes. Of course. I apologise. Good morning. My name is Marquez. Agent Marquez with the Federal Bureau of Investigation. My badge number is KUU158212222. I need to speak with one of your patients.'

'I'm sorry, Agent Marquez, but it's late and—'

He jumps in on her before she has the opportunity to spout her protocol. Marquez can tell from the pitch and tone of her voice that she is young, possibly new to the position, and he sees an opportunity to cut through the bureaucracy. 'Listen. I need two minutes with one

249

patient. It is part of a federal investigation. I wouldn't be asking if it was not imperative to the case and the safety of many lives.'

But his attempt at instilling a feeling of guilt is futile.

'We have rules here—'

He doesn't let her finish. 'Pass me to your supervisor,' he orders robotically, his monotone expressing his irritation clearly.

'I'm sorry . . .'

'Someone above you. Anyone above you. Anyone who can get me a conversation with Eames.'

The name makes the receptionist turn cold; the flesh on her arm that holds the phone receiver to her cheek goose-pimples immediately.

And then the muffled sound of instrumental music as Marquez is placed on hold.

He stands up from the bench and paces frantically around a secluded courtyard on the East River, over-looking the Queensboro Bridge and Roosevelt Island. He curses the inexperience of the receptionist, swearing to himself.

In this moment of banally sound-tracked angst, he allows himself a thought for January David. Is his involvement necessary any more? Is he too close to this case? Is he as unhinged as his reputation suggests or as brilliant as—

Another female voice cracks through to his earpiece. This time older and more authoritative. She talks down to him. 'Agent Marquez, you should know the procedure. I can't grant you access to a patient based on a badge number delivered over the phone. We have to verify this.'

Marquez tries to talk over her but she is not a pushover.

'Especially a patient at the level you have requested.'

There is a beat as they both take a breath.

'I'm trying to save a girl's life here,' comes his desperate plea.

'This is not a hotel service, Agent Marquez. We are a hospital facility and I'm sure you are aware of the necessity for structure within these walls. The routines, rules and procedures we follow are for the benefit of our patients and the safety of our staff. I cannot grant you an ear with Mr Eames without following the appropriate channels of enquiry.'

She makes herself very clear.

Marquez says nothing. He roots around his mind for an angle but knows he's blown it.

'Besides,' she continues, 'the patient has already had his allocated phone conversation this week.'

Marquez already knew that.

January

—◆—

Tuesday
**UPPER EAST SIDE, MANHATTAN, NEW YORK,
21:42 EST**
London, 02:42 GMT

What was Marquez doing in my wife's building?
        That is the first question I should be asking.
But I don't.
My objectivity is marred not by love, but by loss. Only
loss.

I have spent hours in my room going over the last Eames
case and I think I know what I am looking for. I know
what his last two tricks will be. If The Smiling Man has
left me, then so be it. I did this job for years without his
help. I'm still the same man.
    Only Audrey thinks she has changed.
    People do not change.

I return to Audrey's building and gaze high into the grey-
blue Manhattan sky, the straight lines of the architecture
framing a vision of angelic purity I had forgotten. She is
as unmoving as I appear to be merciful. The clouds in

the sky hover silently over my judgement, telling me that I can forgive.

Audrey makes no gesture. She merely holds an expression that is right for this moment. It doesn't tell me to stay away or that she is not ready but it does not ask me to enter either.

We remain transfixed. Drinking each other in. Neither one of us thinking about Eames or Marquez or Girl 9 or 8 or 7 or 6.

5, 4, 3, 2 . . .

She steps back from the window and I feel my chest wrench forward, drawing me across the road to the giant doorman.

He swings the door inwards as my right foot hits the first stone step. 'Mr David,' he tells me.

I nod.

'This way, please.' He ushers me ahead of him through the glass door into the monochromatic art studio of a lobby, then overtakes me and heads towards the lift. Instead of pressing a button, he takes a key from his pocket and turns it in a slot above the other floor levels. He pulls his arm away, the door closes and the lift starts to ascend, leading me, at once, to my past and my future, but, more importantly, away from the present.

As the lights skip from one number to the next, counting up Eames' victims, I tick in and out of courage and fear, hoping that the last number does not signify that Audrey will be his final trick.

That I will have to lose her all over again.

The lift doors open on to a marble square that leads to Audrey's oversized, heavy front door. She has left it ajar.

And I am enticed.

I am exactly how she wants me to be.

Where she wants me to be.

I push the door open with one hand, remaining in the doorway to survey the area before I enter. It's instinctive.

Directly ahead of me, lit from behind by a solitary bulb in the kitchen, is the silhouette of a woman I once knew. I recall the form of those firm thighs, the way she drops her weight on to her left hip to give her more curve. I take one step inside her apartment and she begins to glow. She shouldn't glow. She should be a shadow. A spectre. A demon.

But she glows.

I hate that she glows.

As I move further into the apartment I can make out the cut of her black dress and the shape of her breasts.

Her arms hang loosely at her sides but her hands are restless, as though wanting to reach out and grab hold of me but resisting the impulse. The next step I take, I spot her eyes blink once.

And I am hers.

I have no choice.

Two more strides and my hands reach out to her face, sweeping across her cheeks, guilty with tenderness. I cup the back of her head and firmly pull her red mouth towards mine, pressing my face into hers with all the hatred of a man betrayed. Her hands finally find something to do, transforming into claws that dig in to the flesh of my back through my shirt.

This is a passion that says *I've missed you.*

I need you.

Holding her face imprisoned between my hands, all

the while kissing her erratically and desperately, I force Audrey backwards until she thuds against the kitchen counter – identical to the one in our London home – her back bruising instantly. She groans slightly at the initial pain, but I can sense we both enjoy it. She savours the hurt she believes she deserves while I feel satisfied to inflict the punishment. I want to harm her and hold her. I want to damage and protect her.

Her hands drop from my back and move round to my belt buckle. I remain in the same pose, not flinching despite her provocative grasp. Her red lipstick is smeared across her face and I can feel the syrupy trace that has transferred to mine. Her hair softly grazes the backs of my hands while I hold her in place. And I inhale the scent that vanished from my home like it is the oxygen I need to breathe.

The memory of her overloads my senses and paralyses me. I lose all awareness of myself for a few seconds and think of nothing. I need this more than I need Audrey or sex or to solve this case. Just a moment of pure nothingness.

I kick into consciousness to find Audrey wedged between me and the corner of the counter. Her dress is hitched up; she is panting slightly and looking down towards our connection. I am inside her. My hands are still holding her exquisite, pallid face but hers have moved up to tangle in my hair.

I've been here before.

The last time we were intimate.

She tore a clump from the back of my head.

I finally release my grip on her to bat her hands away, and the force against her wrists sends her arms crashing back to her sides. She tries the move again and my reflexes kick in; I strike her hands away. This is not the past. This is now. This is different.

We both want control.

We both want Audrey to suffer.

It becomes a game. She attempts to grasp my hair and I beat her advances away each time, pushing harder against her chest until she is lying back awkwardly over the kitchen unit. I pin her hands down and thrust heavily upwards inside her. Slowly at first then speeding up, gripping her wrists tighter and tighter.

Loving her with my eyes.

Hating her with my hands.

She says my name out loud as I push deeper into her, and I stop suddenly. It feels odd to hear her voice. It is exactly the same as I remember it, yet it sounds foreign. We both pause in tableau as though capturing this moment. Time has ceased.

Nobody is dying.

No one is being killed right now.

Eames does not exist.

And then we're on the floor and she is bucking on top of me; my back is cold against the tiles and squeaks with every thrust that gradually pushes me out of the kitchen area, the friction burning my skin into the marble. I'm numb to this pain.

And then we're in the hallway. Audrey is now standing, bent over, resting her weight against the wall; I am behind her, our bodies slapping together in pleasure only yards from the room her son sleeps in.

Eames' son.

And then we're in her bedroom, in her bed. I can't pick out any details. I don't know what it looks like, how it is decorated, the style of the furniture. There is only us.

And the sex has changed. Shifting to a tenderness neither of us could have foreseen from the pseudo-abuse in the kitchen followed by the faceless, wordless pounding in the hallway.

She lies on her back; I'm on top, between her slender thighs, which splay to the sides, allowing me to move freely. I hold myself above her, my arms locked straight, my hands near her shoulders, and I look down at her, moving in and out of her slowly.

But she won't look at me.

Maybe she can't.

Part of me doesn't want her to. The same part that doesn't want to hear her voice. I want to make love to the woman she once was and I want to fuck the woman she has become. I try to tell myself that I loathe her. That way I can get through this.

I'm not like Audrey.

Her eyes are closed and her head is turned to one side, leaving me with a view of her perfect profile, her mouth half open as though on the brink of an exhalation that will never emerge.

I continue my rhythm, hoping she will look up at me. So that our eyes can meet as they did while I looked up at her from the New York City street. I will her to face me, so I know that we are together, that her mind is not wandering and picturing something else, someone else, some other time.

Her head shifts position. She is looking towards the ceiling but her eyes are still closed; her mouth remains open in preparation to scream. Her thighs start to grip tighter against my ribs. I feel everything tighten.

And her eyes open.

The bright, red *oh* of her mouth stretches slightly into a half-smile, almost turning her lips into a heart. Her eyes glisten against the light source I have not noticed.

Then she lifts her arms and digs her nails firmly into my back, trying with her might to pull me closer to her. I resist at first but she squeezes my sides with her legs and arches her back several times in quick succession, altering the angle of my penetration.

She claws me harder and I can resist no longer.

Audrey's feet are now wrapped around the small of my back; my chest rests heavily against her breasts. I face her pillow, our cheeks touching as she peers upwards.

'I'm sorry,' she whispers quietly into my ear. 'I'm so sorry.'

And a single tear forms in her left eye, swims down her cheek and on to the pillow while I up my tempo. Part of me is confused or annoyed that she has chosen this moment to apologise. Part of me is grateful to have heard it at all. And another part merely knows that we are both close; this time is nearly over.

I consider finishing in a more degrading position. Pulling her by her hair so that she is face down, pinning her arms out wide, forcing her legs apart with my knee before entering once more from behind. Crushing her down into the mattress as Girl 4. But that is what Eames would do. That is what Audrey would like. What she sees as apt.

That's not me.

I feel her pulsing around me and the circle of her lips finally relaxes in silent orgasm. We lie in that position for a few moments. I am breathing heavily from the final exertion while Audrey's eyes shut once more.

Wednesday
UPPER EAST SIDE, MANHATTAN, NEW YORK, 08:49 EST
London, 13:49 GMT

The next thing I know is that it is morning and I am alone.

A note has been left on Audrey's pillow; her side of the covers has hardly been disturbed.

The note has been written on the back of a postcard. The picture on the front shows the Statue of Liberty and I ask myself whether my wife now feels free.

Have I freed her?

Myself?

I take the postcard and lift it up to the light coming in from the window. I can finally see the room now that Audrey is not here. A woman's voice is muffled beyond the door but it is not Audrey's.

The note simply says *A. x*

I smile at her audacity and hear the woman's voice outside in the hallway again.

Audrey has placed my clothes in a pile on the chest at the foot of the bed so I do not have to conduct a scandalously naked search around the various locations of her apartment for stray socks. My shoes have been placed on top with my mobile phone that now contains my wife's personal number. I scroll through the contacts and find it under the letter D.

The bedroom door opens silently and I tiptoe out into the reality of a well-lit apartment, feeling somewhat delinquent for spending the night with my own wife and having to sneak out of her home.

Suddenly, I have a face I can attach to the muffled voice. She is young, in her twenties, petite, pert, attractive, blonde. She blushes at the sight of me and I have to remind myself that I am indeed clothed. She lifts her eyebrows in a way that informs me she knows who I am; Audrey has forewarned her of my presence. She nods subtly over her shoulder at the front door.

Then I hear another voice.

Younger.

Much younger.

A small boy toddles over to the woman Audrey will refer to as Phillipa when we next speak. She scoops him up. 'Come on, Walter. Let's go flying.' She vrooms him off to another room.

I glimpse one side of the young Eames and my heart stops at the sound of my father's name.

I need to get out of here.

I've lost my focus.

This has become about a personal quest rather than the case I was brought here to solve. If I had been in the right mindset, if I had paid more attention, if I'd been thinking of Girl 10 instead of fucking Girl 4, something would have clicked when I held up that postcard only moments ago.

I would know how Eames intends to take my wife away from me again.

I slink out of the front door like some perverse sex addict and tap the button for the lift several times, though it needs to be pressed only once.

Back in Audrey's apartment, the phone rings. Phillipa

answers and talks to her boyfriend, Marquez. She tells him about me, about what Audrey did last night.

And the toddler sits quietly in his playroom, not knowing that the man outside his home should have been his father.

Audrey

—✦—

I needed that.

To be with January again. Not answering questions or raking over old ground, taking a scalpel to recently healed wounds. I needed to apologise and have him accept my words.

I am taking his reaction as acceptance.

The fact that he was still around when I awoke tells me where his heart is.

But the hard work starts now. I've got him here; it has taken almost two years but I've got him. I have to convince him to stay or agree that I should return to London.

There is so much left for me to finish.

Two more girls. Two more tricks.

It's still happening and I couldn't stop it now even if I wanted to.

But I walk to work as I usually do, stopping at the nearest Starbucks, ordering my coffee, handing them my aluminium cup, as always – they call it *aluminum*. The only difference is that, today, I am smiling. I have taken a heaped spoonful of happiness. The medicine of orgasm. The linctus of triumph.

Eames may be running his own to-do list – his final four – but mine does not tessellate with his plans. And that is going to piss him off. My proposed future does not involve Eames in the way that his objective concludes with my presence. I cannot kill again. I can't. I'm not like him.

Imagine how angry he'll feel when he sees another spade card with a black cross through it. Think how betrayed and sick he will be to have come so far. Take a moment to contemplate how naive I truly am to believe that he does not have a contingency for revenge.

Everything he does leads to me.

Everything I do ends with January.

Work is as it always has been. The team is either placing candidates into new jobs, interviewing applicants or scalping new clients who require roles to be filled. I did not have to leave early. I wrote that on the note to January because I had to say something. I had to leave him there. To test him. With my absence. With the presence of Walter. With the temptation of Phillipa, who seemed hung-over this morning.

I don't want to play games with the man I love, but I have to be sure. I have to get this right. I messed everything up last time. I pushed him further away and closer to his sister, as if that were even possible.

At 18:03 New York time, January will call me from his now charged mobile.

'Meet me for dinner,' he'll say abruptly. Not in a

suave, taking-control-of-the-situation manner, but quite coldly.

'Sure. What time?'

'Eight. Meet at my hotel for drinks and then we'll move on,' he will suggest in the same tone.

Without seeing his face and looking into those tired eyes, I can't place how he feels. It is somehow put out yet alluring. Are we going to make love in his hotel room first? That could be romantic, I guess. Does he want to talk things through before dinner? I can't judge it over the phone.

I'll explain that there is a great Italian restaurant near me or that perhaps we should go to the Carlyle on 76th. He'll say that he doesn't want to go to a place I have been or that I go to often. He wants to go somewhere else. Somewhere new.

It has to be new.

He doesn't even care if the food is bad, just that we are together.

He'll give me the name of his hotel. It is not a great hotel. But I will tell him that I'll meet him in the bar. And even though he'll then hang up the phone, I will continue to speak into the mouthpiece, telling him that I love him.

January

────◆────

Wednesday
MIDTOWN, MANHATTAN, NEW YORK, 09:31 EST
London, 14:31 GMT

Last time, when Eames was working his way around London, picking up women, luring them in with his charm and potency, then killing them, brutally, The Smiling Man would appear to me before each girl was killed. I had twenty-four hours to interpret his messages. This was the pattern.

With the exception of Girl 4.

And Girl 7.

Both of these *girls*, these women, were Audrey.

He never appeared for Audrey.

I want him to appear to me now. Because I want this case over with. I want to catch whoever thinks it is clever to be working with Eames. I want to capture the idiot who does not realise that they are not working in a team, that they are being controlled by him, just as everyone is. They have been seduced. I want to end this.

And if The Smiling Man does appear to me, I will know that Audrey is safe. If he does not materialise and I sleep through the night, I have to assume that she is in danger. That she will be next.

The only other way that I can guarantee her safety is to be with her. If I fall asleep in bed and have a dreamless night, at least she is there with me; I can protect her. I can save her this time in the way that I could not before. The way that I could not protect my sister.

So my only choice is to pretend that I have forgiven her, that I want the past to remain in the past, that it will be easy to move on.

But I can't just click my fingers.

I'm not the magician here.

We need to talk. But not until I have stopped Eames. Not until I have his partner in handcuffs. Not until I have worked out the reason that Agent Marquez called me in the first place.

I return to my hotel with a roll of tape and a map of Manhattan. The stack of paperwork that Paulson faxed over sits in a pile on my bedside table. It needs to be on the wall with the duplicate crime scene photos, the map and any screwed up, scribbled-on napkins or beer mats. I need to see everything I have so I can work out what I am missing.

Eames

———✦———

W hen a man is caught for killing women and he tells you that it was for revenge, for what *they* did to him, for calling him ugly, for telling him it was wrong to wear women's shoes, for being a whore, that's not me. I'm not a fucking cliché.

I'm not giving up because you caught me.

I haven't found the Lord, my saviour, since being here.

I do not doodle or sketch or paint and try to pass it off as some kind of art. My art is the way I kill, the manner in which I take my victims.

You are thinking of me now. I can feel it.

Tomorrow, Detective Inspector January David, you will find Ms Harbin dead. And you will keep on finding her all day long. And you will be standing next to an agent you no longer trust, maybe even suspect; the man whose call I missed last night while you were otherwise engaged, no doubt sinking yourself between the legs of the woman who betrayed you in more ways than you are ever likely to know. And you will understand that time has almost escaped you again. That there is only one more opportunity.

You think you can save her this time.

So, sleep well tonight, Detective Inspector. Drink your wine and eat your meat and walk your streets arm in forgiving arm. And pretend that none of the things you know are important any more. And tell that plump-lipped cuckoo that you never stopped loving her. Tell yourself that you can protect her now. Become the liar. Feel like the only two people in the world. Live in the moment. A tableau of absolution.

I am not giving up because you caught me.

You never caught me.

And you cannot save your wife.

It is no longer her plan.

Everybody thinks they want the answers, that they would like to know how the magician performed the illusion; they want to know the mechanics behind the trickery. You don't want this, Detective Inspector January David. You don't want to see behind the curtain. It will ruin the surprise.

Girl 10

———◆———

Wednesday
**EAST VILLAGE, MANHATTAN, NEW YORK,
09:40 EST**
London, 14:10 GMT

I feel like death.

Champagne headaches are the worst.

As I move beneath the covers, I'm alerted to a tightness on my stomach and I feel the crust that has formed around my navel with my left hand. The guy I brought home last night pulled out and hosed me down with his lust. I can see him now, his eyes shut, his back arched, his mouth in a perfect circle as he gripped his own dick and pumped out a climax over my skin. It was the least sexy thing I have ever experienced.

And now he's gone. He must have woken up early as the light entered the room. The buildings are not as tall here as they are elsewhere in the city; we get the sun first. He was either ashamed of his performance, though I doubt that as I made exaggerated sounds of pleasure to irritate my current roommates, or he decided that I did not appear to be as beautiful as I did last night. He was probably picturing Phillipa the entire time he was thrusting himself inside me.

I scratch at my stomach and brush the yellowing-white flakes on to the bed sheet I fully intend to change despite only having a couple of days left before I am supposed to move out.

Despite only having one day left to live.

It still seems like there's so much to do. The boxes along the opposite wall are only half filled. The drawers need to be taken apart today and I have to get most of my clothes packed and washed. This is the sort of time when I need a boyfriend or any kind of friend to come over and help me out a bit. Maybe Phillipa will help. She owes me for this headache, at least. This is probably the right time for me to start thinking a little more independently because I'll be on my own soon enough.

I hear my roommate outside the door say something like *He couldn't get out of here quick enough*. And her boyfriend fake-laughs. Then she mentions something about me *only just getting this job* and it reminds me that I have to call in sick, just like Girl 8 did the day she was killed by Eames.

I'm creating a pattern.

Maybe I'll just tell them I'm running late. Put off the packing a little longer.

Today I am Eleanor Harbin. I have blonde hair that drops below my shoulders. I'm average height and build. I am newly employed in a job that has its pressures but is ultimately more enjoyable than my last, and I am moving to a new apartment with a large lounge, old-fashioned decoration and dated kitchen appliances.

Though it appears to be a time of immensely significant upheaval, I feel content. Like this is the new start I have so desperately required but have been too blinded by ease to notice.

None of this matters.

Nothing important happens today.

Tomorrow I will be another statistic. My name will be replaced with my gender and a number written beside it. *Girl 10*. I'll be Eames' latest victim. His newest art installation. I won't be moving into that new apartment or returning to the job I have recently secured. I'll be a barcode. A dot on a map. A series of black-and-white photographs tacked to a whiteboard for detectives to stare at.

I'll be Zig-Zag Girl.

The Bones

⚜

Wednesday
VIOLENT CRIME OFFICE, LONDON, 16:23 GMT
New York, 11:23 EST

The last skeleton to be excavated had been underground for decades.

A young girl of six.

The sick bastard's first victim.

Apparently the soil in that area is not too acidic or peaty. Forensics had told Acting Detective Inspector Murphy that it could have been another fifty years before things became dry and brittle.

They were *good bones*.

Aria Sky's body, like any body, had started to decompose as soon as her heart stopped beating. Chemical changes within her had caused a difference in Ph levels and cells started to lose their structure. Her body had immediately begun to cool – *algor mortis*, the guy in the lab had called it before repeating its meaning to Murphy in layman's terms.

The seasoned child suffocator sensed the change in her temperature before he took her out to the park; that is why he wrapped her in a blanket.

He wrapped them all in a blanket.

And they all wore a boiler suit.

So that he could keep their clothes.

Aria was still fresh when the fat fucking animal walked her through the gates of Regent's Park; the signs of decomposition were not yet visible. But he still applied make-up to any exposed areas of skin in case she changed colour, in case autolysis caused her to blister. She would break down four times quicker than she would when buried underground, and the weirdo wanted to spend the day with her in the open air.

It wasn't until after lunch, after the sausage roll he ate and the apple juice that she would never drink, that her muscle tissues became rigid and incapable of relaxing. It was at this point that the sack-of-shit killer told himself that he had loved her too much.

By the time Alan Barber had pissed on Aria's foot, she was bloating. The bacteria in her intestines were already eating away at her insides and the pressure of the gases forming had forced liquid to spill from her mouth, nose and anus.

The forensic analyst explained that they were lucky to find her so soon. She had skin and muscle and eyes, and her teeth were still in their gums. They could detect the bruising with the naked eye and it was clear how she had been killed even before he cut a Y-shape into her chest.

The difficult but *most interesting* thing, he said, were the bones. These were laid out on metal trays, side by side, gradually transforming into skeletal figures.

All of them buried at different depths at different points in time.

Each one a young child whose age never reached double figures.

Every tiny structure a sculpture of death and time; a blueprint for a life not lived.

Six sets of bones.

Six victims.

Six families about to receive an answer.

Audrey

—✦—

B lack. I'll wear black. It seems appropriate. Jan likes me in black. He did, once. Can he have changed that much in this time?

Phillipa agrees to stay on and take care of Walter this evening; she seems perkier than she did first thing this morning.

'I'll pay you double,' I tell her, overplaying it so that there is no need for negotiation.

'That's very kind of you.' She screws her face up slightly as though the talk of money is taboo in this situation. 'I'm happy to stay here with Walter, he'll be asleep anyway, it's really no trouble.'

'Thank you, Phillipa. I appreciate it.'

'Important meeting?' she asks, smiling, raising her eyebrows. She would have seen January as he left; they may have even spoken to one another.

'Sorry?' I buy myself a little thinking time.

'Tonight? Is it an important meeting?'

'You could say that, yes.'

I pause. Partly for effect, to build what I am to reveal but also to gauge my employee. I don't want to overstep the mark. I trust her with my son and I value her discretion but we are not friends. She works for me.

'My husband.'

'Your . . . husband. I didn't know you were . . .'

'Married?'

'Well, yes.'

'It's a little complicated.'

I've always assumed that she did know that I was married. That she knows about Jan. What he does for a living, what his past is. That she knows about his sister going missing and she has read about the Eames case. That she knows that I was part of the performance. And I assumed she was too polite to mention anything. Too professional. But that she, like everyone else, is unaware of how the series of murders was orchestrated, how the strings were pulled.

It is the reason I came here. Everyone in London knows. Here, they move on. They forget. Phillipa is exactly the kind of girl that Eames would prey on. She is the kind of girl I would have chosen for him. Young, nubile and innocently dupable. Eames would have enjoyed her. I know what he likes.

'I don't mean to pry. Sorry. Please, get ready, do what you have to do, I'll fix Walter's dinner.'

I close my eyes and nod in gratitude.

'Do you need anything? A coffee, wine, Valium?' She laughs at her own silly suggestion and I watch her face light up as it always does. Then I think of my own face and how I have to clean off the day before reapplying make-up for the evening.

I should wear black. Black is sexy. Black means

business. This isn't a married couple going out for dinner, this is a date. A time to impress.

I will wear black.

And hope that is what he still likes.

When I eventually emerge from my bedroom, made-up and anxious, Phillipa gushes over my appearance. She uses phrases like *gorgeous* and *knock-out*. She puts a spoonful of pulverised something or other into Walter's mouth and says, in a patronising-to-children way, 'Doesn't Mommy look beautiful, Walter?'

He nods innocently and I watch as Eames' eyes move up and down within my son's unknowing skull.

I try to picture January's eyes there instead but all I see are pools of tragedy.

Eames is watching me.

He knows where I am.

Always.

'Have a great time tonight, and don't worry about Walter, everything will be fine.' Phillipa speaks softly, her right hand clutching my left shoulder as though she is my rock, my emotional support.

There is a moment of silence that follows as I struggle for something to say in acknowledgement of her encouraging tone. She pauses, turning over the words in her mind to ask whether or not I will be returning home this evening.

I tell her that she can use anything she wants in the spare room. To treat it as her own.

Then the door closes behind me and I'm in the lift rehearsing my greeting and checking myself one last time in the mirrored surfaces, peeking over my shoulder to peruse the view from behind. It all seems so staged now.

I can't remember the last time it was effortless, when anything was natural.

January's hotel is cheap, one of the worst in this area. He's situated between Midtown and Central Park but none of the places he'd want to go are here and there's certainly nothing for me, even though I'm still a relative newcomer.

He is sitting at the bar on a high stool and doesn't look to have made any more effort than he ever has for our date, if that is what it is to be called. He has aged over the last couple of years, but not to his detriment; he still sports the handsome dishevelled look better than anyone.

His glass contains a clear, bubbling liquid. From the piece of lime floating on top I can tell it is a vodka and tonic rather than a gin and tonic but I would've expected whisky or wine. Maybe he has changed. Maybe I am stuck in the past.

I start to doubt my outfit. But then his reaction to my appearance is exactly as I had hoped. He stands from his stool like the gentleman he is, takes my hand as though he is going to twirl me in front of the bar staff and drunken patrons, and pulls me in close, his right cheek touching mine as he kisses the air beside my ear.

He wags a finger politely to the barmaid. 'Hi. Yes. Can I get a large glass of Chardonnay for the lady . . .' He stops then looks at me. 'I'm sorry. Is that OK? You still like Chardonnay?' he asks, seemingly nervous. As though I have been missing for years and my tastes have changed dramatically.

'No. Chardonnay is fine. It's perfect,' I reassure. And I perch myself on the stool to his left.

'Vodka and tonic for you?' I screw my eyes up playfully as though implying something is *going on*.

He laughs. 'They have so many different vodkas here that I just had to try some.'

He's right. There is a vodka section on the bottom shelf with five or six different brands, some placed beneath ice-blue lights to make them glow and seem more appealing. Along the front of the bar, one brand has fifteen bottles of varying flavours from liquorice to mandarin to one that is apparently the flavour of Brooklyn.

My wine arrives and Jan hands over a ten-dollar bill.

Now I am nervous.

What are we going to talk about?

I'm sorry I screwed a serial killer and got pregnant with his child? I've missed you? I wish I'd done things differently? I have changed? I don't want to be that person any longer? Please take me back? You fucked me so well last night?

I fidget, pulling the hem of the dress down to protect me. January picks up on my body language immediately. That's what he is trained to do. I'm hoping he is also distracted by my legs.

'I don't want to dwell on things.' He is blunt and laconic and commands my attention immediately. He explains that the things that went on in the past – he doesn't mention Eames by name – are exactly where they should be. In the past.

He tells me, 'What you did is unforgettable' and I start to cry. I don't bawl; I'm in a public place. I fix my stare on him as he continues. My face is stoic, but I let a tear crawl from one eye. 'I won't forget it and I don't think that I should. But I can forgive you. I have to. I have to find a way if this is going to continue. If we are going to get this back.' He swigs his vodka as a visual full stop to the clearly rehearsed speech.

January is showing less emotion than I am. His eyes do not reflect the immensity of the words he utters; his body shows no signs of yearning in my direction. I assume he has practised and practised until the words have become stale, until he can deliver them with a level of clarity and apathy that gets his point across without breaking down and looking weak or vulnerable.

I have to believe this otherwise I cannot understand it.

He orders another drink for me, though I have only taken a few sips of the first glass, and two for himself.

We never get to a restaurant.

Two hours later, I'm startled awake as Jan inhales all the oxygen in his chintzy, dust-filled hotel room.

January

———◆———

E verything is doused in a hue.
Instead of endless darkness, there is light. A white covered in either a grey wash or fading into sepia. The Smiling Man steps out in front of the chair and he too is monochromatic. He looks smart in a tuxedo, less threatening. But that smile, that relentless grin and those unblinking, bulbous eyes are a reminder to be on guard; there is nothing that can be done to stop his disquieting game of abstruse charades.

But I am not there.

He does not perform to me.

The chair is empty.

No blindfold or music or shuffling feet, left to right.

Left to right.

There is a crack and his ankles break to the right, his knees dropping left. Then another thwack of broken bone as his thigh snaps, sending his hip in the opposite direction.

He is trying to convey the name Harbin. He wants to say that she will die in the next twenty-four hours.

He wants to help.

I already know it will be the Harbin Zig-Zag Girl trick, bent and manipulated into an Eames-style murder.

Or Paul Daniels.
Or David Copperfield.

I stand naked in the bedroom with the evidence taped to the floral wallpaper. Audrey is in the other bedroom sleeping. If I have the correct list of tricks, there is only Daniels and Harbin left. I have kept Copperfield because those are the tricks he used for Audrey. And I can't believe he is finished with her.

The only person that knows I am here in this hotel is Marquez. If something happens to Audrey, it will point the finger directly at him. I don't want to believe he is corrupt. I don't want to believe any cop is corrupt, but I can't rule out that he has another agenda. If Audrey is here, I believe she is safe.

I don't have The Smiling Man this time to help me or cloud my judgement or give me information or get in the way of the investigation. But I have Audrey. And I have experience. I have the disposal of the FBI network.

And I have Eames.

I return to the woman, her body forming sand dunes underneath the cheap, synthetic material of the hotel sheets as she lies in perfect afterglow.

She stirs.

'Are you all right, Jan?'

'I need to go,' I inform her.

'Go? Where? What do you mean?'

'I'm working a case.' I glimpse that look of disbelief and then one of recognition as she witnesses the imbalance between my personal and work life.

'A case? Here in New York? You're here for a—'

'Audrey.' I raise my voice to cut off her trail of thought. It's clear that she thinks I have come to New York to track her down, that my only reason for being in this city is to rekindle something with my cheating wife. I don't have time for it. I am here to solve this and keep her protected in the meantime.

'I will explain later. I need to make some calls. I need to go,' I repeat, throwing my arms inside a jacket. 'I'm sorry.'

I walk around to her side of the bed where she is now sitting up, the bed sheets pulled up to cover her breasts to shield them from the cold, I assume, rather than obscure them from my view. And I kiss her on the mouth.

'I'm sorry.' I say it once more. Perhaps it is true.

Then I turn my back and pace to the door, grabbing my mobile from the dresser as I exit. I need to speak with Paulson to go over what Eames said last time they met; I need him to go in there again. Now.

And I have to get hold of Agent Marquez so that he can give me a list of every woman with the surnames of Daniels and Harbin on this fucking island.

The List

—✦—

A gent Paulson should be sleeping but he has just gone all in with an ace/king, suited, before the flop. He is still playing online poker at night, for real money, six games at a time. This particular game is high stakes for most but of medium risk for a player of his quality. He is about to lose over fifteen hundred pounds, which, for a cop on his salary, should make his eyes water, but he understands that you have to take these hits sometimes.

Then his phone rings.

And he doesn't have to look at the name flashing on the screen to know who it is.

'Jan,' he answers, confidently.

'You're up,' comes the response at the other end.

'Of course I'm up. I'm always up.' He smiles to himself at the feeble poker pun.

'I need to know what he said last time.' Paulson can hear January breathing heavily as though pacing or running, but he doesn't sound like he is outdoors.

'Eames? I told you everything before.'

'I need to know exactly.' He drags out the last word to accentuate his point.

'OK. Let me get my pad. I transcribed it.'

'Do you have it on tape?'

'Yes.'

'Play it to me.'

Detective Inspector David speeds down the hallway of the eleventh floor, the sound of rustling papers and drawers slamming coming from the phone receiver. He hits the button on the lift and, though it lights up to indicate the lift has been summoned, he presses it several more times in quick succession to inform the machine that he is in a desperate rush.

Someone will die in the next twenty-four hours unless he can stop it.

He needs more information.

Paulson comes back to the phone and prepares his friend for what he is about to hear before pressing play.

January still feels that sense of failure and anger at the sound of his adversary's tones.

'Who is doing this?'

'Well, I am of course.'

'Who is killing these girls?'

'Eames.'

'What is the location of your next victim?'

'Oh. All over. Anywhere. Everywhere. A little bit here. A little bit there. You need to be looking more closely at the police in that city.'

'That's it.' January exclaims, morbidly excited. 'That's the clue.'

'It is?'

'Yes. I'm sure of it. I don't know what it means, but I just know that he is telling us something with that.'

The last sentence stood out to January David the first time he heard it. The first half was too laid-back and vague for Eames. He was usually so calculated with his diction. And the second part seemed to allude to a distrust of the police force. January forced that idea on to Agent Marquez after seeing him leaving Audrey's building. But something is telling him that is not the case; at least, so he hopes. He still believes that Marquez is acting suspiciously but feels that Eames was trying to convey a different message.

This is his instinct.

His hunch. His gut.

The thing he relied on before the visions of The Smiling Man.

Could Eames really be working with a cop?

'Thanks, Paulson. I think I've got what I need. But you have to go in and see him again. It has to be now. Get into that place as soon as you can. You have to squeeze him for her first name. Her surname is Harbin or Daniels. I know that much. Get what you can out of him. Use him.'

January David could narrow the odds further with the help of The Smiling Man's crooked, serpentine form; the vision that would alert him to the Zig-Zag Girl trick by Robert Harbin. He could abandon the search for the Daniels girl. By not seeing The Smiling Man, he is being forced into convention, to detect, to unravel.

When these visions started, January David rejected them as hokum. The next case, he trusted in them so completely that it blinded him. He has to learn to use them alongside his already established skills as an investigator.

Detective Paulson holds the pause button down.

'No worries, Jan. I'll leave right away. You want to hear the rest of the conversation? It's very short, just Eames insulting me, telling me I'll be back in to see him again, which I guess is true.'

'That's it for now. Call me as soon as you've seen that piece of shit again.'

'No worries.'

'Listen, Paulson. I know there were more bodies in the park, I saw it in the news. Let's discuss later. When London is awake.'

'OK. And then I'll tell you how Murphy still thinks it's the uncle.'

January sighs and shakes his head before ending the call.

But Paulson's dismissal of the rest of the conversation with Eames will prove costly.

'You want a deal, is that it? You tell us where the next victim is supposed to be killed and you get something in return, am I right?'

'No, Detective, use your sense. You insult my sensibility, I just want to help.'

'We're done here.'

'Thanks for visiting, Detective. Must dash. Would you come again?'

*

Eames was toying with Paulson; he would never have risked it with Detective David. He talked of *sense and sensibility*. He said *dash would*. He was informing the fat, unworthy rival that the victim's name was Eleanor.

He was telling Paulson that he is not smart enough.

January David steps into the lift, leaving Audrey where he thinks she will be safe.

From Eames.

From herself.

The doors close slowly but the descent is smooth. He has no reception on his phone while in there. So he thinks of Audrey in his run-down excuse for accommodation and he wonders whether he was ever really in her league.

As soon as he steps into the lobby, three bars light up in the top left corner of his phone screen and the 3G logo changes into the symbol for a wireless Internet connection.

He calls Marquez.

'Detective David, it's late—'

'Harbin,' he interrupts. 'I need a list of Harbins in Manhattan. I need them right away.'

'How do you—'

'And Daniels. All the Danielses. I already have the Davids,' he interrupts again, taking the lead, showing his authority. 'I need that list now. I don't want to meet at some obscure location. I want you to bring it to me in the bar next to my hotel lobby. Can you do that, Agent Marquez? Can you help me put an end to this?'

Marquez looks to his left at the beautiful woman lying next to him.

'I'll be there in ten.'

He hangs up. And, just as January David did moments ago, he leaves his naked girlfriend sitting up in bed wondering what was so urgent. Then he walks out, leaving Phillipa to ponder that question. Alone. In Audrey David's spare bed. Two doors away from the room where Eames' son sleeps soundly.

Eames

———❖———

Thursday
BERKSHIRE, 03:18 GMT
New York, 22:18 EST

I am woken up by the male nurse they always send to me.

They think I like him, trust him.

And they call this a hospital. Do they not understand what I am?

'You have a visitor.' He sighs. All the crazy people should be asleep now. He should be sitting behind a bank of computer monitors, his feet on the desk, talking about nothing in particular with an inadequate security guard. Instead, he is being told to traipse up to my secure room and prepare for a late-night visit from my fat friend.

'What time is it?' I ask, feigning grogginess. He leaves himself off guard as a result, his concentration lapses; he has been taught to be more aware than this. I could take him out now. But where is the skill in that? Where is the artistry?

Besides, I'm supposed to like him.

I think he believes the myth too.

Imagine his face when he realises that I think of him in the same way I think of my own excrement, of the mattress I sleep on, of puppies and babies and screaming old ladies. Think how duped they'll all feel if I sink my teeth into his throat or suck out his eye.

How put out will they be if I leave him alone?

'It's the middle of the night.'

'Yes, but what time exactly?'

He glances at his watch and takes his focus from me again. It's no fun when a victim makes it easy. That's what I hated about Girl 2. Carla Moretti. She was never worthy of my gift. She didn't deserve to be killed by me. She deserved to die, but at the hands of a lesser artist.

'Eighteen minutes past three.'

That's still yesterday in New York.

They can't have found her yet.

'I have a visitor at eighteen minutes past three?'

'Not yet. He tried to say that he was on his way. That he'd be here in forty minutes. Too much red tape for that but he'll be here first thing. Just wanted to give you some time to get sorted.'

'Thanks,' I say, as though I do actually like him.

I feel nothing for him. He is my pillow. He is my contracting sphincter. He is war in a country that I have never heard of.

'Seems you're very popular recently.'

I raise my eyebrows as though agreeing with his sarcasm.

He continues, 'Front desk said you had a late-night call from a friend of yours last night. All the way from New York.'

I smile knowingly, and the dopey halfwit reciprocates as though we have shared a moment. He thinks it's a woman, an admirer, one of these sick fucks who write letters to me all the time trying to connect with me because they think I have no one when, really, it is them who are hungry for companionship of any kind.

I am their excitement.

I am their story over dinner.

I am the gossip in a huddle as your child goes off to school.

Think how glad you'll never feel that I didn't write back.

The dolt backs out of the room, suddenly recalling his training and the fact that I am supposed to be dangerous. If I wanted him dead, he'd be dead. He pushes the heavy door shut as though sealing me in hermetically; my life in a vacuum. His eyes are all I see through the minuscule rectangle that leads to the long sterile corridor of apparent derangement.

I have a few more hours according to the gullible Neanderthal. I already know what I am going to say to DS Paulson, the unworthy substitute for Detective Inspector January David, so I lie back down on my uncomfortably thin mattress and stare through the ceiling, imagining Audrey and what she is doing right now. Thinking of the son I have never met. Speculating as to why I am being contacted a day earlier than I agreed with my New York minion.

This was always the risk of working with a partner.

Suddenly they think it's all about them.

January

━◆━

Marquez brings the list.

He slaps a pile of papers down on the bar in front of me next to my whisky. I've decided to go back to the drink I know I can work with.

'I'll take whatever he's having,' Marquez calls across to the grouchy barmaid nearing the end of her shift.

'You're on duty, Agent Marquez,' I taunt.

'That's not stopping *you*.' He sits down.

'I'm not *officially* here, though, am I?'

The barmaid delivers his tumbler of golden liquid. She has put three ice cubes in his glass. We have only recently discussed the blasphemy of idiots who would ask for rocks with this particular tipple. She seems to wink at me without closing her eyes. I can't help but smile.

With the arbitrary welcome over, I jump back into work mode.

'What have you got for me?'

He points at the top page on the pile of papers and swigs at his alcohol, his sigh suggesting a difficult day has just evolved into something worse.

There are pages and pages of names.

Horrabin, Horobin, Harbin, Harbine, Harbyn, Horbyn. For some reason of etymology I am clearly not aware of, the list also includes those with the surnames Yan, Zhang, Huan, Jiang and Yuan.

'What the fuck is this, Marquez? Why are you wasting my time with this shit? I'm trying to collect as much information as possible from every source *we* have available to us . . .' I push the papers away from me, down the remnants of my Scotch and move to stand up.

'Jesus Christ! You didn't give me a spelling of it over the phone. I got what you asked me.'

'But this doesn't help. How does this help?' I have raised my voice but the bar is almost empty and those still in here are too drunk to care about our spat. The barmaid looks on from a distance and hopes for a fight.

Audrey is still upstairs.

I'm protecting her.

I want to ask him whether he is deliberately sabotaging this so that the killer can get away or so that he can go and kill this Harbin girl himself, but I have to keep him close. I have to think of Audrey.

Could he really be killing these girls himself to further his career, or at least get it back on track? And if he is, who is he going to set up for the murders? Me? Does Eames really even know about this? Is Marquez the cop that Eames is telling me to *look out for*?

I can't trust Eames.

'It doesn't help. It's just the start. I then looked into the trick you mentioned and found the actual spelling. Harbin. H.A.R.B.I.N.' He speaks as if I didn't already know this.

He's waiting for me to say, *And?*

'And so the list looks a lot different this time.' He pulls a single piece of paper from his pocket. It is folded into quarters. Marquez flattens it out on the bar-top.

I start to run my finger down the newly printed text.

'Eighteen,' he says, sounding more like a New Yorker than ever before. Just like that cop at Central Park where Girl 9 was killed.

Eames jumps into my head.

You need to be looking more closely at the police in that city.

'Is that it? Eighteen.'

'It's a very English name, Detective. I know that we are an island of immigrants but it seems the Harbins of the world were doing fine just where they were.'

'So what's with all the theatrics of the huge list? You should have just given me this straight off the bat.' I have never used this expression before; this city is rubbing off on me, or I am becoming part of it. 'You have to understand that we have less than no time to catch the guy that is doing this. They could kill the Harbin girl in twenty-three and a half hours, or they could be doing it now to the Daniels girl. Time is something we do not have. All we have is facts, history and our combined experience.'

I run through everything I know from this case and the last to help profile our next victim. These are young women in their twenties. Vivacious and independent. Sexually open and active enough to take a stranger home for a night. So far they have all been white women, but that may be coincidence or because of the surnames they have been born with. We can't rule out married names. The frequency of this second spate of killings suggests more of a time constraint. Perhaps Eames' partner is more desperate. Perhaps Eames is building up to something.

I tell Marquez that the occupation of the victim is inconsistent. Girl 1 worked in banking her entire adult life; Girl 3 worked at the BBC; Girl 8 was in PR. They were middle-of-the-road; that's what makes it so hard to pinpoint them. Of course, their jobs are key. That is how they are found and chosen. That is the path that will lead me to Audrey. The real Audrey that I am still unaware of.

Marquez and I take the pile of paperwork to a table in a corner of the bar and work through the list, crossing off those who do not fit with the profile.

This is the moment that Audrey enters.

I introduce her to Agent Marquez and they both pretend they have never seen each other before. Nervously, I explain what we are doing together at this time of night, that we are narrowing down where this cut-price Eames plans to stage their lacklustre trick next. Unknowingly, I am insulting my wife's skill level with regard to murder.

'I should go,' she says quietly, 'let you get on with it.'

'No, no, no. You have to stay here. With me.' I stand up from the table and Marquez follows suit.

'Am I at risk?' Her beautiful dark eyes widen in what looks like legitimate fear.

'Mrs David, the evidence does not point in your direction.' Marquez steps in. 'If you would feel safer, I can escort you back to your home.'

She looks at me and I nod to confirm her safety. 'I'll come back to you once we've finished.' I place a reassuring hand on her shoulder and she obliges.

I look out the front window as Marquez puts her into a giant black SUV with tinted windows and drives uptown to the apartment he has just come from. Where Audrey can bolt her door to feel safe. Where he can collect Phillipa and explain the danger camouflaged by the Manhattan smog. Where Audrey can be alone with Eames.

I turn my attention back to the lists of residents and registered voters on this insomniac island, concentrating on the Harbins. That is my best hand. That's where the pattern lies. That is where I find the name I think belongs to the next victim.

Girl 10.

Eleanor Harbin.

The Weight

——◆——

Paulson awakes and does not care that he has missed out on exercise. This can be his rest day. Though he will hardly rest.

The coroner has confirmed that there were six bodies beneath the ground in Regent's Park and the media and social-networking sites will be getting the word out quicker than they ever have in the past. He has to revisit the institution holding Eames today and try to break him, so that January can find the next girl before she is killed. And he still has to work with Murphy who is pissed at him for going behind his back and requesting the dig but is also sheepish that the results have now blown the case wide open.

This is the pressure that January David feels every day.

This is why he is the boss.

Paulson does not want it and Murphy is starting to realise that his ambition is not equal to his proactivity.

Aria Sky is dead. She was suffocated and buried in the ground next to a public toilet. That is known. That is fact. Her father was not responsible. That is another truth. What isn't known is whether he could have been involved in another way, whether he knew what was going to happen. It is also unclear how her mother was so oblivious to her capture and whether her uncle was where he says he was at the time of the kidnapping. The Sky family members have been the only suspects so far. The other five bodies have cast doubt over this. Murphy will find it harder to make something stick. Maybe Aria's family did kill her. Maybe it is coincidence. Maybe there are two cases here. Maybe that old, unhinged predator has seen the news and perches himself on the end of the bed, crying as he looks at the hangers that hold the key to the identity of all six victims.

Paulson's phone rings.

'It's me,' says Murphy.

Paulson sits up but does not reply.

'We should have a date on the oldest bones at some point this morning. I'm going to haul the Skys back in. See what they know, how they react to more bodies.'

'It's not them.' Paulson finally speaks, his voice a sigh, bored of repeating himself.

'We don't know that. I'm bringing them in. Meet me—'

Paulson cuts him off. 'I have something to do this morning. I'll be back before lunch.'

And he terminates the call before his acting superior has the opportunity to respond.

An hour later, Eames is telling him that he is too late, he can't stop Girl 10 from dying now, that he should be thinking about the next girl.

'She is the last,' he taunts. 'There's not a lot I can tell you about her. I have not made up my mind just yet. Still deciding whether I should make her freedom disappear or simply turn her into a lemon.'

Paulson makes a note of everything Eames says this time, and holds back his desire to strike him in the face.

'I see you're no closer to solving your case about that poor missing girl.'

'I'm not here to talk about that.' Paulson feels his eyes widen. This is a personal attack on him, he feels.

'Well, at least you know it's not her family now that you've dug up those other bones.' He waits for a response but nothing comes. 'Were you there when they found the remains, Detective Paulson?'

'Of course I fucking was.' Paulson doesn't want to lose his cool but Eames has turned the conversation away from his own case on to that of Aria Sky.

'So was he.'

'What?'

'So was your killer, Detective Paulson. He would have been watching you.'

'What do you know?'

'For certain? Nothing. Just that he would want to have witnessed that. Just that he doesn't realise he needed to see it. And if he did, things are getting worse for him. You'll need to find him soon before he kills someone else, or kills himself.'

'You think this sicko is like you?' Paulson smirks uncomfortably.

'No!' He leans forward. 'I would never do anything to a child.' Eames leans in to Paulson, his eyes fixed on the detective's face. He holds it for a moment then drops back casually into his seat.

'Well, that's very honourable of you,' Paulson says sarcastically, now that there is sufficient distance between them – he has lost weight but Eames can still move faster than him, even with the handcuffs.

'Look, Detective. I've already told you everything you need to know in order for your boss to stop the last girl from dying, and I'm telling you this: the killer you are looking for is a man with an affinity to that park; the answers are not with the families of these dead children, they are in that park. *He* is probably in that park right now. He may go there every day. You should have solved this already. He wants to be caught.'

'There's nothing like an expert opinion.' Paulson is trying desperately to be aloof but Eames sees it only as recklessness.

'Just tell your boss to keep an eye on his wife, eh? There's a good lad. I think our time is up.' Eames stands.

The guard takes him back down the corridor and into his cell. Fuming, Paulson watches him, wanting the last word. But he knows that Eames has helped. That he is an expert.

As Eames is led through his door, a man in a sharp dark suit appears at the other end. He is the sponsor. Murphy's go-to guy. Paulson does not recognise him but sees that he is holding a brown envelope that he gives to the guard who obligingly passes it on to the prisoner.

And then he is gone.

His work is done here.

Inside the envelope is a single playing card.

The jack of spades.

January David only has one day left with his wife.

January

---◆---

There are two Eleanor Harbins.
  It is not the most common first name and, after some digging and a little help from the FBI database, we find that it's the same person. She's registered at two different addresses. Both in the Village. One in the East; one in the West.

I tell myself that I have cracked Eames' code. That this is what he meant when he said that we'd find her *all over, anywhere, everywhere*. I fit my findings into the pattern and say that this is what is meant by Zig-Zag Girl. For a moment I forget the second part of his sentence, the part about looking more closely at the police in this town.

It doesn't matter that I am wrong about the method or motives. She is the right girl.

And she is still alive.

Marquez is with me in the bar with his list of Danielses. He's crossing off anyone that does not fit the profile. He drove Audrey back to her apartment and assured me that she is safe. He tells me that he offered to post someone outside her door but that she refused. I don't know whether that is true but it does sound like something Audrey would reject.

The Audrey I think I know.

He was longer than I expected but informed me that he then drove the nanny back home too. He didn't want her roaming the streets. She is young and attractive and fits the bill. He doesn't tell me that he knows her. That they are together.

He also lied about where he took her. He didn't want her at her known address in case she was a target. So she was moved somewhere safe. Some place that nobody would find her. Only Agent Marquez knows where she is.

And, instead of looking more closely at the police in this town, I tell Marquez that I have something.

'It's a hunch, but I think it's her.'

'A hunch?' he asks, screwing up his face.

'They're not usually wrong.'

There is a beat while he runs through protocol in his head or at least pretends to.

'Where are we going?' he says in resignation.

I point at the creased paper in my right hand. 'These are the two addresses. You take that one and I'll take this one. There's no time to waste.' I fold the paper and place it in my trouser pocket.

We exit the hotel through the hotel lobby and head out on to the street. It's the first time I have noticed the light creeping back into the city. Marquez jumps into his car and speeds off downtown. I hail a cab and head to the other address.

Only one of us can find her.

Only one will be able to save her and stop this murderous run.

As we travel south, splitting the island in two, Eleanor Harbin is at home, safe. And very much alive.

Girl 10

Thursday
EAST VILLAGE, MANHATTAN, NEW YORK,
07:27 EST
London, 12:27 GMT

'Fuck you, you bitch.'
   These are the words I woke up to twenty-seven
minutes ago as the not-so-happy couple commenced their
first argument as co-habitués.

Eight minutes ago, it turned into make-up sex. I can
hear him saying, 'Yeah, yeah, yeah' as his balls slap
against her ass, telling me that he doesn't think the
argument has finished until he has blown a load inside
her.

I left the apartment two minutes ago, holding the
handles of a cardboard box filled with a few CD cases
and books and candleholders. This is the first part of my
move across town away from the self-destructive,
co-dependent relationship up the stairs behind me. This
is my excuse to get out.

The only other item in my box of curios is the purple
scarf that Phillipa lent me the other night when we went
out. I text her to say that I still have it and that she can
pick it up any time from my new place. I use punctuation

to create a smiling face so that she knows I am happy about the move.

I am happy.

This is the start.

I descend the steep stairs on to the street, away from what once was home but is now bitter memory. I walk away from it. Away from the secrecy and whispering and destined-to-fail set-up of my former friends and the late-night moaning and early-morning hate-fucking. I move away from the address that Agent Marquez will arrive at in two minutes and I head towards January David.

Don't let her kill me, Detective.

This is not supposed to be the end.

January

—⊹—

Thursday
WEST VILLAGE, MANHATTAN, NEW YORK, 07:31 EST
London, 12:31 GMT

Agent Marquez arrives at his destination first.
He pulls his vehicle in closely to the kerb, parking it next to one of the trees that line the street. He jumps out and closes the door behind him in one swift movement that they must teach you at the FBI Academy in Quantico. He leaps up the steps two at a time and hits the buzzer that says *Harbin/Hayes*.

He waits for five seconds then presses the buzzer another twenty times in quick succession. Then he hits his hands against the door.

Inside, Ms Hayes is bent over, her forearms resting against her mattress, her feet pushed up to their toes to create the perfect height and angle for her still-angry boyfriend to thrust himself in and out.

She wonders who it could be and why Eleanor has not answered the call. Then her boyfriend grunts and reminds her where she is and the role she is playing. 'Oh my God, here it comes. Here it comes.'

And then she's hanging her head out of the window and asking, 'Who the fuck are you?'

'FBI, ma'am. I'm here to speak with Eleanor Harbin. Can you let me in?'

She disappears from the window and Marquez pushes his way through the door as it buzzes then makes his way up to the apartment.

Ms Hayes has wrapped a thin gown around her to cover her modesty. Her boyfriend remains in the bedroom waiting for his penis to stand down.

'What's this about, Agent . . .?'

'Marquez. Is she here? I need to speak with her.'

'Sure. Her room is just there.' She points at the closed room to the left. 'El. You have a visitor,' she calls out, knocking against her door. Agent Marquez is now standing in her hallway. 'El?' she asks, rapping against the wood once more.

Agent Marquez moves her gently to the side and opens the unlocked room.

It is empty.

'When did she leave?'

'I don't know. I didn't hear anything.'

'Did she stay here last night?'

'Yes. Definitely. What is this all ab—'

'Shit!' Marquez swivels on his heel, pulls out his mobile phone and calls me.

'She's not here.' That's all he says.

'I'm still in the taxi. Almost at the other address. Get over here.'

I hang up, give the driver twenty dollars, tell him to keep the change and leap from the car, not quite shutting the door with the fluidity that a trained federal agent would exhibit, and I run to Eleanor Harbin's new address.

Hoping she will be there.

*

I repeat the same routine as Marquez. Pushing her buzzer, which still has the name of the previous tenant taped next to it, waiting, pressing the button again and again and again. Eventually sliding my hands down the wall, hitting the doorbell of every resident in the block until I'm let in.

Nobody answers her door.

It takes me three attempts to break through with my shoulder. Neighbours can hear and are starting to call the police or snoop at the action.

'Eleanor!' I shout. 'Miss Harbin,' I continue, hoping not to find her strung up or stabbed or tied to the railings of her balcony. Or whatever Eames has in store for his latest trick.

But she's not here.

She is nowhere.

She is in between. Somewhere on a street or underground or being dragged behind a bush.

Eleanor Harbin is dead.

Soon, I will be finding her all over.

Anywhere.

Everywhere.

And I'll be looking more closely at the police in this town.

Eames

—✦—

G irl 10 was different.
     She had to be.

Detective Inspector January David had to think he was close this time, that we are playing a game and he has a chance of winning. That I am inviting him to beat me. To save these lives.

Imagine how idiotic he will feel when he realises that he is making all the same mistakes that he did the last time.

When you catch a serial killer and they say that, in some way, they wanted to end it, they wanted it to stop, that is because they were caught. That's not me. I still haven't been caught. This girl, the next girl, the one I have called *the last*, she is only the last on this list. This is only my game. It is nothing to do with a detective or his slut wife. I don't care about them. I can't.

January David is not my equal. He is no match for me. He does not trouble my thoughts. And his overweight lapdog even less so. He will find this out soon.

*

By now, the New York authorities will be searching for Eleanor Harbin, checking her phone records, contacting friends and relatives to determine who spoke to her last, who saw her last.

She is dead. I know it. Detective Inspector January David knows it. They will start to find her body soon. It has been left all over. Anywhere. Everywhere. And he will buy in to the misdirection all over again.

Did your father teach you nothing?

I am bored now.

It is time that January David met the real Audrey.

It is time for Audrey to know the real Eames.

The orderly or dogsbody or guard – shh, don't call them that, this is not a prison – arrives at my door. He opens it and steps inside. He is holding something in his right hand.

'Afternoon.' He smiles.

I don't smile back.

'Just as I asked?'

'Just as you asked,' he responds, like a child searching for his father's approval.

'You are a good man,' I flatter. And the fucking idiot believes me.

They're all idiots. They think they can stop me killing in the same way they think they can stop some of these sickos wanting to fuck kids or other men or corpses. The only person that can stop me is Audrey, but the eleven of spades in my hand tells me that she can't. She won't.

Killing one is no different from killing a hundred and one.

Audrey David.

You're up.

Audrey

—◆—

Thursday
**UPPER EAST SIDE, MANHATTAN, NEW YORK,
09:16 EST**
London, 14:16 GMT

I didn't sleep much last night. A night filled with passion and forgiveness that transformed suddenly into anxiety and cold solitary. And now I am behind on everything I had planned for this morning.

But it doesn't matter.

Because Phillipa is late.

Agent Marquez escorted her home, just as he had done with me. He's a federal agent, so she must be safe.

But she has never been late before.

I don't even have a moment to worry about her whereabouts before Walter has thrown his breakfast spoon on to the floor for the eighth time, I accidentally lean into my coffee flask, spilling it across the kitchen surface, and there is a knock at the door.

'I am so sorry about being late. I hardly slept at all last night.' She paces straight into the open-plan space and hangs her things on the hook by the door just as she always does, then moves over to the kitchen, and on

312

auto-pilot wipes up the coffee, places the fallen spoon into the dishwasher and takes another from the cutlery drawer, placing it in Walter's left hand.

'There you go, little man,' she says to him as a greeting, her bright, straight teeth like pearl gravestones.

'But you had time to colour your hair?' I question, staring at the infinitely more beautiful brunette nanny I now have working for me. She acts like it is nothing, and Walter continues to eat his breakfast, oblivious to the change. She probably thinks it makes her look uglier. So that she doesn't fit Eames' victim profile.

'Oh, gosh, that wasn't this morning. I couldn't sleep last night, as I said. I was just trying to keep my mind occupied. Trying to tire myself out.'

I nod, sceptically.

'I'm not even sure I like it that much.' She fluffs it slightly with her hand as though she does actually like it. It's almost as dark as mine. I don't know whether she is fishing for a compliment or commenting on my own appearance.

'It'll probably just take some time to get used to.'

That's all I'm giving her.

'Anyway, you're here now and that's all that matters.' She smiles.

'Look, thank you so much for last night, it was—'

'Oh, don't mention it. It was my ple—'

'It was very good of you to stay so late. I'm sorry you had a tough time sleeping. I will not be late home today and you can head straight back. OK?'

'It's not a problem, but thank you.'

I kiss Walter on the head and leave.

A cold I wasn't expecting hits me as I step out on to

the street and I suddenly understand why Phillipa arrived so wrapped up.

Someone would have found Girl 10 by now, part of her, anyway.

Her head has been left just a few blocks from here.

Come on, Jan. Look how close Eames is. He is getting nearer to me.

We're so similar now.

One of us has to die for the other to live.

January

———✦———

W e're playing catch-up.
    There is a constant high-pitched hum, like crickets, only not. It's the city. It's morning. And it's cold.
    It's not crickets.
    An out-of-shape female police officer drinks a large Sprite in the front of a police car parked out the front of the academy. The number of the car is 4481. The writing on the door says *$10,000 reward for the arrest and conviction of anyone shooting a New York City police officer. Call 1-800 COP SHOT.* I never think about the fact that I am unarmed in London.
    Marquez is waiting by the building next to the academy. An Asian woman hangs out of the window above, smoking. She is trying to peer over the green awning that separates her view from the crime scene. Marquez signals to one of the cops that I can pass under the police cordon.
    'It's her legs, Detective.' These are the words he greets me with, his five o'clock shadow looking more like seven

315

o'clock stubble. If he is trying to make something happen, trying to rebuild his career, he needs to stop the body count.

The sign on the door of the oncologist says *No pharmaceutical or healthcare reps allowed in this office.* In the alleyway down the side, I see the legs of Eleanor Harbin, detached from the rest her, wrapped in plastic.

The humming continues. I feel as though I am the only one bothered by it.

Maybe it is the amount of air conditioners hanging from the windows in this city.

'Over there.' I point at the building opposite, the Cabrini Medical Centre. 'Look at the view they have of this alleyway. It's a hospital, one of their cameras must point this way. Looks as though it is slightly tucked away for the Academy CCTV but you might have a sighting of this guy dumping two legs on the street.'

'I'm sorry, who are you?' one of the uniformed cops asks, forcing himself not to step intimidatingly closer to me.

'He's with me,' Marquez steps in. 'Bureau consultant on this case.'

Then he talks only to me, stating that they are pulling the feed from the training complex cameras for the last few hours, and he sends two colleagues over to the hospital.

'I've just got here myself, Detective.'

'There will be two more of these.'

'What? She got six legs?' the cop who questioned my credentials jokes, and a handful of others laugh.

'The death of an innocent girl is no laughing matter, no matter how many times you've seen it.' I direct my glare at him and his chest drops like a chastised child.

'If the killer is following the Robert Harbin Zig-Zag Girl trick, then he is going to divide the body into three sections.'

As I finish explaining what will happen, another bear of a police officer steps up behind me.

'Agent Marquez?'

'Yes, Sergeant?'

'There's a body outside the Midtown North Precinct.'

'A body?'

'A torso. No legs. No head.'

Marquez and I run to his vehicle and speed uptown, following the trail of carnage.

Everything Eames has told me has been true.

He has never lied.

The Confession

—◆—

M urphy is not the best detective in the world.
He's not even the best detective in the interrogation suite at this moment.

But he has his uses.

He can provoke a reaction.

' He can break a person down; he did exactly that to January David when he thought that he was responsible for the Zone Two killings a couple of years back.

And he is doing the same thing right now to Aria Sky's uncle.

'Her body is still intact, Sky,' Murphy bleats, reducing the suspect to a surname, like he knows him. Subconsciously, the suspect thinks, *Fuck, he knows me. He knows what I did.*

Paulson says nothing.

'The results will be back from the lab soon enough to see just how close she was with her uncle,' Murphy continues. Something in him is trying to *make something stick* but somewhere within this hungry-for-success detective, no matter how undeserved, is a man who wants the truth. He can't tell Paulson that. Can't break down the walls. Be vulnerable. Human, even. He still has time to please his sponsor, to get the job done right.

Aria Sky's uncle looks away in disgust at Murphy's comment. He's trying not to bite.

'If you want to stick with the story that you were asleep, then that is fine. But you want to be careful. Not everyone will hold out as long as you, and if you prove to have been lying about that then you could have been lying about a whole load of things.'

Murphy sits down. He has been standing up for the entire interrogation so far.

Paulson is seated, looking ahead into the air to the right of Aria's uncle.

He's thinking about the park.

'What the fuck do you mean? What did she say?'

Murphy doesn't answer. He leaves a silence and waits for the suspect to fill it with his guilt.

'It's all right for my brother; he had witnesses. He was off gambling in front of cameras and people.'

Murphy's got him.

Aria's mother is in the interrogation room next door. Paulson and Murphy haven't even spoken to her yet. Murphy wanted to let her stew. Said the mothers were always harder to crack. That they are the strong ones.

The uncle goes on to say that he knew his brother was gambling. His brother had confided in him. He'd acted as his alibi on occasion. On the day Aria was taken, he knew where his brother would be and that meant his sister-in-law would be at home, alone with Aria.

So while Aria played out the front, after she had said hello to her uncle, he was pushing his brother's wife against the work surface in the kitchen. While the four-year-old Aria – five in June – sang outside the front of the house, smiling, innocent, her mother's hands were pressed against the washing machine as her brother-in-law entered her from behind, the top of his thighs slapping against her soft buttocks, slow and hard at first, then faster and faster still.

While the fat man with the sick mind was snatching another girl from her skipping-rope game, while he wrenched purity from safety and plunged it into depravity – the innocent girl, the gentle child – the mother was groaning, her head lightly bruising against her washing machine as the uncle emptied a sackful of his lazy swimmers inside her. They would expire long before her own insides died of heartbreak, of guilt.

That is why they lied.

They blame themselves.

As they should.

'You don't have to tell my brother, do you? It would kill him. It would end him,' the disloyal uncle pleads.

Murphy stands up, saying nothing but showing his own distaste for the entire situation; he is worried about the sponsor's reaction. Paulson follows him out of the room.

'We can let this go now, eh, Murph? It's not the uncle. I'm sure she'll 'fess up now.' He points at the door behind which Aria's mother is sitting, worried, still guilty.

Always guilty.

Her husband was a gambler, a money-waster; he was depressed. He was depressing. She sought comfort and love and passion and companionship. When she looked out of the window, hoping to see her daughter still playing, she was gone. Everything was gone.

She may not have killed Aria Sky.

But that does not mean she is not at fault.

It is not necessarily true that she does not know who killed her only daughter.

January

—◆—

A n aged woman, wearing all black, walked into the
St George Greek Orthodox Church. She eked up
the stairs slowly then disappeared under the brown semi-
circular awning without even glancing at us.

A man in his thirties jogged by in a New York Yankees
T-shirt and hat. Sweating. Oblivious. Irritated that we
were blocking his usual route.

And the Chinese woman in the organic laundry was
on the phone the entire time Marquez and I were there
at the Midtown North Precinct, also called the 18th
Precinct.

Opposite the dilapidated police station, tucked behind
the church entrance, underneath the handwritten sign
saying *Do NOT chain or lock bicycles to railing or fire scopes.
The landlord*, there were six black bags filled with rubbish
– Marquez called it *trash* – and dumped in the centre was
the petite torso of Girl 10.

It will match the legs we recently uncovered.

Inspector Beau Bryant has the dyslexic landlord in for

questioning at the moment while two of his team run through the camera footage from the station and the Judicial District Court building next to theirs. It's a more professional outfit than I witnessed at the police academy, but these guys are qualified, they have experience.

While we wait to hear something conclusive, Marquez has me on another of his sightseeing tours, it would seem.

The woman's badge says *Renita E.*

She tells us, 'The lift is automatic. Please don't press the buttons.'

It stops when we hit the eightieth floor.

Marquez takes me over to a set of binoculars numbered 2385 and points downtown to where Eleanor Harbin's legs were uncovered. He then swings his arm over to the west of the island and indicates the spot where the torso rests on a bag filled with old, uneaten fruit and boxes of fast-food dregs.

'Now, if we move back this way' – Marquez speaks authoritatively, windmilling his arms back to the east – 'then we should be able to pinpoint the third part.' He is careful not to impart information with tourists around. 'That was the Zig. We need to work out where the path will Zag.'

We step over to observation point six, binocular number 2389. The view is astonishing. The art deco Chrysler Building, Grand Central Station tucked neatly below the protruding Met Life structure, Central Park where Girl 9 was found under a pile of birdseed. We could have looked at this on a map but Marquez was right to do it this way. We need to be a part of the city. In it. Beneath it. Submersed in it. To breathe with the streets and buildings. So that we may absorb the information that only the kerbs and doorways speak of.

I don't need the binoculars to pick out the white Italian Renaissance Revival buildings of the Upper East Side. I don't need a second more thought to pinpoint the position of Audrey's building and the location of Eleanor Harbin's head.

'What is the closest precinct to that building?'

'Where your wife lives?'

'Eames wants to scare her. To let her know that he is close, that he is coming for her. What is the closest precinct to her building?'

'Shit. If we want to stay in line with the first, uh, part, then I'd say it's the nineteenth.'

'Well, what the fuck are we still here for?'

Audrey

—✛—

C arey, my camp assistant, doesn't react to my tardiness when I enter the office.

I'm the boss. It's been a long night.

And a busy morning.

Nobody in the office has heard the news yet; if they had, they'd be flinging emails to one another and eventually one would end up in my inbox explaining that parts of a girl's body have been found zig-zagging across Manhattan.

It's only a matter of time now. A cop will tell his wife what he's seen, that he will probably have to work late as a consequence. His wife will tell five friends over coffee. A mutated version of events will end up on a social-networking site. The topic will start to trend. The media will get involved. They will inform the television-watching public. They will show photos of the crime scene and moving images of the detectives working the case. They will question Agent Marquez and display his name at the bottom of the screen.

January will want to protect me from all of this but he will soon have footage of someone dumping parts of the body. He will see that it is a woman, hiding herself from the cameras she knows are there. He will see that she is pushing a child's buggy in front of her – at first the police will dismiss her as an unlikely candidate before rewinding and watching her actions again – and they will deduce that this was probably the thing used to transport the birdseed for Girl 9 in Central Park.

I'm going to lose January again.

All of this will have been for nothing.

I have to think about myself now, and my son.

I continue the morning as though everything is normal, responding to mail, putting in calls, setting up meetings for next week, ignoring that my actions in London two years ago have finally caught up with me.

When Carey bursts into my office, flustered, shaking, wafting his hands about in an overly animated fashion, on the brink of tears that a young girl from the Village has been decapitated, when he informs me that she is one of our clients, I'll have no choice.

I will have to do exactly what Eames wants me to do.

And call the police myself.

January

---❖---

**19TH PRECINCT, MANHATTAN, NEW YORK,
09:43 EST**
London, 14:43 GMT

The 19th Precinct is sandwiched between the fire department's 16 Ladder Company and the Kennedy Child Study Center.

Eleanor Harbin's head is sandwiched between two more bags of discarded waste in a dumpster outside the blue front doors of the police station. It is wrapped in opaque plastic.

Marquez is the one to uncover it.

It has gone unnoticed all morning.

Inside, the precinct is much different from the last. It has the same wall of faces commemorating those lost or hurt during the World Trade Center tragedy that coats the entrance of each precinct, but this is less shabby than the Midtown North building. There is a kids' corner with toys and concrete seating, for a start, but this is a wealthier part of town.

The two cops behind the front desk are talking.

'I haven't been home in two days. Don't complain.'

'You might not make it home today either,' Marquez interrupts, flashing his badge and explaining what we have found and the seriousness of cordoning off the area and getting a team here to work the crime scene. 'We'll also need your camera footage right away.'

I spot a poster in the background that says *$100 cash for guns. No questions asked.* And once again I am very aware that I am the only one who is unarmed.

The station's inspector appears from a door at the back of the room. His name is Matthews. We've already met. He was one of the policemen at Central Park when I tried to see Girl 9's body.

'Mr David. Still here.' He smiles, not realising the severity of the situation.

I want to correct him, tell him that it is Detective David, but it's not worth it; we need to work together to get this finished.

Marquez jumps in. 'Yes, he's still here. Doing your job. You've had a severed head outside your front doors all morning.'

'And who the fuck are you?' the inspector asks, puffing out his chest, his jovial tone replaced with acrimony and paternal protectiveness towards his officers.

Marquez flashes his badge as though it gives him the right to behave in this way. Matthews suddenly registers the words pertaining to the package we just found in the dumpster.

'What? A head?'

'We've been finding bits of this girl all over town this morning,' Marquez exaggerates.

Matthews gives the two officers on the front desk a look that says *shut it down*, and they march out the front without a word.

His phone rings and Marquez walks over to the corner where the toys are stored. Inspector Matthews talks to me to fill the time.

'Hey, David. About the other day at the park.'

'Just doing your job, Inspector. I understand. Can't be too careful.' I hope my amiability goes some way to soothing the relationship between the two law-enforcement agencies.

He shrugs his giant shoulders in what I assume is agreement and thanks.

My unofficial partner returns.

'They pulled some footage from the hospital downtown like you thought. Said they can't get a positive ID. The perpetrator hid their face but it looks like a woman.' Marquez pauses, expecting some kind of reaction, an intake of breath, words of incredulity. 'That wasn't the fucking profile, eh?'

Makes sense, I think.

'Look, Matthews. I need to see if your cameras can get a better view of her face. She'll be the one with the push-chair dumping some innocent girl's head in your dumpster.' He can't resist a final dig.

And then I'm back in the car with Marquez heading downtown to God knows where and Marquez is telling me that I should call my wife.

Paulson let me know that Eames told him I should be spending as much time as possible with Audrey.

He hasn't lied yet.

Maybe that is what I should be doing.

Something stops me wanting to follow the advice of a madman. I won't do what he wants. It could just be misdirection. What's true is not always what is real; that is what I have to remember.

I think of Audrey and shut my eyes for the first time since I last saw her.

It is only a moment. To collect myself, centre my thoughts.

But all is black.

And I am blindfolded, and tied to a chair.

The Park

—◆—

Paulson starts with the boats.

Kids love the boats.

Aria loved the boats.

The twisted, deviant, no-good shit who took the gentle child while her mother was being pounded in the kitchen still loves those stupid fucking boats.

They won't help Paulson solve this case. But it's a start. It's the closest he has come to cracking it.

January David didn't have much time to speak to Paulson; he was in the car with Marquez and had been startled from a moment in the dark with The Smiling Man.

'Looks like we're after a woman here, Paulson. Or at least someone dressed as a woman.'

'Shit. You're close.'

'I hope so. I think Eames' partner is probably going to go after the last victim soon. He or she can't waste any time now that we're on to them.'

Paulson doesn't say anything.

'Yeah. I'd imagine some time in the next twenty-four

331

hours,' January adds as though answering a question, hinting to Paulson about his recent vision.

'The Smiling Man is back?'

'Looks that way.'

'What does it mean?'

'Not sure yet. Just on the way to view some CCTV footage. Almost there. Anything new on your case?'

Paulson explains to his on-sabbatical-but-still-his-boss that the family of Aria Sky seem to be off the hook after a confession from both the uncle and the mother that seems to corroborate and confirm their location at the time Aria was taken.

'The answer is somewhere in that park,' Paulson suggests, hoping that January will agree. So that he doesn't have to explain that he is following the advice of Eames.

'You're right.'

Paulson tries to hide his relief and sighs away from the phone.

'Go there, Paulson. Go to the park. *Be* Aria. *Be* her killer. Don't go there with anything or any specific place in mind. He could have been there all day with that little girl, hiding. Hiding in plain sight. London Zoo would probably be too crowded but maybe in the vicinity. I can't remember everything that surrounds it but perhaps a play area.'

Paulson is a detective who does not rely on hunches or feelings; he is more scientific and calculated. This is the reason he works well with January David. He complements his style. He looks for patterns. He wants to solve a puzzle. But right now, he needs to adapt. Adopt the role of January David.

Rely on a little luck.

Sometimes it is the only thing that can break a case.

'I've got to go. I think you're close too. Keep me posted.'

January hangs up and Paulson heads straight to the boats at Regent's Park. Because he thinks that kids love boats and he wanted to try this out for himself. He resigns himself to the fact that January is probably right; the zoo is a better starting point.

The old, disturbed child-snatcher lies on his bed hugging the school uniform that hangs on a child-sized hanger. This is the outfit that Aria wore when he took her. It still smells of her. Of cleanliness and fun. Of grass and scuffed knees. Its space is in the right-hand side of the wardrobe because she was the last person he killed and buried in the park. The garments to the left just smell old now. They reek of the past.

Paulson passes the restaurant where the killer ate and bought the dead child a carton of apple juice, but he doesn't go in. As he approaches the large drinking fountain set at the centre of a crossroads, he sees that one of the many dog-walkers is allowing her animals to climb on the ledge and lap at the liquid meant for humans.

He thinks about flashing his badge and moving her on.

He wonders whether Eames would want to kill her because of this.

Paulson does not fully comprehend Eames' warped code of honour, his apparent scruples, his prejudice towards other murderers and felons.

To his left, Paulson hears the sound of excited children and sees the tops of buildings over the trees that line the outskirts of the zoo. To his right are open playing fields, but an area is closed off while they erect a stage for an upcoming event. On the far side are swings and a soft-floored area for toddlers to play.

He feels watched.

Paranoid that the killer knows where he is.

But nobody knows where he is. With the exception of January, who suggested the excursion but is across the Atlantic; Murphy, who is allegedly finishing paperwork at the station but is actually meeting his so-called *sponsor* and Eames, who seems to know everything. None of them can help him now.

Paulson walks past a bench to the left of the path. It is set within a semi-circle of gravel. A thirty-something couple sit there silently, reading different books. His is something humorous; hers promotes the word CLASSIC in large letters.

A few paces on he reaches a gate that acts as the exit to the zoo, guarded by a girl in her twenties who looks disinterested and pierced and tattooed. Her hair has blue highlights.

He stops.

The killer would not go into the zoo. Too many people. Too many cameras. Still, it would take for ever to go through all the footage they must have of that day.

Paulson turns back and walks behind the reading couple. He pauses at the top of the gravel arc and peers through the gap in the trees. There is a rock. There's a pool of water. There are crowds. And there are penguins. He can see into the zoo. It's free. It's obscure. And the foliage is open and low.

London Zoo is fully aware of this view from the outside of an attraction that costs seventeen pounds for a child over three years of age. The fence is not too high at this point either.

On the wooden fence a foot ahead of Paulson's gut, partially covered by the leaves of an overhanging branch, there is a sign. A bright yellow diamond with black writing.

CCTV – 24-hr Surveillance.

There is a camera pointed at Paulson's face.

The same camera that pointed at Aria.

At her killer.

Paulson has narrowed the search considerably.

He's got him.

A little bit of luck, but he's got him.

* * *

Agent Marquez drops January David back at his hotel. Says he has some things to sort out, clean up. He tells January to *freshen up. Get some rest. Go and see his wife.* He says he'll be back in an hour.

January knows that Girl 11, the last girl, could be dead by then.

Marquez takes his car back downtown to the apartment only he knows about, the one he is calling a *safe house.* As he drives, he thinks of the girls that have died, the image of each one embedded into his psyche for ever.

Girl 8 hanging from the ceiling. A floating corpse replica.

Girl 9, her eyes pecked out in Central Park.

Girl 10 zig-zagging her way from station to station.

And he thinks of his career. And how he is just trying to get things back on track.

How he is trying to make things happen for himself.

How easy it would be for someone to pin this all on January David . . .

Marquez pulls up outside the unknown building and locks his car, looking over his shoulder. He twists the key quietly in the lock, steps into the hallway and presses the door silently closed from the inside.

He checks the bedroom first, then the living room, the kitchen, the bathroom, all without saying a word. He paces quickly back into the lounge and calls her name. Once. Twice. Three times, shouting it this last time.

She's gone.

His girlfriend is gone.

He lost her.

He lost Phillipa Daniels.

Agent Marquez had Girl 11 and he let her go.

Part Four

Reveal

Girl 11

---*---

I left.
   I couldn't just stick around in that strange apartment where he wanted me to be, needed me to be, so that only he could find me. So that he had control of the entire situation.

I didn't even stay the night. I waited for an hour. He wasn't coming back for me. He had too much work to do. He needed to make too many things happen. I refuse to sit around waiting for something to happen to me. You think everyone in this city is scared to go too high in a tall building since *that* day? No. We live on. We don't tiptoe through life in fear. And I won't do that just because my surname happens to be shared with a balding British magician.

Besides, Ms David was at home. She would never leave Walter alone in her apartment. I was perfectly safe.

*

And now I am exactly where I am supposed to be. At work. At Ms David's. Looking after her beautiful son, Walter, instead of being cooped up in my boyfriend's secret lair.

I can't live like that.

It's just not me.

Walter has woken up from his morning nap. It is only thirty-five minutes but it really does revitalise his mood. Ms David had a routine when I first started to work for her but I have changed it. Walter is a different person now; he's growing and learning so I have adapted it slightly. She knows. She agrees. I run everything past her that involves her son. Mostly. She is an amazing and successful woman, she doesn't need to know every single detail. I respect her too much for that.

His diaper is dirty. That's what woke him initially. I clean him up and he sits on my lap for a while as I read the same book three times in a row. When he wriggles, I know he has had enough, he wants to get down. He wants to go into the playroom. He wants a drink. He's almost ready for lunch.

I know all his cues.

I'll really miss him.

He's a special boy.

Such kind eyes.

I would make the most of our next hour together if I knew. If it had crossed my mind that I would be the next to die. But I can't think that way. Nobody should live their life at the bidding of fate.

Plans change.

People make split-second decisions that turn order into chaos.

Chaos into order.

I continue with normality.

My routine.

I'll be fine.

January

———✦———

Thursday
MIDTOWN MANHATTAN, NEW YORK, 11:08 EST
London, 16:08 GMT

E ames is a liar.
    He told me that I should spend as much time with my wife as I can. He was insinuating that she would be the next on his pathetic list. That she would be the last girl to die in his sadistic homage to great illusion.

But I saw The Smiling Man.

It was a fleeting visit from my threatening, subconscious menace but he gave me enough information in that short while to deduce that the girl to die had to be a Daniels. Just by the mere fact that he was appearing to me was enough to relieve me of any doubt concerning Audrey's safety.

The Smiling Man never appeared to me when Audrey was taken last time.

He only reveals himself when someone is going to die.

Both times that Audrey was taken by Eames, The Smiling Man was absent. That is a pattern.

Audrey will live, I tell myself.

Audrey docs not dic.

*

As he took away my blindfold, I was immediately greeted by the smell of lemons. This transformed immediately into the aroma of waste, of rubbish, of mould and expiration. The Smiling Man placed one of his giant hands into his right trouser pocket. Before he could produce the contents, I went cold and awoke to a concerned federal agent in the driver's seat next to me and a ringing mobile phone with Paulson waiting at the other end.

So I know it is outside. I know that Paul Daniels uses a lemon in his Chop Cup trick. I know he works the crowd with the speed of his patter and his sleight of hand. I know that he fishes around in his trouser pocket, apparently moving a ball around by magic.

So it can't be Audrey that dies.

But I call her, anyway.

She's at work.

'I'm not sure that work is the best place to be right now,' I suggest. 'Take a half-day. Go home and wait. This will be over soon and things can go back to normal.' I hear myself saying the words and wondering just what *normal* means. Does Audrey think I am stating that I want things to be the way they once were? That's impossible now.

I just need to keep her safe.

See this thing out.

'What's going on, Jan?' she asks innocently, as though she doesn't know that another girl has died. As though she never picked her out from a list of candidates on her files. She put Eleanor Harbin in her new job. She agreed with Eames that the girl would have to be cut into three and displaced around New York.

But, sometimes, fact and fiction work as a team.

I explain the things that Agent Marquez and I have

found this morning. The things she already knows. She says *uh-huh* and *OK* and *mm-hmm* as though I am giving her instructions on how to work a new DVD player, like I am asking her to take notes.

'Audrey, are you listening to me?'

'Yes, Jan. Of course. You're worried, I get it, but you've said it yourself that you don't think I am in danger.'

'It's just a precaution.'

Because I couldn't protect you last time.

'You're close to catching this guy? You think you know who is doing this?' She suddenly sounds worried, more eager.

'Yes. I'm almost there,' I lie.

And she knows.

'Look, Jan. I've got to make a few calls, then I'll leave. I promise.'

'I can come and get you, I'm back at my hotel. Marquez is . . .'

Where is Marquez? He said he'd be back shortly. That I should get cleaned up. That was it. We don't have time to waste. Girl 11 will be dead in a few hours. She is the last one. The end of the psychotic masterpiece.

I know what Eames was trying to do. He mentioned *making her freedom disappear*. He was talking about liberty, the Statue of Liberty. He was referring to the David Copperfield trick where he apparently made the monument disappear in front of a live audience.

'Mirrors,' Murphy told me.

Mirrors.

When Eames said *turn her into a lemon*, he was citing the Paul Daniels illusion. The ball moves from his hand to his pocket to under a cup. It disappears and reappears and turns into a lemon. Eames wants me to think that he is still undecided. That he still has the power to choose whether the next victim will be Audrey or the as yet unknown Daniels girl.

I don't believe that he will choose my wife again. It is more important to him to finish this list than it is to gain another point over me.

That is why I am not worried for Audrey's safety.

Maybe I want her to be caught again. Punished.

Maybe I just want to rescue her.

'Marquez is following a lead.' I finish our conversation with another lie.

'I'll take a car if that would make you feel any better.'

'It would,' I lie again.

'OK. Well, I'll see you later, then. It'll be over soon.'

I picture her at work behind a grandiose desk, swivelling from side to side as we talk on the phone. And not once do I marry that image of her to the woman in the footage, dumping parts of a young girl's body on the street.

I still think The Smiling Man is informing me about Eames.

But he's not.

He's telling me when my wife is about to kill.

Audrey

—◆—

'How close are we at your end?'
This is how I open my next phone conversation.
I make the call as soon as January bids me farewell – that
awkward moment where I stopped myself from saying
'I love you'.

'A slight problem, Ms Silver.' He uses my maiden name
to keep things anonymous.

'I'm not paying you to hear about problems. You are
there to end this. Wrap it up.'

'The uncle confessed. It was unforeseen.'

'I don't want your excuses.' My tone is superior and
cold. 'What is your contingency?'

There is a silence.

I fill the void with a thought of Eames, locked away
in his windowless room, wanting me to finish this
off for him, to see it through. And I feel something for
him. I can't say what the emotion is. Love. Pity. Guilt.
Apathy.

'Well?' I prompt.

'Ms Silver, there are protocols to follow in this event. I assure you, our man on the inside is—'

I cut him off. 'Lean on him. Time is running out. This has to be over right now. This time tomorrow, I want to read of an arrest. I want to see a picture of *our man on the inside* beaming at this prestigious collar.' In my head, I make quotation marks with my fingers as I say *our man on the inside*.

'Is there a reason for this sudden urgency?' he questions. His tone is so unflustered that it aggravates me.

'The reason is because I said so. That's all you need to know. That is why I came to you. If you want the last instalment transferred—'

'Now, Ms Silver, there's no need to be rash. You want something to stick, you want this to end in a day, then it will be. I give you my word.'

As though that kind of decree holds any weight with me.

'Stick a foot on Murphy's neck. Leave it there if you think it will do the trick. This has been dragging on for a couple of years now. It ends tonight.' I am decisive and he is quiet.

I hang up the call before he has the opportunity to irritate me further with his composure.

I have to make sure that January cannot return to London. He has to be unable to go back to his old life. I want him to stay here. With me.

The only way that I can get everything I want is to make sure that Phillipa does not die. For this to all work, there can be no Girl 11.

The Lean

—✦—

Thursday
VIOLENT CRIME OFFICE, LONDON, 16:11 GMT
New York, 11:11 EST

The sponsor is less composed when the call ends.

'Fucking bitch.' He puffs out his cheeks with aggressive exhalation and shakes his head in pseudo despair.

He knows who she is. *Ms Silver* was hardly the toughest codename to crack, but he doesn't know why she would want this. Why she would want to ruin her husband's career after wrecking their marriage with her infidelity.

Looking into the case, he couldn't expose a reason for 'Ms Silver's' apparent scorn, apart from slight neglect on account of DI David's occupation.

But it is not, nor has it ever been, his place to ask such questions. He is paid, and paid handsomely, to do a job. And right now, he has been asked to step on Murphy's neck.

'Shit. What are you doing here?' Murphy jumps up out of January David's seat. His first thought was that it was him; that his boss was back.

'Calm down, Detective. This is important.' The sponsor, the man who walks in shadows and the corridors of power, has regained his composure.

348

'What if Markam . . .?'

'Don't worry about Chief Markam. There's nothing he can do to me, I assure you.'

'I wasn't thinking about you,' Murphy responds like an invertebrate.

'I told you that you have to make something stick. I've heard that you've let the uncle go . . .' He lets it hang in the air like a matador's red cape.

'How can you already know that?' Murphy speaks quietly but the question is neither under his breath nor directed at the sponsor.

The well-presented man takes a step towards January David's desk, the detective's sister still in the top drawer along with the bottle that holds his coping mechanism, and Murphy is caught in two minds: should he step away in fear and self-preservation or show some steel and stand his ground?

He takes a step back.

His neck further from the sponsor's foot.

'What is your next move, Detective Sergeant Murphy? Now that you've let the uncle go, what is your plan?' His tone is accusatory.

'To find out who took the girl. Get the guy that killed her.' Murphy has felt pushed around for the last few years. He makes outrageous claims and suggestions at times. He has ideas above his station. But he does want to solve the crime. He wants to put the right person behind bars.

The sponsor smirks.

'And how close do you think you are to finding the *real* perpetrator? A week? A year?'

'DS Paulson thinks he might have something on camera. We're waiting to see what he turns up.'

'You've got a day.'

'What?'

'A day, Detective. One more day to show us that you are the right man for this job, that you deserve the boost we can provide you with.' He pushes away from the desk and stands back.

'And then?'

'And then you're fucked. You're on your own. I never existed. And you won't want to try to suggest that I ever did. Because I don't.'

Murphy pleads pathetically, uttering reminders of all the underhanded missions he has been tasked with. Manipulating evidence, accusing his boss of murder, ignoring direct orders and leaking stories to the press.

'I'm working quickly. There are procedures in place that I have to abide by.'

'I can cut through the red tape. Just get me someone to hang this on in the next twenty-four hours or less.'

'Even if they're not guilty.'

The sponsor wants to say yes. He wants to say that he just doesn't care. That sometimes good people die and bad people get away with it. Everything balances out in the end.

'I want to hear that you've got someone in the next day or sooner. That is all I am saying.'

And he starts to walk out, his foot never getting close to Murphy's neck. He has his own way of conducting business and he has always found it more productive than physical violence.

'So I should contact you somehow? When I have something.' Then Murphy repeats himself for effect, accentuating the first word to feign his own confidence. '*When* I have something.' His expression is caught somewhere between a smile and pure worry.

The sponsor stops at the door and turns back.

'You can't contact me, Detective. And you don't need to. I'll know. This will be the last time we speak. Whether you are successful or you fail in this task. The only time you will hear from me again will be if you decide to believe that I exist, if you ever talk about me.' The sponsor looks into Murphy's eyes to ensure his message has registered.

He sees the same expression he's seen on the faces of tens of men he has delivered the same speech to before.

'Goodbye, Detective Murphy. I do hope we never speak again.' He delivers this last line pleasantly, in the same way he would thank someone for hosting a dinner.

And then he is gone.

And Acting Detective Inspector Murphy is left in the clutter of the violent crime office. Alone. The amber from a streetlight forming a zebra-crossing on the stained carpet through the partly closed blinds. He sits back down in the seat he does not deserve to grace, and he contemplates the meaning of success. And the likelihood of failure.

Audrey

—◆—

Thursday
AU RECRUITMENT OFFICES, MANHATTAN,
NEW YORK, 11:17 EST
London, 16:17 GMT

'Carey, can you get me a coffee and a jug of ice-cold water, please?'

'Sure thing, Ms David.'

I remove my finger from the intercom as my enthusiastic PA trots off to fulfil my request for refreshments.

The CNN website is already reporting the story of Eleanor Harbin, and Agent Marquez has managed to feature himself in many of the photographs. Making things happen. I wish *our man on the inside* back in London had the same level of motivation to back up his desire.

Because Girl 10 was cut up into pieces, the authorities, the reporters, the alarmed public, are all guessing what to expect of Girl 11. They hear the words *Chop Cup* and immediately think of another body broken down to bite-size.

That's not what we had in mind.

It's not how I planned it.

That's not Eames.

When Carey returns with my black Americano, I am

352

flicking through résumés of candidates to fill the position now left open by the unfortunately named Miss Harbin.

I'm detached when I should be feeling afraid.

'Thanks, Carey. I'll be taking a half-day today.'

'Are you feeling OK?' he asks, genuinely concerned.

'Yes, yes. I'm fine. I'm just going to catch up on a few things at home. I'm still contactable on my mobile phone should anything come up.'

'So, just hold off all your calls until tomorrow?'

'Yes. I'll be back in the morning, I just have a few things to get sorted before the weekend. Patch it through to me if you think it's important.' I pat a reassuring hand on his shoulder as if telling him that I trust him to hold fort in my absence. That's all he needs.

I drink an entire glass of the iced water in one go, then take a sip of the black coffee, which would be too hot had I not just temporarily numbed the inside of my mouth.

And I call Phillipa.

I tell her I will be home for lunch and she acknowledges in her usual, perfect, pretty manner. She informs me that Walter will be thrilled.

'I just have a few things to finish up here and then I'll catch a cab back.'

'You want to speak to Walter?'

'No, no. It's fine. I won't be long. See you around twelve-ish.'

And I hang up on Girl 11, knowing that this can all end if she lives. That it will mean Eames is defeated, I am free from his spell. It's over. I win. I can be with January.

When all it will take to end this nightmare, this game of one-upmanship, this pestiferous plan to obtain all the things I've ever wanted, is to let a beautiful and demure being continue with her simple life, when all I have to do is let it go. Well, that's just not me.

I'm not a failure.

I don't quit.

When I return to my apartment, my son sleeping peacefully on the sofa, the television turned to a hush though the cartoons still play, I will know what to do. What is necessary.

I will want to kill Phillipa Daniels.

The Cheap Seats

—◆—

Thursday
**LONDON ZOO, REGENT'S PARK, LONDON,
16:24 GMT**
New York, 11:24 EST

Paulson had paced down the exit path towards an intimidated young woman apparently standing guard, a ring in her nose and several studs running up her ears.

'I need to come in.' He flashed his badge and the girl's eyes widened in recognition. Paulson wasn't even out of breath. His weight was down, his fitness up.

'Er, OK, officer.' She stepped aside and gestured with a hand to push through the barrier.

'Where do I go for the park keeper?'

'I'm sorry?'

'The park keeper. A supervisor. Someone in charge of this place.' He was getting impatient. All the time looking over towards the site that the camera was pointing at.

The girl radioed in her query.

And now Paulson is here, in a room full of TFT monitors, some split into four sections, each showing a different area of the zoo. Apparently, it is difficult to find the person in charge but a member of the security team

355

– Don, aged forty-two, just over six feet tall, grade-one horse-shoe of blond stubble pinching his head, a wiry strength, never got into the police – arrived within a minute to greet him and bring him to the hub.

'What date and time do you need? We store everything digitally on our servers and keep the video for three weeks. As long as it wasn't longer ago than that, we'll have what you're looking for.'

He sits down at one of the terminals and taps at a computer. Paulson glances around the room and thinks of his own set-up at home. He imagines himself playing forty games of poker at once; he's starting to understand what real pressure feels like.

'The coroner has her death down as last Wednesday.'

There is a discomfort in the room and Paulson realises that he hasn't explained what he is looking for.

'This about that little girl?' Don asks, his toughness melting away with sympathy.

'That's right.'

'Well, let's find this fucker, then.'

He clicks and drags and opens files, and, eventually, a high-definition image of the gap between the trees that overlooks the penguin enclosure fills the centre screen. Paulson can't bear to sit down, he's too restless. This has to be it.

'You want the cheap seats camera, right?'

'Huh?'

'We get people watching the show from back there for nothing. Just a name we give it. Restricted view.'

Paulson nods, though he has no time for banter between distant colleagues.

Law enforcement, twice removed.

Don fixates on the monitor and starts to roll a ball in

356

his right hand. It looks like an oversized mouse but the ball rotates and the video corresponds with the gestures, moving forwards and rewinding depending on the speed of Don's hand movement.

Each time a figure stops to overlook the penguin pool, Don stops scrolling. And Paulson says, 'No.' So Don scrolls some more.

'This guy?'

'No.'

'This couple?'

'Nnnno.'

He swipes across the ball a little too fast.

'Wait, wait, wait. Go back. Back!' Paulson raises his voice. 'There.'

On the screen he sees a man, overweight, his hair thinning but parted to one side. He watches the penguins, then he bends down out of shot for a few moments before reappearing with someone else. A girl. In his arms. Paulson recognises her face immediately. It is the dead Aria Sky.

He almost throws up, whether through the relief or the magnitude of the discovery or the horror of this deceased young girl being taken to a free show at the zoo. Her eyes are shut and she is being hugged by a man who believes them to be friends.

'Can you zoom in on that guy?'

'It's HD so there won't be much loss in quality.' Don flicks a wrist and presses a few buttons on the keyboard, proud of his statement.

You sick fuck. I've got you now.

'Can you print that off and—'

'Way ahead of you, brother.' Don feels awkward using that term; he never says it. He's nervous. His job suddenly means something to someone.

A printer whirrs.

'I can't send you the footage because the file will be too large but it is burning to a disc as we speak. Can you wait ninety seconds?'

Paulson produces a mobile phone from his inside jacket pocket, hits a speed-dial number and shows Don his right thumb.

'Murph. I need some details.'

Paulson explains what he has found in the most succinct way he can think of. Murphy wants to get the image to the press immediately. Like always, engaging his mouth before his mind.

'I don't even want the family to know yet. Let's not get anyone skipping town, eh? Find Alan Barber. He might know this guy. We don't want the family filled with vengeance or hope or fear: nothing good can come of any of those emotions.'

Murphy agrees and tacitly surrenders the lead role in this case.

For now.

Paulson puts the phone away and takes the still-hot disc from Don, thanking him for his help, all the time knowing that he should be thanking Eames.

Still unaware that he has become part of the trick.

Girl 11

Walter looks adorable.

His left cheek is slightly squashed against the sofa cushion, pushing his face into a half-smile. He takes long, lung-filling breaths in through his nose and back out the way it came. He is asleep. It has only been a minute or so but already his eyes seem to be moving behind their lids as his little imagination conjures up stories he won't be able to articulate.

I stare at him for a moment and smile at his innocence, his unknowing of the world in which he finds himself learning something new every day. The biggest problems he has to face are fatigue and hunger. There are so many complications ahead for him that he has no control over. I wish things could be different for him.

In the fight between nature and nurture, there is only ever one winner.

I turn down the television, despite his sleeping through the racket of exaggerated sound effects and caricature

359

voices. It won't be nice for him to wake up to that. He's such a sensitive boy.

I tiptoe into the kitchen and tidy away the mess I made preparing a snack for him before his nap. I want the place to be spotless when Audrey gets back. So that she knows I have everything under control. So that she can trust me.

I don't think she liked my choice of hair colour.

I'm not sure I'm a fan either.

I wipe the crumbs from the work surface with a cloth into my cupped hand and then brush them into the sink before washing my hands.

She will be home in around twelve or fifteen minutes. That gives me just enough time to go to the bathroom, straighten out my clothes and hair, touch up my make-up, and look presentable for her return. So that she knows she picked the right person for this job. I want her to know that I care about myself, about her and Walter.

I drop seven scoops of Blue Mountain Java into a cafetière and fill it with hot water. It needs four minutes to steep, allowing the flavour of the coffee to infuse adequately.

I check on Walter one last time and return to the kitchen with my mobile phone.

'Hi. Police, please. Yes. Thanks.' I wait.

A woman answers and asks me about the nature of my call.

'I'd like to report something. There's an upturned trash can on Union Square.' I pause but the woman at the other end is also waiting.

So I continue.

'I think there's a dead body inside.'

I hang up the phone, plunge the coffee and stare at the front door until it opens.

360

The Drunk

Thursday
CAMDEN, LONDON, 16:52 GMT
New York, 11:52 EST

Alan Barber is not important to Aria Sky's life story, not as a person, a personality; it is only his actions that carry significance.

He only knew her in death.

And he can help put her to rest.

Alan is drunk already. It is before five o'clock and his trick to take glasses of gin from alternating brands is not fooling anyone. This is the tenth time he has been in here since he found Aria in the ground next to the locked public toilet. It is just one week since he pissed all over her.

When Paulson and Murphy enter the bar, he is regaling the barman with the story that has defined the most recent chapter of his life.

He looks sad.

Drunk and sad.

'I wish we'd never followed that girl, you know?' he drools at the bartender. 'It was (unimportant friend's) idea. But, then, if we hadn't gone that way . . . maybe it was lucky in the end. You think it was lucky? I don't feel lucky.'

The man behind the bar continues to wipe surfaces, unpack clean glasses from the dishwasher, load the dirty ones and cut the segments of citrus fruits for the expected rush over the next hour as discontented workers spill out of their offices.

Alan Barber is talking to himself out loud.

He feels alone, with only the memory of Aria's piss-drenched foot for company hanging over his head like the gin bottle of Damocles.

'Mr Barber.' Paulson rests a soft hand on Alan Barber's back as he approaches the bar with Murphy in tow.

'Detective.' Alan Barber tries to stand and shake Paulson's hand.

'No need to get up.' Paulson can see he is unstable on his feet.

'I've told you everything I know, officer. I really have. I've been going over and over it in my head since it happened and there is nothing new.' He looks at the bartender then shoots a pointed finger at his glass and nods slightly. Another gin arrives. 'Would you like a drink, detectives?'

'No thanks, Alan.' Paulson uses informality to bring the possible witness to ease, to make him feel he has a friend. Alan Barber needs a friend right now. 'I just want to show you a photograph and you tell me if you know this man or have ever seen him before, OK?'

'OK.'

'Your statement was fine. I don't want to go over it again. I just want to know whether you have ever seen this person before.'

Paulson slides the printout across the bar, avoiding the rings of condensation from Alan's previous tumblers of alcohol. And he looks at Murphy in anticipation.

Murphy takes a breath and then holds it. Time has been moving faster for him since his talk with the sponsor.

'I've seen him.'

'You've seen him?' Paulson stands from his barstool. He looks at Murphy once more and thinks he smiles but his face is all wide eyes and nothing else.

'Yeah. A few times.'

'Where?'

'About. Shops. The street. He's local. Doesn't drink in here all the time but I have seen him.' Alan lifts the sheet of paper, turning it towards the bartender.

'Oh yeah,' the bartender chimes in, 'he comes in here. Not a regular. I don't know him by name like Alan here.' Alan Barber smiles like it is something to be proud of. 'But I've definitely seen him. What's he done?'

'Killed a bunch of kids.' Murphy finally speaks and his aim is to shock.

'This is the guy?'

'We believe so, yes.' Paulson takes the reins again.

'When was the last time you saw him in here?' Murphy jumps back in, still reeling from the success of his interrogation of Aria's uncle. He looks at Alan then the barman, then back once again to Alan.

'I'm not keeping tabs but it must have been some time in the last week,' concludes the barman, whose name is irrelevant.

'He was here that night.' Alan Barber speaks to his own lap.

'That night?'

'The night I, er, *found* the girl in the park. He was in the toilet at the same time as me. At the urinal.'

'Fucking hell, Barber. How many cases could we crack just from you taking a piss?' Murphy is on edge. Too much is riding on this and his best hope of success seems to lie in the bladder of a drunk.

Paulson signals for Murphy to back off.

'Thanks again for your help, Alan.' Paulson plays the friend again.

'Really? I helped?'

'Sure did.' Paulson hands a ten-pound note across to the barman. 'Another drink for my friend here and one for yourself.' Then he urges Murphy outside.

'How has that drunk helped in any way?' Murphy confronts Paulson.

And Paulson explains.

From the small amount of information that Alan Barber offered, much can be extrapolated. The killer is local. He frequents the same pub but clearly not often enough to be known: this is probably intentional. There will be another handful of bars in the area where people could say the same thing.

He was here the night after he killed Aria Sky. He remained within walking distance of the body, he showed his face, he got out. Either he is complacent after all this time and believes he cannot be caught or he wants to be caught. He wants to stop. Both are equally terrifying.

Alan Barber said that he knew the man from the streets. He is of this borough, which means that he may be recognisable to others who live in this particularly close-knit London community.

'I'd go *all in* on the Skys knowing exactly who he is,' Paulson states with the certainty of a top poker player. 'Let's get Higgs to watch this place in case the suspect shows his face again. And we can take a trip to see Aria's mother.'

Eames

——◆——

When someone, usually a woman, sends a letter to a murderer or rapist and hopes they will respond to the apparent kindness and altruism, it's me they wish to hear from.

They are wasting their hope.

When they say that they are just looking for a pen pal yet enclose a picture of themselves in a bikini or low-cut top, it is not me they are fooling.

I am not lonely.

I would like to see a woman, to feel her skin against mine, to gorge on the flesh of her breasts and bury myself between her legs. We all need to fuck. But sex is secondary. I just need to kill.

They call these people hybristophiliacs.

Because they love their labels.

Shhhh. It's not really a hospital.

I received sacks full of these letters when I was first incarcerated in this fake health centre, this masquerading clinic. I read them all, of course. Some were clearly well

365

meaning. Others, the yearning to escape, to live in a relationship where the man is attentive and writes letters of love, odes to the lady in question; they want to reside in that state of perpetual courtship, the initial throes of a relationship.

And I'm the one who is locked away . . .

I read them all because I was waiting for Audrey. We had agreed beforehand that she would contact me in this way and I would have to respond to a great deal of the letters to keep hers hidden within the curls and slants of handwriting. It was always the plan to finish the list.

Her plan.

My plan.

Our plan.

But then I received a letter telling me that I was special, that even though I did those things, though I strung a woman up with invisible wires or asphyxiated a young lady with a mouthful of cigarettes or cut a man's dick off and let him bleed to death inside a locked chest, though I did all these things that I have never denied, she somehow *knows* that I would never hurt her. That what we have together is significant.

When you claim in your letter that this is the first time you have written to a serial killer, to me, this is not the first time you have tried this. You have sent this to many of us.

Imagine how wrong you'll be when I'm drawing the blade of a knife across your throat. Think how appealing a dating website will seem when you realise there is no relationship, that you mean nothing to me. That you are this toenail or my bed sheet or the guard outside my room.

You are the eleven of spades.

You are a piece of card in a deck of fifty-one other cards. You are my alibi and my motivation.

These women are like the bored wives and daughters I used to screw in Hampstead. But they are worse. They are not looking for the taste of something different; this is not a moment of release.

They tell me that they empathise with the horrible things I did. They want to live out their fantasies through me, to experience the sensation of killing indirectly. To kill without having to actually kill.

They want to *be* Eames more than they want to be *with* Eames.

And I respond to all of them, putting another Eames in another town or county or country. Passive soldiers wanting to be seduced and manipulated.

Imagine how naive you are to believe that you are the only woman I lie to.

Phillipa was different.

I saw her potential in the same way that I noticed Audrey's. Both are beautiful and proactive. Both with an urge that lies dormant within. Both are fine prospects for transforming passivity into aggressiveness.

They would kill for me. In my name. Not to provide any doubt to my case. Not to thwart the attempts of forensic teams looking for a DNA match; they know it is not physically me: I am here, in my cage. Neither is it to look like a copycat murderer.

That's not me.

That's not Eames.

They are my arms and my hands. They continue my legacy. They spread the mythology. They make me into a movement. I am immortal.

I cannot love either of them more than the other because I cannot love them. In the same way that I can feel no hatred.

They are gum on my shoe.

They are the frame of a door.

They are tree bark.

One of them will die today.

And I do not care which of them will perish.

Detective Inspector January David, you still don't get it, do you?

January

---•---

T hen Marquez is banging on my door and shouting my surname.

'Where have you been?'

He doesn't answer.

'Come with me now. There's another body.'

'What? Already? That can't be . . .'

I'm shocked that it happened so quickly. Deflated that I didn't get there on time. Irritated that Eames managed to finish his opus. But relieved that it can't be Audrey.

'Leave your fucking jacket, Detective,' he barks, raising his voice in frustration, 'we've got to get down there.'

'It has my key-card and phone inside the pocket,' I justify, stepping back in the room for just a moment to pick it up.

Marquez seems particularly nervy about this.

Like he knows what to expect.

The German couple step out of the lift.

'*Guten tag,*' I greet, trying to make up for my previous

369

inability to communicate. They smile courteously and Marquez jumps into the lift and hits the button for the ground floor repeatedly, only ceasing when the doors close and we are alone.

'There's been an anonymous call about a body in an upturned trash can at Union Square.'

'OK. Is there a body?'

'The call has only just come in. That's where we're going now.'

'Where have you been?' I ask again.

And he ignores again.

'Sounds a lot like that Chop Cup trick, doesn't it?'

'Yes. I suppose.' I can tell that he is getting aggravated by my composure.

'You suppose?'

'Well, of course it fits in with the idea of producing an item from underneath an upturned cup, and the upturned bin, sorry, trash can, will certainly provide the same aesthetic . . .'

'But?'

'But it doesn't really fit in with the theatricality of the other scenes or the performance aspect of the trick itself. Maybe there was a time constraint. Perhaps Eames' partner is getting lazy or is not as thorough.'

We hit the ground floor.

'Well, get in the car and we'll take a look for ourselves.'

We arrive at Union Square.

The area has been closed down but a crowd has formed and Marquez informs me that we're lucky it's a Thursday because the farmers' market doesn't operate today.

Then he jibes, 'Theatrical enough for you, Detective?'

I roll my eyes.

There are bins throughout the square but one does sit on the opposite edge to where we stand and it has been turned upside down.

Nobody has approached it. Local law enforcement are present and try to tell Marquez that he should wait for the bomb squad but Marquez is solely focused on the large black receptacle everyone is frightened of and intrigued by.

He walks over, stands next to the can for a few seconds, takes a deep breath and prays that his girlfriend is not underneath.

She's not.

Of course.

Nobody is.

The Anomaly

———◆———

It deserved more attention.

At twenty-six years of age, living and working in London, Canary Wharf, zone two, Girl 5 sat happily within the demographic of an Eames victim.

Almost.

Girl 5 was Richard Pendragon.

He was young and hard working and earning a healthy wage in the financial sector. And it only took one evening of too many drinks combined with a surreptitious drugging to find himself waking up contorted in the complete darkness of a locked chest. Very little air, and even less room to move. The hessian of the sack he was tied up in was syrupy and stained with the blood from the area where his penis was once attached. He didn't even feel the pain, at first.

He went to work one day as Richard Pendragon.

And returned the next, dead, as Girl 5.

Nothing helps highlight a pattern more than the one thing that does not fully tessellate with the sequence.

The anomaly was never properly addressed.

Audrey made sure of that.

The sponsor was given his instructions and the orders were passed on to Murphy. He accused January David of committing these crimes. He arrested his superior on suspicion of murder. He was trapped now. He was *in*. No turning back.

Then Girl 6 was found, speared through the gut, apparently levitating in her garage.

And Richard Pendragon became old news.

Forgotten.

Eames has not forgotten him.

He lies in discomfort on his too-thin mattress, staring at the perfect white of the ceiling, and plays a re-run in his head of the kill hidden in the middle of the other women in this sequence.

A tap at the glass jolts him from his reverie. The face through the window is that of his apparently favourite guard. He has food for Eames. Something grey and stodgy and bland, with boiled, too-soft vegetables.

The door opens slightly and Eames sits up, pushing himself backwards, away from the door so as to appear less threatening.

The giant, gullible dolt enters and grins back at Eames.

But Eames is not smiling *at* the guard, he is looking through him. He is still daydreaming about Richard, about Girl 5. He is laughing at inadequacy. How the anomaly of Mr Pendragon is of the greatest significance if only January David would look back rather than forwards all the time.

He scoffs at the detective in his mind for pining over Audrey for the last two years. For not knowing who she really is. What she has done. What she is doing.

And he pities him for dismissing Richard Pendragon so easily when his death was the greatest clue of all. When Girl 5 would tell him exactly why Eames is doing all of this.

January

—◆—

Thursday
UNION SQUARE, MANHATTAN, NEW YORK, 12:01 EST
London, 17:01 GMT

Marquez should look confused.
  The trash can is empty.
But all I see is relief.

'Expecting somebody?' I inquire brashly. The crowd is dissipating with the perplexed expression I expected from the federal agent. They were hoping to witness death.

'I'm sorry?'

'You look relieved. Like you were expecting someone you knew to be under there. I know that look. I've given that look.'

'If anything, I'm relieved that there is not another corpse on the list,' he offers, beating a lie-detector test but not my own radar for deception.

'I'd have thought you'd be more shocked.'

'What? That there's nobody under here? Prank call. Kids cashing in on the spectacle of the case, no doubt.'

'You're wrong,' I state. I thought about easing in with, *I'm not so sure about that*, but we don't have time.

Marquez screws up his dark eyes at me. He's battling to retain some composure after being called out on his blatant solace that Phillipa was not crammed underneath the giant thimble that he doesn't want to rock me too much.

'This is part of the trick.'

'Part of the trick?'

'Chop Cup, Agent Marquez. Lifting the cup to realise that the ball is no longer there, that it is, in fact, in the magician's pocket.'

'So, we need to find where the magician's pocket is?'

'Maybe. Or maybe the ball was never in the pocket.'

'You're not making any sense, Detective David.'

'Who did you expect to find in there?'

He doesn't answer.

'Who did you think had died, Agent Marquez?' I raise my voice enough that some of the crowd who have turned away, disappointed, are now looking back over their shoulders.

'Not here, David.'

'Why are you not on to the phone company to get the number that called this in?'

'Not here.' His own voice gains volume.

I wait. With so much illusion and misdirection and subterfuge, I need to find something true.

'Come with me.' He walks back across the square and I follow closely.

So that he can tell me he has been withholding information.

He can explain just how much he has fucked this up.

And, while we waste more time talking about things that should have been known from the start, the last girl will be killed.

Audrey

❦

Thursday
**UPPER EAST SIDE, MANHATTAN, NEW YORK,
12:11 EST**
London, 17:11 GMT

I tip the driver twenty per cent.
     Fifteen per cent is average but I add on a little more because he will expect that based on my address. Giving too little or too much would make me a memorable fare, and I don't want that.

I want to be forgotten.

Forgiven.

The stocky Mexican security guard smiles broadly, his bright teeth poking out from under a full moustache. He welcomes me back, calls me by my name and asks how I am feeling today.

'Fine. Thanks. Just taking some time off to spend with Walter, you know?' I lie.

'Oh, yes, Ms David. I know very well. I have four girls of my own.'

He laughs as though we have shared a joke that nobody would understand without being a parent. I reciprocate the best that I can but I can only muster fakery and continue my walk to the lift.

I turn the key for the top floor and the music fades into white noise as I think about my son. What possible chance does he have with the two people that combined to bring him life? Have we already mapped out his destiny? Will January make it any better? What about Phillipa? What difference does she make?

I push through the front door of the apartment, immediately turning to face it so that I can shift the two bolt-locks across and place the chain in its holder. This has become habit since the killings. This is my new routine.

When I turn around, Phillipa is in the kitchen waiting for me, with her faultless smile and smooth skin and newly darkened hair. She looks the way I wish I'd looked ten years ago. Better than I looked.

She is a constant reminder of my failures.

'Walter's asleep on the sofa,' she whispers, wide-eyed and as enthusiastic as ever.

She holds up a mug of fresh coffee and the heat rises, forming beautiful wisps of vapour that blur her features temporarily.

I'll have to kill her.

Girl 11

—◆—

I've done everything perfectly, everything that I am supposed to do.

I have fed Walter, played with him, shown him affection and taken the time to help him grow. I've read him books and used games to develop his dexterity. He's worn out and satisfied and fast asleep for Audrey's return.

She locked the door as she entered. It has become quite a habit with her since the girls started dying. I have to unbolt them again every time I leave and I hear her shift them back to a locked position before I even enter the lift.

She seems scared or paranoid that somebody is going to get in.

That she is being targeted.

Like before.

Audrey looks at me gratefully as I hold up a fresh coffee for her. She smiles with her amazing heart-shaped mouth.

I grin through my fatigue. It has been a long, tiring night and morning. And I have done everything perfectly. Everything I am supposed to do.

I left Marquez's apartment for the sanctity of my own home. He's sweet enough but he's really only there to serve a purpose now. It was my way of telling him it's over.

I dyed my hair darker; there are still stains in my bathtub, but I look more like her now. Not in person. I'm much younger, my body is tighter, more toned. But on a camera, from the side, from behind, I look enough like her to cast doubt and suspicion. Enough that my idiot ex-boyfriend or her inadequate ex-husband might suspect that she was visiting different police stations across the city this morning to dump parts of El's body. I had to use the same model of pushchair that she owns, and it's not cheap.

Part of me thinks that I should throw the hot coffee into her face.

Eames told me that I should just drug it. 'She trusts you now,' he said.

I look down at the drawer by my waist. I know there is a knife in there. I could use it. That would be quicker but ultimately messier.

That's not my plan.

Audrey leaves her coffee on the side and exaggerates a tiptoe over to the doorway of the living area to see Walter sleeping. As she gazes in at him, his back lifting slightly with every quiet breath, I move over behind her, the scarf I took back from Eleanor wrapped around my hands, and I loop it over her head, tightening it around her neck, pulling her backwards on to the floor.

I thought it would be somewhat poetic to use the scarf as a weapon.

I whisper a growl in her ear. 'I know who you are.'
She chokes. 'But he is mine.'

And I put my final ounce of strength into squeezing
the last life out of her.

Girl 4.

Girl 7.

Girl 11.

The Mistake

—◆—

M arquez comes clean.
About everything.

He explains that he was a young and bright prospect at the agency. There was praise from his first week at Quantico and it continued throughout training into the line of duty. He was being fast-tracked to the top.

Then he made a mistake that cost him dearly, in more ways than one. He fell for a witness in a big case. He was assigned on protection detail. It wasn't the kind of job he signed up for but it required a level of constant focus that he had clearly displayed. But he got too involved.

'You know, you're with one person all day every day over a period of time. It can get intense.' He tries to justify himself to January David just as he has been trying to do with everyone since it happened.

Since he lost his focus.

And she died.

She was killed.

'So, I'm drinking a lot more and this woman approaches me in a bar I go to when I'm in town and I can't believe it. I mean, she is gorgeous. Better than I deserve. But she's interested in me and she doesn't freak out when I tell her what I do.'

'You told her you worked for the FBI.'

'I've been fucking things up a lot, in case you haven't noticed.'

January nods and takes a sip of whisky from the double-measure the barman placed in front of him.

'Anyway, you tell me that the next girl has the surname Daniels and I freaked out. I didn't want it to happen again. So I kept her a secret and I thought I'd put her somewhere safe. She isn't answering her phone to me and I don't know where she is.'

'So you thought she'd be underneath the—'

'Yes. I mean, fuck, David, I am focused on this case. I need this case. Crack this and it will go a long way to redeeming my screw-up. You know?'

'Sure,' January agrees, not averse to the occasional procedural faux pas himself.

'It's the reason I brought you in.'

'To use me for your own gain,' January quips.

'Yes. I suppose.' He looks beaten up.

The truth of Marquez's statement sways January David. It gives him no reason to doubt anything that has been said in the bar. There is no profit in deceit at this point.

'You're worried. You haven't spoken to her all day. I get that. But you know her. You know about her. You're the FBI. You must have enough information and resources to locate her.'

'I do, but this case . . .'

January knows all too well how easy it is to choose work over the commitment that comes with a personal relationship.

'Who is she, Agent Marquez?'

'You know her.'

'Who is she, Agent Marquez?' January David leans forward on his barstool hoping he is not about to hear the name he is thinking.

'It's Phillipa. Your wife's nanny.'

'You fucking idiot.' January slams his empty glass down on the bar. He thinks about the CCTV footage and he doesn't think of Audrey like Eames had planned. He thinks of Phillipa Daniels.

'I know where she is,' he adds.

And as he speaks, his heart and stomach swap places.

He let it happen again.

Audrey has been captured.

And this time she will die.

Audrey

She whispers in my ear.
He's mine.

And I hear Eames. He's telling me that my son will no longer be with me. That he is coming to reclaim what is rightfully his. I think like Eames now. I know what he wants, what he needs.

I am right about Eames, but that is not what Phillipa meant when she said those words. She was talking about the prisoner in the near-empty room with the small glass window. She was talking about the killer she somehow empathises with. She thinks that he loves her, that he would never harm her the way that he has hurt all the other women.

Now she is killing for him.

She thinks she can make me Girl 11.

But I don't know this. I can't consider the intricacies of their affair, how it came to be, how it developed, how I was used, how she was used, because I have a scarf

385

around my neck, choking the life out of me. Cutting off my airways. Starving my brain of oxygen.

I have no time or opportunity to reason with her, to tell her that Eames does not love her, that he is incapable of that emotion. I cannot explain to her that we can both win, both get away with the terrible things we have done in the name of love and success.

If she does not kill me and I do not kill her, Eames will lose. He will not be able to claim Girl 11 and he will not complete his trick, his masterpiece. He will be remembered as sadistic and psychotic, and worse than that, a failure.

But this cannot happen now.

Because I am being strangled. She has already started this.

And I mistakenly believe that she is trying to take my child from me.

He sleeps through the commotion.

I sense the noose slacken just a touch. Phillipa is weary. She has cut a body up this morning, wrapped it in plastic and dropped it off in a zig-zag across the city.

I know that.

It is the same plan I formulated with Eames.

A moment of slack is all I need. It is all a mother being threatened with the abduction of her child requires. I push upwards, my feet flat on the floor, one between Phillipa's legs, and I arch my back violently, the top of my head crashing into her chin.

It hurts us both but she releases the scarf a little more.

We are almost on even terms.

I roll on to my side and try to crawl away, but she still has hold of me by my neck. She screams something incoherent as she yanks me to the floor, my hip crashing against the marble that I just had to have in here.

I swing an arm wildly and it catches her in the face, allowing me to shuffle forward another couple of feet. But she does not let go. She holds a handful of material in each hand like a horse's reins, trying desperately to reel me back in.

She should have listened to Eames.

She should have poisoned me. It's what I would have done to her.

It is not about *how* the victim dies, it is the theatre, the staging.

Phillipa whips the scarf and my face hurtles towards the floor this time, but I instinctively put my hands down in front of my nose and cushion the fall.

Pulling in the opposite direction to someone who is attached to your neck is not the answer. I realise I am getting nowhere. January used to say that *sometimes the best form of defence is attack*. Something must have sunk in because I launch myself in Phillipa's direction, my arms like windmills, trying to make contact with any part of her.

She never lets go. And I take some hits myself but eventually I grab a clump of her artificially brunette hair and yank her head to the floor. I grip it tighter and force it back to the marble with my entire weight falling down on top of her.

She's hurt but she won't let go.

I hope I have dislodged some of those pretty white teeth.

Still with the thought that she wants to separate me from my son, I pull her across the floor to the kitchen area. She tightens my noose a little but not enough that I feel the need to gasp for air.

I open the drawer with my left hand, her hair still in my right, blood falling from her nose and mouth, and I pull her against me tightly, her back to my breast. She breathes heavily. I have a chance here. I could attempt some rationality amid this chaos, tell her that nobody needs to know what we have done. That he doesn't have to win.

It's then I realise he already has.

I swipe the sharp blade across her throat then jab the sharp point in and out six times for good measure. I swear I hear the blood bubble and pop, but she goes limp fairly quickly.

I let go and she falls.

It's over.

I sit back on my heels and take a breath. But, as I look up, Walter is standing at the entrance to the kitchen, silently observing the brutality of the aftermath.

He doesn't say a word.

The kid never had a chance with his current mixture of genes, and now, I've directly ruined him. It's too late.

I take the mobile phone which looks like Phillipa's, from the kitchen counter, and I dial 911.

'Hello? Yes. Police please. I think there's a dead body in an upturned trash can in Union Square.'

The Tale

———✦———

'I hope you know what you're doing here,' Murphy warns Paulson.

'Just follow my lead. Accept everything.' He sounds like January David.

Paulson looks down at the printed picture of the filthy predator and he wants to throw up. He wants to take him in with a smashed-up face and broken ribs and tell Chief Markam that *he must have fallen*. He wants Markam to give him the look that says *I know you hit him, but it's all right*.

Murphy is anxious. He wants the collar. But he knows that he won't be the one to hang if Paulson fucks it up.

They park the car several houses down the street so that the Skys don't know what they are driving; it's an unmarked vehicle. Paulson walks at the same pace as Murphy without sounding out of breath. Murphy considers complimenting his partner on his discipline in getting healthy, but figures that it will not be accepted as genuine so opts for silence instead.

'Here we go.' Murphy knocks on the door then hits

389

the bell. He sees the mottled silhouette of a man. Aria's mother is to the right in the kitchen where she let her brother-in-law screw her from behind while her only daughter was kidnapped and killed.

'Oh, what the fuck do you want now, Detective?' the uncle blasts. 'We've told you everything we know.' He's speaking deliberately loudly so that the rest of the family are aware of the police presence at the door. Then he lowers the volume and focuses solely on the bloodshot eyes of Acting Detective Inspector Murphy. 'And don't think I don't know that you fucking entrapped me with that statement. We're grieving, you sack of shit.'

Paulson steps a hefty leg between the two men.

'Is Mrs Sky at home? We have something she needs to see.'

'You've got him?' His eyes widen with intent.

'We have something, yes. Is she around?'

'I'll get her.'

The uncle shuts the door on the two officers and returns a minute later with Aria's mother and the cuckolded brother.

'What now, Detectives?' She sounds exhausted in every sense of her being.

All cried-out.

'Do you know this man, Mrs Sky? Mr Sky?' Paulson shows the black-and-white photo taken from the zoo.

'Well, it looks a bit like—' The mother starts to speak. The father cowers in the background as he always seems to do.

Then he speaks up, interrupting his wife.

'No. We don't know who he is. What is this all about?' Everyone is taken aback by his sudden authority.

Paulson explains that the picture was taken from some

CCTV footage after the time that Aria was taken. He goes on to explain that they have every reason to believe that he may be the man to have taken their daughter. He then lies, stating that it is protocol to speak directly with the family first as these crimes are often committed by a family member or somebody close to the victim's family.

'Well, we don't know who it is,' the father reiterates, his wife leaning her weight against the door in anticipation of her closure on this matter.

'OK, Mr Sky, Mrs Sky. Thanks for your help. Sit tight, we may have some news for you very soon. Thank you all for your help,' Paulson says, turning and placing the folded sheet of paper back into his inside jacket pocket. Murphy glares at the uncle until the door is shut in his face.

'What now, smart guy?' Murphy queries, the internal angst manifesting as lines of blood in his eyes and beads of sweat on his brow.

'Now, we get in the car and we wait.'

January

—✦—

I speak with Audrey on the phone.

She sounds calm. Normal. Not like she has just repeatedly inserted the blade of a kitchen knife through the neck of her nanny, severing her vocal cords, blood spilling out on to her hands as her son, Walter, gazes on in bewilderment.

She's detached from the situation.

'Where are you?' I ask quickly.

'At home. You told me I should come home.'

'Yes, yes. I did. That's great. Is Phillipa there with you?'

'No. I sent her home. I don't need her if I'm here. Is there a problem?'

'No. No. It's fine. You've done the right thing. Just stay where you are, OK?'

'OK, Jan. You're sure everything is fine?' She plays her role to perfection.

'Yes. I'll call you in a bit. Just stay there.'

I shut my phone.

And inform Agent Marquez that his girlfriend is not

there. That she has left and is on her way home. I suggest that we make our way to her address, if he knows it.

He sighs. Then nods.

Then answers his phone and bolts out of the door at high speed and I sprint after him, back to the upturned can at Union Square.

The Tail

T he uncle's car starts.

Just as Paulson had anticipated.

He sees the reverse light in the rear-view mirror as the car performs a three-point turn to exit the street.

Murphy looks at Paulson in disbelief, the greyness of his worried skin lightening with encouragement.

They hang back. Far enough to not appear suspicious but within range to keep a close tail on the car. The driver suspects nothing. He has only one thing on his mind.

The uncle's car stops. It pulls into a space outside a long row of townhouses. Paulson has no space to pull in so keeps on driving past, eventually slotting in further along the road. He adjusts the side mirror to look back down the street. The man is out of the car and walking along the path towards them.

'You think he spotted us?' Murphy warbles.

'Just stay calm, Murph. He didn't see us.'

And then the man they are surveilling takes a left up five steps to the red front door of number 36. He raps the knocker three times and waits. Paulson does not take his eyes away from the mirror, scrutinising the scene. Viewing the figure who is present only as a shadow beneath the orange glow of the streetlights that are already flicking on. Hoping the door opens.

It does.

And the figure disappears inside with a flurry of punches to his chest.

'Shit. Go go go go,' Paulson shouts to Murphy as he exits the car quicker than a man of his size should be able to.

The detectives hear the words *You fucking cunt!* in an angered garble as a previously unseen, overweight male falls out of the doorway and hits the stairs with a thwack, landing with his face to the night sky.

A split-second later, his attacker descends the stairs. He drops his knee on to the chest of the man whose bloodied face matches the printout in Paulson's pocket, and he punches him repeatedly. Right hand. A left. A right. Left. Right. Left.

Murphy lunges forward to pull the man away but Paulson stops him.

'Leave it.'

The man from the car, now pummelling the disgusting, semi-conscious children's nightmare is not the uncle – he has been left alone in the house again with Aria's relieved mother.

It is Aria's father.

The meek man at the back of the crowd.

The guilty gambler.

'That's enough,' Paulson shouts at Mr Sky. He doesn't want to mention his name because he plans on letting him go. He'll say that the man was attacked and the perpetrator ran off. He is letting a bereaved father vent. He's giving him some catharsis.

Mr Sky backs off. Standing up above the man who killed his daughter. He looks down at the sicko and feels no better about the situation than when he landed his first punch.

His daughter is still dead.

His body returning to a state of drought.

Drained of the ability to feel, to love.

He lifts a knee and brings it crashing down at speed, his right foot connecting with rib cage; the sound of bones splitting dances across the colder particles of air.

Paulson pulls the father away.

'Who is he?' Paulson asks.

Then he asks again, this time shaking Mr Sky by the arms.

'Stanley Becker. His name is Stanley Becker. Just a local. Known in the area. He killed my daughter.' And Mr Sky finally has some release. He cries. He leans back against a stranger's car and he weeps for his child, for his guilt, for his wife. He slides down the car door until he is resting his knees on the grey concrete of the Camden pavement.

Paulson points at the crumpled husk of a man and signals for Murphy to get the father out of here.

Neighbours are starting to peer out from behind blinds and net curtains. Some are exiting their front doors to take a closer look at the beaten, groaning body.

Murphy returns from placing the father back into his brother's car and telling him to drive home and ice his knuckles.

'You want to do the honours?' Paulson offers Murphy.

The crowds grow larger and more inquisitive. This has to be by the book now.

'Stanley Becker, I'm arresting you on suspicion of the

murder of Aria Sky. You do not have to say anything but it may harm your defence . . .' Murphy rattles off the caution robotically yet smiling within.

Paulson calls it in.

He says they'll need a medic.

Then he lets Markam know that it is over.

It's never over.

January

———✦———

The girls cried, 'Wolf!'
Girl 11.
And Girl 4.

Marquez runs through the street at full speed, barging pedestrians to the side, knocking handbags from ladies' shoulders. But this time he does not approach the upturned can with caution, he continues his pace, using the momentum of his own body to knock the bin over and reveal nothing once again.

'What the fuck is going on here, David?' he shouts at me, as though I am to blame.

'You need to calm down. This is a game with him. He somehow knows your weakness and he's playing on that.'

'Who? Eames?'

'Yes, Eames. He took Audrey from me twice when I was the lead investigator on his case. I don't know how he knows about you but he clearly does and he's trying to push your buttons.' I don't think he can handle my theory that Eames knows about Marquez because Phillipa was in contact with Eames. It's the only possible explanation other than Marquez himself working with the psychopath.

Two sentences ring in my head.

Sometimes you need to make things happen for yourself.

You need to be taking a closer look at the police in that town.

Marquez seems too convincing to be duplicitous. I may once have believed it but not now; this must be part of a misdirection. Still, I'm acutely aware that I am the one without a firearm.

Yet, it is my suggestion that the two of us travel immediately to Phillipa's residence, break in if we have to, and put this charade to bed. I even tell the highly trained federal agent that there will be no need for backup.

Audrey

—◆—

Thursday
**UPPER EAST SIDE, MANHATTAN, NEW YORK,
12:20 EST**
London, 17:20 GMT

Walter runs.
What else is he supposed to do? He's not even two years old yet.

'Wait. Walter. It's OK. It's Mummy,' I call after him but he screams as he runs towards his room, unknowingly trapping himself.

I approach him tentatively and evenly paced, like he's a wild boar. His eyes are full of tears, the liquid film disguising for a moment the Eamesness that lurks within him. The evil is diluted. Reflected as me.

I feel that I should be crying but I'm not.

'It's OK, darling. Phillipa is fine. Mummy is home now so Phillipa is going to go back to her house. She'll be back in the morning.' I'm careful not to say that she hurt herself or that she fell because the police are more brutal here. They'd question my son. He should be allowed to remain innocent for as long as his biology will allow.

He hasn't noticed that I have been moving slightly closer with every word I've uttered. Soon, I am near

400

enough to pull him into my chest. The same chest that his nanny rested on while I cut through her trachea with the knife I have used to dice carrots and open tough pizza boxes.

I stand up with him still holding on to me and we embrace for a minute. Me, making him feel secure. Him, ensuring I start to worry about the time. And mess.

I lower him into his cot-bed. I know he has only just woken up but the bars are still high enough to keep him contained while I clean the blood from the marble, fold my treacherous nanny into a ball and place her inside a black plastic sack, before winding her tight with duct tape to keep her rigid then encasing her in another black bin bag.

I leave three items on the kitchen surface.

Eleanor Harbin's scarf, fresh with enough forensic evidence to suggest a struggle and my own possible strangulation.

Eleanor's mobile phone, which Phillipa took after killing her. There are missed calls on there from Agent Marquez. Her last text is to Phillipa, explaining that she has her scarf to return.

A photo taken from the south of Manhattan depicting the Staten Island Ferry port with the buildings of the financial district in the background. On the reverse side I write the number 4.

January will know what this means.

This is his final test to see whether we can be together.

Then I place Walter into his pushchair and rest Phillipa's body in the extension seat that attaches behind and below Walter's own seat.

Just as I'd told Eames that I would.

Just as I was supposed to with the three sections of Eleanor Harbin's remains.

As I would have done with the bags of birdseed had Phillipa not replaced me.

If January hadn't come back to me so soon.

I unbolt the door and take one last look over my shoulder at the apartment where my new life was supposed to begin but, instead, turned back into shit.

January

Thursday
ALPHABET CITY, MANHATTAN, NEW YORK,
12:26 EST
London, 17:26 GMT

The neighbourhood reminds me of some of the cheaper boroughs in the south of London or the overpopulated ethnic areas in the East End. Rent is inexpensive here. Apartments are adequate. Phillipa would stick out in a crowd here. She's not black or Polish or Jewish. She doesn't even look like she's from New York. If anything, she seems to have been transplanted from a beach in Miami or California somewhere.

Marquez kicks through her door before I have time to finish telling him that *it sounds like nobody is home*.

We have no warrant. I have no jurisdiction. And only Marquez has a gun.

I have to keep telling myself that he is not involved, that this is not a massive error in judgement from me. Though I believe we will uncover evidence to support my theory, I can't help but wonder why The Smiling Man would point me towards her death.

Her apartment is sparse. A small amount of furniture, the least amount possible to survive. Marquez informs me that this is his first time here. They always do it at his place or a hotel.

There are two pans in the kitchen. A kettle. A two-slice toaster. The cooker is turned off at the wall. The fridge has milk, juice, butter and fruit in the bottom left drawer. She doesn't need any luxuries. She has it all at her job. A penthouse suite. Expensive, quality food. A coffee maker. Perfumes and make-up that Audrey would never notice being used.

The bathtub has been stained with a dark hair dye.

Phillipa's flat is unenlightening until we enter her bedroom.

Fitting the rest of the apartment, it is bare. A single bed. A pine wardrobe and a desk that is covered in papers and envelopes. And, in the back left corner, six packs of cards.

'Split-ace decks,' I exclaim, picking up one of the boxes and opening it.

'What?' Marquez asks, irritated, edgy. I look at the spot under his jacket where his gun is holstered.

'The same cards that David Blaine uses.' I flick through, counting. 'There are cards missing.'

I take up another deck and repeat the routine.

Cards are missing.

In each box, there are cards missing.

Marquez finds a piece of paper covered with hand-written letters and numbers:

A♥ 1♥ 2♥ 3♥ 4♥ 5♥ 6♥ 7♥ 8♥ 9♥ 10♥ J♥ Q♥ K♥
A B C D E F G H I J K L M N

Another scrap shows the second half of the alphabet with the corresponding diamond card laid out above.

'It's the simplest fucking code in the world. How did we miss this? Why do we not know that Eames was receiving these cards?' I say out loud to myself.

He makes it so easy for us. Too easy.

I don't yet know that Audrey had set this up. I may never know how the sponsor was involved or how Phillipa found a way to keep this part of the plan going even when Audrey had ceased to act on it. But I know that the missing cards from these packs were informing Eames.

'Sort out one of the packs and find which cards are missing,' I order Marquez.

We rifle through the packs and conclude that the cards missing correspond to the letters that spell out Georgina and Eleanor.

Georgina Burton and Eleanor Harbin.

Girl 9 and Girl 10.

Eames would have already known their last names from the planning of the tricks and correlating them with the surnames of the magicians. We find that the nine and ten of spades are also missing, representing the number of the victim. Probably a confirmation that they were dead.

There is a file with letters from Eames. Love letters. Letters of support. Letters describing her fake relationship with Agent Marquez. They talk about me and Audrey. They are addressed from a mental hospital in Berkshire, England. They are the proof we need to lock Phillipa away for a very long time.

'What about the cards that spell out Girl 8 or Girl 11?' Marquez questions, quite rightly.

'Well, Eames would not need to know who the last girl would be. He would know because it is the only trick left.'

'And Girl 8?'

'I don't know, Agent Marquez. Maybe Phillipa committed the first one to get his attention. We are not going to know until we find her.'

I watch as a part of him dies. I moved in the same way when I found that Audrey had betrayed me with Eames. Languid. Removed. I remember how the sense of loyalty dissolved and disappointment took over. Followed by blame, then self-condemnation.

Then anger.

I freeze to the spot as Marquez reaches into his pocket; my eyes are fixed on the bulge of his gun. I'll act in whatever way I see fit. My best form of defence would be to attack him. Fast.

He takes out his mobile phone and says, 'I've got to call this in. Get this place locked down and swept. Get a team over here to help find Phillipa. Alert the transport authority. We'll have to wait until they get here.'

I hear the defeat in his voice. I've spoken in that very tone. He's detaching himself.

It's for the best.

Marquez walks off to speak to the appropriate authorities and leaves me alone with the evidence that I should not be touching, contaminating.

But I'm a detective. I can't switch that off.

I swipe through some of the letters, hoping a word or phrase will jump out at me.

Nothing.

I open her cheap pine wardrobe. It looks the way I would expect any twenty-something female's wardrobe to look. Packed so tight with clothes that the hangers can no longer move. Shoes piled high beneath. One of the shoeboxes contains newspaper clippings of the initial investigation. They mention me and Audrey and Eames. But I don't find this, and it would not tell me anything new about Phillipa Daniels.

I move back to the desk and start on the drawers. The top is locked but it is not the greatest security and I turn it open with the nail file standing up among the biros in her penholder.

Inside are four sets of handcuffs. They don't appear to be the FBI-issue cuffs though it crossed my mind that she would use them during sex with Marquez. Beneath these I find a fold-out map of Franklin County and Crum Hill. I unfold the map but nothing has been circled or marked in any way.

Marquez still talks on the phone in the other room.

Along the right edge there is a sizeable knife and another pack of split-ace cards, this time sealed. And one of Audrey's business cards.

The last item I find in this eclectic mix of psychopath curios is an opened pack of postcards. A pack of ten. And only nine remain. They each have the same image on the front. The Statue of Liberty, as seen from the southern tip of the island, surrounded by water, lifting a torch and touching the sky, which is a shade of blue I am yet to witness since arriving.

It is the same postcard that I assumed Audrey had left me after our first sexual encounter in New York.

She never left me that note.

It was Phillipa.

She was telling me that she was going to kill my wife.

That is what I am supposed to think when I open this door. I'm meant to call Audrey now and get no response. It is intended that I now worry for her safety.

Eames knew that Phillipa would kill for him; she

exhibited those character traits through her correspondence. He knew that she would relish taking out Audrey. But he knew that Audrey would prevail and, though she wanted out, would be drawn back in through taking the life of Girl 11 and completing the list.

And he knew that I would open this drawer.

And he knew that I would focus on the postcards.

And he knew that I would buy the misdirection again because I feel so fucking guilty about allowing Audrey to be taken, just as my sister Cathy was taken from me.

And he knows that I will soon come to know the real Audrey. The scheming Audrey. The manipulative Audrey. The killer Audrey.

And I'm ignoring all the other items in the drawer that he had Phillipa leave for me.

The final clue to the Eames endgame.

Part Five

Prestige

Eames

———◆———

Time is moving slowly.

There has been no confirmation of Phillipa's death.

I hear the shuffling of feet outside in the corridor as the fake psychiatrists and neurological fraudsters strut past the minuscule glass rectangles, judging those they pretend to observe and help and treat for mental deficiencies and malfunctions.

Imagine how futile they will consider their own existence to be tomorrow.

Think how terrified they will be to leave this building. To walk to their cars. To return to their families. To turn the keys that open their homes.

I see their scrutinising eyes reach my small window and I know it is six o'clock. Audrey will have killed again and part of her would have enjoyed it, no matter what she protests. Detective Inspector January David may have even opened the drawer by now.

My final message.

Come on, Detective. It's all there. Just ask somebody, anybody, where Franklin County is. Ask them where to

411

find Crum Hill. They will tell you. They will pronounce it *Burk-sheer* rather than *Bark-sha*, but you'll realise this is a message from me.

Look at the items, Detective Inspector January David.

What are they telling you?

Do you get it now?

I wish it were you.

The pinhole pupils of the alleged health professional watching me lie on my bed, my hands behind my head, staring at the sky I cannot see, move on. And time stops for me. The next marker will be the guards' rounds at eight. Then lights out at nine-thirty. Followed by the sleepless monotony of eventless moments bleeding into one another.

This is the hard part. The waiting. Putting my trust in somebody else to do the work that I was destined to perform. Silence and darkness are not friends to me. They fool with time and interfere with space. I have needs. Do not allow me to dwell on this, to think about it, meditate, dream.

I want to kill.

I need to fucking kill someone.

So, sun, rise from your horizon line and bring forth a new day. A new chapter.

A new trick.

Stop tampering with hours and minutes.

Let a second last only for a second.

All I need are three of them.

Audrey

Thursday
**UNION SQUARE, MANHATTAN, NEW YORK,
13:04 EST**
London, 18:04 GMT

I can see the upturned bin and I know that Phillipa did this after dropping her friend's legs off at the police academy near Gramercy Park. Because that is how we planned it.

I walk past it a few times before committing to the plan. The air smells of a million competing restaurants and the cold air bites at my skin to tell me that I am doing wrong. Then my mobile phone flashes its screen at me again as January tries to reach me.

He'll be worried and guilty that Eames has got to me again but he'll know the truth soon. He'll know that I love him. And that should be enough. I wonder when he last thought of his sister. Is he consumed by this case, by me? Am I the most important thing in his life right now? Not ever, but right now, at this moment. Is this the point in Jan's life when he loves me the most?

And will it be enough to forgive me?

Again.

I stop the buggy at a forty-five-degree angle to the

413

large bullet-shaped container that Phillipa so graciously prepared for me. What did she think she was going to do with Walter? Leave him in the apartment until someone uncovered my body?

I crouch down and talk to my son who sits wrapped up in his seat, his nose and cheeks turning a healthy shade of pink, and I yank the ball of Phillipa Daniels out sideways. She hits the floor with a thud that the city drowns out and a rustle that mingles with the leaves.

I stroke Walter's cheek with the back of a forefinger of my gloved hands as though I love him. Then I stand up once more, move around to the handles, place my boot on to one of Girl 11's toes to hold her in place and scoop her head into the cone where Agent Marquez has, so far, found nothing.

All performed in one swift movement as I walk away from the scene.

Eames showed me how to do this.

He said I should practise.

I exit via the south-west corner, passing the statue of Gandhi, and it is done. Eleven tricks transformed into eleven sadistic performances. Nine murders. Eight young, vibrant women cut down in their prime. One unfortunate man castrated from this mortal coil.

All that remains is a murderous illusionist, gaining in notoriety. Edging towards infamy. An audience is left asking how this happened. Repelled by events but somehow excited by the unknown. Guessing a plethora of theories involving mirrors and trapdoors and twins and contortionists.

And me. Audrey David. Girl 4. The stooge. The patsy. The woman in the audience raising her hand to take part.

The one who steps on stage and declares that she *has never seen the magician before*.

That's who I am.

I place my foot on to the pavement that runs along Broadway and take my first step towards freedom.

The Wait

---+---

S tanley Becker kills children.
He is ill.

Or that's just the way he is.

He belongs in a white room with a simple bed frame and tiny window with a view of nothing but another pale wall. Like Eames. And he should be made to live, to endure this torture at the hands of vengeful prison guards disguised as healthcare professionals.

But, at this moment, the kid-killer Stanley Becker is being treated by real doctors at St Pancras Hospital.

It was the nearest to the scene of his (allegedly) random attack.

They are specialists in mental health but that is not the reason he is here. Paulson wants the suspect's nose set back in place and his ribs checked. Then he wants to sit by his side to ensure that nothing happens to him. He doesn't want Aria Sky's uncle or mother getting into the ward and holding a pillow over the sicko's face to act out some emotional sense of justice that will dissipate with the murdering bastard's final breath.

Paulson does not want a family torn apart even further by another avoidable mistake. He is happy to wait. To let Murphy go back to the station and report to Markam. To file the arrest and take whatever glory he needs. To allow him the prestige he believes is so important. Paulson will wait on the front line.

Murphy organises a team to sweep the home of Stanley Becker. He will take the lead again as acting DI. He will be the one to bring the contents of that wardrobe to the light of day. But he has no idea of the scope of its significance.

Paulson rests his weary frame in the chair next to the hospital bed, his eyes at the same level as two broken ribs. He looks at the man lying down, bruised and broken, draped in a lemon-coloured blanket, looking like a victim. This disgusting creature who crushed the innocence from Aria Sky.

The gentle child.

She would have been *five in June.*

And he feels pride in himself. And relief. And he thinks of January David who is still searching for that emotion, filling it with small victories on a hopeful path towards discovery. He wonders about Detective Sergeant Lamont, the officer in charge of finding Cathy, January's sister, back in '85. Did he do everything possible to find her? Did he venture outside his comfort zone of investigational practice?

Where is he now, and does he have that same aching that consumes Cathy's brother?

Paulson thinks in order to stop his eyes closing. He is used to late nights playing poker, seeing a game through to its conclusion, retaining focus to the last hand dealt at the last table.

He will see this through until morning.

Becker will be discharged from the hospital and detained.

This story will overtake Eames' success in the UK papers.

But Paulson will visit him one final time.

January

———✦———

I flash my badge at the doorman as though it gives me the authority to barge in here.

I run past his counter in the lobby and press the button for the lift to the right, next to the large black-and-white canvas of a wilting daffodil, breaking apart in the breeze.

'Sir, sir,' he calls after me. 'Wait a moment, sir.' He trots over to me.

'I need you to unlock the penthouse for Ms David.'

'I'm sorry, sir, but I can't do that.'

'You recognise me, right? I was here the other night.' He looks me up and down and then his gaze flashes over the features of my face.

'I'm sorry, sir, but I—'

'Look.' I flip open my warrant card, which indicates that I have no jurisdiction in these parts but it also serves to confirm my identity; I brought it out this time. 'I'm her husband. Detective Inspector January David.' I point at my name and title. 'I have reason to believe that my wife is in danger. I need you to unlock the lift to take me to the top floor.'

'Your wife is not in danger, Mr David,' he says, coolly.

'I have reason to believe—'

This time, he cuts me off. 'She left about a half-hour ago. With the baby. I helped her take the buggy down the stairs to the street. It was heavy. She turned left towards Fifth Avenue. But that is all I know.'

'And you're sure about this?' It's such a pointless question.

'I helped her myself, Mr David.'

Fuck. What is going on? She did as I said and came home from work. She sent Phillipa away and now she has left with her son. Eames' son. If I hadn't had to wait around at Phillipa's flat for the FBI to show up, I would have got here before Audrey had a chance to leave.

'I still need to get up there.'

'Not without a police officer from this city. I'm sure you understand.' And the jumped-up piece of shit returns to his spot behind the front desk.

Eight minutes later, Inspector Matthews from the 19th Precinct is standing in the lift with me and the timid security guard, turning the key that will take us to Audrey's level.

Her front door has been left ajar.

'You can go back down in the elevator now,' he instructs the sheepish doorman. Then he pulls out his gun and prods the door open. I stand behind his wide shoulders. Behind the weapon.

'The place is clear. It's fuckin' huge, but it's clear.'

And I make my way over to the kitchen counter where

Audrey has left the items. My second message from a psychotic killer in the last hour or so.

I start to reach for the phone. Inspector Matthews shouts my name and startles me. He tells me that the device could *go off*. I turn it on. There is no passcode to get into the main screen. The speed dials are the usual. Mother. Father. Work. Girl's names that mean nothing.

Her last text was to Phillipa in the early hours of the morning before her death. It says that she still has Phillipa's scarf but is transporting it across town to her new place.

I see the scarf on the kitchen counter.

Phillipa killed Eleanor Harbin between houses, probably as Marquez and I split the two addresses. We were at each place she was registered to be living while she was being strangled in the middle then cut up, probably, at Phillipa's sparse dwelling.

'You'll want to bag that scarf as a possible weapon,' I inform Matthews, 'and this phone is evidence pertaining to the severed head found in the dumpster outside your precinct.'

'And that?' he asks as I pick up the photograph.

It looks like nothing. Another picture of a Manhattan skyline. I turn it over and notice the number four written in Audrey's hand.

And everything makes sense.

The Smiling Man does not represent Eames at all. He is leading me to Audrey.

To Girl 4.

Maniswomanismaniswomanismaniswoman.

I can see Girl 1, attached to her bed, standing up. Then

The Smiling Man running at me with a bullet in his teeth as the chair appears next to me.

Audrey watched as Eames shot Dorothy Penn through the mouth.

I can visualise Girl 2, pierced with arrows and my intuition telling me that Audrey witnessed the culling of Carla Moretti through the window.

Girl 3 writhes on the wooden floor of her West London flat while The Smiling Man fills my mouth with cigarettes, and then nothing for Girl 4. Because she didn't die. She was never meant to die. She made this happen.

'Everything OK, David?' Matthews seems concerned and I realise I'm gripping my temples with my right hand, the hand he uses to hold his gun.

I can do nothing to stop these images swarming around my brain.

The Smiling Man did not visit my dreams to hint at Girl 9 in Central Park or Girl 10's body zig-zagging across the metropolis. Because Audrey did not kill them.

Eames was using them both.

My chest goes cold and I have to force my stomach not to expel itself onto the solid marble tiles beneath my feet.

Audrey hadn't actually killed anyone herself in London. She could chalk up Phillipa's death to self-defence when all the evidence is collected, when they find her body – I already know that she is dead, because The Smiling Man told me – but Girl 8 makes her a murderer. My wife is a murderer.

Is it my fault? Did my life, my work, my quest to find Cathy, somehow impact her?

Or has this always been inside of her?

Was Girl 8 even her first kill?

'What is that picture?' Matthews asks again.

She signed it with the number four. Because she is not Audrey, not the Audrey I know or once knew or first met. She is implicit in this case. She has become Girl 4, the victim, the perpetrator. She tells me with a single digit that she is not the woman I think she is.

She confesses.

The picture itself is a reflection of the postcard I saw in Phillipa's drawer. The same one she left on my pillow after reigniting my passion for Audrey. This is the image of Manhattan, the scene of these crimes, taken from Liberty Island.

Audrey is looking back at me from her freedom.

But it is not just a photograph. I know Audrey better than anyone.

This is an invitation.

I know where she is.

'Detective?'

'Oh, this is nothing. This is mine,' I deceive, not handing Audrey over to the authorities.

Passing her test.

The Wolf

—✦—

Thursday
**UNION SQUARE, MANHATTAN, NEW YORK,
13:34 EST**
London, 18:34 GMT

At first, Agent Marquez is worried for January David. If this had been another report of an anonymous caller, he'd have ignored it. Probably. Though it was the third time that the boy was eaten by the wolf. This had been reported by a young man who had stayed next to the trash can after making the call to the authorities.

Marquez could see immediately that the upturned rubbish container was not empty like it was the last time. Or the time before that. He was tired from running around the city all night and day, worrying about a girlfriend who never cared for him, only to find that he'd spent the last couple of nights screwing a hot girl who was using him. For information. For an alibi. To set him up. After all, he had all the resources and information on the victims. He had census information and FBI databases that he could have used to pick out who could be killed.

And he was trying to save his career.

Make something happen.

'Step back, please,' Marquez asks the confused black

424

guy still holding the remnants of greasy paper that had been wrapped around his burger. He wanted to dispose of it responsibly. That is when he noticed something was wrong.

Marquez lifts the giant bullet up and the body, wrapped in plastic, remains in position for a few seconds before flopping to one side, the head hitting the concrete.

He kneels down, his left knee taking all of his weight as it freezes to the cold concrete. He pokes a pen through the black liner, making a small hole, which he then prises apart to view the contents. The man with the burger wrapper wants to look away but finds himself leaning over the agent's shoulder.

There is a mass of dark hair, some clumped together and wet with blood.

And Marquez is worried for January David.

He thinks it must be Audrey.

Girl 4 and Girl 7 equals Girl 11.

He recalls the words that January David relayed to him. Eames was deciding whether to *make her freedom disappear or simply turn her into a lemon*. Marquez pulls the rolled-up corpse's hair away from her face, tucking it gently behind her ear and sees immediately that the identity of the victim is Phillipa Daniels.

Eames turned her into a lemon.

Marquez wants to feel shocked or upset. But can't bring himself to feel either emotion. He should experience anger or loss, but the young woman lying at his feet, sporting the latest in garbage couture, is a stranger to him. He never knew her, really.

She was a slumber party.

A black hole.

A dance in the dark.

Now it is the end. Time for him to regain his status, his standing within the FBI. He knows who did this and that is all he needs to know. This is the reason he brought January David over to help with the investigation.

He too knows where Audrey David is.

And he wants to make her freedom disappear.

January

———◆———

W hy, Audrey? Why do it?
      Because you're the big-time independent woman making it in business and you think you're fucking invincible? Or is it just something else for you to conquer? He made you do it? Is that right? You were caught under his spell like the other girls? Are you lonely? Did I not pay you enough attention? Are you simply psychotic?

Do you think you will get away with this?

It's over.

These are the words I want to say to her. These are the sentences I want to throw in her direction when I get off this boat. It's so cold I'm in pain. The air touches the water where the East River meets the Hudson and picks up a frost, carrying it to my extremities.

It's over?

The boat winds around a corner that isn't even there and parks snugly against the island. The statue looks much smaller in person. In films and photos it seems majestic against the sky. A beacon. A symbol of this powerful

427

nation. On the ground, even looking up at it, the grandeur is blown away with the wind that chaps our lips.

People ahead of me *ooh* and *aah* on the jetty. They hook their headphones over their hats and listen to the facts blurted into their ears as they take the ninety-minute audio tour.

I can see the reason I am here.

She is standing alone, behind the buggy; the boy I could never accept as my own child sits heavily on her jutted-out hip. They are wrapped up in coats and hats that I was unprepared for. They are too close to the water.

Why, Audrey? Why did you do it?

To impress a man who does not have the capacity to love you in return? Are you so much like him now that you, yourself, have forgotten how to feel for another person? What did it feel like to kill Kerry Ross? Did you enjoy it? Did you do it just to get me here?

She did it just to get me here.

Don't put this on me. Do not say that you are killing for me.

It's over.

Is it over?

She smiles as I approach her. She thinks she has won. That I am here alone and I can forgive her. I can understand that.

I extract the photograph taken from this spot that I took from her kitchen work surface. It is folded in half. I wave it at her. I see her shoulders release tension. She thinks I am here to forgive her. To understand her madness. That love outweighs the law.

'Jan. You came.' She smiles, I sense, nervously.

'I'm here.' My response is ambiguous. I'm still walking.

'That's probably close enough, don't you think?'

I watch her right hand move to the back of the buggy. The boy who is not my son sits on her left hip. Her hand remains there until I stop. She is shaking.

Am I the only one in this city without a gun?

'I know how much I mean to you, Jan.'

'We've been through a lot.' I continue my line of ambiguity.

'Don't play me, Jan. I can see you're here and you are here alone. There must be a reason you haven't turned me in.'

'Well . . .'

'Either you want answers and you want to take me in yourself, or you trust me. That I would never hurt you. That I love you. You understand why I had to do these things.'

She never looks at the kid. Not once. It's as though he is not even there or he is an appendage of herself. And not in a good way. Not in the way that she feels he was made from her and that he is a part of her. Like he is her elbow or a split-end or a cracked nail.

I see his eyes and I see Eames but this is still her son. If she is incapable of demonstrating the appropriate level of maternity towards him, how can I believe that she feels anything close to love for me?

But I say, 'I know that you love me. Of course I know that. I want answers so that I can understand why you did those things, Audrey. That is all I want.'

This is now a negotiation. I have to give her some truth. And I have to have some closure.

'What? You want to know how I did it? Is that it? The detective in you needs to know the specifics?'

'No. I know how you did it. You didn't do it. He did. Eames did it. He had all of you doing as he wanted.'

'No!' she shouts. 'No. I told him how to do it. Where to do it.' Walter starts to cry the moment she raises her voice. And still she doesn't look at him. 'We used my company database to find all the girls with the right name, the right goddamn personality. He couldn't do it without me.'

Her face looks different. It's still the same luminously pale, smooth skin stretched tightly over the cheekbones. It is still those plump red, killer lips and those eyes that are ninety per cent lashes. But she looks different. There's a harshness there that wasn't there before, or I did not notice it.

I look at Walter and feel for him in this situation.

The boy I can't love.

The boy with my father's name.

'I know all that,' I lie. Audrey had to put the final piece together for me. I had no idea how they were scouting these girls. It must have been so easy. 'I don't care about that.'

'You don't?' Her hardness softens and I see the Audrey I love creep back into the scene, filling the lines around her eyes.

'Why, Audrey? Why do it?'

There, I said it.

'For you, dummy,' she says sweetly, like she has just bought me a box of chocolates. 'So you could move on from the past, realise what you have now. Stop pining over your sister.'

This is where she loses me.

'Stop pining over my sister? I'm not pining, I'm looking. I'm looking for my sister, you maniac.'

This is where I blow it.

'What have I got now? A wife who conspires with a known killer? Who, herself, also kills? Great. Throw in a bastard child and I've won the fucking lottery.'

This is when she looks at Walter.

This is when she pulls out the gun.

'I have to take you in, Audrey. It can't be any other way.'

It seems like a stupid thing to say now that I have a weapon pointed at my face but it's windy out here and she has only killed up close, with her hands, as far as I know.

And I have noticed Agent Marquez appear from the right of my periphery. Like he has been waiting at the statue's feet for this moment.

I take a step forwards and she flicks the safety off.

I'm no longer sure that a bullet will not penetrate my skull or heart.

Walter wails.

Marquez moves in closer and draws his gun, aiming it at Audrey.

I don't want him to shoot. That is not justice.

'FBI. Put down your weapon, Ms David,' Marquez shouts from a distance of around forty feet.

Audrey looks to her left over Walter's head at the approaching agent and smiles. Her face changing yet again. She cranes her head back to me and tilts it to the side as though saying, *Such a shame.*

Is it over?

She knows Marquez will not fire his weapon while she is holding a child. Her son. A toddler. She knows this. But she turns away from me, out of my life, and faces Marquez before bringing her gun around and pushing the barrel into the tiny temple of her first-born child.

The tourists at the top of the statue hear my intake of breath.

Marquez stutters.

The Audrey I knew is long gone.

She steps backwards a short pace. Marquez's words get lost in the breeze as it bounces across the East River.

'Audrey. Don't do this. Don't let it end this way,' I plead.

'You idiot, Jan. It was always going to end this way. You should never have come here. You shouldn't be here.'

'Put the gun down, Ms David,' Marquez persists.

'Go home, January.'

I don't know what she is talking about. I put it down to her delusion.

She has been backing away with every word.

'I do love you, Jan,' she says again. I think she is just flitting between her many faces.

'Aud—'

In one swift motion, everything ends. In chaos.

Audrey tosses her son forwards into the East River.

She jumps in herself, in the opposite direction.

Marquez fires two bullets at her.

And then my body is rejecting itself as a result of the sharp shock of the cold river as I jump in after the child I am supposed to feel nothing for. There is screaming from the statue and the boat and the grass and some people don't hear because their audio tour is turned up to the maximum.

My clothes are heavy. Marquez stands at the side, watching, shouting, looking in the opposite direction. I was taught to keep my head above the water in this situation. To always look where you are swimming. But I see him beneath the water and I dive down.

Later, I'm sitting on a brick wall, holding Eames' son, hugging the child, keeping him warm. He's alive and so am I. Audrey hasn't surfaced. Marquez won't stop looking. He keeps saying, 'She'll come up, she'll come up.' Like repeating it with confidence will make it happen.

I don't care for this boy. I can't. But I won't let go of him until I know he will be OK. He's an orphan now, in theory.

'I hit her,' Marquez bleats. 'She'll come up.'

I look at him but say nothing. I rock the boy named after my father in my arms.

'She'll come up,' he confirms again, only to himself.

For the next twenty minutes, I rock back and forth. I say *ssh ssh ssh*. Marquez paces. Audrey is far away. Tugged along by the undercurrent.

The Statue of Liberty looms large in the grey New York sky.

The medics will arrive shortly to deal with the boy.

Audrey David's freedom has disappeared.

Girl 12

—✦—

The hardest part for any magician is the deception.
It is never the trick itself.

You are actively deceiving your audience, your partner, your lover. And, in order for them to want to be misled, they have to care.

The assistant is never really sawn in half. No blade of a sword ever passed through the body of an innocent spectator. Men cannot fly unassisted. Nor can they levitate for a short moment. You want it to be true, but it is not. You want to be fooled. You want to know how things are done.

You need to know why.

When a woman is fixing a padlock to the front of the chest, her male counterpart is not trapped within a rope-tied sack. He has already made his escape and is waiting for the curtain.

This is illusion.

This is practice.

And whenever a gun is fired, nobody is ever in danger.
The bullets are not real.

The Statue of Liberty does not disappear.
    She is always there.
    She has been there the whole time.

January

Friday
NEWARK AIRPORT, NEW JERSEY, 00:20 EST
London, 05:20 GMT

Then I'm out of there on the first flight. Maybe it's the last flight.

It's a new day.

Marquez escorts me to Newark Airport, still seemingly bewildered at how everything seemed to conclude. He found out that his girlfriend had used him and killed two people, one of whom was a friend. He later found her with a slice taken from her neck, wrapped in plastic and dumped at Union Square Park, obscured by a trash can. He seems surprisingly level-headed for a man who has just dealt with such discoveries.

He informs me that he worked it out just as I had and made his way to Liberty Island. That he definitely hit Audrey with one of the bullets. That Walter is being taken care of and will be placed into the foster system and treated and monitored at the expense of *the Bureau*. He confirms once more that Audrey will come up, probably somewhere downriver.

I can't think about that. I don't know who she is. I can't understand her reasons for throwing her son the way that she did. Maybe it was another of her tests. She knew I would jump in after him. Perhaps she thought I would take him on, give the kid a chance at something better, something more than his biological parents could provide.

'Thanks, Detective David. Thank you for everything,' Marquez gushes, I assume, sincerely.

'I'm not sure what I really did to help. People still died.'

'It's over now. That's it. She's gone. Eames is still locked away. There are no more tricks.' He speaks in the same manner as he does when trying to convince himself that Audrey will *come up eventually.*

All I can do is fake a reassuring nod.

I don't know what to believe.

It's too late or early to contact Paulson and let him know that I am on my way back. I think he'll be sleeping after another night of online poker, not sitting awake next to the man who killed Aria Sky, waiting for him to wake so that he can drag him to a cold cell. So I text him saying that there's so much to talk about but this case is over and I'm coming home. I want to see his reaction when I explain Audrey's part.

I turn my mobile phone off.

I won't read Paulson's response until I land.

'Well, Agent Marquez,' I speak, stepping slowly towards the departure gate, putting my phone into my hand luggage, 'I guess that this case has polished the edges of your reputation.'

'It hasn't done it any harm.' He smiles.

'I hope to never hear from you again.' I reciprocate his laughter but there is a truth in my comment.

He shakes my hand. 'Someone will keep you informed of the boy's progress, as you requested.'

I don't respond.

'Thanks again.' He finally releases my hand.

I pull the boarding pass from my back pocket. 'Good luck, Agent Marquez.'

He should have left it there. Ending with pleasant banality.

'I don't believe in that. We make our own luck, right?' And he winks before turning in the opposite direction, his shoulders rolling back, his chest puffed in pride.

And I am left with a sense of unease as I hand the woman my passport.

And the world continues to move forwards. Stories evolve, are born, or die. While I sit at the only bar and drink and drink.

Eames

⇒✦⇐

O ne. One thousand.
  Two. One thousand.
Three. One thousand.
That's how long it takes.

When a disgruntled performer dons a mask and claims to be able to reveal how a trick has been performed, the truth behind the deception, I see a coward. I see facade. A disguise I would like to kill.

There is no pride in this.

Of course, people will believe what you tell them, even if you have lied before. Because they want answers. Inherently, we are all searching for a truth.

I would never unveil the mechanics of an illusion.

That's not me.

But the truth is grey. The truth is that I am being led into a packed visit today and nobody even notices that the ridiculous overalls I am forced to wear to take away my identity, my status, are far too big for me.

In all honesty, they do not notice that a small triangular part of my bed frame no longer supports the springs when weight is added to the mattress.

And Detective Paulson waits in the large room of madhouse guests, to inform me that it's over. To thank me for my help in catching his child killer.

The guard walks me down the corridor with my hands cuffed stiffly at the wrists. He pushes the door open and there is the noise of conversation and colours and brightness and love and fear, all mingling amiably.

One. One thousand.

Two. One thousand.

Three. One thousand.

I step into the theatre.

Detective Paulson is sitting at the same table as before. I knew he would be. He is a creature of habit and procedure. I move my hands, rotating my wrists by one hundred and eighty degrees, feeling the chafe of metal against my skin. They feel tight today. The centre section is rigid rather than connected with a loose chain.

I sit down opposite the detective. The guard leaves us alone and joins a colleague at the door we entered through moments ago. I had hoped it would be Detective Inspector January David but had to prepare for this eventuality.

'Detective,' I greet him pleasantly, confidently. And I rest into my chair, my hands in my lap.

'Mr Eames,' he responds, trying to rile me immediately, knowing that I prefer to be called simply *Eames*.

'Caught your man, have you? You're quite welcome. No need to come all this way to thank me.'

'He's in a cell now. We're going to let him stew for a

couple of hours. Get used to living like a caged animal.'
I swear I see his eyes glint as he looks directly into mine.
Thinking he has won.

But he's tired. And slow. And all this talking, all this
bravado, is the same as having my assistant pretend to
lock a padlock on the chest.

'I'm glad you caught him. Some animals need to be
locked away.'

The detective then takes great delight in passing on
that my killing spree has come to an end, that January
David knows how I did it, how I used that girl and
how I was working with Audrey. He says it is over.
That I lost.

Then he thinks he is clever and finishes with the words
final curtain.

And I know he wants to leave.

I tell him, 'That wasn't the trick.'

'What?'

I repeat, moving my head closer to his, speaking softly.
'That wasn't the trick.'

Then I count.

One. One thousand.

Two. One thousand.

Three. One thousand.

And then there is screaming and crowds and guards are
ushering a group of people in the same direction, pushing
them out of the door while all the patients – you can't
call them inmates – are left in the room for safety. One
of the guards is calling for medical help. There's blood
everywhere.

There has been an attack.

*

Some of the visitors take a seat in the waiting area to calm themselves. Others leave immediately and head for their cars in fear. They hate coming here as it is.

Back in the room I was recently led into by the giant guard who thinks we are friends, the medic still has not arrived. The other two guards are clueless about how to proceed. The room is full of felons and they see their duty as keeping a watchful eye over this danger, keeping themselves alive, rather than the man slumped over my table, wearing the company overalls that distinguish sanity from lunacy.

They stare at the prisoner, with his hands cuffed together on the table, his head slumped down, blood draining from the hole in his neck.

And they think, *Who cares if this psychopath dies?*

Imagine their faces when they realise it is not me. That I wasn't lying when I said that I could take the handcuffs off whenever I wanted. That I could place them over the wrists of Detective Paulson once I had stabbed the triangle of metal from my uncomfortable bed into his neck and removed my oversized outfit and placed it over his clothes.

Think how uncomfortable they will all feel for being impressed, for wondering how I performed it even though I had already demonstrated my ability and intention with Girl 5 and Richard Pendragon.

This is illusion.

This is practice.

This is metamorphosis.

And now I am walking straight out of the front door.

The driveway is long. I start to walk. It will be a little while before they realise I have escaped. I can make it out on foot.

A car pulls up next to me and stops.

A window drops down and a woman's voice calls out.

'Are you OK?' she asks.

I bend down so that I can see her.

'That was pretty scary, huh?' she offers.

'Gosh. Terrifying.' I have to stop myself from smiling.

'Do you live nearby?'

'Oh, no. I'm just going to walk to the station. Grab a train back home. It's not too far,' I lie.

'Jump in. I'll give you a lift. Get away from this place as quickly as we can, eh?' Her eyes are large and brown and freckles pepper a smooth thirty-year-old skin.

I open the door, sit on the heated leather seat and pull the seatbelt over my shoulder. She pulls away.

I'll kill her at the train station.

I can hardly wait.

The Fourth Girl

―✦―

His face is bruised. His nose is broken. His ribs are cracked. But it is the cold that is getting to him. Stanley Becker has been moved from the comfort of a hospital bed to the confines of a personal cell where his only company is the memories of his failures.

The deranged idiot doesn't even think about Aria Sky or the other six girls he has killed over the years, almost one per decade; he thinks about Annie. And the books she used to read and the questions she would ask him and her interest in his drawings. And the one time she didn't speak to him because it was the school holidays.

And her face after he'd finished beating it.

And the strands of her soft hair left in his hand.

Murphy looks in on the fat piece of shit and he has hate in his eyes. He enjoys watching him shake and grimace as he tries to still himself to prevent his ribs from stabbing at his lungs. Murphy doesn't care if the animal is sorry. It makes no difference if he wanted to be caught. That excuse has never washed with him.

If you want to be caught, walk into a police station.
Don't make it a game.
This will be an interrogation to relish.

Chief Markam knows almost everything. He has been in contact with the FBI. He knows of January David's involvement. He knows that he is ready to return to work. He knows that Audrey was involved and he explained the details to Paulson and Murphy, ruining January's story.

He doesn't know that Paulson is dying. That he is losing blood rapidly while rapists and kidnappers and torturers and arsonists look on with an inability to care.

Markam has no idea that it is not Eames the guards are standing back from, that they are allowing an officer of the law to bleed out. That he has been the lynchpin in two huge investigations but did not crave the prestige of a Marquez or a Murphy. He just did his job and he did his job well.

And, for another twenty minutes, nobody will know that Eames has escaped. Walked out of the front door. By that time, he will be gone, and would already have killed.

'Great job, Detective Murphy,' Markam compliments, the words sticking in his throat.

'Thanks, sir. We've got him. And we've got enough evidence to bang him up until he dies. I don't see him putting up much of a fight in interrogation.'

'I think you'll be surprised. Look at Shipman.'

'True.'

'His lawyer on the way?'

'Doesn't want one.'

'Sounds like mischief to me. At least you'll have Jan here.'

Markam is lying. He doesn't know for sure that January David will return to work straight away but he knows that Murphy is claiming the glory for cracking this case and he wants to ruffle his feathers.

'He's coming back?' Murphy tries to stifle his annoyance but it just comes across as awkward.

'He's calling when he lands,' Markam lies again. 'Leave him to stew a little longer in there. We'll pull him out in a couple of hours.'

Markam walks off, leaving Murphy reeling and stranded. He has done everything asked of him and has been left with nothing. He cannot contact the sponsor to question January's return. The sponsor is gone. He is no longer on Audrey David's payroll. Murphy has shot himself in both feet and will now be made to walk through a pool of vinegar.

And none of this will matter.

Not to January David.

Because there is one piece of evidence that is considered the nail in Stanley Becker's coffin. The wardrobe of death. The six tiny hangers, each with an outfit to represent a life, a time. Each dress or skirt or shirt or cardigan taken from an innocent child. The one furthest to the right was taken from Aria, the most modern attire. To the far left, the outfit of the first young girl he squeezed to death for not being Annie.

The inside of the wardrobe smells like every charity shop you've ever entered but the fibres from the material will correspond with the bones that are still being tested.

There will be five other names to add to that of the gentle child.

January David will be interested in one.

The outfit hanging in the centre.

The Fourth Girl.

The girl that Stanley Becker snatched from the front of her home in the eighties.

The fourth girl he buried in Regent's Park, whose bones are now rid of their flesh and sinew.

The young, naive girl that once fit the polka-dot dress.

January

T he stewardess announces over the tannoy that all
  passengers should remain seated with their seat belts
fastened until the plane comes to a stop and the *fasten
seat belts* sign has turned off.

Then I hear the click of thirty seat belts.

Next, she tells us all to wait until we reach the baggage
carousel before turning on our mobile phones.

That's when I turn on my mobile phone.

It takes a minute or two for it to realise that we are back
in the UK. That I am home. The place I should have stayed.
Three bars of reception pop up at the top left corner
followed by the 3G logo, which instantly disappears again.
Then a response from Paulson to the text I sent him before
I left Newark.

Five minutes ago, he was also in the sky being flown
by the air ambulance straight to the Royal Berkshire
Hospital where a vat of O+ awaits his arrival.

His text informs me that they *caught the guy who killed
that girl*. He thanks me for my help. He says he's *on his
way to visit Eames for the last time*. I had wanted to do
this. To finish things and close it off myself but decided

448

that Eames would want me to do that. So it's better that Paulson does it.

He deserves it.

Another text vibrates onto my screen from Murphy.

'So, I hear you are coming straight back in . . .'

And then six missed calls from Markam and a voicemail.

Something is happening.

I dial back to Markam, unclip my belt, stand up and walk into the galley where four flight attendants, three female, one male, sit, waiting for the plane to taxi to the correct gate. I pull the curtain closed behind me. The male attendant looks shocked and pins his back to the seat. A blonde, overly made-up woman stands and raises her voice.

'Sir, you can't be back here. Please return to your seat.'

I flash my badge at her and point my finger aggressively at her seat. She understands my sentiment and returns.

'Jan.' Markam answers the phone after two rings and confirms my name.

'Chief. What's going on?'

'I need you at the station. I know you've just touched down but you have to come back. It's time.'

'What's so important that it couldn't wait until I landed?'

'I'd rather not discuss this with you over the phone. There's a taxi waiting for you at the gate. You'll come straight here.'

'Fuck that, Chief.' There's still alcohol in my system from the departure lounge pumping around my body, masquerading as courage and presenting itself as stupidity.

'Detective Inspector David,' he interrupts with authority, 'DS Paulson has been injured in the line of duty.'

'Injured? What does that mean?' I start to panic.

Everything I touch dies.

'He was stabbed . . . in the neck.'

'What?' I clench the phone in my right hand and punch the door of the plane with my left, shouting, 'fucking fuck, fuck, fuck'. One *fuck* for every jab.

When I return the phone to my ear, Chief Inspector Markam is repeating my name over and over.

'Where is he?'

'He's in the best hands.'

'Where is he?' I raise my voice again to my superior.

'There's nothing you can do for him now, Jan. He's being operated on. We are getting constant updates. He's alive at the moment.'

I breathe. It's the only thing I can do.

'The best thing that you can do is get off that plane, get into the car I've sent and get to the station. You need to lead this manhunt.' I can see Murphy's sigh of disappointment in my mind.

'I'll be with you as soon as I can. Call me if you hear anything.'

And I end the call, turning around, resting my back against the door and looking up towards a God I'm not sure exists. The flight attendants all have the same expression of uncertainty.

Another text comes through from Paulson. A continuation of his first. I go cold when I see his name on the screen, knowing his current state.

Killer's name is Becker. Heard of him? Kept a little memento of each victim. Need to talk about this with you when you get back. You should come in straight away. Talk more when you land.

It is Murphy who greets me at the station.

My cab driver sensed my mood from my monosyllabic responses to his jovial questions.

'Good to see you, Jan.' Murphy shakes my hand firmly. 'We've got to catch this fucker and make him pay.' He seems genuine. It is a side of Murphy I had forgotten. He actively wants to seek out the person that did this to Paulson. Maybe their relationship changed while I was away but there is a determination in his eyes I thought had been long extinguished.

'We'll get him, Murph.' I tap his shoulder reassuringly as we turn to the entrance. I don't yet know it was Eames. Markam wanted to tell me that part.

In the office, everything is as I left it. Though Murphy has been using my desk in my absence, he has taken great care in restoring things to the state I would expect.

'Markam is on his way to fill you in on the details. Get you up to speed.'

'OK.' I sit at my desk and open the top drawer. I see my Scotch and Cathy's case file.

Everything back to normal.

'Paulson said he wanted to talk to me about this Becker guy.' I make conversation, trying as best I can to fall back into investigative routine. Attempting to take my mind from the status of my best friend lying in an operating theatre.

'Oh yeah. Sick fuck. Killed a bunch of kids and buried them in the park.'

'I know about that but Paulson wanted me to know

specifically about the things he kept from his victims,' I prompt.

'The Wardrobe of Death, they're calling it.'

'Who are *they*?'

He ignores my question and continues. 'Liked to bury them in a plain white boiler suit and keep their last outfit in a wardrobe in his room. Hung up like he expected them to come home.'

'Fuck, that's . . .' I can't find the word.

'Sick. I know. Damning evidence. Looks like he's been doing this for decades.'

'Why would Paulson want to talk to me about it? Sounds pretty conclusive.'

'I don't know, Jan. I've got pictures of it if you want to take a look. Maybe speak with Markam first.' He knows what is coming and in his own little way is trying to protect me or keep me focused or prepared.

I convince Murphy to let me take a look before Markam gets to the office. Naively I tell him that *it can't hurt*.

He hands me a brown folder from his desk. There are eight photographs. One that shows the entire wardrobe with all the outfits dangling like lost souls on wire. The others depict the clothes individually.

The fourth garment knocks me cold.

It takes me back to 1985. To Detective Lamont. To repeating, 'I was inside making a juice. When I went out there, she was gone.'

Back to 'Hang on, Cathy. Hang *on*.'

All the way back to my sister.

At this moment, nothing else matters.

It doesn't matter that my best friend and partner lies helplessly at the hands of mercy and faceless surgeons.

Or that the man who did it to him has escaped from an apparently high-security mental-health facility. It doesn't matter that I left his son to waste away, waiting for an adoption that will never come; even at eighteen months, he is too old, everyone wants a baby.

It doesn't matter that my wife may have been used or may have orchestrated the murder or a series of people to get my attention. Or that she jumped in the East River and never came up. Or that I may never know Special Agent Marquez's true involvement.

I think I am looking at my missing sister's dress.

Cathy David's polka-dot dress.

If it is hers, then she is dead and a stranger is scraping at her bones in a sterile room somewhere in this city to confirm what I do not want to hear.

And downstairs, in a cell, is the man who may have killed her.

For the first time ever, it dawns on me. I hope he didn't do it. I want this to be a grotesque coincidence. I want some other family to get the closure I think I have been craving all this time.

I search for facts and strive for what is right and just. But I have been lost.

At this moment, I have discovered my own truth.

I don't want to find my sister.

Acknowledgements

Huge gratitude once again to everyone at Random House for getting behind another January David story, particularly Francesca Pathak and Philippa Cotton for your work and enthusiasm for this book. And to my editor, Ben Dunn, who has taken three very different journeys with me. Thanks for still being my champion and getting excited by my ideas.

To Sam Bulos, my agent, my therapist, my friend, who even reads the things I write that should never be seen. You do more for me than any agent should and I thank you for your continued belief.

Mum, Brendan, Marc and Karen, thank you for everything ever. In addition to that, thank you for your tireless support over this last year; you have helped keep the dream alive.

It is useful, as a writer, to have friends who also write, to talk to about writing, who understand the process. I'm fortunate to know Claire McGowan, Tom Wood, Stav Sherez and Sarah Pinborough. It is also useful to have writers to drink with. The list is the same.

Thanks to my brother, Alex, for walking many cold miles on the streets of New York and enduring that unforgettable Central Park downpour, all in the name of research. And Brooklyn Lager.

To Phoebe and Coen. My light and my courage. My greatest creations.

Writing is a solitary affair. Having a supportive partner can make everything so much easier. Someone who understands my moment of despair after pressing *send* on a new book and how that can, and usually does, turn into weeks of self-loathing, yet realises that a large glass of whisky is necessary the moment a book is completed, regardless of the time of day. Someone that props me up, praises or delivers those cold, harsh realities. Someone that pays the bills and buys the food. Fran, you are my muse and I can never thank you enough for your love and support. You're my best story.

Also starring January David

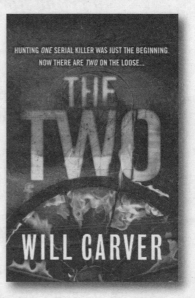

Both out now!

dead good

*For all of you who find
a crime story irresistible.*

Discover the very best crime and thriller books on our
dedicated website – hand-picked by our editorial team
so you have tailored recommendations to help you
choose what to read next.

We'll introduce you to our favourite authors and the
brightest new talent. Read exclusive interviews and
specially commissioned features on everything from the
best classic crime to our top ten TV detectives, join live
webchats and speak to authors directly.

Plus our monthly book competition offers you the
chance to win the latest crime fiction, and there are
DVD box sets and digital devices to be won too.

**Sign up for our newsletter at
www.deadgoodbooks.co.uk/signup**

Join the conversation on: